KISS OF THE BETRAYER

A BRINGER AND THE BANE NOVEL

KISS OF THE BETRAYER

A BRINGER AND THE BANE NOVEL

BOONE BRUX

Entangled Publishing, LLC
2614 South Timberline Road
Suite 109
Fort Collins, CO 80525
Visit our website at www.entangledpublishing.com.

Edited by Erin McCormack Molta and Kerry Vail
Cover design by Heather Howland

Print ISBN   978-1-62061-035-0
Ebook ISBN   978-1-62061-036-7

Manufactured in the United States of America

First Edition December 2012

CHAPTER ONE

The Shrouded Forest, Outer Faela, Inness

"Come out, come out, wherever you are." The demon's taunt circled through Jade's veiled hiding place. "You can't escape." Leaves rustled, shuffling under the demon's feet. Its call drew closer. "You can *never* escape."

Jade ground her teeth together and squeezed her right arm, cringing against the searing bite racing up her limbs. After all these years, she'd still not gotten used to Bane burn, as she called it. Her gaze darted around her small hiding spot inside the hollowed tree trunk, searching for something to draw the demon's attention away. Dampness seeped through the seat of Jade's pants and sent an involuntary shiver up her spine—whether from cold or anticipation, she couldn't say.

A stone lay half-buried beneath the layer of rotting leaves. Careful not to make a sound, she picked up the rock and let it drop into her palm.

"You know I'll find you," the demon called from farther away.

With achingly slow movements, Jade scooted low enough to get a clear shot through the branches. She waited, listening. Nothing. *Cursed demon.* The stretching silence chipped away at her patience. Not a single leaf fluttered beyond her cover, but the needle-like bites on her skin told her the demon huntress was near.

Jade drew her hand back and focused on a spot several yards away. Concentrating, she closed her eyes and sought the ancient words. An earth magic chant, normally dormant until she needed it, filled her mind and rushed from her lips in an indistinct hiss. She snapped her wrist forward and released the stone.

As if thrown with full force, the rock sailed through the opening in the branches and disappeared into the shadows of the surrounding woods. A small crack echoed when the stone hit what must have been the trunk of a tree.

She held her breath but didn't have to wait long. Three running steps thundered toward her hiding place. She tensed, ready to fight. The loud thump of the demon's wings extending was followed by a rushing uptake of air. The dark shadow soared above her and headed toward the sound of the rock. It banked left and disappeared into the wall of trees.

Not waiting to see if her ruse worked, Jade scrambled from her spot, the twigs tearing the green kerchief from her head and scoring her back with their sharp points. She didn't stop to retrieve the material or examine her injuries. Escape was her only thought.

Any second, the demon would realize she'd outsmarted it and return to the hunt, more determined than ever. Jade raced in the opposite direction, never running in a straight line for too long. She snaked a path through the trees in an all-too-familiar pattern meant to throw her pursuer off her trail. The woods blurred. Her chest tightened and her breathing became labored, but she didn't stop.

Prickles nipped at her skin, which meant the danger was still near. A stitch of pain jabbed at her side. She wrapped an arm around her waist, but it didn't help stem the discomfort. She craned her neck to look over her shoulder. Only the dark woods yawned behind her—empty—demonless as far as she could see.

Hope jabbed at her, teasing her into slowing her step, mocking her with the possibility that she'd actually eluded the Bane. She scanned the canopy. Still no demon. Her jog slowed and finally stopped. Blood pounded against her chest like a drum, ricocheting into her ears. She dragged in a deep breath, willing her body to recover.

A rivulet of sweat ran down the back of her neck, beneath her loose and tangled hair. She pushed the damp strands from her face. Her gaze raked the trees and sky for movement. Nothing. The demon lived for this kind of challenge. It loved to taunt its prey, which was her at this moment, into doing something stupid, namely standing around like an idiot the way she was now.

Jade began to jog again, ignoring the pinch in her side but not ignoring the raw burn that swept across her skin. Pain was the one thing that could divide her attention and make her lose focus. Over the years she'd mastered tolerance for many of life's discomforts— cold, hunger, loneliness—but pain refused to be conquered.

She massaged her ribs. Just a little farther and she'd reach the sanctified grounds of the small chapel. There she'd be safe and could rest.

The throbbing pain suddenly flared, her only warning before large talons wrapped around her upper arms and lifted her from the ground. Jade screamed, her stomach lurching toward her feet. Her body swung wildly, the demon's wings pulling her higher, cresting the tops of the trees.

Nausea rolled through her. "Put me down!"

A high-pitched cackle erupted from above. "Are you sure about that?"

Next to pain, she hated heights most. Vomit crept up her throat and she swallowed hard, fighting against the demon's hold. Swirling air from the flapping wings battered her.

"You promised, no flying!"

The demon cackled again. "Promises are meant to be broken."

"Damn it, Rell, put me down!"

"You're no fun."

Jade bit her tongue when the creature flipped its body to point head down. The sting had hardly registered before they fell into a spiral, plunging toward the earth. Her stomach slammed into her throat. Heartbeats hammered against her chest as the ground raced up to meet her.

Please, Sainted Ones, let me die now.

They circled low over the smooth rise of a hill. Without warning, Rell let her go and Jade suddenly found herself toppling through the air. A scream ripped from her throat but turned to a heavy grunt when she hit the ground hard and tumbled across the rise in a tangle of limbs. Stiff vegetation scraped a layer or more of flesh from her arms. A thorny bush blocked her path and she crashed into it, its sharp branches enveloping her. She groaned and rolled away from the plant's painful embrace to lay with her arms and legs thrown wide.

Stinging cuts licked her body. "Fucking demon," she muttered.

The wild pounding in her chest slowed as the shock from hovering ten feet above the tree line faded. Jade rolled to her stomach and kissed the wet grass. *Thank the Sainted Ones.* She lay with her face pressed against the cool ground for a few seconds before pushing to a sitting position, babying her battered ribs.

The demon circled and flared its green wings, alighting on the top of a boulder. Curled black talons rasped along the stone.

"I'm going to kill you," Jade said.

"That's not a very nice thing to say." The creature folded its green wings behind its back and gave a feminine pout. "Besides, you can't. I'm invincible."

Jade struggled to her feet and pulled a dagger from her boot. "You know I hate flying."

"Yes," the demon drawled. "I do."

"Then why did you throw me to the ground from ten feet up?"

"You told me to put you down." The demon shrugged. "I was only doing what you asked."

"I could have broken every bone in my body. Where's the fair fight in that?"

"Bless the Sainted Ones, but you complain a lot. Whoever said being hunted by a demon was fair?" A wicked grin spread across the creature's face. Its tiny spiked horns flicked toward the knife clutched in Jade's hand. "Are we going to fight now?"

Exhaustion and aches battered her body, but Jade ignored them. She might not be able to best Rell, but getting in a few good punches would help cool her ire. "Oh yes, we are most definitely going to fight."

"Oh goody." The demon's grin widened to a fanged smile. It jumped from the boulder and the scrape of talons against rock whispered across the clearing. "This is my favorite part." Muscular legs rippled under the thin iridescent fabric that clung to her legs with each step the Bane took toward Jade. "I love your misplaced hope of beating me."

"That's the wonderful thing about being human, Rell—my

optimism."

The demon edged to the side, trying to work its way behind her, but Jade knew this maneuver. Tensed for the attack, she backed in a circle, keeping the demon in front of her.

"Remember hope, Rell?"

She stressed the demon's name, trying to distract it.

The creature turned its head and spit, and then tracked its yellow eyes back to her. A sneer curled across the full upper lip, daring her to continue.

Not taking the warning, Jade spouted some of her best verbal barbs. "The joy of a new day? The feel of the sun on your face?"

Fangs glistened in the gloom of the darkening woods. "You humans are consumed with feelings." Rell's voice rose to a mocking whine. "Is this right? Is that wrong? I don't have to worry about any of that now."

"I know you." Jade pointed the knife at the demon. "You miss being human."

"And you talk too much." The demon crouched. "Let's fight."

She attacked. Jade dove to the side and swiped her knife in a wide arc as she came to her feet. The blade grazed the demon's arm, but Rell only laughed. With a powerful leap, the demon launched onto the boulder and spun to push off, hitting Jade full force and taking her down. The blade flew from Jade's hand. A smooth green arm slid around her neck and tightened like a large snake crushing its prey, cutting off her air. She gasped and clawed at the forearm and elbow, but the pressure didn't ease.

Blood pounded against Jade's skull and black dots danced in front of her eyes. She kicked and flopped, trying to get free.

"Why would I miss being a weak human female?" Rell whispered. "I serve no man. Answer to no master."

The zing of a blade being drawn sang through Jade's descent into unconsciousness.

"Release her," a strange voice said.

Rell's grip eased enough for Jade to suck in a partial breath.

"Release her," the voice demanded.

The demon's imprisoning arm loosened and Jade fell to the ground. She rolled to her back and coughed, gulping in the cool, blessed air. The black dots faded and her vision cleared enough to see the silver tip of a blade pressed against Rell's neck.

"We've got company," the demon said, staring down at her.

Jade struggled to her feet. A young man of about seventeen held the sword. His eyes were wide with fear but his hand remained steady. The knot at his throat bobbed up and down with compulsive swallowing, his jaw clenching and unclenching.

"Run," he said. "I'll deal with the demon."

The creature laughed. "Yes, run along, Jade, so the boy can *deal* with me."

Jade's gaze cut to Rell. "Don't hurt him."

"Run," the young man said again. "This abomination needs to die."

The demon laughed again. "It's too easy."

"Rell." Jade whispered the demon's name, holding the creature's focus on her.

Rell's eyes narrowed, pinning her with their yellow intensity. With slow movements, Jade gripped the point of the man's sword and moved it away from the smooth, green neck. The blade sliced her hand but she didn't release it.

The man fought her. "What are you doing? Run, you stupid cow."

Anger blazed in the reptilian eyes, and before Jade could act,

Rell spun. Like a striking snake, the demon knocked the blade from the man's hand and closed black talons around his throat, lifting him off the ground. His toes dangled an inch above solid earth, kicking, searching for a foothold. He choked and sputtered.

"Rell!" Jade shouted. "Put him down!"

The demon's lips pulled back in a snarl. "Why should I?"

"Put—him—down." She enunciated each word, trying to pull Rell from the blood lust, but the demon didn't budge. "Please." With a soft touch, Jade laid a hand on the demon's wrist. "Please. Don't give in."

Rell's nostrils flared, seeming to struggle against her plea. "But the pull is so strong."

"Fight it." Jade took Rell's face in her hands and forced the demon to look at her. "Fight it." Her fingers caressed the smooth and delicate cheek of the demon. "Let him go."

Sable brown brows furrowed against the inner struggle so apparent on the demon's face. Rell stared for several long seconds, the man's efforts to escape weakening. Yellow eyes swirled to green and back to yellow. With an anguished cry, the demon tossed the man across the clearing. He landed with a grunt and lay on his back, wheezing. Jade didn't move to help him, but instead lowered her hands, holding the demon's gaze. This was the most dangerous time.

"Go," Jade said quietly to the man.

He coughed. "You control the demon?"

She opened her mouth to tell him to shut up but before she could utter a word, Rell shot across the distance to tower over him.

"Nobody—" Talons clawed the ground next to the man's leg—"controls the demon."

He scrambled backward. Jade raced across the clearing and jumped between them, bracing her back against the demon's chest to stop another attack. "Go! Now!"

His gaze darted from her to Rell. Finally jumping to his feet, he fled into the woods. They stood, back to chest, watching until he'd disappeared.

Jade released a heavy breath and turned. "I'm proud of you."

Rell gave a snort of disgust. "You should have let me kill him."

"Why? Because it feels good?"

A fanged smile pulled across the creature's mouth. "No, because the jackass called you a stupid cow." The demon reached and brushed a sweaty strand of hair from Jade's face. "Nobody calls my sister names—but me."

CHAPTER TWO

The Iron Crown Tavern, Faela

Luc dodged the barstool flying past his head but failed to avoid the man's uppercut. A meaty fist slammed into his jaw, sending him backward into a crowd of scantily clad women. Their shrieks filled the air, but thankfully their soft bodies cushioned his descent. Plump bosoms pressed against his head and the smell of heavy perfume over body odor enveloped him. The group stumbled under his weight, but settled without injury in a loose pile on the floor.

"Ladies." Luc smiled, wincing at the pain in his jaw. He struggled to stand but the room spun around him. His hands conveniently fondled as much exposed flesh as possible before finding his feet. "I'm grateful for the assistance."

The women giggled and trailed their hands across his shoulders, down his back and over his butt. One dark-haired lovely cupped his crotch before lowering her hand.

Luc's smile spread. "Weeell," he slurred. "Maybe I have time for a little—"

Hands gripped his collar and the waist of his pants, lifting him upright and off the ground. With an animal roar, the behemoth tossed Luc like a bag of grain. His body was hurled across the room, the low, black beams of the tavern just inches above his head. A rickety table broke his fall and collapsed, sending wood, ale, and its occupants scattering.

Luc lay among the splintered timber, the tang of blood in his mouth and a fierce pounding in his head. How had his evening gone so awry? One minute he was enjoying a pint and the attentions of a particularly friendly lass, and the next, he found himself ejected from his seat by a most *unfriendly* man.

"Stay away from my woman." The stranger towered over Luc, pointing a fat finger at his face. "Do you hear me?"

Luc struggled to sit, the pile of wood shifting under him. "I beg your pardon, sir." The skin around his lower lip felt tight and hot. "I didn't realize the lady was with you." He held his hand out. "Some assistance, please."

The brute glowered at him.

"Truly sir, you have my deepest apologies for any affront I might have caused."

The man grunted and clutched Luc's hand, hauling him to his feet.

"Thank you." He brushed the chips of wood from his leather tunic and wiped the spatters of ale from his face with his sleeve. "It was all a misunderstanding." He smiled up at the giant. "You misunderstood my friendly nature as flirting with your woman and I misunderstood the way she kept rubbing my cock under the table as her availability."

The brute roared and Luc threw his punch, connecting with his attacker's stomach. The man doubled over, meeting Luc's raised knee, but he was made of sterner stuff and barreled forward, taking Luc down.

The massive weight of the stranger knocked the breath from Luc's body. Punches rained down on his face, splitting his lower lip. Pain ricocheted through his body with each blow. With a hard jab, he landed an elbow strike in the man's neck. Air rushed from the stranger's lungs and he coughed. Luc punched him again in the jaw, which seemed to have no effect other than to make the brute angrier. A snarl squeezed from between the man's gritted teeth a second before he grabbed Luc's head and beat it against the floor.

Luc managed another direct hit to the thick jaw, causing the stranger to release his skull and reel backward. Black dots danced in front of his eyes and he struggled to sit up, but he was still trapped under the weight of the man. With no escape, he lifted his arms to block the incoming assault but gained little relief. Kicks followed punches, battering any exposed body parts. Luc curled into a ball, shielding himself from the free-for-all, which now felt like multiple hands, multiple feet, and multiple people.

The sound of breaking bottles rang from somewhere seconds before shards of glass showered him. The beating suddenly stopped, followed by a thunderous crash next to him.

Taking advantage of the lull in his thrashing, Luc uncurled and rolled over to push up to his hands and knees. The tang of blood mixed with the stale taste of ale. His stomach roiled and he coughed, making it difficult to breathe. The swelling around his eyes impeded his vision and the hot throbbing of his cheek vibrated from his temple to his teeth. He reached for the table to help him stand, but missed. Strong hands wrapped around his biceps and jerked him off the ground.

"Not again," he moaned, squinting through bloated lids. In the tavern's dim light he could barely make out the two cloaked figures holding him. "You're not going to hit me, are you?" His head swam from the pummeling and the numerous pints of ale he'd consumed. "Cuz, I must say, I feel I've had my fair share tonight."

Each stranger secured one of his arms around their shoulders and dragged him toward the door. Luc's legs wouldn't cooperate with his mental command to stand and fight. None too gently, they jostled him up the narrow stairs and out onto the dark street. Cool air brushed his face.

"No more fighting for you tonight," a deep voice ordered.

"Damn, and I was doing so well, don't you think?" He laughed and winced, then swung his head toward the speaker. A black hood shielded the man's face, making it impossible to identify him. Luc stumbled, but they held him upright. "Did my father send you?"

"No," the other stranger said.

Luc craned his neck, trying to bring the second man into focus, but the action only made his head bobble uncontrollably. The world spun and thunder ricocheted inside his skull. He inhaled, trying to settle his stomach. The smell of rotting fish and seawater filled his nostrils. Vague recognition cued him to the fact that they were traveling along the docks. Ships creaked and rocked against their lines and the noise from the tavern faded into the lapping of waves.

Their footsteps sounded hollow and overly loud against the wooden planks of the pier. With great effort, Luc concentrated on not stumbling.

Another cloaked figure stood at the end of a gangway, watching their approach. The image wavered and slowly settled into focus. The person appeared smaller than the two men holding him.

Luc's fighting spirit rallied. He could probably overpower the smaller one if need be. The strangers shifted, hefting him higher.

Luc's stomach muscles clenched against the piercing ache in his side. Maybe he could take the little one, but he sincerely hoped he wouldn't have to.

Progress up the gangway was slow. Luc tried to widen his swollen eyes, but gained only a fraction of an inch more clarity. He tripped and lurched forward onto the deck of the ship but the men steadied him, taking most of his weight. The surroundings looked familiar. He knew this ship. He was almost certain.

"Where are you taking me?"

"Bed," one of the strangers said. "To sleep it off."

"Well now, that's very decent of you," Luc said, giving his supporters a grateful smile. "Do me a favor, friends. Don't tell my father. He'll kill me if he knows I've been fighting again."

One of the men chuckled but didn't respond further.

They maneuvered across the deck and around a large blackened hole in the center. The faint odor of charred wood hung in the air. Luc took exaggerated steps away from the hole, the gentle rocking of the ship making it difficult to traverse a safe path. A small door stood open with the smaller stranger waiting at the side.

"This is Rhys Blackwell's ship." The need to defend his friend's vessel flared but quickly fizzled. Every movement took energy— energy he didn't have. "I hope for your sake he knows you're using it? Probably does. He knows everything. And Siban, I can't get away with anything—always knows when I'm lying."

They ignored his drunken ramblings and they half-walked, half-dragged him across the floor of the captain's quarters and set him on the bed.

Luc's injuries coalesced into one giant ache. He groaned and melted into a boneless mass against the bedpost. The cool wood pressed into his aching cheek and prevented him from falling forward.

The smaller figure stepped inside the room, locked the door, and threw back her hood. Black curls tumbled from the covering and pale blue eyes sparkled with concern.

"Ravyn?" Luc tried to widen his lids. He pointed. "Ravyn."

The two men pulled their cloaks over their heads and tossed them to the side.

"Rhys! Siban! What are you doing here?"

"Saving your ass, my friend." Rhys knelt in front of him and gave a low whistle. "You need to quit stopping fists with your face."

Luc laughed and winced. "Got in a good punch or two. Did you see it?"

"Impressive," Ravyn said. She joined Rhys and knelt, pushing Luc's hair out of his face. Her fingers traced his swollen eye. "Very impressive."

She cupped a hand against the side of his face and whispered words he couldn't understand. Heat spread along his cheek and down his neck. The throbbing eased, bringing blessed relief from the headache that had started at the base of his neck. The room began to spin.

"Lay back on the bed, Luc." Ravyn's voice lulled him, zapping any argument he might have considered working up. She swiped her hand across his forehead and pushed the hair away from his face. "Everything is going to be all right."

His body went willingly and settled against the soft down tick. The scent of lavender wafted from the pillow when he laid his head on it, reminding him of Ravyn. Her fingers lingered against his skin before she rose to stand next to Rhys.

Even in his drunken state, Luc was glad he couldn't fully make out their expressions. He thought he'd caught a hint of uncertainty in Ravyn's expression. Maybe it was disappointment or pity. He was suddenly grateful that his eyelids were nearly swollen shut. Nobody spoke. Shame crept over him, but he'd lost the capacity to care what people thought of him long ago. Drink melted his pride and numbed his morals.

"Is he strong enough?" Rhys asked, looking at Ravyn. "Maybe we should wait until he sobers up."

"I think these are just bruises and cuts and a lot of ale." She looked at Rhys. "But I'll heal him first. We can't risk anything going wrong. I'm already guessing at too much."

"What are you talking about?" Luc tried to sit up, certain he needed to be involved in whatever plan his friends were discussing. "I can help."

Rhys lifted Luc's hand and held his wrist in a tight grip. "Test him."

"Test me for what?" he slurred.

Rhys threaded his fingers through Luc's, pulling his hand open. Before Luc could react, Ravyn stepped forward and sliced his palm with a knife. The lamplight caught the blade and Luc recognized it as Ravyn's immortal dagger, the weapon used to convert a Bringer to full power.

"Son of a—" Luc cried.

Rhys released him. Luc snatched his hand back to stare at the blood that welled but didn't spill from the gash across his palm. He clenched his fist against the pain.

"Why the shaggin' Saints did you cut me?"

"In death there is life," Ravyn said. "In sacrifice, return."

A tingle sparked in Luc's hand. Heat raced along the cut. He opened his fist and stared at the slash. Pain snaked along the wound but his protest died on his lips. Threads of euphoria pushed against his muddled mind.

"All barriers destroyed and evil be spurned," Ravyn continued.

Luc let his hand fall open to rest on the bed and looked at Ravyn, blinking several times to bring her into view. White light pulsed around her and ribbons of gold coiled outward, dancing around him. The burning of the cut faded away to be replaced by an overwhelming feeling of love.

"No hindrance remain, from our blood be renewed."

He tried to sit up again, needing to go to her, but Siban pushed him back down. Her words were like a warm rain spilling over Luc, drenching and cleansing the stain on his soul. A tear slipped from the corner of his eye but he didn't wipe it away.

"That which was taken settle in those who Bring true," Ravyn finished.

"Ahhh!" Luc clutched his hand to his chest "What's happening?"

His two friends knelt by the bed—Rhys, his best friend, at his feet and Siban, the mixed-blood Tell who Luc had recently come to think of as a friend, by his head. Ravyn stood.

"Relax, Luc." Ravyn's voice penetrated his pain. "We're almost finished."

Rhys laid his body across his legs as Siban stood over him and pressed his biceps to the bed.

"Finished?" Luc held Ravyn's gaze, wanting nothing more than to go to her. He struggled against the men's hold. "Release me."

A spark of reality pushed through the haze of euphoria that gripped him. Being pinned down, unable to move, was tantamount to complete submission. Never was he *completely* at somebody's mercy. He kicked and twisted against his restrainers. The sensation of being bound pushed away all traces of confusion. Panic rose.

"Damn you, let me go!" His shout filled the room. Surely,

somebody would hear him. "Why are you doing this?"

He thrashed about, needing to get free, but the men shifted their weight to pin him fully to the bed.

"Hurry up," Rhys growled.

Ravyn stepped to the bed and Luc froze, trying to understand the scene before him. Blue light glowed around the blade of the dagger she held—pointed directly at his chest—her intent clear.

A single word hissed from him. "Why?"

"Because we need you." Ravyn's voice quivered slightly.

"But are we not friends?"

"Yes, Luc." The sweetest smile pulled at Ravyn's mouth. She leaned in and kissed him gently on the lips. "The best of friends."

Before he could reply, she straightened and brought the dagger down, plunging it into his chest, burying it deep. The blade bit into his skin and burned a path to his heart. Searing heat spread across his chest as blackness closed around his vision.

One word slipped from Luc's lips before darkness claimed him. "Betrayer."

CHAPTER THREE

A light scraping and a heavy whoosh sounded behind Jade. She didn't turn, knowing all too well who was there.

"Where is he?" Rell said.

Jade pointed to the rocking vessel. "On the ship, drunk—again."

Two hollow steps thumped against the wooden pier, closing the distance between her and Rell. "Are you surprised?"

Jade looked over her shoulder at the demon. Rell's yellow eyes peered through the dark. Her sister was petite, like she had been as a human, but as a demon she had a temper to rival any titan.

"No." She shook her head. "Nothing he does surprises me anymore." Her gaze scanned the dock area, making sure no late night tavern-goers stumbled close to her hiding spot behind a stack of crates. "Why are you here? You might be seen."

"Never fear, little sister. I'm very careful." The demon folded her leathery green wings behind her and reclined against a wooden box. "Besides, it's safer here than near Vile."

"Why?" Jade turned back to the ship, irritated by the demon's intrusion. Her sister demanded so much of her attention. At times, it seemed her whole purpose in life was to serve Rell.

"He's angry—very angry."

Jade shuddered at the thought of the Demon King. She'd seen him once when she was eight years old. Though Rell had ordered her never to leave the hot pool cavern where they hid in the Shadow World, curiosity had gotten the better of her. One day, when her sister had left to hunt for food, Jade had crept from the cave and down the forbidden corridor to the Bane hive. Heavy footsteps had thundered along the passage, giving her a few panicked seconds warning of a demon's approach. She'd slipped into a narrow gap in the rock wall and backed into the shadows. Even today that memory made her blood run cold.

From Rell's description, she'd recognized the Demon King immediately. Vile had stopped, halted by another demon's call. His massive body had filled her view, his webbed wings soaring beyond her sight. At first she'd thought his blue skin was marbled with black. But then he'd turned, exposing his wide chest to her, and she realized the marbling was an intricate pattern of symbols she didn't recognize.

After Vile's footfalls had faded, she'd rushed from her hiding place. Too afraid the king or another demon would find her, she'd sprinted back to her cavern. Never again did she venture beyond the hot pools where she felt safe and never did she confess her disobedience to Rell.

She pulled herself from her childhood memory. "Why is Vile angry?"

"The Blackwell Bringer. It seems he's a full-blood, in possession of all his Shield powers."

Jade spun to face her sister. "What happened?"

Rell laughed. "Oh, Jade. You should have seen him. He was

glorious, shifting in a blink of an eye to a dragon, breathing fire and all."

"Shhh." Jade put her finger to her lip but recognized the dreamy expression flittering across Rell's face. Even as a human, her sister had been prone to dramatics. "Somebody will hear you."

"The way he wrapped his body around the woman." Rell wound her arms around her torso, heedless of Jade's warning. "Protecting her."

Dread pulled at Jade. "What woman?"

"The female Bringer. The woman you pretended to be friends with."

The desire to contradict her sister's assumption that her friendship with Ravyn was a ruse nearly slipped out, but she bit her tongue. Let Rell believe what she wanted. It made no difference. In the end, the only important thing was keeping her sister rooted in the land of the living. Each time Rell spoke of love or their childhood, she seemed almost human again.

"His face." Rell's yellow eyes swirled with green. "You should have seen his expression when he thought the Bringer woman was dead." She curled her talons into a fist and placed it against her heart. "Such love. Such anguish." Her voice dropped to a whisper. "I could almost taste it."

"Ravyn was hurt?" A pang of concern shot through Jade.

"Not hurt—dead."

Jade shook her head. "But I saw her tonight. She looked unharmed."

"Really?" The dreamy look melted from Rell's face. "How can this be? I saw her drive a blade into her heart and fall into death's sleep."

"Well…" Jade crossed her arms again, trying to fit the conflicting information together. "She's not dead."

"I'm beginning to understand." Rell tapped her chin with a talon. "During one of Vile's rants he let slip about an immortal weapon. It seems your Bringer friends have more surprises up their sleeves than we originally thought."

"How did Rhys find the Shadow World?" Jade asked. "Especially the entrance leading to the throne room. Isn't that opening hidden unless you know where to look?"

Rell gave her a fanged smile. "He had help."

Jade furrowed her brow. "What kind of help?"

"Bane help."

"You?"

Her sister laughed. "Hardly. No, the demon who helped Blackwell had a lot to lose." She paused. "Or gain."

Jade thought for a second. What demon was brave enough to foil Vile's plans? Only a few Bane came to mind. Most of the demons were minions and not capable of doing much beyond the bidding of their king.

"Sha-hera?"

Rell smirked. "No. Though that bitch definitely has designs on the throne."

"If not Sha-hera..." Jade trailed off. *No, it's not possible.* The name barely topped a whisper. "Icarus?"

A smile spread across her sister's mouth, her almond-shaped eyes sparkling in the dark. "I daresay the good son is tired of being under his father's thumb."

"I don't believe it."

"I saw him. He didn't know I was there. If he had, I wouldn't be standing here now." Rell crossed her arms and nodded. "But I saw him help the Bringer escape."

Vile was horrifying, but Icarus defied description. He was beautiful in an unworldly way. Where most demons were reprehensible, Icarus's allure was intoxicating and deadly. Once, when Jade had been a teenager, she'd encountered Icarus. He'd come upon her as she bathed in the hot pools in the Shadow World. She'd thought he'd kill her, or at the very least steal her soul, but he'd only watched, crouched at the edge of the water, silent.

How long he stayed, she couldn't say. To her, the experience had lasted hours. The memory of that day still filled her with fear.

"Much has happened since I left the ship," Jade said. Her gaze leveled back on the glowing windows of the captain's quarters. She thought about Luc. "And many things have stayed the same."

The demon tilted her head. "You sound disappointed. You're not having doubts are you?" She laid a hand on Jade's shoulder. "He must pay for what he has done to our family—for what he has brought upon me."

Jade wasn't so sure anymore, but instead of voicing her opinion, she simply nodded, knowing it would be enough to placate Rell.

A cry erupted from the ship. Jade pivoted and crept to the edge of the crates to peek around the corner. "I'm going to try to find out what is happening."

"Have a care, sister."

Jade looked over her shoulder and nodded. She needed to stay hidden because when she killed Luc, she wanted no connection to him. Without another word, she crouched and darted to a group of wooden barrels. When no shout of discovery went up, she raced to the gangway and tiptoed along it, silently easing onto the wooden deck.

Low voices floated through the door of the captain's cabin, but she couldn't make out what they were discussing. What she needed was to see what was happening inside the cabin. Besides peering through the crack in the door, the window at the side of the ship was the only other option.

She skirted piles of rope, barrels, and the large hole in the center of the deck, making sure to walk lightly and keep the clip of her heels quiet. From what she could tell, none of the ship's crew was aboard. Though this was not unheard of, the fact still put her on alert. Shipping was a cutthroat business, and it was a foolish owner who left assets unguarded.

Jade climbed onto the roof of the captain's cabin and lowered herself to lie on her stomach, hanging her head over the edge. If she could inch her torso lower, she should be able to get a clear view into the cabin.

She bent her elbows, ready to push forward, when the door beneath her banged open. Panic swept through her. Her grip slipped, causing her to drop to her elbows with a dull thud.

"Who's there?"

It was a male voice, one she didn't recognize. Probably the man she'd seen with Rhys Blackwell earlier this evening.

Footsteps thundered on the deck, pushing her into action. Jade jumped to her feet and with four long strides, leapt from her hiding place onto the rope ladder leading to the crow's nest. Her grasp slipped and the rope bit into her palm, leaving a stinging trail. She clawed at the rungs, finally gaining a hold. Her intent had been to slide to the ground and make her escape in the direction she'd come, but he was instantly below her, as if he'd deduced her intent.

With no route for escape, she began to climb, picking her way up the unsteady weave of rope. Sweat ran down her neck despite the cool evening and her stomach lurched to her throat. A small whimper squeezed through her lips. With each foot she ascended, it became more difficult to release the ladder.

Don't look down. Don't look down.

The ladder swayed under the weight of the man when he launched himself onto the ropes, dislodging Jade's foothold. Her legs swung wildly, searching for a solid perch. She glanced down to see him maneuvering along the woven mass as efficiently as a spider traverses its web.

She looked upward. The crow's nest hovered four feet above her now, though she didn't know what she would do once she got there. She cursed her shortsightedness for not braving a leap into the inky black water instead of taking this dead-end path.

Finally, her fingers touched wood and she slapped her hand through the small opening of the crow's nest. It took all her strength to pull her nearly paralyzed body through the narrow gap. Tremors vibrated up her legs as she worked herself into an unsteady stance. Flashes of heat and nausea washed over her. The black water stretched out in front of the ship and blended with the night sky. There was only one escape.

Gritting her teeth, she shoved her arms in the air. The words lodged in her throat, refusing to be spoken until she heard the man's heavy breathing directly below her.

"Rell!"

Silence greeted her, but the prickles of heat told her the demon was close. She closed her eyes. *Come on, sister. If there was ever a time to not let me down, it's now.*

The bite grew and Jade swallowed hard against the pain. A hand slapped the floor of the crow's nest near her foot. Her eyes sprang open and she stomped on the searching fingers, eliciting a colorful string of curses from her pursuer. His hand disappeared from sight. Time was nearly out.

"Rell!"

The familiar down-stroke of air sounded behind her at the same time a large hand snaked out and grabbed her ankle, knocking her off balance. She screamed and slammed against the curving wall, catching herself before she toppled over the side. The dark shadow ghosted across Jade's periphery and again she jammed her arms in the air. Her ankle jerked out from under her the same instant sharp talons wrapped around her wrist.

For a second Jade hung in the air, suspended between the demon and the man below her. Whether from the strength of Rell's grip or the shock of seeing a Demon Bane, the man's hold slipped free and Jade found herself floating out over the Sea of Alba.

"Rell!"

The man's voice broke through Jade's fear. The stroke of the large green wings faltered. Jade craned her neck to see him. Was this somebody Rell knew or was it his attempt to draw them back? He stood watching their escape from the lookout, but he made no further effort to capture her.

Movement below them drew Jade's attention. Ravyn and Rhys raced from the cabin, their gazes searching the deck of the ship until tracking upward to the man.

Rell gave several powerful pulls of her wings, sending them out of range of hearing and into the cover of the night. Jade tried not to dwell on the fact that nothing but her sister's strength kept her from plummeting to her death. They skirted the shore, avoiding the populated areas and the possibility of being seen. Cool, salty air buffeted Jade's face and the din of the city faded to the rhythmic lapping of the waves. The tight grip around her wrists and the position from which she dangled made Jade's arms ache. She flexed her fingers, trying to ward off the encroaching numbness.

Once well past the sprawl of the city, Rell banked right to fly inland. They circled low over a clearing in the trees. With unusual gentleness, she dropped Jade from only a few feet up and landed beside her.

Jade's legs trembled, threatening to give out. She plopped onto the damp grass and stuck her head between her knees. Deep breaths eased the sick feeling working its way up her throat and after a minute of thanking the Sainted Ones for her escape, she looked up.

Rell stood quietly, her wings folded behind her back and her gaze focused on a spot near the small stone chapel several yards away. The whirring of the katydids hummed low, a familiar and comforting sound. The terror of the evening's events melted from Jade, replaced by the awareness of her sister's silence. If not for the protective way Rell held herself, arms wrapped around her torso, Jade would have thought she was merely contemplating tonight's excitement. She thought back to the man on the boat.

"Do you know him?"

Her sister's jaw clenched, a rare sign of the demon's vulnerability. After a second, she gave a tiny shake of her head. "No, I don't *know* him."

The way she stressed *"know"* meant there was more to the explanation than Rell was revealing. But after years of living with the demon, Jade also knew not to push for more until her sister was ready.

Jade stared at her sister. Not for the first time in the past few weeks did doubts about their plan plague her. Things had changed since she'd met Ravyn. Becoming her friend had made the impossible dream of having a normal life seem possible. Hope blossomed where an endless existence with her demon sister now flourished. The thought of tossing aside her current reality, one that bore no roots and flowered no friendships, sent a tremor of forbidden longing through her.

Rell turned to face her. "You're reckless."

Jade stiffened against her sister's criticism but held her tongue.

"Perhaps *I* should be the one to kill Luc."

"No!" Jade struggled to her feet. "I won't let you risk slipping farther into the darkness." She reached for Rell's hands, needing to keep her sister rooted in the rational world. "You can't afford to take such a chance."

Tension eased from the demon's stance, her gaze switching from their connected hands to Jade's face. "So you still agree to kill him?"

"Yes." The word turned sour in Jade's mouth. Rell was determined to exact revenge on Luc, no matter the cost. Jade couldn't allow the insidious darkness that spread through her sister to take over completely. "I will kill him." For years Rell had kept her safe and fed despite the danger of discovery. Saving her sister's soul was the least Jade owed her. "Tomorrow—I will do it tomorrow."

Jade released her sister's hands and rubbed her arm where the demon's talons had dug in, the night suddenly taking on a bitter chill.

"Good." Rell took a deep breath and released it. "And finally justice will be served." The demon crouched. "I will be waiting."

Jade stepped back and Rell launched herself into the sky. No sisterly goodbyes or hugs, just the cold detachment Jade had come to expect from the demon. Within seconds, the night sky had swallowed Rell's ascent. Emptiness as heavy as a large stone weighed in the pit of Jade's stomach, but she pushed aside the doubts troubling her.

For the betrayal of her family, she *would* keep her promise to her sister. She *would* kill Luc Le Daun tomorrow.

Chapter Four

Luc sat on the edge of the bed, cradling his head in his hands. Every movement he made was a stinging reminder of his night spent at the tavern and the new dragon tattoo emblazoned from his hip to shoulder. The ship rocked gently from side to side, the motion doing nothing to soothe his ire. "Why did you do it, Ravyn?"

"We need you." Her answer held far more confidence than it should have, or maybe it was her misplaced optimism that he'd rise to the challenge now that *they'd* made the decision to bring him to full power.

Luc lowered his arms and glared at her. "What gives you the right to take without my permission?"

"We didn't take, Luc, we *gave* you your full Shield powers." She shook her head. "I don't understand your reluctance."

"Not reluctance," he barked. "Insistence. From the very first time you and Rhys offered to bring me to full power I've told you no, but you didn't listen. You've turned me into something I never wanted to be." He stood and walked to the window. She didn't understand what she'd done. None of them did. "Something I have no right to be."

The soft clip of her booted footsteps approached. She stopped beside him. Her concern brushed along his skin like a mother's touch, but he steeled himself against the craving to be consoled by her. Each day Ravyn's powers seemed to grow and at times it took all his strength not to give into her every request. Though envious of the deep bond of love Rhys and Ravyn shared, Luc did not envy Rhys in this one matter.

"Why don't you have the right to be a Bringer, Luc? It's your heritage."

"You wouldn't say that if you knew me, Ravyn." He continued to stare out the window, fighting to keep the dark memories at bay. "I've done things…" He stopped, unable to share his shame. "I'm not worthy."

"Every person has sins. Things they're not proud of." She ran her hand up and down his arm with comforting strokes. "Without those experiences, how would we learn right from wrong?"

He gave a humorless laugh and looked at her. "One day you'll realize not everybody is worth saving."

"No." Her pale blue eyes flared, and that one word burned with conviction. "Men like Powell don't deserve forgiveness, but you're not like him."

If only she knew how wrong she was. Though his crimes didn't include kidnapping and serving up an innocent woman to the Demon Bane like Powell had done with Ravyn, the effects of Luc's transgression still cut much deeper and hurt the very people who had trusted and loved him.

Luc studied her face. A thin black line ran from just below her lower lip to the indent above her chin, a Tell tattoo she'd received after gaining her full powers. She peered at him and he wondered what she saw. The woman found good in *nearly* everybody. Anger over what she'd been through during the past few weeks threatened to cool his resentment toward her.

His gaze slid back to the window and the crowd bustling along the dock in the late afternoon heat. Ravyn was like family to him, a maddeningly meddling sister.

"Your Tell powers don't give you the ability to see into the past." He crossed his arms and focused on his anger, not wanting to concede he had no other choice but to embrace being a Bringer Shield. "Not everybody is meant for, or even wants to be, a hero."

Ravyn sighed and lowered her hand. "I'm sorry you feel that way."

He didn't look at her, but felt the loss when she turned to leave, taking her warm presence with her. The door gave a quiet *click*.

Seconds ticked by but he didn't move, continuing to stare absently out the window at the teeming dock. He was a Shield. Nothing could change that fact now. Not complaining, not wishing, and certainly not dredging up the ghosts from his past. He exhaled, releasing some of the tension in his knotted muscles, and pressed the heels of his palms to his eyes.

Rhys had never been anything but good to him, seeing something more than he could see in himself and always putting duty before personal desires—until he'd found Ravyn. Both she and Rhys had wills of iron wrapped in a velvet covering and were exactly what the Bringers needed—all Bringers but him.

"Ehhh!" He slammed his palms on either side of the small window. "I need a drink."

He yanked open the door and stepped onto the deck. Shouts and the rumble of wagons boomed around him. He stalked down the gangway toward *The Iron Crown*. People scattered from his path.

His mood darkened at the thought of being brought to full power. Would they change Siban against his will? Already his Tell ability to sense truth was strong, but he'd rejected all suggestions to be brought over. Though Siban never lamented about being imprisoned by the Bane for two years, Luc suspected that he waged a daily war against those awful memories. To give someone plagued by darkness such great powers would be foolish indeed. Luc made a mental pact with himself to defend Siban if they ever found themselves in the same position as last night—even if the Tell hadn't had the consideration to return the favor.

Luc cursed through gritted teeth. Damn his inability to change the course of events.

A woman in a faded red gown stepped in front of Luc, blocking his path. Her bosom spilled over the top of a worn, gaping corset that had been made for a much smaller woman. Strings of greasy brown hair lay plastered against the side of her face and neck. She propped her hands on her ample hips and attempted a seductive smile, which was anything but.

"Time for some fun?" she asked.

Even at his lowest, Luc never engaged the services of the dock whores. Too many diseases, not to mention the chance of being robbed and beaten. Robbed and beaten? According to Rhys, that wasn't something he'd have to worry about anymore. With his full powers, killing him had just become very difficult.

He reached into the small pocket of his leather vest and pulled out a gold liat. The woman eyed the money hungrily.

Luc flipped the coin at her and she snatched it out of the air like a frog snatches a fly. "Go home," he said.

The whore stared at the coin, turning it over in her hand to examine it. She stuck it in her mouth, bit down and then looked at him with a confused expression. "You'll not be wantin' somethin' for this?"

"Yes." He assessed her for a long moment. Stains on her underdress and her unnaturally plump breasts told him she still had a babe on the teat. "I want you to go home." He flipped her another liat. Her eyes widened as she caught the second gold piece. "And purchase food for your family."

She stared at the coins and then back at him, her eyes narrowing. "And you don't want nothin' else?"

"No."

She straightened, lifting her chin an inch. Pride, he recognized it in her stance. Strange thing about pride, it crossed all boundaries. The lowest doxy would rather sell her body than accept charity. Yet a nobleman could whore himself to a king for land and title, slaughtering innocent people in the name of his sovereign, and never miss a night's sleep.

"I don't take charity."

"I'm paying you to go home and take care of your children." He paused and held out his hand. "But if you prefer to work the dock…"

Her fingers tightened around the coins, more money than she'd make in a week. "Well, if you're makin' me leave, guess it's not charity."

He lowered his hand and stared at her. She dropped the money between her breasts. The coins clinked, sliding between the mounds to settle somewhere in the sweaty recesses of her bosom. She tipped her head at him in silent thanks, turned and sauntered away.

Luc pushed through the crowd, not looking to see if the whore had left. He'd done his good deed and whether she complied with his demands or not was no concern of his. At the very least, he hoped her children would have full bellies tonight.

Thankfully, *The Iron Crown* was crowded. Jade slithered through the crush of drinkers and settled in a dark corner across the tavern from Luc. He sat slumped, staring into his mug of ale, turning the cup in slow, continuous circles. His wealth of blond hair was plaited into a thick braid that hung nearly to his waist and showed off the sculpted features of his face. Jade huffed and chided her appraisal. What was his handsomeness to her? Nothing more than a distraction she didn't need.

She'd followed him from the ship, had watched when he'd tossed the dock whore not one, but two pieces of gold. But what had surprised her most was when he'd walked away from the woman. Damn him for doing something good.

Her hand moved over the knife secreted inside the waistband of her pants, under her tunic. The cold metal pressed against her side. Usually the weapon comforted her, but today it felt like an unwelcome intruder.

The minutes ticked by but she didn't move, waiting for Luc to leave. Tonight she'd fulfill her promise to Rell and be done with it — no regrets. Tomorrow, just maybe, she'd be able to start a new life.

Funny how the prospect of his death no longer held the same draw it had months ago. A sense of betrayal crept through her. Avenging her family had always seemed simple, but now the act was layered with repercussions. Could she kill Luc and spend the rest of her life pretending she'd not been involved? Could she build her friendship with Ravyn, knowing all the while it had been her hand that had caused her new friend's grief? Jade shook herself from her dark ruminations and turned her attention back to Luc.

He was different tonight. Not even the tavern whores could pull him from his brooding. When the wenches sidled to his table he didn't look up, only shook his head and continued to stare into his cup. Jade pushed away the jab of pity for him. He had everything and had taken everything from her. She hardened her conviction. She would end this tonight.

Luc stood and tossed a coin to the serving wench. Jade tensed and slid from her chair. Her heart beat in her throat as if she'd been running for her life. She gripped the solid hilt of the dagger through her rough tunic, her thumb caressing a chink in the metal at the butt of the hilt. The repetitive action helped to calm her nerves and center her focus.

She wove a path through the crowd and moved in behind him. He was so tall. His head nearly reached the low beams of the tavern. She swallowed hard, praying she could bring him down with one strike.

The smell of warmed leather encircled her. His braid grazed his lower back and her fingers itched to run the golden rope across her palm. Instead, she steeled her resolve and snaked her hand under her tunic to pull the knife from the waist of her pants. No weakness. No second-guessing herself.

A group of drunken men began to sing and sway, staggering into her. She stumbled, nearly dropping the dagger, but righted herself.

Luc was almost at the door. He mounted the two stone stairs and stepped onto the muddy road. The sun hung low, half hidden by the horizon. Her attack had to be timed well. The darkening sky would be an advantage. She shoved the few stray strands of hair that had escaped back under her kerchief and pulled the hood of her tunic more tightly around her head.

She followed as close as she dared, clutching the knife in a death grip, ready for her chance. He stopped and vigorously rubbed his arms as if set upon by a chill. His gaze wrenched upward, searching the sky.

Luc began to turn. Jade froze, her breath catching in her throat. She couldn't let him see her, didn't want to witness the recognition in his eyes when she took his life.

Without thought, she drew back her arm and thrust the knife deep into Luc's side. The blade pierced the leather of his vest and sank into hard flesh. She stood, unable to move, horrified by the sickness rolling through her body and the blood pouring over her hand. He stumbled, jolting her from her shock. Jade twisted her wrist and pushed him forward, pulling the knife free. The strike had landed fatally true to its mark. Luc fell against the stone wall of the tavern and clutched at his side.

Warm, sticky blood coated her hand. The realization of what she'd just done made it impossible to catch her breath. Luc dropped to his knees but didn't collapse completely. Her hand holding the knife trembled and tears burned at the back of her eyes. It hadn't been as she imagined. Where she thought she'd feel satisfaction and relief, she only felt repulsion. There was no honor in stabbing a man from behind.

He slowly turned his head. She took a step backward. Why wasn't he dying? Luc struggled to stand and she stumbled several more steps. When he gained his feet, survival instincts took over. She spun and fled.

"Stop."

His command drove her to run faster, as did the footsteps pounding from behind. Panic welled. She ducked down a narrow alley and without looking back, wove a confusing route through the dark labyrinth of streets.

The concealment of her hood fell away and her boots slapped through puddles of muck. She dodged people and piles of garbage. Fetid air filled her lungs. Her breath thundered in her ears and she struggled to silence the cries of panic welling in her chest. A dog chased her, nipping at the back of her legs. With a solid kick, she sent the yelping mutt tumbling, ending its pursuit.

She ran through the narrow passages for what felt like miles. Rounding a corner, she slammed her back against the rough stone wall to listen. Heavy footsteps followed in obvious pursuit. How was he chasing her? How was he not dead?

Instinct spurred her forward. She turned corner after corner, trying unsuccessfully to weave an evasive path. The streets closed around her with barely enough room for one person to pass. Luc's footsteps echoed off the tight walls, making it hard to tell how far behind he trailed. She stopped and turned sideways, slipping into an opening between two buildings. Rough stones pulled at the rag covering her head and tunic. She slid along the damp stone until coming to a carved section in the wall, where she ducked in. He'd never fit into such a tight space.

Her breath came in gasps. She looked down and stared at the knife still clutched in her hand. Unable to stomach the feel of the weapon, she opened her bloodied fingers and let the dagger silently slide to the ground. Her attack and escape had been well planned — she'd thought — but events hadn't happened as she'd imagined.

Limping footsteps stopped at the end of the building. She pressed her body deeper into the hole, listening to the person who panted no more than three yards away.

"I can feel you, you little bastard. You won't escape."

She flinched but stayed her impulse to run. Feel her? That was something she hadn't planned on, had never thought of. Luc was a Bringer, she knew this from Rell, but never had he shown any signs of power. Did he sense her because of her contact with a Bane? She'd never considered herself tainted, but of course she was. If Luc could feel Rell's influence, what about Ravyn and the others? They'd never expressed any concern.

Stupid, stupid. Nothing was ever as it seemed. She had an uncanny ability to rationalize her actions only to have them turn around and bite her later. Anger stirred. Her blind loyalty to Rell constantly put *her* in dangerous situations, but rarely cost her sister anything.

Jade pulled her tunic over her mouth to dampen her heavy breathing. Grunts and swearing filtered between the buildings. She closed her eyes and prayed for Luc to leave.

The minutes ticked by. His muffled inquiries to her whereabouts eddied around her, but either nobody had seen her slip between the walls or they weren't turning over one of their own to a privileged prig.

After several agonizing minutes, she heard his uneven gait move away and his footsteps fade. In what direction, she didn't know. Tremors shook her body and she released the neck of her tunic. Blood covered her hand. She pried her fingers apart, flexing them against the hardening layer.

The coppery smell filled her nostrils. All she wanted was to wash away the congealing crust, but she dared not leave her hiding spot. The feel of Luc's flesh giving way under her knife lingered like feathery spider webs she couldn't brush away. She rubbed her palms against her pants, trying to erase her deed, but the crime wouldn't be so easily expunged.

The narrow walls trapped the smell of blood and rotting waste, nearly choking her, pushing her patience and sanity to the limits. She kicked at a rat that wandered too close to her boot. The rodent skittered away, but didn't leave, continuing to paw through the moldy remnants of bread and what looked like a turnip.

She needed to get clean. Never had she felt so dirty. Not just from the filth coating her, but the sins soiling her soul. Despite her near-paralyzing fear, she crept from the alcove and pressed her back against the wall, inching her way down the gap. People passed by but she heard no limping steps, nor the deep timbre of Luc's voice. She poked her head out into the main alley and glanced in the direction she'd come.

The dimming light outlined the shapes of women lounging outside a tavern. Laughter and the gruff voices of men wafted from the surrounding buildings. A child's cry floated from an upstairs window directly across from where she hid, but was quickly silenced by a soft melodic song from a woman. Jade glanced in the opposite direction. No Luc.

A cluster of women passed, giving Jade the perfect cover. She stepped from the gap and blended. The group moved along the narrow street, laughing and talking loudly. At an open doorway, they stopped to speak to another woman. She eased around them and continued down the road, far away from *The Iron Crown* and Luc.

Her pace increased. If she could get to the small, abandoned chapel within the Shrouded Forest she could hide, safe from Luc, and for a while, safe from Rell.

Wooden huts replaced the crush of the city as she darted along the rutted road toward the woods. A border of trees lay dark against the horizon and she began to run. She glanced over her shoulder, the feel of somebody watching her goading her faster. Like a welcoming friend, the tangled arms of the Shrouded Forest enveloped her.

She wove the same kind of path she did when Rell practiced hunting her, never in a straight line. After a few minutes, she stopped and turned in the direction she'd just come. Light from beyond the forest was no longer visible. The trees sealed her away and allowed some of her tension to ease, but in its place, the reality of what she'd attempted took hold.

She stared, unseeing, into the gloom. Emptiness consumed her. For so long she'd been driven to avenge her family, the deed all she and Rell talked about and everything she'd trained for. Now that she'd tried to kill Luc, doubts plagued her. She'd never stopped to consider what it meant to take another person's life, never thought about the cost to her own soul. It had always been: *It had to be done.* Luc *had* to pay for his betrayal.

Rell thirsted for vengeance. With each cruel deed she seemed bent on performing, Jade volunteered in her place, hoping to slow her sister's descent into the world of the Bane. For so long she'd fought to keep Rell rooted to humanity, but never once noticed her own slipping away.

A twig snapped, jolting Jade from her thoughts. She crouched and searched the forest. Nothing moved in the murky grayness. A shiver ran across her skin, the woods' coolness suddenly feeling a lot less welcoming. Maybe the follower was Rell, or a deer. Jade didn't dare call out in case someone or something else stalked her. Other creatures lurked in the forest, none of which she wished to encounter. She cursed herself for not keeping the knife. Now her inability to stomach its feel seemed idiotic.

Another twig snapped. She spun and ran in the opposite direction. Footsteps thundered after her, closing fast. Her muffled breathing blended with the crushing of leaves and the blood pounding in her ears. She hurtled a fallen tree and dodged a tangle of spiny bushes. Leaves and branches thrashed behind her. With a quick cut to the right, she raced toward an opening in the trees. Beyond the clearing the woods thickened to an almost impassable mass. If she could evade her pursuers long enough to lose herself in the tangled undergrowth, she might be able to wait them out.

She broke through the trees and was halfway across the clearing when someone hit her full force, taking her to the ground. The breath burst from her body from the weight of the person landing on top of her. It took only a second to realize who the attacker was.

Luc.

She squirmed out from under him and tried to crawl away, but he grabbed her ankle and yanked, pulling her through the wet leaves. She flipped onto her back and kicked him in the face. He grunted and fell sideways. She clawed at the ground and tried to stand, her panicked whimpers mingling with her gasp. Sharp thorns dug into her hands, but hysteria dulled everything except the need to escape. Before she could gain her feet, Luc tackled her again, smashing her against the wet earth. She smacked at him but he caught her wrists and pinned them to the ground.

"Thought you could get away?" She bucked but he straddled her, rendering her completely helpless. "Not so brave now tha…" His words trailed off as his eyes settled on her face. "You."

Jade twisted under him with no success. "Get off."

"So you can stab me again?"

She stopped fighting. "I didn't stab you," she lied.

Luc sneered and wrenched her hands up, holding them in front of her face. There was no hiding the blood. He released one of her wrists and grabbed the neck of her tunic, pulling it away from her chest. She looked down. A dark handprint stained the neck where she'd pulled the tunic over her mouth.

"Tell me again how you didn't stab me."

"I warned you on the ship that I was there to kill you."

A shadow ghosted across the sky. She fixed her eyes on Luc's face, trying not to follow the figure's descent. Luc hissed, inhaling deeply.

"Cursed minion." He lowered his face toward hers. "It burns to even touch your tainted skin."

Saying nothing, she willed herself not to react, knowing help was almost there.

"Why?" he growled.

She pinched her lips together.

He shook her. "Why?" Anger rolled off him in waves. "Who paid you to kill me?"

Before she could answer, Luc was lifted from her body and tossed across the clearing. Jade jumped to her feet just as Rell landed and crouched in front of her. Luc hit the ground hard and immediately rolled to a stand, taking a fighting stance.

The scene before Jade shifted to something surreal. For years, Rell had raged against him. Now, here he was, squaring off with her demon sister. Before now she had never questioned her role in his death. Sacrificing for Rell was something she did without thought or question, but with her sister bent on engaging Luc, Jade felt helpless to prevent Rell from taking his life and sinking farther into the hold of the Bane. Helpless to stop a chain of events that no longer felt right and would cost her sister more than the satisfaction of revenge would provide.

"Not just a minion," Luc ground out. "A servant."

The disgust in his voice was like a slap in the face. Rell straightened, but the tension in her body let Jade know she was ready for an attack. She folded her wings and stepped back to stand beside Jade.

"Servant?" Rell's voice rang with contempt. She slid her arm around Jade's shoulder. "Sister."

Luc's eyes narrowed, his gaze darting from the demon to her.

"What's the matter, Luc? Don't you recognize me?"

"I don't consort with the Bane, demon."

Rell laughed. The sound pierced Jade's ears and she wanted to turn and run from the scene before her—from this violent, lonely life.

"No," Rell said, lowering her arm and freeing Jade. "You merely leave innocent girls to Bane cruelty."

CHAPTER FIVE

Luc stared for several seconds but didn't relax his bearing. The large green eyes and heart-shaped face were familiar, but the small spiraled horns and glimmering green skin contradicted everything he thought he recognized. Round, firm breasts clad in a leather harness and sculpted muscles could not be attributed to anyone he'd ever known.

His gaze slid to Jade. No longer argumentative and defiant, she now looked scared.

"You speak in riddles, Bane."

"Really?" The demon laughed, the sound empty of humor. "Do you so easily forget the girl you once loved?" She took a step toward him, the iridescent blue-green drape of material hugging her hips and thighs. He crouched, sinking deeper into his stance, ready for her attack. "The girl you promised to marry one day?" She took another step, but he didn't move. "The family you betrayed to the Bane?"

"W–what?" Her words undid him and he straightened, ignoring the sting burning along his arms. His mind rebelled against the very idea that his haunted past stood before him. "What did you say?"

"How much did they give you to betray my father, Luc?" The demon tilted her head to the side, her voice caressing him with false easiness. "A thousand gold liats?" She prowled toward him. "The promise of power?"

He stumbled back a step. "Esmeralda?"

A smile curled the corners of her mouth, exposing her fangs. She stopped and held out her arms. "In the flesh."

"No." The weight of his past pressed around him. Unable to believe the demon standing before him had once been the woman he'd loved, he shook his head. "You're dead."

"Wishful thinking on your part, but as you can see, I'm very much alive." She turned and pointed at Jade. "You remember my little sister, don't you?"

His gaze cut to Jade and for the first time he recognized the seven-year-old he used to tease, the little girl who had followed him around like a puppy, always poxing him and Esmeralda at the most inopportune times.

Luc gripped his head, digging his fingers into his skull in an effort to bring this new reality to focus. This was not possible.

"I never betrayed you, Esmeralda." His answer sounded unconvincing even to him. He lowered his arms. "I wouldn't have done that."

"Tell my father that." The demon's eyes grew wide. "Oh wait, you can't. *He's* dead."

He lowered his head, unable to meet her accusing glare, and blinked back the stinging regret. That night would be forever burned into his mind. "I was coming to see you—to ask for your hand." The words lodged in his throat. "But my friends convinced me to first have a drink in celebration." His gaze cut to her face. "I lost track of time."

"Ah, your friends." Her head nodded slowly, as if contemplating his explanation. "Still blaming others for your actions, I see."

"No, I don't blame anybody for my mistakes." He took a step toward her, holding out his hands pleadingly, needing her to understand how deep his regret cut. "I was so happy, Esmeralda."

Her lip twitched in a sneer. "Pretty words spoken so easily."

"My father had given his approval to our marriage and entrusted me with documents to deliver to your father. A wedding agreement, I think." He had never discovered what the papers were for, only that the information within them had directly led to the murder of Esmeralda's father. "I drank too much, gambled too much, and lost the very coat off my back, including the documents I was to give your father."

The demon shrugged. "It doesn't matter, Luc."

"I searched for you, Esmeralda." He lowered his arms and took a step toward the demon. She tensed as if to attack. "I never stopped."

"Where, Luc? Where did you search? In the taverns? Or perhaps you looked for me under the skirts of all those whores you slated your lust with." Esmeralda bared her fangs in a feral snarl. "You never looked, because you were the one who led the Bane to my father."

He exhaled heavily, the fight going out of him. "I never stopped hoping." No excuse could erase his failure. "I'm sorry, Esmeralda."

"Esmeralda is dead," the demon snapped, her yellow eyes bright and accusing. "No matter how many tears of regret you cry, I am a demon." She slowly lowered to the ground in a crouch. "Because of you, I will forever battle the darkness that threatens to consume my soul. None of your heartfelt apologies can bring back my father."

Her smile turned feral. "My only comfort in life will be the memory of your face as I bleed the life from your body."

All these years he'd blamed himself for her death. The guilt bit doubly hard knowing her fate had been worse than death. There was not recompense for his failure, no fix for his night of indulgence. The woman he'd loved had paid more dearly than he'd ever imagined.

"And now?" he asked.

"I kill you." Her statement held no inflection of emotion. It was said as absolute fact, an imminent event.

"Rell?" Jade said. "Please."

The demon spun to face her sister. "Please what, Jade? Don't tell me you've changed your mind."

"Don't do this." Jade's voice wavered. "The cost to you is not worth it." She paused. "He is not worth it."

Esmeralda hissed. "If you had done as you promised, he'd be dead and I wouldn't have to clean up your mess."

Luc saw Jade flinch from her sister's words.

"You will not be able to kill me," he said.

Rell's gaze snapped to him and she gave another humorless laugh. "You're still arrogant."

He stayed her with a hand. "You're not strong enough."

"You underestimate me, traitor." Her muscles flexed. "I'm going to enjoy proving you wrong."

"Rell, stop," Jade shouted a second before Esmeralda sprang.

Luc had little time to prepare before the demon came at him, talons and fangs bared. He dove to the side and rolled, wrapping his arm around Rell's legs. She spread her wings and pulled herself upward. Her ascent lifted him off the ground, but with his full powers he was as strong as she was and far heavier.

They plummeted the few feet back to earth. He landed on

his knees and released her legs and then tackled Rell, pinning her under his body. Jade attacked, nearly knocking him off her sister, but he held tight. She grabbed his braid and pulled, sending shocks of pain through his head. He let go of one of Rell's shoulders to palm Jade's chest, and shoved. Her grip slipped free of his hair and she tumbled head over heels away from him.

Rell raked at his face, her talons leaving a stinging path across his cheek. The warm blood pooled and ran down his face. She smiled and swiped at him again, but he caught her wrists and restrained them.

"You cannot win, Esmeralda." He used her name, hoping to draw out some of the girl he'd known thirteen years ago. "I'm a Bringer."

She stopped fighting and looked at him. Her gaze leveled on his cheek. If she weren't a demon, bent on killing him, he'd say her expression was one of sudden hopelessness.

"Your face." The words choked from her throat. "It's healing."

The gashes still hurt but it was no longer the sting of an open wound. Tingles of fire burned along his cheek. He let go of her wrist, still ready for her attack, and touched his face. Rounded welts marred the once-smooth surface but there was no longer wet blood, not even a scab.

He lowered his hand and pushed off to stand, stepping away from her. Jade lay on the ground, propped on her elbows, watching him.

"You have your powers?" Rell rolled to her hands and knees, her eyes boring into him. "But how is that possible?"

He said nothing. She was still a demon and even his guilt wouldn't allow him to reveal the one secret that could turn the tides against the fight with the Bane.

"Tell me," she hissed.

She stood and took a step toward him. Gone was any resemblance to the girl Esmeralda. Greed burned in her yellow eyes. He felt her push of compulsion. If he hadn't been brought to full power, he would have told her everything, or been dead.

"Tell me." Urgency drenched her words.

He turned, walked to Jade, and offered her his hand. Anything to avoid the regret Rell's crazed look of need stirred in him.

Jade glanced from her sister to his hand. She hesitated and then accepted. Warmth and an almost imperceptible tingle passed from her hand into his. He pulled her to her feet. Jade blinked and tugged her hand free. Had she felt it too?

"Luc," Rell barked. He turned and faced her. "You owe me an answer. How?"

He pushed aside the call to purge his soul of wrongdoing and confess everything to her. His answer would never even the score and could cost thousands their lives. "I'd never tell a Bane."

"Bane because of you," she snarled at him. "Nothing has changed. The glorious Luc Le Daun is still only concerned for himself. Even when given the chance to make right your past, you still betray me. I might not be able to kill you, but I can certainly cause you pain."

"No!" Jade jumped to her feet and stumbled to stand between Luc and the demon. "You can't win. Go." She wrapped her arms around her body. "I won't let you risk your soul. Go."

Esmeralda stared at Jade for several seconds, unmoving. Perhaps the light played tricks on him, but he thought the yellow glow of the demon's eyes darkened to green. He narrowed his gaze, but when Esmeralda's stare slid to him, her eyes were once again those of a demon.

"I *will* find a way to kill you." She unfurled her wings and again crouched. "You may thank my sister for your reprieve tonight, traitor."

With a powerful leap, she soared through the treetops and disappeared into the night.

Chapter Six

Jade watched her sister ascend until the canopy of leaves swallowed Rell, leaving her alone with Luc. Pain bit into her palms as she squeezed her hands into fists and tried to control her panic. Would Luc retaliate? After all, she had tried to kill him.

He stared at the sky as if waiting for Rell to return. She bit back the urge to tell him he'd be waiting a long time. She knew her sister's demon nature too well. There would be nothing but revenge on Rell's mind. Forgiveness was a rare occurrence.

Only once before had her sister shown compassion to a stranger. Though Rell rarely spoke of him, when she had, it had been with a dreamy air. Jade had deduced two things: that he was human and the bond between them had been far more than curiosity.

Then one day, suddenly, Rell told her to never speak of him again. The days that followed had been dark, her sister sometimes sitting for hours in silence like a stone gargoyle. Something inside Rell had been forever changed.

Worry poked at Jade now. Hopefully, tonight's events hadn't pushed Rell more deeply into the demon realm. At least Rell hadn't killed Luc, for certainly his murder would have frayed and weakened the delicate thread of humanity that still bound Rell to her old life.

Luc turned and glared at her. Jade tensed.

"You'll come with me," he said.

She shook her head. "No."

"We have much to discuss."

"What? Catching up? To discuss old times?" She wrapped herself in her anger. "We have nothing to say to each other."

His gaze darted around the clearing, avoiding eye contact with her. "These woods are not safe."

Not with you here. "So *now* you're concerned for my safety?"

He crossed his arms over his chest and stared at her, unblinking. She stilled her impulse to fidget and instead mirrored his action. She wouldn't let him bully her.

"You can walk beside me, or…"

He let his threat hang in the air. Not again. Last time she'd defied Luc, he'd thrown her over his shoulder, bum in the air, and carried her through town. Heat infused her cheeks at the memory. *Bloody barbarian.* How could her sister have loved him? Stubbornness and a twinge of desperation bolstered her determination. She would *not* go with him.

"Or what? You're going to manhandle me again? Or maybe tie me up and drag me back to town?"

A few telling seconds of silence stretched between them. "If it comes to that."

Her foot inched toward the tangle of trees.

He lowered his arms. "Don't."

She stepped to the side, gaining a full body length's distance from him. "I won't go with you."

"Yes." He glided toward her. "You will."

She spun, but before she could run, he gripped the neck of her tunic and yanked her off her feet. The edge of her collar bit into her skin, choking her. His other arm wound around her waist. She flailed in an unsuccessful attempt to free herself. Hard muscle slammed into her back as he pulled her against him. Her feet dangled above the ground.

"Now." His breath warmed her ear. "Will you walk, or shall I carry you?"

The collar of her tunic tightened against her throat, cutting off most of her air. She tried to wiggle free but the pressure around her waist increased. Her head pounded from the lack of blood and breath fighting to flow free, but still she couldn't allow herself to give in. Never would she be at his mercy.

Her right temple lay along his left cheek. With a painful blow, she smashed her head against his face and delivered a hard thrust of her elbow into Luc's rib. A grunt erupted against her ear and his hold loosened, but not enough to slip free. With as much power as she could leverage, she fisted her hand and delivered a blow over her shoulder, punching him in the neck.

He gasped for air and released her. Her body fell forward and she landed on her hands and knees. Like a dog, she scrambled away from him and toward the cover of branches.

"Oh, no, you don't," Luc choked out.

Jade's body lifted from the ground, her arms and legs pawing uselessly in the air. He flipped her like a rag doll and once again she was hanging, head down, over his shoulder. His arm pinned her legs against his chest, immobilizing her.

"Put me down!" She pummeled his back and was rewarded with a solid smack to her backside. She flinched but the sting only lasted a second, almost instantly replaced by the soothing caress of his hand. She gasped, both at his boldness and the pleasurable sensation he was creating. "Damn you."

Her words sputtered against the smooth leather of his vest. With every step he took, her face bounced off his back and her indignation grew. Saplings and thorny branches brushed her cheeks, increasing her humiliation. For a split second she wished her sister would defy her nature to plot revenge and come back to save her.

Jade gripped Luc's long braid and yanked. He smacked her rear end again before reaching around to reposition his white-blond rope of hair over to the front of his shoulder. Each breath she tried to consume was volleyed back out of her body by his bouncing gait.

"My head aches from hanging upside down." She waited for some sign of sympathy, but he continued to weave his way through the dark and twisted trees, saying nothing. "Did you hear me? I think I'm going to vomit."

Her half-truth failed to move him. Tension bled from her and she gave up her fight. Her body hung limp. She resigned herself to the possibility of being carried ass-end-up through town. Scrub and brambles passed below her with each long stride.

A movement in the trees to her right drew her attention. It was only a flash and then gone. She squinted into the murky dimness of the surrounding forest. There it was again. A shadow within a shadow.

"Luc." He said nothing but his step slowed. "Luc," she whispered, the quiet call more effective than her previous shrieks.

Luc stopped. Forms emerged from the protection of the trees. Thieves. Any other interruption would have been welcome, but she knew these men, recognized them from the docks. They were not only dangerous—but deadly as well. Luc was tough to kill, but she certainly was not.

Luc's hands slid up Jade's thighs and tightened, slowly pulling her back over his shoulder to set her on her feet. His gaze remained riveted on the four men blocking his path.

"Thieves," Jade whispered. Without releasing or looking at her, he slowly spun her to face the men. She gasped. "And there are three behind us."

Twigs snapped and four more men emerged, two from his right and two to his left. They were completely surrounded.

"What are we going to do?"

She'd asked the question as if certain he'd protect her. There was only one problem.

"I have no weapons."

Jade looked over her shoulder and spoke through gritted teeth. "You *are* a weapon, idiot."

Her meaning jolted him. By all accounts he *was* a weapon, only he didn't know how to use his newly gifted powers.

Anger flared. Over the past two weeks Rhys had casually discussed his own transformation to a Shield. Luc had listened to the stories but hadn't taken the details to heart—hadn't realized his friends were setting him up to also be changed. He pushed his resentment away. Betrayal was a distraction he couldn't currently afford.

He sifted through his and Rhys's conversations, searching for something he could use. Shields were protectors and their powers engaged when others were in danger.

Nice and vague.

With the Bane he felt the prickles of fire under his skin. Now all he felt was a heavy awareness of danger, but no sudden intuition on how to transform or even use his abilities. It seemed being brought to full power didn't automatically give him instant knowledge.

A large man stepped forward, dragging a woman behind him. She fought his hold, but her feeble attempt was no match for his brutal grip. He thrust her forward and she crumpled to the ground a few yards from Luc, wrapping her arms protectively around her waist and folding in upon herself. Familiar brown eyes stared up at him.

"I'm—" Small whimpers hiccupped from the woman. "Sorry."

Luc recognized her immediately. The dock whore.

"Shut up!" The man kicked her, the toe of his boot catching her in the stomach.

She gasped and doubled over, slowly sliding to the ground, where she lay struggling for breath.

An unfamiliar heat surged through Luc and engulfed him. His body shuddered from the force of the fire pouring through his veins. At that moment, all he wanted was to beat the man until rivers of his blood soiled the ground. Shocks pricked his fingertips. He flexed his fingers against the unfamiliar sensation. Jade took a tiny step toward him, pressing her back to his chest, as if she knew his intent. The warm presence of her body kept him rooted, dousing the rage, and preventing it from overpowering him.

"Saw how generous you was to her today, my lord." The large man nodded toward the whore. "Ya seemed rather lonely at the tavern and I thought, now there's a nice fellow who needs a friend. So I had Shillings here…" He flicked his head toward the skinny lad to his right. "Follow ya." He slapped the young man on the back and smiled. "Best tracker this side of the Alba Sea."

Shillings gave his master a gapped smile that betrayed his dim-wittedness but also held a hint of maniacal pleasure.

Luc's mind raced for a way to protect both women. "If all you wanted was to rob me, why bring the whore?"

"Call her insurance." A gapped and rotting smile stretched across his thin lips. "Since whether she lives or dies depends on your answer, I figured you'd be less inclined to refuse our kind offer." Laughter rippled around the circle of men. "So what do ya say, my lord? Want to be our friend? All it will cost you is your purse."

Luc trained his gaze on the leader of the group, but as the heat circulated through him, his other senses heightened. Awareness of each thief's movement and position aligned itself within his consciousness. He knew despite the leader's posturing, the man was not the most dangerous of the lot. The need to protect Jade rivaled the urge to batter each of these ruffians to a bloody pulp, protecting the whore only slightly lesser.

Luc kept his voice low and his meaning clear. "I have enough friends."

"Well now, that's too bad." The leader wrapped his hand around the hilt of the dagger sticking out of his pants and pulled it out. "But I'll be takin' your purse just the same." His eyes drifted to Jade. "And the woman."

Blistering heat coiled through Luc's hands. He squeezed his fingers in an effort to stem the flow. The fire pushed back, painfully demanding its release. "Leave now before I lose my temper."

The men erupted in laughter. Sweat beaded on Luc's skin, his powers fighting against the weak rein he had on them.

"Thanks for the warning," said the leader. "But we'll take our chances."

The circle of men tightened. Jade pressed flush against him. There was no way to protect her. Knives and daggers were pulled from the thieves' hidden pockets and sleeves. Back near the trees, another thief notched an arrow.

"Do something," Jade said, making no attempt to keep her voice low.

The fear in her words pushed at Luc. Opening his hands, he let the fire pool in his palms. The freedom that releasing his fire caused was unexpected and euphoric. He fought for control, barely maintaining his command over the energy. A hundred battles never prepared him for the heady rush of knowing he couldn't lose this fight.

He pivoted and flung two balls of fire at the men positioned behind him. Like dry timber, the flames engulfed their layers of clothing. Screams filled the woods. They pulled at their garments, unsuccessfully trying to rip the flaming cloth from their bodies. Seeking help, the burning men ran open-armed and flailing toward their comrades. The other thieves dove out of the way in an effort to avoid the flames. Luc saw two men duck back into the forest and disappear. Nobody moved to help and finally, the human torches fell to the ground, where they continued to burn, unmoving.

The smell of charred flesh assaulted Luc. One of the watching attackers fell to his knees and vomited. Jade spun, but Luc stepped aside in an attempt to block her view of the horrific scene.

She darted around him and froze. A look of shock blossomed on her face. Too late, he grabbed her arm, trying to pull her back against the protection of his body. A heavy thump sounded and Jade convulsed. She stumbled backward and slammed into Luc, her knees buckling. As she crumpled, he caught her in his arms.

"Jade?" He cradled her to him. "Jade?"

Her eyes grew wide and Luc followed her gaze. The shaft of an arrow protruded from her chest. Her mouth opened and shut a few times before forming words.

"I'm hit."

He lowered her to the ground, trying not to disturb the arrow. Anger rolled through him like a dust storm across the desert plains of Alba. He looked up, his sight narrowing on her attacker. Rage took over, blotting out any thought for his safety. Without hesitation Luc jumped to his feet and cast a ball of energy toward the archer. The strike veered wide, blasting a tree into a hundred pieces. The man dove, but gained his feet to flee into the shadows.

Unable to stem his fury, Luc blasted anything that moved, sending fire into the dark recesses of the forest. Flames erupted around them. The thieves scattered, leaving the whore, who still cowered on the ground.

The uncontrollable lust for destruction roared through him. He searched the clearing for his enemies but saw no one. His gaze fell on Jade, the need for conquest instantly bleeding out of him. He knelt, forgetting the thieves and growing flames. Shivers racked her body.

"Don't worry, Jade." He smoothed her hair from her face. She looked ghostly white in the fiery glow. He glanced at the spreading fire. "It's going to be all right."

She mouthed something he couldn't hear and reached a trembling hand toward the arrow. Not wanting her to tear open the wound, Luc stayed her hand.

With as much care as his panic would allow, he scooped her into his arms, making sure not to bump the protruding shaft. The whore stumbled to her feet, clutching her arm, and approached them. Fear flared on her face—whether from him or the growing fire, he couldn't be sure.

"The fire spreads," she said.

Smoke billowed around them, thickening the air. Jade coughed and cried out. Luke laid her on the ground again and gripped the bottom of her tunic. He yanked, tearing a wide strip of material, and tied it loosely over her mouth and nose. Following his lead, the whore reached for the bottom of her skirt and did the same.

He glanced around, looking for some familiar marking to guide him out. Nothing was recognizable. Flames licked the surrounding trees. Best to head the direction the thieves fled. He lifted Jade again and looked at the whore. "Follow me."

The woman nodded and fell into step behind them. If she remained calm and obeyed him, she'd survive to see her children. Heat seared his skin as the underbrush caught fire and swept across the ground like spilled wine. He hoisted Jade higher and breathed into the crook of his arm, the smoke nearly choking him. In an effort to stay ahead of the flames, he wove his way around the twisted trees and gnarled brambles.

He stopped and looked around. "Damn it."

Though these woods were not unknown to him, the fire distorted their path. Loud pops echoed through the treetops.

"These flames are spreading faster than gossip travels through court." The woman's voice was steady despite the growing danger. She stepped around him and veered to the left of their previous direction. "There's a dirt path not too far ahead."

Luc followed, surprised by her calm demeanor and quick pace. Blood spread across Jade's tunic. Each breath rattled in her chest. He *had* to get her to the boat. Ravyn could help her. Ravyn *had* to help her.

Within minutes they stepped onto a narrow trail. A blaze of orange illuminated the treetops, turning each leaf into a small light. The footpath glowed for several yards before plunging into darkness. Obviously familiar with the forest, the whore guided them out into the cool, black night.

The crackle of the now-raging forest fire sounded behind them. Luc didn't have time to worry about the destruction he'd caused. His Shield instincts to protect and save replaced his anger and guilt about his and Jade's current situation. She needed help. Town was far enough away to not be in danger from the blaze, but some of the closer huts might suffer.

The three traveled in silence. The whore ran from hut to hut, beating on each of the doors and giving warning. Luc didn't stop, pushing forward to get Jade to the ship. Each time the woman caught up with them and took the lead.

She led him through sections of town Luc had never been in before. The strong smell of the sea sent waves of relief through him and signaled they were close to the docks. Despite his urging, the whore wouldn't leave, following him onto Rhys's ship. He'd deal with her after he took care of Jade.

"Ravyn?" Luc's voice billowed across the deck of the ship. "Ravyn!"

The door to the captain's quarters flew open. "Luc? What happened?" In seconds, she was at his side. "Oh no." She stepped from his path. "Lay her on the bed."

He carried Jade to the same bed he'd occupied only a day earlier. Despite the warm glow of candlelight, nearly all the color had bled from Jade's complexion.

Ravyn followed him into the chamber and knelt beside the bed. The whore hovered near the door, but didn't enter.

"What happened?" Ravyn said.

"Thieves."

He kept his answer short but knew Ravyn would not let the subject go so easily. His sins pressed around him like a pack of wolves from which he couldn't escape. To tell her about Esmeralda would not only lay open his failing, but betray Jade and her sister a second time.

He stared at Jade's still form, now so frail and near-death. She was a colossal tyrant stuffed inside the tiny body of a woman. She annoyed him, had always annoyed him, even as a child. He didn't trust her, but he wouldn't fail her again, even if that meant lying to Rhys and Ravyn.

"Can you save her?"

"This is a grave injury." Ravyn turned and stared at him as if searching for the answer to some unasked question. "What are you not telling me?"

Curse her new Tell intuition. The greatest talent of the Bringer Tells was knowing when someone lied. After she'd been brought to full power, Ravyn had developed an overabundance of the gift—or curse, depending on whether he was on the receiving end of her scrutiny.

"Nothing."

"You're lying." Her eyes narrowed. "We'll speak later." She flicked her head toward the door. "Take the woman and wait outside."

"I'll stay and help."

Ravyn shook her head. "I can't concentrate with you here." She lowered her voice. "I'm still learning to control my powers and right now my Tell instinct is screaming that there is more to this story than you're telling me. I can't focus."

She looked at Jade and examined the entry point of the arrow. Luc stood and backed away.

"Close the door behind you," Ravyn called over her shoulder as she slipped her immortal dagger from her boot.

CHAPTER SEVEN

A heavy chill enveloped Rell, pulling what felt like the last bit of heat from her body. Rarely did she venture into the lower regions of the Shadow World. When raising Jade, it had been safer to live near the surface in warm caverns, far from the concentration of the Bane. Most demons never hazarded beyond the main level of the throne room, choosing to exist near the king.

She shuddered from the heavy presence gathering around her, like being watched when she could see no one. The dark, narrow corridor appeared empty, but one could never be too sure in the bowels of the Shadow World.

She ran her hand up her arm, attempting to rub away the ominous foreboding filling her. The action helped stay her impulse to skitter back to the surface and hide in the safety of her hidden caverns, where hot pools bubbled and warmed an otherwise bitterly cold world. She focused her thoughts on Luc and fed off her desperation to exact revenge.

Icy rivulets of water oozed down the rough slab walls and disappeared into thin cracks along the base, cut by eons of constant dripping. The crisp air burned her nostrils with each deep breath. She exhaled, trying to calm her rapid heartbeat. Dampness seeped through her muscles and into her bones, causing them to ache.

She wouldn't be here if not absolutely necessary. This section of the Shadow World resonated with everything she hated about being a Bane, everything she could never accept about the change that had been forced upon her. This was the true demon realm.

Only twice had she followed Icarus to the lower levels, needing to satisfy her curiosity about where the deadly demon traveled. Protecting Jade had required her to ferret out secrets and know who moved where in the netherworld.

Sha-hera's army dwelled here, planning and plotting in the war room. Luck had been with Rell so far, having neither drawn the attention of nor made an enemy of the succubae army captain. Rell stopped and scanned the passage in both directions. Still empty—or so it appeared.

She leaned against the wall and gathered her courage. What she was about to do was sheer madness, but she needed Icarus's help; and though he didn't know it yet, he needed her help as well.

She glanced around and slipped into the gap separating two behemoth slabs. If one didn't know the passage existed one would have passed right by. Rough stone scraped against her wings as she inched to the end and exited into a small circular chamber. A rock staircase beckoned her forward. Her heart beat faster. Again she chided herself for the madness of her plan.

Small stones crunched under her foot when she placed it on the first step. Her quiet shuffle up the narrow stairs sounded overly loud.

Rell paused, listening for movement above her. Raised voices filtered down the spiral opening. A female voice, more than likely

Sha-hera, bantered with a male. Was it Icarus? The arguing grew louder the higher she climbed.

At the top step, Rell stopped. It wasn't Icarus, but Vile.

From where she stood, she could peer directly into the succubae army's plotting chamber. Several of Sha-hera's commanders lined the wall, their stances rigid. The Demon King and Sha-hera faced each other on opposite sides of a large stone slab, debating over several sheets of parchment. Each drawing looked to be a map of some kind. Rell squinted. Not maps, layouts of buildings and grounds. What were they plotting?

Vile slammed his fist against the table. "I speak but you do not seem to hear me. So I will say it again. Your plan is flawed, and will not work."

Rell leaned toward the opening, making sure to stay clear of the torchlight that brushed the first foot of rock ledge on which she stood. With controlled impatience, Sha-hera clenched and unclenched her hands behind her back. Tension radiated between the two powerful demons, but Sha-hera wisely made no further argument.

The sensation of being watched skittered along Rell's skin. For a moment she'd forgotten her purpose, but when she turned the reason came rushing back.

Icarus was there, standing in the shadows, watching her. His golden gaze held her in place, making it more difficult to breathe. Suddenly, success of her plan paled against the cost her encounter could reap. She mustered her courage and took a step forward.

His mouth peeled back in a silent snarl. Her steps faltered but it was too late to retreat. She focused on her anger at Luc and managed three more small paces. Icarus straightened away from the corner he'd been leaning against, his body tense as if readying to fight. Rell glanced away and peered into the army's strategy room, giving her bravery time to rally.

Turning to the demon, she inched forward slowly and raised a talon to her lips. His snarl relaxed slightly but his stance did not.

On silent feet, she closed the distance between them. He could have been made of stone if not for the suspicion burning in his eyes. His aura was palpable, radiating a power that thrummed against her skin. He was like no other demon she'd ever encountered.

"We must talk." Her voice was almost inaudible but she knew Icarus had heard her by the way his gaze narrowed even further. "It is urgent."

He stared at her for a long moment, assessing the situation with the skill of a demon who knew treachery firsthand and trusted no one. She held her breath. Never had she been this close to him. Never had she dared. His skin was black and smooth like polished leather, perfect and unblemished, each muscle sculpted to perfection. His almond-shaped eyes followed the contours of his high cheekbones, giving his face perfect symmetry. Stunning—and deadly.

Icarus's hand snaked out and wrapped around Rell's arm. She didn't resist when he dragged her toward him. He pivoted and pushed her into the corner, his warm body pressing against hers. She stifled her surprise when his skin touched hers. Instead of being cold and hard like marble, heated velvet covered her. Warmth seeped into her body, sending tingles across her skin.

The voices below fell quiet. Icarus's gaze cut from her face toward the ledge and then back to her. His hand moved to her chest, pressing her more firmly against the wall. She opened her mouth but the words died in her throat when a heavy thud thundered behind Icarus.

He didn't turn but his eyes narrowed, boring into her with the silent command to remain quiet and hidden.

"Why not come and join us, Icarus?" Vile's voice filled the small cove. "Lurking is beneath you."

Icarus straightened, his hand sliding across her chest, gently raking the leather that covered her breasts with his talons, and turned. Fear paralyzed every muscle in Rell's body.

"I find the company you keep not to my liking, Father." He braced his shoulder against the wall, effectively blocking her in. "Besides, you don't appear to want my participation."

From the sound of his movements, Rell knew that Vile moved deeper into the space. She pressed against the rough stone wall, the rocks poking painfully at her skull. The demon's presence seemed to swallow the air around her. She closed her eyes and sent up a prayer of help to the Sainted Ones.

"I care not about your strife with Sha-hera." Vile paused. "You each have your duties and I expect you to accomplish them." The threat in his voice was unmistakable. "Any conflict that threatens the success of *my* plans shall be dealt with swiftly and without mercy."

Rell stared at Icarus's profile. His expression was unreadable. Though he didn't openly challenge his father, neither did he cower from the threat. His posture remained rigid and unyielding. She had been right to think that Icarus held no love for the Demon King.

"I am aware of your methods," Icarus said.

"Are you?" Three footsteps paced away from where she hid and stopped. The sweep of Vile pivoting swished along the walls. "Because if I didn't know you better, I might think you have designs on my throne."

Icarus gave a convincing laugh of surprise. "I have no wish to rule your mongrel horde, Father—until it is my rightful time."

Silence stretched between them but Icarus remained unmoving, his gaze peering steadily forward.

Vile's answer was pitched low, cutting through the strain. "For your sake, I hope that is true—son."

The sound of wings extending was followed by retreating footsteps. A rush of air hummed from what must have been Vile leaping from the ledge.

Another few seconds passed before Icarus's stance relaxed. He turned his head and leaned toward her.

"Hot pools." His lips brushed against her ear. "Go."

He stared, unmoving. No emotion showed on his face. Rell gathered her wits and stepped around him, wanting nothing more than to get as far away from the Demon King as possible.

She eased toward the stairs, but stopped to glance one more time into the war room, making sure to remain completely in the shadows. All appeared as it had when she'd first entered. Before she could slip away, Vile's gaze traveled upward and stared steadily in her direction. Could he see her? With a measured step backward, she eased out of his visual range and crept down the stairs.

As silently as possible, she moved down the passage until she reached the first corner. Rell stopped and looked behind her. Nobody followed. She turned the corner and picked up her pace, fairly sprinting by the time she reached the upper level of the Shadow World.

Moist, warm air settled on her skin when she entered the cavern and slowly seeped through the chill of the Shadow World. The chamber's ceiling soared, a welcome change from the tight, low passages winding through the lower levels. Layers of steam billowed off the water.

Rell paced around the edge of a bubbling pool. Would Icarus come? Or more important, did she want him to come? There was definite contention between the king and his son. Taking sides might be too big of a price for revenge.

A vent of warm air hissed next to a large, flat-topped boulder. The rock had always been Jade's favorite spot to stretch out. It was the closest thing she'd had to a bed. Rell climbed on top and perched like a waiting vulture, her arms wrapped around her knees. She spread her wings and let heat from the vent blow over them, the gentle vibration relaxing her muscles and thawing her body. Even her talons were cold. She rested her chin on her knees and waited.

The minutes dragged by, fueling her folly of asking Icarus to help her. The slow bubble of the water and quiet hiss of the vents were the only sounds.

Then she heard it. Stone crunched beyond the doorway. Her head snapped up, her gaze riveted on the entrance, her heart beating against her chest. Seconds passed and then he was there.

Icarus's body filled the arched entrance. He ducked his head and stepped through the doorway. Spike-tipped wings scraped along the stone arch of the entrance.

Rell didn't move, waiting for some indication of his mood. Icarus ignored her, turning to examine the chamber. Satiny black hair hung in a long tail down his back. Five gold rings banded the silky strands and glinted in the green-blue glow of the cavern's pools. He flared his wings, stretching them to the warmth of the cave, and held his arms out to the side. A gold bracelet glimmered at each wrist. He flexed his fingers. She watched, surprised by his reaction to the heat. Was it not only her then who hated the bone-chilling burn of the Shadow World?

Icarus pivoted to face her, wings still spread. The demon was magnificent, every line of his body sculpted with perfect symmetry.

Desire stirred inside her. Rell straightened, taken aback by the twinge of lust. She'd seen other demons fornicating, but she had never partaken. Turned before her maidenhead had been taken, she had never had the chance to explore the sensual secrets between men and women.

Never once had she desired any of the filthy beasts that littered the throne room. Even her vengeance against Luc was born of anger, not lust. There had only been one man, until now, who had stirred her blood. She'd risked so much for him, saved him from a fate worse than death. But he was lost to her now and it hurt too much to think about him.

Rell stood, pushing away the memories of what could never be and the yearning she felt for Icarus.

"Where is your sister?"

She gasped, desire evaporating. Of all the things she'd expected him to say, asking about her sister wasn't one of them.

The smile he gave her was a cross between amusement and a predator cornering its prey. "You kept her here." He sauntered toward the largest pool. "Raised her from a child."

Rell eased from the rock and folded her wings behind her. "How do you know this?"

"I know many things that go on in the Shadow World." He skirted the edge of the pool and stopped to crouch, dragging his talons through the steaming water. "Once she bathed here."

"But, she never mentioned the encounter."

Swirls of water eddied around his hand. "I believe I frightened her."

"Why did you leave her..." Rell searched for the right word. "Unharmed?"

Icarus stood, the amusement draining from his face. "Why did you summon me?"

This was the reason all demons feared him above any other,

even Vile. Like a coiled snake, Icarus seemed to wait for his chance to attack. Always poised to take down his enemy, even when none existed. She discarded her question and focused on her mission.

"I offer you a proposal."

His eyes narrowed. Another way Icarus differed from Vile. Where the king would mock with wide-eyed surprise, Icarus approached with suspicion.

"Speak."

Rell swallowed hard and forced herself to hold his gaze. "I know you helped the Bringer escape."

He cocked his head to the side. "Not a proposal." The velvety purr of his voice licked at her, reawakening her sensual need. "Is it to be blackmail then?"

"No." She shook her head slowly. "I care not that you helped him." Her mind scrambled for a common thread to bind them. "I would have helped him myself if it would have foiled Sha-hera's plans."

His face relaxed back to its inscrutable beauty. "I'm listening."

"The Bringer woman still lives."

Icarus went still. "Impossible."

"Not impossible. My sister has seen her."

"How?"

"I don't know. She appeared dead when you—" She searched for a better description, something less accusatory about the time Icarus had carried Rhys Blackwell and his woman out of harm's reach. "When I last saw her with the male Bringer."

Icarus paced along the edge of the pool as if contemplating her words. "You're sure of this?"

"Yes." Rell dared a few steps toward him. "And there's another."

He stopped pacing and looked at her. "Another full-blood. A man."

"Besides Rhys Blackwell?"

She nodded. The silence in the cavern stretched, growing louder as they stared at each other across the green, bubbling water.

"Why do you tell me this?"

Why *was* she telling him this? What did she truly know about his reasons for helping the Bringer? Too late to retreat, she decided to follow her hunch. She relaxed her stance and locked her hands behind her back in hopes of appearing confident.

"You want the throne and I wish to help you."

His bark of laughter ricocheted off the walls, causing Rell to jump.

"You are most direct."

She shrugged, maintaining her air of confidence. "I am observant."

His smile faded. "Maybe too observant."

"Perhaps." The threat was not lost on her. She shrugged again. "But not in this matter." With slow, measured steps she sauntered toward him. "I can help you."

His eyes followed her. "At what cost?"

She stopped a few feet from him. "There's no cost when what we want is the same." She took a step closer. "You seem to need a full-blood and I want to rid myself of one."

"Why?"

Anger erupted, rolling through her before she could contain it. She stepped away, fisting her hands. "Because this is his fault." She held out her arms, indicating her demon form. "He betrayed my family and stole my future."

"A woman scorned." Icarus tilted his head, assessing her. "I think you loved him, yes?"

She lifted her chin and lowered her arms, not wanting to admit how Luc's actions had betrayed her trust. "I was naïve."

"And now?"

"Now…I will have my revenge."

An expression Rell couldn't identify passed across Icarus's face. Sympathy? Understanding? Compassion? These attributes were as foreign to the Prince of the Shadow World as wings on pigs.

She tensed as he glided toward her. His knuckles gently grazed her upper arm, admiringly, as if savoring the feel.

"You're different." He grasped her arm and drew her toward him. "Not cold like the others."

Shivers of pleasure rippled across Rell's skin. The iron velvet of Icarus's body molded with hers and she was helpless to do more than stare into his eyes, watching as gold swirled to silver and back to gold. His gaze caressed her face, searching for something. He ran the back of his hand along her cheek like a blind man trying to identify a familiar object.

"Touching you stirs…" He paused.

"Stirs what?" she prodded, needing so much to hear his declaration of desire—his longing meant only for her.

"Memories where I have none." His words caressed her.

She furrowed her brow, confused by his words. He lowered his hand back to her arm, his eyes refocusing to their penetrating stare.

"We will work well together, I think." One arm wrapped around her back and held her tightly against him. "I accept your proposal."

Of their own accord, her arms inched around his waist. She watched and waited as he slowly lowered his head. His breath brushed her lips. So close. She stretched up, offering herself to him.

"But know this," he whispered. His mouth captured hers in a searing kiss, his rough tongue sweeping inside to stroke hers.

The bones in her body seemed to melt. Luc had kissed her when she was a young woman, but the memory paled in comparison to the demon's branding.

As quickly as he'd launched his sensual attack, he pulled back and stared at her. "If you betray me, I *will* kill your sister."

Her breath came in pants, all words failing her, not because of his threat but because of his effect on her. She nodded and then lifted her chin, asking for another kiss. A knowing and somewhat amused smile crept across his lips, but he gave her what she wanted.

Again he lowered his mouth to hers, this time more slowly as if savoring and teasing her at the same time. It had been so long since somebody had held and gently kissed her. She pushed the memories from the past away and concentrated on the feel of Icarus.

His knuckles brushed along the sensitive skin of her neck, shoulder, and across the swell of her breast. The light pressure of his talons scraped across her leather harness, sending sparks of desire through her nipples. He cupped her breast, eliciting a small moan from her. Icarus deepened his kiss. She tugged him more tightly to her. His warmth seemed to drive away the darkness that threatened to swallow her.

She ran her hands up his lower back to stroke the powerful wings folded against him. The evidence of his desire pushed against his black leather breeches, stiffening against her stomach, his kiss becoming more demanding. Heat coursed through her body and the need to be closer, to rub against him, overwhelmed her. She gripped the thick edges of his wings, wrapped a leg around his thigh and pressed herself to him. He groaned, his hand traveling down to cup her rear end. No space existed between them, but still she wanted more.

Without warning, Icarus broke their kiss. He stared at her, his breathing labored.

Her voice sounded weak and desperate. "What is wrong?"

"You." He eased her hands from around his waist. "I can't think clearly when you are…touching me."

She didn't disagree. The intensity between them had been like nothing she'd ever felt, but neither was she sorry for what they had shared. For several glorious moments she had felt human.

"There is much at stake for both of us." He stepped around her.

She followed his movements, somewhat surprised by his apparent lack of control. Perhaps she had more leverage with the demon than she thought.

Icarus stopped a few yards away, straightened and turned to face her again. "Until this is over and I have what I want, I will not let myself be distracted."

Rell raised her eyebrows in question "And afterward?"

A predatory smile tugged at the corners of his mouth, but he didn't reply.

CHAPTER EIGHT

Luc stared across the ink-black water. How much time had passed—an hour, two hours? He glanced toward the door, willing Ravyn to come out.

"She your woman?"

He'd been so lost in self-loathing he'd forgotten the whore was still there. She sat on a crate, one arm resting in her lap while the other hand plucked at the frayed end of her dirty skirt.

"Who?"

The woman flicked her head toward the cabin door.

"No. Just an acquaintance." He turned and leaned his hip against the ship's railing. "Why?"

"Don't know." She shrugged and continued picking at the hem of her skirt. "You didn't accept my offer this morning. Wondered if it was because of her. You don't exactly seem like the faithful type, but in the forest I got the impression she was your woman."

"She's not." He glanced out across the water again. "Far from it."

The woman harrumphed.

He straightened, his gaze snapping back to the whore. "Why are you still here?"

"I don't want to leave until I know your friend is all right." She looked at him, her face pinching into a sour expression. "Feel like this mess is my fault. I should have been more careful around Pascal. He has eyes everywhere. There ain't nothing that happens on the docks that he don't know about and that Shillings…" She shook her head. "He's one nasty piece of work. Do just about anything for Pascal."

"None of this is your fault." Luc sighed and rubbed his hands over his face, then lowered them. "It's mine." When would he stop ruining Jade and Esmeralda's life? "It's always my fault."

"I find there are usually no extremes in relationships, even friendship. One is not always right or never wrong. I doubt things are *always* your fault." She shrugged. "But I could be wrong."

"You are," he bit out. "And we are not in a relationship."

The whore gave a nod that said less about agreeing with him and more about knowing something he obviously didn't.

"She hates me." He picked at a worn strand of rope that lay draped over the side of the ship. "For good reason."

Her eyebrows lifted but she didn't look at him.

"You don't believe me?"

She smirked and looked up. "Who am I to question your story? All I know is what I thought I saw." She shrugged again. "The heart wants what the heart wants." She let go of the worn hem, stood and stretched, arching her back. "I find there ain't no use fightin' it."

"Rubbish."

She didn't argue with him. An awkward silence grew between them, her words chipping away at what little calm he maintained. It was nonsense to think Jade harbored anything but hatred for him.

Complete foolishness.

He crossed his arms and glared at her. "You're very blunt."

The woman gave a quiet laugh. "So I've been told."

"Not surprising," he mumbled.

He found the whore to be a complete puzzle. Willing to sell her body to make a living, but wouldn't accept charity, intelligent, with a rough kindness that grew out of hard times. He lowered his arms and relaxed his stiff stance. "What's your name?"

She bit her bottom lip as if contemplating whether to lie. After a few seconds she said, "Delphina."

"Pretty name."

"It's the one beautiful thing my mother gave me before selling me to a pleasure house."

Words momentarily escaped him. He was well acquainted with the seedy side of life. Had been facedown in it more times than he cared to remember. But to come face-to-face with the stark rawness of what happened to the innocents rallied a sense of morality and honor he didn't know still existed within him.

In an effort to lighten the mood, he changed the subject. "Thank you for your help tonight—after the thieves fled."

Delphina smoothed one hand down the front of her skirt, not meeting his gaze. "I didn't do anything. Like I said, I caused more trouble than I'm worth."

Her words echoed the same thoughts he had about himself. He fumbled with the frayed end of the rope, plucking apart the threads. Her unwillingness to accept praise was understandable. Each day was a struggle to live, with few kind words and even fewer offers of freely given help. There was no reason she should believe him to be sincere.

"You helped lead us out of the forest and probably saved Jade's life."

She lifted her gaze and gave him a hard stare.

"I'm fairly certain those men didn't give you a choice," he continued before she could protest.

"You're very understanding." She walked toward him and stopped a few feet away. One arm cradled the other and she eased a hip against the rail. "There's something different about you. I've seen a fair bit of earth magic in my day, but what you did was like nothing I've seen before."

Luc contemplated lying to her, but knew she'd see through his deception. "What do you think you saw?"

She cocked her head, slanting him a suspicious look. "You'd just say I was mad if I told you, so I think I'll keep my ideas to myself." She winked at him. "Till I know for sure."

The door to the cabin opened before he could reply. Ravyn stepped out, holding a bloody rag, and closed the door behind her. Dark stains spattered the front of her green leathers and bluish circles pooled under her eyes.

"How is she?" he said.

"Alive." The stiff set of her shoulders told him her mood hadn't lightened. "Sleeping."

Luc sighed. "Can I see her?"

"No." He flinched from her sharp tone but she ignored him, cutting her gaze to Delphina. Ravyn smiled. "I guess I have you to thank for saving my friends."

Delphina blushed under the praise. "Weren't nothin.'"

"Well, I disagree. These two have a penchant for getting in trouble. They were quite lucky to have your help."

Luc pinched his lips together. Even Ravyn knew this situation was his fault, and she was angry with him. Arguing wouldn't help.

She turned her attention to the rag, scrubbing it against her knuckles in an effort to clean off the blood. "So what really happened?"

"We were attacked by thieves. Jade took an arrow." Luc kept his answer short, trying not to inadvertently betray Jade and Esmeralda by providing too many details. He pointed to Delphina. "She helped us find our way out of the forest."

Ravyn arched an eyebrow, still not looking at him. "Were you lost?"

"No, my lady," Delphina piped in. "He set fire to the forest with that blasting thing he does. Took out a couple of ruffians."

Ravyn's head snapped up. "Blasting?"

Luc set his jaw against her censuring tone.

"I saw what I saw." Delphina waved a hand in the air. "You may think me mad, but you won't be changing my mind."

"I had no intention of trying." Ravyn tossed the rag onto a barrel and looked at him. When Luc opened his mouth to explain she held up a hand, effectively cutting him off. "No lies and no half-truths, Luc."

"I'd met…" He motioned toward Delphina. "Her earlier in the day."

Ravyn propped her hands on her hips and pinned him with a questioning stare. It was amazing how she could trumpet her disapproval with a single look. He ground his teeth together.

Delphina came to his defense. "Not like that, my lady. He gave me two gold liats and told me to go home and feed my children."

Ravyn's expression softened.

"I was going to do his bidding," the woman continued, "but Pascal and his lot seen my transaction with his lordship. They thought him an easy mark."

Ravyn nodded, letting her arms relax at her side. "Then what happened?"

"Pascal tracked him to the bar." The woman gave Luc an apologetic smile. "You weren't very difficult to find."

"I see." Ravyn stepped toward Delphina, putting Luc on alert. Her eyes leveled on the woman's arm. "And I assume he threatened to hurt you if you didn't help him?"

Luc recognized the subtle way Ravyn blocked Delphina's path. It was a position he'd found himself cornered in far too many times—usually when Ravyn wanted something.

"Pascal used her as a bargaining tool," he said. "If I gave him my purse he wouldn't kill her."

"He sounds like a wonderful man." Inches separated her and the whore. "May I examine your arm?"

Delphina flinched, her eyes darting from her arm back to Ravyn's face.

"I promise I won't hurt you," Ravyn said.

Hesitantly, Delphina extended her arm. Ravyn encircled the woman's hand between hers. At first contact Delphina jumped, but she didn't pull away.

Luc shifted, unsure if he should stop or help Ravyn. Was she planning on healing Delphina out where prying eyes might be watching? He knew Ravyn's healing abilities had grown since she'd come into her full powers, but he also knew her to be a bit careless. Rhys's demand that they keep the Bringers' existence a secret didn't appear to be something she planned on heeding.

He took a step toward her, meaning to casually mention Rhys's wishes. "Uh, Ravyn?"

"Hush, Luc." A subtle compulsion to keep quiet hit him, cutting off any further attempt.

It took a second to realize what she'd done, and another few seconds to recover from the realization of how easily she'd silenced him. She'd always been stubborn. Now it appeared she had the ability to back up her obstinacy.

If she won't listen to Rhys, she sure isn't going to listen to me.

Luc made note not to be around when she explained to Rhys about revealing the Bringers to a questionable dock whore.

Ravyn closed her eyes and released a slow breath. The depth of her compassion resonated around them, humbling Luc. He reproached himself for never considering that Delphina might be hurt. Now he could see the way she cradled her arm was from injury and not insecurity. *Unfeeling bastard.*

The woman glanced at him in silent question. He gave her a slight nod, wanting to ease her worries. It was a small act of kindness he could give her. She held his gaze, the indecision clear on her face. The fist she pressed against her thigh slowly relaxed, her shoulders following suit. She turned her attention back to her arm.

Nobody spoke. Water sloshing against the side of the ship and the distant din of the late-night crowd were the only disruptions in the whispered words of the healing chant.

Delphina gasped, her eyes growing wide. "Sainted Ones, your hands is like a steamin' kettle." She gripped her upper arm as if to stop the healing burn. "I can feel the heat travelin' right up my arm."

"It's all right." He placed a hand on her shoulder. "She won't hurt you."

Her eyes rounded to the size of gold liats, but she nodded, accepting his reassurance.

Luc started to lift his hand from Delphina's shoulder but stopped. Pulses of heat radiated through her coarse wool dress. He closed his eyes and absorbed the residual healing. Snaps of fire shivered up his arm. The world shifted and for a brief moment the three of them were connected. Golden ribbons of light flowed from Ravyn's hand and wrapped around and rushed into Delphina's wrist. The healing light spiraled up her arm, burning away the dark patches of pain.

From the top of Delphina's shoulder, the light entered Luc's hand. It warmed and surrounded him, circling through his body and erasing not only wounds, but his exhaustion as well. After a minute, he let his hand slide free and stepped away, extinguishing the vision of golden light.

Ravyn's abilities had grown. She seemed capable of calling upon her powers with almost no visible effect. The distance between the mixed-bloods and those who possessed full power was not lost on Luc. When Nattie, Rhys's mixed-blood Redeemer, healed, it was like being dragged back to health by a team of horses. Ravyn's healing didn't wrench, but soothed, like a baby in the arms of its mother.

Time passed until finally she released Delphina's hand and opened her eyes. "Better?"

The woman held up her arm and rotated her wrist. A smile spread across her face. "Better than before Pascal got a hold of me." She flexed her fingers. "You have some powerful magic, my lady."

"Please, call me Ravyn," she said, ignoring the veiled question. "And you are?"

"Delphina."

"Delphina." Ravyn repeated the name with a sort of reverence that made the woman stand a little taller. "What a beautiful name. How old are your children?"

"Twelve, six, and a year, my lady. Two girls and a boy."

Ravyn's smile held a hint of longing. "Where are they now?"

"In our room." Delphina rotated her wrist again. "My oldest is watching the younger two."

In the short time he'd known Ravyn, she'd never shown signs of wanting a family. Luc had certainly never heard Rhys talk about a life other than being a Shield.

Things between he and his friend had changed since Ravyn arrived. Though Rhys had always been more responsible and focused, Luc had chalked up his attitude to being more than three hundred years old. Still, somewhere in the back of Luc's mind, he'd ignorantly believed he and Rhys would remain unmarried together.

Such was not the case. Now he stood on the outside of Ravyn and Rhys's private circle, and if they had children, the distance would grow. Luc shook off the pang of jealousy that thought drew from him.

"May I beg a favor from you?" Ravyn brought her hands together in a praying pose and touched her middle fingers to her lower lip. "Would you consider staying on the ship with your children?"

Delphina stopped examining her arm and lowered it. "I don't take charity, my lady."

Ravyn laughed. "Trust me, my request is purely selfish. You would be doing me a great favor. We are in need of somebody we can trust. The ship will be undergoing repairs, and well… to be honest, I haven't found the workers around here very trustworthy."

"Too right, my lady." Delphina bristled, waving her newly healed arm in the air. "Most would just as quick steal you blind as do an honest day's work."

"Then you see my dilemma." Ravyn turned her palms up in a helpless plea. "I need somebody with my interests at heart. Somebody firm and strong. And who's more firm than a mother?"

Delphina glanced between him and Ravyn as if trying to sniff out a ruse. It was so like Ravyn to try and save the world one person at a time. Luc decided to help her out—for the sake of Delphina's children, not because he was kind. And besides, it was a good plan.

"I agree," he added. "We could use an extra pair of hands around here."

Ravyn's eyes radiated her thanks, but she kept her expression serious. "Indeed. But…"

"But what?" Delphina said.

"Well, I couldn't allow you to continue your current…" She stumbled over her words. "Your current line of work—for reasons of safety."

The expression on the whore's face sparked a protective instinct inside Luc. A lifetime of burdens seemed to slide from her shoulders.

"I—I'd be willing to give that up." She blinked hard, her voice betraying a slight tremor. "And my children are welcome as well?"

Ravyn gave an exaggerated sigh of relief. "If they don't mind pitching in whenever needed, we'd love to have them." She tapped her index finger to her lip. "Now, I can pay you two gold liats a week." Delphina opened her mouth, but Ravyn held up her hand, cutting her off. "I know it's not much. You're probably used to a lot more, but remember food, lodging, and clothing are all provided for you. Unless you have other debts, your income will be yours to spend as you wish."

Delphina stared at Ravyn and then looked at Luc. "Is she serious?"

"Quite serious." He shook his head and propped his hands on his hips. "But don't think every day will be peaceful." His gaze cut to Ravyn. "Things can get dangerous."

Delphina's laugh was empty of humor. "I spend my nights

spreadin' my legs for the likes of Pascal just to keep my children fed and hidden away in a cold, dark room." She mirrored his stance. "I think we can handle a little danger."

"Good." Ravyn smiled. "Would you like Luc to help you fetch your children and belongings?"

Her eyes widened. "Now?"

"No time like the present," Ravyn said.

"Uh, no…thank you." The woman looked shocked, which Luc suspected was hard to do. "I like to keep my head low." She slid a glance his way, giving him an apologetic half smile. "Sorry, but you are anything but unnoticeable."

"If you're certain," Ravyn said.

"Don't have but one bag. If I leave now we can be back within the hour."

Without a backward glance, Delphina climbed onto the walkway and left.

He and Ravyn watched their new boarder sashay across the dock and disappear down a dark alley.

Silence stretched between them until he couldn't stand it. "That was very kind of you."

She shrugged. "You would have done the same thing."

"I didn't even think to check her for injuries." He snorted. "Let alone give her family a safe home."

Ravyn faced him, her expression difficult to read. "Luc, what do you know of Jade?"

The abrupt question took him aback. He schooled his reaction. "Not much. She dresses like a boy. Seems to have a bit of a grudge against me."

"So you're unaware that she's a Bringer?"

His mouth fell open. "What?"

"A Bringer. Did you know?"

A dozen reactions swamped him. Denial. Jade couldn't possibly be a Bringer. He would have known. Question. If she was a Bringer then Esmeralda was as well. Fear. A Bringer turned Bane—what did it mean? This revelation added a deeper level of mystery and danger to the Bringers' quest.

Luc stared at Ravyn, grappling over how much to tell her. He needed to speak with Jade first. Had she deceived him? Was her alliance truly with the Bane and she was using them to worm her way into the Bringers?

"No. I didn't know." That at least was the truth.

"What are you not telling me?"

"Damn it, Ravyn." He glared at her. "Stop prying."

"I'm right, though. Aren't I?"

He sighed, his shoulders sagging. "Let me deal with some things. Then we'll talk—all of us, Rhys, Siban."

Her gaze narrowed. "What kind of things?"

"I need to speak with Jade first." He could almost see the questions speeding through her mind. It was her nature to help, or at the very least pry. "Please," he added, hopefully pushing her into compliance. "Just let me talk to Jade first."

Ravyn pointed a finger at him. "Fine, but I expect answers. You're not fooling anyone." She lowered her hand. "Too many things about your story don't add up, Luc, and I won't let you endanger others with your carelessness."

Her words hit the mark. "I may have my faults, Ravyn, but even you can't argue with my dedication to the Bringers."

"Oh really? How about the fact that you don't want to be one? Maybe you can explain your reasons for that when you tell us the rest of your story." She took a step toward him. "I know deception when I feel it, and it's pouring off you in buckets."

Her words felt like a slap in the face. He'd fooled himself into thinking he didn't care if Rhys and Ravyn respected or trusted him. Yet her harsh words proved him wrong. He did care. With great effort, he corralled his hurt and anger. "May I see her?"

After a tense moment, Ravyn stepped aside. "She's still weak. Don't tax her overly long."

He nodded and eased past her.

"And Luc…"

He stopped but didn't turn.

"I had to bring her to full power."

He swung on her. "What?"

"She would have died otherwise." Ravyn squared her shoulders. "As it was, I barely saved her."

The realization of how close Jade had come to dying hit him, as did a chaos of emotions he was unprepared to deal with. He pushed the tsunami of feeling into the ever-expanding space of things he didn't wish to acknowledge and looked at Ravyn. "Thank you for saving her."

She gave a single nod.

He turned back to the cabin door and gripped the handle. "I hope she is more grateful than I was."

A trace of desperate hope laced Ravyn's answer. "As do I."

CHAPTER NINE

Jade opened her eyes and screamed. Luc's face loomed no more than a foot above her. She pressed her head into the feather tick, trying to put distance between them and calm her racing heart. Waking up in the chapel was so much more peaceful. "What are you doing?"

"Checking to see if you're still breathing."

"Why wouldn't I be?" She braced her palms against his chest and pushed. "Get off of me." Pain burned across her palms and she flinched. "Ow." She yanked her hands back and shook them. "What did you…" The words died in her throat when she caught sight of suns etched into her palms. She raised her hands and stared. "What?"

"Jade." The seriousness in Luc's voice dragged her eyes away from her hands. Gone was his usual arrogant confidence. Now he appeared uneasy, as if caught committing a crime. "We need to talk." He cast a quick glance at the door and lowered his voice. "About you and Esmeralda."

She ignored him and turned her palms to him. "What is this?"

"Tattoos." He said nothing for a long time, as if waiting for her reaction. When she didn't reply, he said, "Do you recognize them?"

Her head spun. What had happened in the forest? The last thing she remembered was intense pain and an arrow protruding from her chest. Gingerly, she touched the spot where the arrow had been. Her skin felt raw and tender, but was nowhere near as painful as it should have been. The blanket slipped an inch and she realized she was naked from the waist up. With a quick tug, she pulled the blanket to her chin.

"I don't know." She shook her head. "They're familiar. What are they?"

He paced a few steps and then turned to face her. "They are the marks of a Redeemer."

His words refused comprehension. "I don't understand."

"A Bringer Redeemer."

Still, his meaning scrambled out of reach. "Then why do I have them?"

He said nothing, his silence finally helping her understand.

"You can't mean that I'm a Redeemer?"

Luc stood and paced "Did you not know?"

Was this some elaborate ruse to punish her for her treachery? To create a bond between them that really wasn't there? She shoved her palms at him. "Did you brand me as retribution?"

Luc walked to the bed and leaned over her. "I know you distrust me, but surely you don't believe me capable of taking advantage when you lay dying?"

"Why not?" She slowly sat up, clutching the blanket to her, tightening against the deep aches in every part of her body. "Do you forget how well I know you? And you can't deny being angry that I tried to kill you."

"You don't know me. You know only what your sister has pounded into your head." He smoothed his hand over the spot she had stabbed. "And no, I have not forgotten." He slid onto the chair. "And it seems I never will—no matter what amends I make."

The accusations and years of anger poured forth like a dam that had weakened over time. "You? Try to make amends?" She sneered. "Since when does the mighty Luc Le Daun take responsibility for his actions?"

"Could you please stifle your righteous indignation for a few minutes? We have more serious matters to deal with right now."

"You do perhaps, but not me."

He leaned forward, resting his elbows on his knees. "Those marks are real. You *are* a Redeemer. A healer. The light that saves those on the brink of death."

There was no trace of humor in his words. She stared at the black suns on her palms. The skin around the tattoos was red and swollen, as if burned. "How could I have not known?"

He sighed and the tension eased from his posture. "Do you know which of your parents was a Bringer?"

She closed her eyes against the painful memories of their deaths, but they came anyway. "It must have been my father." She opened her eyes. "My mother taught us simple earth magic spells, but Father was the one who told us stories about the Bringers. We'd fall asleep listening to his tales of the great battle between the Bringers and the Bane." She smiled at the memory of her and Esmeralda pretending to be angels, saving their dolls from danger. "I even dreamt of being a Bringer when I was young." She looked at him. "When I still believed in fairy tales."

"It seems you got your wish."

"I always imagined it to happen differently." She curled her hands into fists. "With less pain."

A sad smile tugged at Luc's lips as he tapped his index fingers together. "We have more in common than you realize."

She didn't like the comparison. "How so?"

"We are both newly brought to power and we are the only ones who know about Esmeralda."

Jade's breath caught. "But if I'm a Bringer, so is Rell."

"So *was* Rell," Luc corrected.

"What are we going to do?"

Luc shook his head. "I think we need to tell Rhys and Ravyn about your sister."

"No." Jade straightened and cringed, her muscles protesting the quick movement. "You promised not to betray us."

"It wouldn't be betrayal, Jade. We can help you—help her." He leaned forward, resting his elbows on his knees again. "Esmeralda is dangerous, maybe more dangerous than one Bringer can handle."

She glared at him. "So you mean to hand her over to the Bringers." She swallowed hard, wondering how much she should reveal. "What guarantee do we have that they won't kill her?"

"I won't lie to you. I can't guarantee anything, only that *not* dealing with Esmeralda will be detrimental to us all."

"I won't betray my sister." She turned away to stare out the small window. "I am done talking. Please, get out."

Silence filled the room, stretching the tension between them, until finally his chair creaked. She resisted the urge to look at him when his footsteps thumped across the floor and stopped.

"Ravyn left clean clothes for you on the desk." He paused. "I will give you time to think on it, Jade, but if you don't tell Ravyn, I will."

Her head snapped around. "Traitor!"

"Yes, I am, no matter what course of action I choose."

Luc pulled the door closed behind him. She flexed her palms and stared at the emblazoned suns. A Redeemer—her. The idea seemed preposterous, yet the proof stared back at her. She knew from Luc's expression that the tattoos were real.

Being a Redeemer changed everything. A tiny shudder of excitement rippled through her. A Redeemer—*her*. Not just an orphan or an outcast sister of a demon. The marks meant she had a purpose beyond revenge. What would her sister say when she found out?

Foreboding doused her bit of excitement and she inhaled against the growing uneasiness. Rell wouldn't see her new powers as something good. Jade clenched her jaw and fisted her hands, ignoring the pain. Her powers would be a source of jealousy or corruption and Esmeralda would find a way to use them for her own selfish purpose.

Maybe Luc was right. Maybe she should tell Rhys and Ravyn. Her sister could be unpredictable. Jade sighed. One day Rell would turn on her, the only person in the world who truly loved the demon. Doubt plagued Jade. Maybe this *was* the time to ask for help.

She sighed. How could she accuse Luc of betrayal when she contemplated it herself? The thought renewed her waning loyalty to Rell. No, she'd find a way to help her sister without letting Rell know she'd been brought to full power. First she needed to speak with her—alone. A difficult task with Luc sniffing around.

Another thought occurred to her. How had she been brought to power? Had it been Luc? Or was Ravyn the key?

Jade drew back the covers and swung her legs over the side of the bed. The room spun and slowed. She contemplated the possibilities and decided not to ask—yet. The information would be another bit that Rell could twist and use. Until Jade figured out where all the pawns stood, she'd rather keep her strategy a secret.

She glanced at the tattoos. There was purpose in her life now. For the first time that she could remember, she felt happy. But she couldn't let Rell destroy her future, nor could she leave her behind.

Jade slowly stood, gripping the wooden post. The scope of these new revelations threatened to overwhelm her. What she needed was a plan, just the first step of what was bound to be many. She needed to get a message to Rell.

With wobbly steps, she made her way across the cabin to the desk and sifted through the pile of clothes. Favoring her injured shoulder, she slid on a white undershirt and a clean brown tunic. She still wore her pants from last night, but decided it was easier to leave them on, despite the blood.

Careful not to disturb the items on the desk, she searched for parchment and quill. A book lay atop a stack of papers. Her hand hovered above the thickly bound tome, her eyes growing wide with recognition. A line of three golden swords embellished the leather cover. The familiar symbols stared back at her and a sick feeling grew in her stomach.

With shaky fingers she opened the book. As she'd suspected, each page was filled with the same ancient script she'd seen inside a book she'd found in the chapel—a book she'd sold to stave off hunger. Silent curses tumbled from her mouth. She'd assumed the book had been left behind or hidden away by someone from the Order of the Saints. Up until now, she'd foolishly thought it a gift from the Saints watching over her.

She glanced at the door. Maybe the curiosity shop owner hadn't sold it yet. Maybe she could get it back. Uncertainty swirled through her mind. If she found the book, should she turn it over to Rhys and

Ravyn or keep it for leverage against Luc's threat to reveal Rell?

A dull ache throbbed around her arrow wound. She placed her hand against it and closed her eyes. Seconds passed and no great Bringer secrets were revealed.

She opened her eyes and gave an unladylike snort. "Some Redeemer you are. Can't even heal yourself."

She released a heavy breath, her shoulders slumping with the weight of the latest events. Things were happening too quickly. What she needed was a plan. The three most pressing issues were talking to Rell, keeping Luc from betraying them, and finding out if the shopkeeper still possessed her book. The last would be the easiest to check on. She'd do that before going to see Rell. First she had to get a message to her sister.

She scrawled a quick message on a small sheet of parchment. Opting against sand, she pressed a blotting paper to her message, trying to absorb the extra ink. She pulled the paper free and set it on the desk. Scared Ravyn would walk in and find her at the desk, she blew on the note, folded it, and shoved it into her tunic pocket. Now all she needed was to hand off the note to one of the street couriers she normally used to get messages to Rell.

The dark wood walls of the cabin seemed to press around her, making the room oppressive. She had to get out of there. Sunshine and fresh air always made her feel better and seemed to lessen any burdens plaguing her.

When she pulled the door open, a squeal of excitement greeted her. A small boy raced past, followed by a much older girl. The two thundered up the steps to the helm, disappearing from sight.

Jade craned her neck around the corner, ensuring another stampede of children wasn't about to trample her. The coast was clear. She stepped out and closed the door behind her.

"Jade." She hadn't noticed Ravyn and the woman from the forest sitting on two low barrels. Ravyn rose and walked to her, wrapping her in a gentle hug. "How are you feeling?"

Two things about Ravyn immediately caught Jade's attention: the black line running from her lip to her chin and the black suns that flashed on her palms when she reached to hug her. They were the same suns she now possessed. Jade said nothing of it, stilling her impulse to grab her friend's hand and demand an explanation about everything, the tattoos, her new powers, her new life.

She returned a quick hug and let go. "I've been better."

The whore from last night sat staring at her. Jade discreetly slid her hands into the pockets of her tunic. The fact that the woman was still with them barely raised Jade's curiosity. Of all the things that had happened since last night, this was the least peculiar.

"And you've been much worse," Ravyn said with a warm smile. "You're lucky to be alive."

"Do I have you to thank for that?"

Ravyn gave a noncommittal shrug. "In part. Thank Delphina. She helped Luc get you to me in time."

"Who?"

"Come." Ravyn hooked her arm in Jade's. "Let me properly introduce you."

She led her to the whore. The woman stood and absently rubbed her hands against her thighs. "Jade, this is Delphina. After you were struck with the arrow, she led Luc out of the forest."

The woman stared at her as if waiting for Jade's response.

"It seems I owe you my life." Jade dipped her head. "I'm in your debt."

Delphina's posture relaxed slightly. "It weren't nothing, my lady."

"It was to me." Jade smiled.

The woman gave a quick lift of her eyebrows. "Suppose it was at that, but I feel responsible for what happened."

Jade shook her head. "Please do not take responsibility for those men's actions."

"I told her the same thing." Ravyn gave her an approving smile. "Delphina and her children have agreed to stay on the ship. With all the repairs needed, having her act as a liaison with the laborers will save us time better spent on other matters."

Jade didn't know what the other matters Ravyn spoke of were, but she would certainly try to find out. "Wonderful." She scanned the deck of the ship. "I believe I met your children a few moments ago."

"Those are my two oldest, Serena and Hayden. Jenna is sleeping right now." Delphina held up her hands to the sky. "Praise the Sainted Ones. Cuttin' teeth. Some nights she keeps us up all night with her crying."

"I was just about to send Luc to the market for supplies," Ravyn said.

Delphina's posture took on a light rigidness. "Like I said, my lady, I can go myself."

Ravyn patted her arm. "Better to not chance Pascal finding you if he and his men are still around. The ship is safe and in the evening you can pull up the gangway." She smiled as if expecting no argument. "Besides little Jenna's complaints, you should have a peaceful and safe night's sleep."

Delphina worried her lower lip and gave an unconvincing smile. "Thank you, my lady."

"Supplies?" Jade said, getting back to the subject at hand.

"Clothes, food, everything she and her family will need."

Now Jade understood the woman's reaction. Pride. She possessed enough of the cursed stuff to know it when she saw it. "You're sending Luc?"

"Yes. I need to meet Rhys, and Luc kindly offered."

Jade snorted. "And you expect him to purchase material?"

"Yes." Ravyn drew out the word as if reconsidering her decision.

"I'd stake my reputation that his knowledge of women's apparel does not extend beyond lace and satin." She pasted on a contemplative expression. "Perhaps I should go." This would give her a chance to get a message to Rell. "I doubt he knows linen from wool."

"I see your point." Ravyn tapped her finger to her lip. "Still, are you sure you're up to the task?"

"Positive. I'm a little sore, but it will give me a chance to stretch my legs."

Ravyn gave her a hard look. "No." She shook her head. "I don't feel comfortable sending you alone. You're still weak." She looked toward the helm. "Luc!"

He appeared above them, holding a squirming Hayden by the waist. "What?"

"Jade is going to accompany you to the market. Let her select the clothing. You get the other supplies."

He stared at her in a way that made Jade slightly uncomfortable, his reaction difficult to fathom. "Fine."

The boy wiggled free, preceding Luc down the steps. Jade cursed her bad luck. How would she get a message to her sister with him lurking about? "I really don't need an escort, Ravyn."

"I'd feel better if Luc was there to watch over you. At least for today."

Having him *watch* over her smacked deeply of irony. As she

held Ravyn's gaze, the impulse to agree overwhelmed her. Her head nodded without her conscious effort.

"Wonderful," Ravyn said. "I appreciate your help."

Luc passed her and stood at the gangway. "Ready?"

"As ready as I'll ever be," Jade mumbled under her breath.

Delphina gave her a sympathetic smile. The woman was observant. How far Ravyn intended on including her, Jade was curious to know. Truth be told, she wondered what her own role within the Bringers would be.

She trailed in Luc's wake as he pushed their way through the crush of the open market. His broad body blocked most of the jostling crowd but made it impossible for her to scan the marketplace for one of the many children she used to get messages to Rell. Usually they lurked in the trees near a crowd or in a shadowed doorway. Somehow she'd need to lose Luc and search the messengers' typical spots.

Before she could duck away, an argument over the last haunch of mutton broke out between two large women. The disagreement quickly escalated. Neither woman appeared to have ever missed a meal, but both seemed determined to claim ownership of the meat.

"It's mine," the larger of the two women yelled.

"Liar!" The other said. She turned and wrapped her arm around the bulky end of the mutton, tucking her prize into her armpit. She leaned forward and dragged her foe several feet. "I saw it first."

A circle formed around the women. Shouts erupted. Silver ducats were waved in the air as the onlookers placed their bets. Each patron gripped the haunch of the meat and dug their heels in, tugging in the opposite direction, grunting like two oxen dragging a cart through the mud.

Luc grabbed Jade's upper arm and hauled her to him. She flinched against the flare of pain in her chest where the arrow had pierced. Her breasts pressed against the left side of his body and a protective arm cradled her to him. The vendor launched himself toward the coveted meat, but the crowd squeezed him out, nearly knocking Jade over in the process. She snaked her arms around Luc's lean waist and held on for dear life. Falling in a crowd like this would probably mean death, crushed by a hundred trampling feet.

"Don't let go," he said over the mayhem.

Still holding her against his left side, he inserted his right shoulder into the ever-tightening crowd and leaned into the wave. She buried her face against his body, letting him practically carry her through the crowd. He smelled good, like leather and *Clovilla*, a local delicacy of warm, spiced cider. It reminded Jade of her childhood, of days before the Bane. Her arms tightened around him.

People bumped and elbowed each other, trying to get a better view of the tussling women. Jade lifted her head just in time to catch sight of the larger woman pressing both feet against her combatant's rear end. With a guttural yell, she shoved. The smaller woman's grip slipped free of the mutton and she careened toward Jade. Luc spun, protecting her body with his, which cast her into a low dip. The woman bounced off him and toppled into the crowd.

Luc made no attempt to right her, instead still cradling her in his arms. His arms lingered around her waist and his eyes traveled across her face, down her throat, and leveled on her breasts that were mere inches from his mouth. Her breathing quickened at the look of desire on his face. Spiders of anticipation skittered across her chest. Her nipples tightened against his warm breath. All the things her body should not be doing for Luc Le Daun—it did.

The crowd faded around them. Awareness of how their stomachs and legs molded together made the warmth in Jade's chest spread to her lower regions. Her eyes locked with his. Was he going to kiss her?

Seconds ticked by. She should move, but her body seemed incapable of obeying her mental command. Luc spread his fingers against her back and slid his hand lower, coming to rest against the upper curve of her rear end.

Her eyes grew wide when he drew her toward him. Logic screamed for her to get away, but her body went willingly, turning to clay in his hands. *Curse his beautiful blue eyes.* Instead of kissing her, he helped her to her feet, but his gaze remained locked on her face. Very slowly, he lowered his hands and took a step back.

Words clogged her throat. "Thank you."

He gave a quick nod. "The market can be dangerous."

Funny, but everything seemed a bit more dangerous when Luc was around, including her treacherous thoughts about the man she was supposed to despise.

The hefty woman waved the haunch of mutton in the air like a triumphant. Ducats were exchanged by the betting onlookers, and the crowd began to disperse, clearing a path for them.

He held out his arm. "After you."

"There's a shop on a side street that sells material." She concentrated on their mission, trying to take on a business-like tone, trying to ignore the lingering feel of his hand on her back. "I've done business with the woman before and she's never cheated me."

He nodded, indicating she should lead the way.

Jade squeezed through the crowd, inching her way to the far side of the street. More hagglers blocked her way, but she skirted the patrons, glancing over her shoulder to see if she'd lost Luc in the crowd. No. He towered over nearly everyone and easily followed her path.

She rethought her plan. The fabric shop and the curiosity shop, where she'd sold the book, were situated side-by-side on the narrow street. Maybe she'd be able to slip into the shop and question the owner about the book while Luc paid for the goods at the fabric seller. It wasn't a great plan, but it might work.

The whining strains of several street musicians wafted around the marketplace, blending into a single disjointed song. Canvas tents billowed in the late morning breeze. Bugs were minimal today, not swarming the way they did on hot, still days.

As they approached the side road where the shops were located, the faintest tingle skittered up her arms. She barely had time to register the sensation before somebody knocked into her. Instantly on alert, Jade crammed her hands inside her pocket, hoping what little money she possessed hadn't been pickpocketed. Her fingers touched a crumbled piece of paper. She glanced around, but the note's deliverer had skillfully melted into the crowd.

Luc followed a length behind her, slowed by the steady stream of people crossing his path. As inconspicuously as possible, Jade unfolded the paper.

The church. Tonight.

She glanced around again, but saw nobody. The message was from Rell.

Jade wadded the paper and clenched it in her fist. As she passed a small shrine to the *Forgotten Gods,* she tossed the note into the burning brazier. Best not to leave any clue that Rell had contacted her.

She turned, looking for Luc. He was still behind her, but his interest was now trained on a dark-haired Splinter dancing near a pub. Jade fished in her pocket and pulled out the note she'd written to her sister. With a glance at Luc, she tossed it into the fire. The dry parchment instantly caught fire and was consumed by the flames in seconds. Her only concern would be getting away from the ship tonight.

It would be her one chance to find out what Rell knew. Jade's stomach twisted in a knot. And then what? What if Rell had always known they were Bringers but had never told her? What if she didn't know but started asking questions?

Jade bit her lip. What in the Saints' names was she trying to do? She needed a plan, and—she glanced at her palm—a pair of gloves.

She walked past the shrine and eased her back against the side of the building to wait for Luc. He'd stopped, his gaze intent on the dancer. Jade knew that look, had seen it in many men before. It was the insidious talent of the Splinter to entice men until they could think of nothing else. Families, fortunes, and lives had been lost to these women. An entranced man would pay any price for the mere possibility of winning a Splinter's affection. Their magic was said to be one of the many dark branches of earth magic.

Better not let Luc fall too deep into the siren's melodic trance. Jade placed her little fingers between her lips, rolled her tongue, and blew. The shrill whistle caused heads to turn and the music to falter. It was enough to break his interest. He turned, scanning the crowd for her. When his search settled on her face, she raised her hands in a silent, *Are you finished?*

Without waiting, she pushed through the crowd, confident he'd follow her. After all, she'd made him look like a brainless puppet. Which she realized he wasn't, but she'd never let him know that. Heavy steps slowed behind her.

His energy tickled the back of her neck, making her hair prickle and stand on end. Like a voice she recognized without seeing the face, she would have known it was Luc without turning to look. His wide body blocked what little sun streamed through the narrow cracks between the buildings.

Jade continued down the street, breathing deeply and struggling to close off the tiny tendrils of Luc Le Daun that were trying to wiggle through her defenses.

She stepped inside the fabric shop and waited for her eyes to adjust to the dim light. Bright swaths of expensive material hung for customers to admire. She caressed a length of nearly transparent, yellow fabric.

"You like?" A thin, rat-faced woman approached wearing an oily grin. "With that hair." She waved a gnarled hand at Jade's head. "And this material, you'll look like walking sunshine."

"It's not for me." Jade glanced at Luc, whose attention was elsewhere, and quickly back to the old woman. "I'm in need of something more durable, less—bright?"

"I got cotton." She scooted behind a table, pulling out a drab length of gray material from under it. "Good for hard work."

"That's hideous," Luc said. The owner scowled at him. "Have you anything else?"

Though extremely blunt, Jade was glad he'd said something. Gray was the color of servants. To present Delphina with such fabric would be an insult.

"Yes, perhaps in blue or dark red? Our friend has recently lost everything in a fire," she lied.

To her surprise the woman's wily look melted into one of compassion. "The fire from last night?"

Luc shifted next to her. She forced herself not to look at him and nodded.

"So sad," the woman continued. "So many beautiful trees lost. Bless the Sainted Ones that nobody died."

"Yes, a tragedy. People should learn to be more careful with their campfires." She couldn't resist the chance to plant a barb. She prodded the old woman for more information. "Were many homes lost?"

"I thought none until you told me of your friend. Life is tough enough. Here now." She dug into a large trunk and extracted several bolts of serviceable material. Red, blue, there was even light lavender. "How about these?"

"They're perfect. I will take three lengths of each."

"Wonderful, wonderful," the old woman chimed. "And I'll include two needles and a spool of thread at no extra cost."

"That's very kind of you," Jade said.

The owner shrugged. "What's the point in having all this if I can't share a little of my good fortune."

Jade scrutinized the shop and the woman's inventory. Certainly it was no king's ransom, but what the shopkeeper had was hers. That was more than Jade could say for herself. She turned to Luc as the owner began measuring and cutting the lengths of material.

"I need to go to the shop next door. I will meet you outside."

"Why?"

Jade cleared her throat and lowered her voice. "Gloves."

It wasn't a complete lie. She did need gloves to cover the tattoos. It was just unlikely the curiosity shop carried them. Her excuse seemed to placate him.

"Don't be long."

She gritted her teeth and gave him a strained smile. Why the man thought he could tell her what to do confounded her, but this was not a battle she wished to engage in. More important matters pressed.

With a quick nod, she pivoted and headed to the door. The bright sun momentarily blinded her when she stepped onto the street, turning the clay wall running along the street a stark white.

Jade shielded her eyes and approached the low, open door of the curiosity shop. The smell of dust, leather, and oiled wood greeted her.

"Hello?"

Nobody responded. Shelves crammed with strange items lined the wall and filled the small area in the center. She picked up a large conch shell and held it up to her ear. Muffled tones ebbed and she could almost imagine she was listening to the ocean.

She replaced the shell and wove her way to the back of the store, stopping to examine a two-headed snake floating in a jar, a heavy piece of glass shaped like an egg, and a brass kaleidoscope. Pointing the tub toward the door, she spun the wheel at the end. Colors and shapes toppled together, forming and breaking apart in a brilliant burst that reminded her of a blossoming flower.

"May I help you?"

Jade jumped, nearly dropping the kaleidoscope. "Oh, uh, yes." She replaced the toy. "I don't know if you remember me, but I was here last month."

The old man squinted and lifted a monocle to peer through a milky eye at her. His skin was tan and wrinkled like old boot leather and his fingernails were long and filed to sharp points. "You look familiar." He lowered his monocle. "What can I do for you?"

She glanced over her shoulder, hoping Luc was still occupied next door. "I sold you a book."

"I buy many books, my lady." He pushed aside the edge of his coat and slid his eyepiece into a small pocket at the breast of his vest. "You'll have to be more specific."

Jade lowered her voice. "It contained symbols and markings."

The old man's bushy brows furrowed into hard lines of concentration. Suddenly, his face brightened. "Ah, yes, a very lovely item."

"What item would that be?" said a deep voice behind her.

Jade cringed, her heart leaping to her throat. How could a man so big move so quietly? "Nothing."

"The young lady sold me a very rare book last month," the shopkeeper said.

"Really?" Luc leaned an elbow on the counter and slanted her a suspicious look. "Tell me about this lovely book."

"Just a book." She crossed her arms over her chest and glared at him. "Nothing special."

The old man laughed. "Oh, not just a book. The symbols and markings were the likes of which I've never seen. The man I sold it to was very pleased to get it."

"Symbols?" Luc slowly straightened.

Her defensive stance melted. "You sold it?"

"Indeed. A wealthy gentleman purchased it. He often sends his man in here to buy or trade items." He pointed a trembling finger at Jade and smiled, his mouth only partially filled with teeth. "And he was very interested in you. Asked a lot of questions."

"Me? Why would he want to know about me?"

"He probably wanted to know if you owned more," Luc said. "As do I."

"Yes." The old man nodded his head. "He said he was a collector. Wanted to know where he could find you." He rubbed his hands together greedily. "Do you have more books you wish to sell?"

"No, I only had one." Her gaze darted between the two men. "I found it in an abandoned church."

Her explanation seemed to placate Luc. He gave a single nod of understanding, but asked no more questions.

The old man's shoulders slumped. "A shame. I would have given you a good price for more."

Luc continued to stare at her, not speaking.

"What?" she said. "I'm telling the truth."

"Can you describe the man who bought the book?" Luc said to the shopkeeper.

"Yes, yes." The shopkeeper licked his lips, as if tasting something wonderful. "He was wealthy. The worth of his robes totaled more than my entire store."

"Did he give you a name?" Jade said.

"No." The owner leaned forward. "And you never told me yours."

She couldn't remember what she had and hadn't said during their haggling. "Nor will I now."

The smile slid from the old man's face.

"How long ago did you sell it?" Luc said.

"Two weeks, maybe." The shopkeeper scowled. "He sold me a dagger on that same day. A lovely piece."

He opened a rickety drawer and pulled out a gleaming dagger. Luc's stance stiffened. She glanced at him, but his eyes remained riveted on the knife in the man's hand.

She followed his gaze. The weapon was beautiful, a true work of art. Three smooth ropes of gold were braided together to create the handle. A dragon in flight was embossed on the small guard that was meant to prevent the dagger user's hand from slipping up the blade. What looked like an extremely thin sharp blade delicately balanced the weapon.

The old man laid the dagger on the counter and smiled again as if sensing Luc's interest. "A real beauty." His voice was full of pride. "It is my belief that I got the better end of the trade."

Jade's fingers itched to touch the weapon.

"May I?" Luc said as if reading her mind.

The old man hesitated. "You are interested in buying it?"

"Perhaps." Luc's eyes never left the blade.

Shivers of apprehension tingled up her arms. She was missing something.

The old man enthusiastically slid the weapon toward him. With the lightest touch, Luc ran his finger along the edge of the blade. His finger twitched. For a second, Jade thought he had cut himself. His hand wavered above the hilt and she wondered if he was afraid to touch it. With a deep inhale, he wrapped his hand around the handle and lifted the knife.

She watched his face, knowing that was where he'd betray his thoughts. His brow furrowed. He twisted his arm, palm up, and opened his hand. The blade never wavered from its spot in the center of his hand. His fingers curled and uncurled around the knife hilt.

After a few seconds, he closed his fist and looked at her. "Hold out your hand."

She clutched her fist against her chest, not trusting that he wouldn't cut her. "Why?"

"I want you to *feel* the dagger." He held her gaze and something in the way he said *feel* piqued her curiosity.

She opened her hand and he laid the handle in her palm. An impulse to curl her fingers around the handle was too strong to resist. The handle grew warm and vibrated against her skin. She glanced at Luc and she knew he had felt the same thing. With effort, she opened her fingers and offered it back to him.

He gingerly plucked the weapon from her hand and turned to the shopkeeper, who was staring at them with a great deal of interest. "How much?"

A crafty smile spread across the old man's face. "Five gold liats."

"Five?" Jade exclaimed. "Are you mad?"

"Done," Luc said and slammed the coins on the counter.

"What?" She spun on him. "You could buy ten daggers with that much."

He glared at her. "But I like this one."

The old man cackled, scraping the money off the counter and pocketing it into a leather bag at his waist. "Nice doing business with you, my lord."

Obviously there was something special about the dagger, something Luc was unwilling to share with the shopkeeper around. She worried her lip. Hopefully he would explain himself once they were outside.

"Do you have any other weapons with these markings?" He indicated the embossed dragon. "I'd be interested in purchasing all you've got."

There was some satisfaction in watching the greedy shopkeeper being offered a large sum of money and not having anything to provide for it. There was even greater enjoyment in watching Luc not get what he wanted.

"'Tis the only one I have, my lord."

Luc slipped the blade into the waist of his pants. "If you acquire more, hold them for me. I will pay you five gold liats for each item."

"Yes, my lord." Greed blazed in the old man's milky gray eyes. "I will, my lord."

Luc turned and walked toward the door without another word.

Jade scrambled after him. A stranger crowded the door, but Luc pushed past him and stepped onto the street, leaving Jade to plaster her body against a shelf of colorful feathers in order to not get run over. She let the customer pass and then followed Luc outside. He stopped and turned toward the shop again, staring at the door.

She glanced behind her but saw nothing out of the ordinary. "What is it?"

"That man…"

She looked again, but saw no one. "What man?"

Luc tilted his head back and stared at the sky, squinting as if reasoning out a problem. Jade didn't know if it was against the sun or in concentration. What she did know was that he was acting very strangely. After a few seconds, he shook his head, turned, and started toward the ship.

"Wait," she said.

He stopped and looked at her, but his thoughts seemed elsewhere. "We need to get back to the ship."

"What about the rest of the supplies?" She glanced around and lowered her voice. "What about the dagger?"

He started walking again. "We'll collect food on our way, but I don't have time to gather the rest."

She jogged next to him. "What's wrong?"

"Nothing."

"Nothing? You're practically running to the ship!"

He stopped and sighed. "I need to speak with Ravyn and Rhys."

"About what?" Her patience was wearing thin.

Luc glanced around and spoke through gritted teeth. "About the book you sold." He paused. "And about the dagger."

She ignored his reference about the book. "What about the dagger?"

He stepped close. "It matches Ravyn's."

"So what? Lots of weapons are crafted in pairs. They were probably made by the same craftsmen."

"Indeed." He leaned in, his mouth inches from her ear. "There's only one problem."

Every time he was this near, her mind seemed to stutter. "W–what?"

"Ravyn's dagger is one of the Bringers' lost immortal weapons."

CHAPTER TEN

Thunder rumbled across the sky and the wind rattled the windows. The storm outside seemed to mirror the mood inside the ship's cabin.

Luc had taken a chance trusting Jade, and from her response it seemed she knew what an immortal weapon was, probably from her father's tales. Too many unknown pieces had been thrown onto the game board today: the dagger, the book she had sold to the shop owner, and the mysterious man who had bought it. His interest in Jade was not from simple curiosity, of this Luc was sure.

Siban leaned against the doorframe, while Rhys and Ravyn stood on the opposite side of the desk from Luc, staring down at the twin daggers. The knives were a perfect set.

"You say you thought this shopkeeper knew nothing about the seller?" Rhys said.

"Just that he was rich and interested in Jade." Luc didn't elaborate, hoping Jade would join the conversation willingly.

He glanced at her. She glared back. He attempted his most sincere look of pleading. With a haughty tilt of her chin, she crossed her arms and looked away. The woman was so damned stubborn.

"If there are more of these weapons in other shops, we need to find them." Rhys glanced at Ravyn. "Are you feeling anything from the daggers?"

She picked up both knives and held them. After a minute she shook her head. "All I can sense is that they are a set, forged at the same time, from the same metal, by the same person. Nothing else."

"Tomorrow we search every shop in Faela that might carry weapons." Rhys ran his hands through his hair and released a heavy breath. "We need every advantage we have against Vile."

"What do you have planned?" Siban's question hung in the air.

Rhys glanced over at the imposing Tell. "We need to attack Vile before he has a chance to rally."

Luc's gaze settled on Siban. Only the slight tightening of his jaw showed the Tell's unfavorable reaction. "You mean to engage him in the Shadow World?"

"I do not expect you to go, Siban. Your time in the Shadow World is still fresh—I know you are not ready. It will be too dangerous for any who aren't yet at full power." Rhys glided around the desk to stand next to Ravyn. "As difficult as it is for me to say it, Ravyn and I will be undertaking the mission."

Ravyn's arm slid around his waist, her eyes conveying the love and gratitude she had for Rhys. "He'd rather I stay home, locked away and safe—but he needs me. We're stronger together."

Luc rubbed the back of his neck and looked at Jade. She refused to look at him, but the tiny sniff and lift of her chin told him she was aware of his censure. He continued to glare. His friends were heading into the bowels of the Shadow World to face the Demon King and she stood there, unwilling to share information that might be helpful to them or even save their lives.

Ravyn drew his attention back to the conversation. "I think it's time you two share whatever it is you're hiding."

Rhys looked at Luc and then at Jade. "Do you have information?"

Silence enveloped the room, all eyes turning to Jade. Her posture stiffened and she rolled her lips together, refusing to speak. The four continued to stare at her. For his own part, Luc was prepared to wait her out. She had no idea how stubborn *he* could be, but Ravyn wasn't nearly as patient.

She released a heavy sigh. "Whatever it is, Jade, you can trust us."

"If you've something to contribute, please, now is the time," Rhys said.

Jade's stiff exterior crumpled a fraction.

"We're your friends," Ravyn continued. "I hope you know that. We'd never do anything to hurt you."

Jade looked at her. "I can't."

"Can't?" Ravyn paused. "Or won't?"

"It's all the same," Jade said. "I can't and won't tell you."

"Are you in some kind of trouble?" Rhys said.

Luc snorted and hooked a thumb toward Jade. "Trouble follows this one."

She glared at him. "You're one to talk."

Ravyn moved around the desk. "We want to help."

"Thank you, but I don't need any help."

"Then..." Ravyn reached to touch her. "Help us."

"Don't." Luc stepped forward, intent on stopping Ravyn from using compulsion on Jade. "She needs to trust us, not be coerced."

If Jade spilled her secrets against her will, it would only create more animosity between them.

Ravyn lowered her arms and nodded. "Please, you're part of our family now."

"Whether you want to be or not," Rhys added, smiling.

Jade's stiff demeanor softened a bit more, her expression changing from anger to helplessness. She swallowed hard. "I can't tell you. I can't betray…"

Luc waited for her to finish the sentence. Instead, she stared at the floor, wrapping her arms more tightly around her torso.

"Betray who?" Ravyn asked.

Jade shook her head, obviously still set against revealing Esmeralda's existence. But things had changed. It wasn't just about them anymore. Innocent lives were at stake.

"Her sister," Luc said into the silence.

All heads snapped in his direction.

"Traitor," Jade hissed.

He didn't reply. No matter what he did, he couldn't win.

"What of your sister?" Rhys said.

She continued to glare at Luc, refusing to answer.

"I once courted Jade's sister, Esmeralda," Luc said.

Ravyn shook her head. "But on the ship from Alba, you never said anything about knowing Jade."

"Because I didn't *recognize* her. It had been nearly thirteen years since I'd seen her." His gaze drifted the full length of Jade's body. "She has changed much since then."

"More than you know," Jade sneered.

"If you were once friends, why such hostility now?" Rhys asked.

It was Luc's turn to remain silent. He wanted to hear Jade's accusation. She'd been so young when her parents had been murdered and he'd yet to hear exactly what she believed happened. The Bringers needed to know about Esmeralda, but he wanted Jade to be the one to tell them. That, at least, she wouldn't be able to blame him for.

"He betrayed us." Jade's tone was steady and cold. "Luc was supposed to deliver papers to my father, but he never came." Her arms tightened around her torso, as if the memories were too painful to repeat. "But the Bane did." Now she seemed either unable or unwilling to stem her angry words. "That night we were attacked, and it was his fault. He told them where my father lived."

Ravyn gasped. Rhys stared at Luc, silently asking if what she said was true. As usual, Siban's stare was steady and revealed nothing of what he thought.

Luc shook his head. "I did betray them, but not like she thinks. My father had given me permission to ask for Esmeralda's hand in marriage and ordered me to deliver important documents to Jade's father, saying it would help pave the way for me. It was the first time he'd ever entrusted me with more than managing my monthly allowance. I had every intention of going directly to their home, but on my way I stopped at a pub and had a drink with my friends to celebrate. One thing led to another and I found myself in a spirited game of cards. After several drinks I forgot about my task." He cleared his throat. "I lost all my money and the very coat off my back to a stranger." Shame pushed against him, still as potent after all these years. "The documents were inside."

"What were the contents of the documents?" Rhys asked.

"I don't know. When my father found out about my gambling and Jade's family, all he said was, "Their blood is on your hands." He didn't speak to me for a month after that." He stared at the floor, trying to talk through the shame that still gripped him. "He was so angry." Luc looked at Rhys and shrugged. "It seemed best to never speak of the incident."

The low moan of the wind whistled through the cracks in the door. Nobody spoke. What was there to say, really? Their deaths had been due to his recklessness. Nothing more mattered.

He chanced a glance at Jade. Her gaze was locked on the window, but he doubted she was focused on the rain beating against the glass. The mournful howl and creaking wood of the rocking ship filled the uncomfortable silence that stretched through the group.

"You said you gambled against a stranger?" Rhys said, breaking the lull.

"Yes." Luc pulled his attention away from Jade and looked at Rhys. "I'd never seen him before and haven't seen him…" He stopped, his mind racing. "Until today."

All eyes turned toward him, including Jade's.

"Today?" Ravyn said. "Where?"

"In the marketplace." He held Jade's gaze. "The man entering the curiosity shop as we were leaving."

Jade's defensive posture relaxed. "The man you thought you recognized?"

"Yes. At first I couldn't remember, but now I'm positive it was him."

"Yes." Ravyn closed her eyes and ran her fingertip across her forehead. "That feels correct." She pressed her fingers to her temples and rubbed. "But…" She hesitated.

To everybody's surprise, Siban added, "He feels false."

Ravyn nodded. "Yes, it all feels false." Her eyes opened and she glanced at the Tell. "The game feels false. The man was there for a reason."

"For Luc," Siban added. "The man came for you."

Ravyn walked to Luc and took his hands. "It was all orchestrated."

"I don't understand," Luc said, his grip tightening around Ravyn's fingers. "Why? Who sent him?"

She tilted her head back and stared at the ceiling as if searching for answers. "I don't know." Ravyn detangled her fingers from his. "I can only tell you what I sense. False that the gambling was legitimate. True that you were his target."

He looked at Siban. "Do you sense anything different?"

Before the Tell could answer, Jade's sharp retort pierced the tension. "No." Her green eyes blazed, her head shaking. "No, he betrayed us." She hugged herself tighter. "He got drunk. That's what he does. Gets drunk, gambles, and wenches." She pointed a finger at him. "It's his fault."

Nobody said anything.

"He has to be at fault," she continued, her voice quivering, "otherwise my whole life…" Jade inhaled and stared at him.

For the first time he thought she might truly be seeing him as the man he was, not who she'd always blamed him for being.

Ravyn inched toward her and stopped a foot away. Like reaching for a feral cat, she held out her hand and touched Jade on the arm. "Or your whole life is what?"

Jade flinched and pulled away. Her head continued to shake in denial. "Nothing."

"What happened to your family?" Rhys asked.

Jade spun and walked to the window, refusing to reply.

"The Bane burned their home." Luc paused, hoping Jade would finish the story, but knew she wouldn't. The last thing he wanted was to describe the grisly details of that night. He cleared his throat. "I found her father's body among the ashes, but never found her mother."

"And her sister?" Ravyn walked to stand near Rhys. His

arm wrapped around her waist and she leaned into him. "What happened to her?"

Luc's gaze slid to Jade. Her body was coiled tight, her spine stiff. It was the only indication she was still listening to the conversation. "She—"

"Don't!" Jade spun and held up her hands to halt him. "You promised."

"No more hiding." He straightened, strengthening his resolve. "I won't see innocent people killed because of a misplaced promise."

"You mean when a promise no longer suits you," she barked.

"And how would you know?" His anger lashed out, making her the focus of his frustration. "You don't know me. At every turn you've betrayed me, yet still I offer you help."

"You can't betray somebody when you hold no loyalty to them."

"You may think what's between you and your sister is loyalty, but all you're doing is serving the Bane."

Jade gasped, her eyes cutting to Ravyn and Rhys.

"Bane?" Rhys said.

"I hate you," Jade whispered.

She stomped toward the cabin door but Luc blocked her path. "You're not leaving."

"Are you going to stop me?"

He pushed his face toward hers. "You think I won't?"

They stared for several seconds, neither willing to budge. Jade's lip curled in a snarl. "I really hate you."

He shrugged. He pushed his face an inch closer, their noses nearly touching, and lowered his voice. "This is about more than you and me. Now sit down."

"All right." Rhys walked around the table and stopped next to them. "Both of you—calm down."

"I'm sorry." Jade looked at Rhys. "It's too late for that."

She shouldered her way past Luc. He turned to follow, but Siban grabbed his arm and shook his head. Jade shoved the door open and staggered against the wind. A sudden gust caught the wood, flinging it open and smashing it against the cabin wall. She hesitated a second and then barreled into the storm.

Siban released Luc's arm and leaned outside to pull the door shut. He pushed the chocolate brown coils of hair out of his face. "We can speak more freely without her here."

Luc exhaled and nodded.

"What's this about serving the Bane?" Rhys said.

Luc and Siban joined Ravyn and Rhys at the table, standing opposite the couple. Luc rubbed his hands over his face and then propped his palms against the edge of the desk. This would not be pleasant but they deserved to know the truth of what was happening. "When the Bane attacked her family, they took Esmeralda. I *thought* she was dead."

"She's not?" Ravyn asked.

"Not completely." He took a deep breath and exhaled, rushing on while he still thought it was the right thing to do. "Actually, she's a Bane Demon."

Silence filled the room as the weight of his statement was absorbed.

Finally Ravyn said, "Are you certain?"

He gave a humorless laugh. "Quite sure. It seems she and Jade have been plotting my death for some time now."

Stunned expressions registered on his friend's faces.

Siban crossed his arms over his chest and shook his head. "And I thought *I* was bad with women."

Luc stared at the top of the desk, unable to meet their eyes. "If it hadn't been for me, Rell wouldn't be a demon, and Jade wouldn't be trying to kill me."

"Rell?" Siban lowered his arms, his gaze settling on Luc with disturbing intensity.

"Jade's sister. That's what she calls Esmeralda." Luc waited for Siban to reply but the Tell remained silent.

Luc sighed and rubbed the back of his neck, the weight of his past growing heavier.

"It's my fault Bowen and Willa are dead."

Ravyn straightened. "Bowen and Willa?"

Luc glanced up at her surprised tone. "Yes, Jade's father and mother."

"No." Rhys's brow furrowed. "It can't possibly be."

"What?" his gaze bounced between his two friends. "Can't possibly be what?"

"Willa and Bowen," Rhys repeated. "It's too much of a coincidence."

"Luc." Ravyn turned to him. "We know Willa and she is very much alive."

He heard her words, but their meaning took its time sinking in. Like a cruel joke that was almost too ludicrous to believe. "No."

Ravyn nodded. "Yes, alive and remarried."

"No." It seemed to be the only word he could form. He ran his fingers through his hair, gripping it at the back of his head and stared, his gaze darting between Ravyn and Rhys. Were they joking? "No."

"I've known Willa for years," Rhys said. "Knew that her husband and children had been killed, but we never spoke of it." He slowly shook his head. "I had no idea Jade was her daughter."

"I can't believe we didn't see it," Ravyn added. "Their resemblance is rather obvious."

Luc lowered his hands, the unbelievable finally sinking in. He turned toward the door. "I need to tell Jade."

"Now?" Rhys asked. "You'll never find her in this storm."

"I have an idea where she's headed." He rubbed his hands over his face. "She needs to know her mother isn't dead."

"We've got to tell Willa," Rhys said.

"I'll go." All eyes turned toward Siban in surprise. "Barring any unforeseen delays, we can be back within a week."

Rhys glanced at Ravyn. "We owe her. She's been nothing but kind to us."

"Of course." Ravyn looked at Luc. "Do you agree?"

Not only was Willa alive, but she could be reunited with Jade within a matter of a week or two. The weight of ever-pressing guilt lifted slightly. "Yes, she needs to know Jade is still alive."

"Leave as soon as possible," Rhys said to Siban. "The repairs to the ship's deck can wait until you return."

"We'll need new lodgings." Ravyn waved a hand absently toward the door. "With Delphina and her three children, Jade, Willa, and Saints knows who else, we're running out of room, besides having to leave the ship."

Luc thought of his father. Surely he would help them, especially upon learning about Willa's miraculous resurrection.

"I'll ask Jacob." He tapped his knuckle absently against the desktop. "He has a manor a few miles from Illuma Grand. It's large enough."

"That would be convenient," Rhys said. "Close enough to keep an eye on the Council, but away from prying eyes and ears. I'd appreciate it if you'd ask him, Luc."

"I will." He straightened and walked to the door, making another command decision. "Right after I find Jade."

Not waiting for the others to reply, he stepped onto the deck. The wind built to a crescendo, as if raging at him to go back inside and forget about her. Rain slanted in a solid, gray sheet across the deck, seeping through his clothes. Within seconds he was drenched.

She could be anywhere, but since she'd sought refuge in the Shrouded Forest after she'd stabbed him, more than likely that was where she had gone now. He'd grown up in these parts, had played in the forest when he was young. She would head for the small chapel she'd spoken of.

She'd be safe there, even from the Demon Bane—from the sister she claimed to love.

Chapter Eleven

The chapel stood like a beacon against the tempest. Drenched and shivering, the only thing Jade wanted was to get out of the rain. The constant pelt of drops had beaten some of the anger toward Luc out of her, but not all.

Snippets of their conversation rolled about in her mind. Though he hadn't been completely at fault for exposing her father, that didn't make him entirely blameless. She stumbled through the door of the chapel and collapsed against the crumbling altar. Slowly, she sank to the floor.

How had things gotten so out of control? Three days ago, her only mission in life had been to kill Luc. The memory of her knife sinking into his flesh still made her stomach roil. Now she was caught up in a battle between the Bringers and the Bane. Where did that leave Rell, part Bringer, part Bane?

Bites of fire ran up her arms. She flinched, sucking in a breath and clutching her forearm in an attempt to stop the spread. Now that she was at full power, her sister's presence hurt instead of being merely irritating. "Damn."

"Jade?" Rell's voice floated through the open entrance. "Are you here?"

She tensed. *Damn*. She had hoped for a few minutes to collect her thoughts before she had to face her sister.

"Jade, I know you're in there."

With a deep inhale, Jade pushed off the ground and walked to the door. Before stepping out, she shoved her hands into the pockets of her tunic to hide the tattoos. "I'm here."

Unable to pass onto holy ground, Rell stood at the boundaries of the church. The unwavering commitment Jade had tirelessly maintained to Rell slipped. Perhaps from the intensity of the day's events, or maybe she was seeing things in a new light, but the sight of her sister set Jade's teeth on edge. Life was black and white for Rell, and the amount of time and effort she demanded made Jade want to hide inside the chapel and never come out.

She schooled her resentment and pasted on a passive expression. There were too many questions she wanted answered. "You wanted to see me?"

Rell glided backward, giving her room to step off the sanctified land, but Jade didn't move. Her sister's eyes narrowed. "Yes. We've much to discuss."

"Like what?" Sharpness laced her words. She might be able to keep her face a mask of compliance, but her voice was not so easily constrained. "I'm tired and wet, Rell." She tried to cover her resentment. "All I want is to get dry and sleep."

Her sister's expression softened. "Then come home with me. The hot pools will warm you."

Jade resisted the urge to rub her arms against the growing burn spreading across her shoulders. "What about Luc?"

"We'll deal with him tomorrow." Rell's eyes slid toward the dark woods to her left. Jade followed her gaze, but saw nothing. With a slow turn of her head, Rell refocused on Jade, her lips pulling back in a placating, yet somewhat feral smile. "It will be like old times, just you and me."

"Why don't you deal with me now?" said a deep voice.

They spun to face Luc. He eased from the shadows to Rell's right.

Jade cursed under her breath. He must have followed her. Would the man ever stop meddling in her affairs?

Rell's smile widened, baring her small, pointed fangs. "Luc, why am I not surprised to find you sniffing around my sister?" She crossed her arms over her chest. "If you can't have what you want, take the next best thing, eh?"

"Shut up, Esmeralda." Jade emphasized her sister's human name, knowing it infuriated her.

"Oh Jade, don't tell me you've fallen for his lies," Rell mocked.

Unlike the last time they'd encountered Luc, her sister's confidence seemed rooted in place. Jade watched her. Something wasn't right. Unable to help herself, she rubbed her arms against the growing burn.

"So why have you come?" Rell's lip curled in a sneer. "Perhaps to save my baby sister from the clutches of her demon sibling?"

He ignored the question and looked at Jade. She shifted under the intensity of his stare. Something in his expression made her want to go to him, but she didn't move. A throbbing ache radiated up her neck and settled at the base of her skull. Unable to resist, she scrubbed at the bites that were growing more painful by the minute. For so much of her life she'd lived in anonymity. Now she was the center of everybody's attention.

"Jade." Luc called over the din of the beating rain. "I have something I need to tell you."

"More lies?" Rell snarled. "Don't listen to him. He wouldn't speak the truth if they were his dying words."

He took a step forward. "Your mother is alive."

Jade stopped rubbing and stared at him. Surely she hadn't heard him correctly. Rain dripped into her eyes, but she made no move to wipe it away. "What?"

"Your mother lives." He pinned Rell with a stare, as if daring her to try and stop him. "After you left, I told Rhys and Ravyn about the night your parents were killed."

"The night you betrayed us, don't you mean?" Rell spat.

He ignored her taunt. "They recognized your parents' names. Said they know Willa. She took care of Ravyn after Icarus attacked her."

"He lies." Rell spun and stepped in front of Jade, blocking as much of Luc from her view as she could without crossing the boundaries. "He's just trying to lure you away from me."

Jade looked at Rell, not really seeing her. Was this some kind of cruel trick he was playing? She pushed past her sister and off holy ground. "You lie. I would have known." She pointed to Rell. "*We* would have known."

"I speak the truth." He pushed wet strands of hair off his face. "I swear it."

Lightning cracked above them, briefly illuminating the sky and his unwavering stare. She took another step toward him. Could this possibly be true? Her breath caught in her throat. It was almost too much to hope for, too big of a heartbreak if Luc were lying. Despite the animosity between them, she couldn't believe Luc would be so ruthless in his manipulations.

"Jade." Rell's voice took on a high-pitched coo. "He lies."

"But…" She turned. "What if it's true? What if our mother lives?"

Hope like she'd not felt in years filled her. The vision of a normal life crystallized, suddenly not as distant and a fraction easier to believe in.

"That's ridiculous." Sharp talons curved around Jade's upper arms. Rell's expression hardened. "Don't listen to him. He's trying to lure you away from me."

The black points dug into Jade's skin. She winced and pulled her arms out of her sister's grip. "Still…" She lifted her chin and faced Luc. "I want to hear what he has to say."

White streaks raced across the sky, the thunder mimicking Rell's expression.

"She lives a day's ride from Alba." He glided toward them and away from the edge of the deep shadows.

The wind whipped a chunk of wet hair across Jade's face. She swiped at the strands, never taking her gaze off Luc. "Why didn't she look for us?"

"She thought you were dead, just like you thought she had been killed." He hesitated. "The ship leaves tomorrow to go get her."

"Jade." Rell stepped in front of her, again blocking Luc from view. "Don't believe him. He's trying to split us up."

"But if mother is alive…"

"We don't need her." Rell took Jade's face in her hands, capturing her gaze. "We've never needed her."

Jade's racing thoughts stilled at Rell's words. The howling wind seemed to cry out in disbelief. She focused on her sister's face, seeing her clearly for the first time. The cunning expression glinted in the golden reptilian eyes. Her placating yet dominant stance blocked Jade's advance toward Luc. With every action, Rell controlled.

Jade tilted her head back, dragging her face out of Rell's none-too-gentle grasp. "What do you mean we've *never* needed her?"

Her sister's smile slipped and she lowered her hands. "Haven't I always taken care of you?"

"Did you know?" Tears burned at the back of Jade's eyes.

Rell straightened, her yellow eyes widening like a cornered animal. "I was the one who protected you. Not Mother." She pointed a curved talon at her chest. "I provided for you, not her."

"Did you know...?" The words choked her. "That Mother was alive?"

The demon's desperation melted to self-righteousness. "Do you actually believe she would have embraced a demon daughter?" Rell backed away, putting distance between them. "Do you see how easily she replaced Father?"

For years, Jade had tried to keep her sister from slipping into the demon world, hoping to save what little bit of family she had left, but it had all been a lie. Rell had always known their mother was alive.

"What do you mean, 'replaced father'?" When Rell didn't answer, Jade looked to Luc. "What does she mean?"

"Your mother is remarried."

Tears rolled down Jade's face to blend with the pelting rain. "You've watched her all these years and never told me."

Rell stopped and held out her arms. "She doesn't want us, Jade. She has a new life. New children."

"That doesn't mean she forgot us!" She pointed at her sister. "You had no right."

Rell's eyes widened a second before she launched toward Jade and grabbed her wrist. Too late Jade remembered the tattoos.

"What is this?" Rell's grip tightened. She threaded her talons through Jade's fingers and opened her fist. "A Bringer? I guess I'm not the only one keeping secrets."

"She didn't know." Luc inched forward. "Release her, Esmeralda."

"I think not." She yanked Jade to her. "Perhaps now I'll get the answers I seek." Her gaze flashed to Luc. "While you get what you deserve. Icarus!"

Jade gasped against the fire racing through her body. From behind Rell, the demon emerged. Unchanged by the years, Icarus was still as frightening as she remembered. She tugged against her sister's grasp.

"Why?" was the only word she could form.

"Because he must pay for his betrayal and Icarus needs a full-blood to secure the throne." She dragged Jade toward Icarus. "The pact serves us both."

"No." Jade fought against her sister's hold and twisted free. Now at full power, her strength had increased. "I won't let you do this."

Icarus crouched, his gaze cutting to Luc as if he were preparing to attack. Heat swept through Jade, followed by a savage hunger to protect and save. A wave of white light rushed from her feet through her body and to her hands, cooling the fire set ablaze by the demons. The world faded and her vision tunneled to the demon that held her. All traces of sisterly bond were replaced by the indomitable need to react. Luc's cry faded in the background much like somebody calling from the other side of a thick, oak door. Her vision shifted and the forest changed from a grove of dark shadows to a glistening realm.

Life pulsed in green streams from the trees. Each raindrop shimmered like hovering diamonds. Tendrils of white-blue light wound their way from her feet across the ground and linked with the surrounding plants, filling her with power.

Shouts and screeches of the battle between Luc and Icarus eddied around Jade but did not sway her focus from Rell. Without thought, Jade called the life essence to her and ordered the gleaming light into her sister's body. Ancient words poured from her lips, the rhythmic cadence blending with the buffeting gale. The brilliant spindles pushed into the demon, wrapping around her arms like glowing vines.

The darkness of Rell's aura traveled to meet the light's invasion. Heavy and suffocating, the dense black began extinguishing each thread before they burrowed beyond the demon's elbows. Rell's knees buckled, taking them both to the ground.

The healing chant pushed from Jade and she bellowed it to the sky, asking for all living things to offer up their healing light. The life essence flared, fueling Jade's efforts. The small vines formed into two thick ropes of light and inched their way up Rell's arms, powering through the dense blackness that surrounded the brilliant white orb at the center of the demon's chest. Rell shuddered and cried out.

Jade released all her barriers, needing to heal the demon, wanting nothing more than to drive her healing light into the pulsing globe in Rell's chest. Nothing else mattered but to burn away the darkness.

Without warning, Icarus's taloned hands wrapped around Rell's arms and yanked her free from Jade's grasp.

Jade tumbled backward, sliding through the wet mass of leaves and grass. The glimmering forest darkened to shadows once again, taking with it the euphoric feeling of power. Her head spun and she lifted her face from the wet grass, realizing she lay back on holy ground. A puff of warm air battered her head. Craning her neck, she looked up, expecting to see Icarus—and froze.

Her eyes locked onto the snout of a giant, golden dragon.

Another jet of hot air from the beast's nostrils buffeted her loose hair. She blinked, unable to do more than stare. The creature gave her cheek a rough bump with its nose and darted its forked tongue out to lick her cheek.

Besides the nudge, Jade didn't move, judging it best not to recoil from the creature's examination. From her angle, she had a close view of the pearly white fangs curving from the dragon's mouth. Twice as big as a Bane talon, the teeth looked made for ripping flesh.

The dragon swung its head toward Rell and gave a deep growl. The demon staggered to her feet, obviously as shocked as Jade was to see a full-grown dragon. The creature's massive body followed its head, trampling anything in its path. Jade flattened her body against the ground, narrowly avoiding the golden spiked tail that swept overhead and missed her by inches.

She searched the area for Luc and Icarus but saw nothing.

The beast tromped toward Rell. With a powerful leap, she launched herself into the sky and out of the reach of the dragon's jaws. Large fans extended from the dragon's body, but didn't have enough room to fully extend. The beast roared, seemingly frustrated with its inability to take to the air.

Bellows reverberated against the trees, causing Jade's ears to ache. She slapped her hands against her head, trying to quell the vibrations rippling through her head.

From out of the darkness, Icarus attacked. With talons extended, the demon swooped close to the dragon, digging his claws into its thick hide. The creature roared again and swung its spiked tail upward in an effort to knock Icarus out of the sky. It missed and crashed into a gnarled tree. Chunks exploded and Jade ducked.

Splinters pelted her like flying needles.

The only safe place seemed to be inside the chapel, but even that would prove deadly if the dragon's tail struck the already crumbling structure. On her hands and knees, she crawled through the doorway and cowered, peeking around the edge of the opening. From that point she witnessed a light show like she'd never seen.

Jets of fire blasted past the treetops and into the dark sky. Thank the Sainted Ones for the rain, or the forest would be ablaze yet again. Fiery threads burned like glowing lacework across the leaves, but never caught fully on fire. Thousands of glowing embers floated to land on the dragon's back and outstretched wings. The sparks hissed, their red core fizzling to black and returning the sky to night.

The low thumping of air against wings echoed in the dark. Jade knew that sound from the times Rell had hunted her. She squinted, barely making out the large form of the dragon. With only her hearing as a guide, she closed her eyes and concentrated. Flapping and the whistle of rushing wind sounded above her. Like two thick-hided animals colliding, the hollow clash thundered from where the dragon had last stood.

Her eyes sprang open at the beast's anguished roar. Again the night sky erupted in flames. The dark form of Rell soared above the canopy and disappeared. Next, Icarus attacked, raking his talons across the dragon's wings.

Jade cried out, the need to do something to help the creature nearly crippling her. She crawled out the door to the boundaries of the chapel. Staying low to avoid the spiked tail, she scanned the sky, looking for the demons. On sanctified ground she was safe from Rell and Icarus. The dragon hadn't hurt her. In fact, she was certain it had checked to ensure she was uninjured.

She'd never seen a real dragon, and after the initial shock wore off, it didn't appear to want to hurt anything but the Bane. Leaves above her sizzled with orange light, giving a low glow to the area. The dragon beat the earth with its tail, causing the ground beneath Jade to pulse and adding to the cacophony of the storm.

Icarus dove from out of the blackness and swooped just out of reach of the dragon. The beast reared onto its hind legs and snapped the air with its powerful jaws. While focused on Icarus, Rell swept below the dragon's mouth and raked her talons across the scaly throat.

Blood seeped from the wounds and ran in watery red rivulets down its neck. An ear-splitting cry pierced the night and shook the trees. The creature spun, searching for its attackers. Jade scrambled backward and pressed her body against the chapel, again avoiding the spiked tail. The dragon stumbled but righted itself. Huge golden fans extended, bracing on either side of the creature like a support. Maybe from the confined space, or perhaps the beast was weakening from the wounds the demons had inflicted, but it didn't appear to have control of its body.

Now steadied between the giant wings, the dragon scanned the sky. How could something so big fight against two demons that blended with the night and attacked with such ferocity and agility?

Jade pushed her dripping hair out of her eyes and watched the dragon through the fading glow. Its head wove from side to side as if following something from above. Jade crouched, sending up a prayer that the dragon would vanquish Icarus.

Emptiness filled her chest. She'd spent most of her life doing anything to keep Rell fighting for her humanity, but now that was lost. Together with Icarus, there would be no way to keep her sister from fully embracing the Bane.

A jettison of fire shot into the sky. Rell spun, barely missing the flames. The creature inhaled and rounded its cheeks.

Jade braced herself, expecting another trail of fire. Instead, the dragon huffed. A spinning ball of light and flames, much like the energy Ravyn fought with, hurtled after Rell and struck her in the back.

Suspended in air, the demon convulsed. Tiny golden veins of lightning coursed around her. Jade ran to the boundaries and stopped short of being clubbed by the thumping tail. Her sister's eyes grew wide, her mouth open but not speaking. It was a horrific sight, but one Jade couldn't look away from.

With a sudden burst, Rell exploded into a million glittering bits.

"No!" Jade stumbled forward but stopped when the dragon's huge head swung toward her and bared its fangs. "Rell!"

What had happened? Was her sister dead? Tears spilled down her face and she sank to her knees. Shame washed through her. She'd wanted the dragon to vanquish Icarus, not Rell.

From above, Icarus dove. With talons bared, he latched onto the golden neck, tearing at the glistening scales. The creature cried out, thrashing in an attempt to dislodge the demon, but Icarus didn't give up so easily.

Unable to reach behind itself, the dragon was helpless against the demon shredding its thick hide. Bile churned and rose in Jade's stomach.

"No." The decree was barely more than a whisper. "No," she said louder.

She struggled to her feet and staggered toward the deadly fight. Pure adrenaline drove her forward. Icarus had caused too much pain. No more. She began to run. With a leap onto the dragon's tail, she pushed off and stepped onto the animal's haunch, and then propelled herself upward.

She collided with Icarus and coiled her arms around his neck. Wings battered her legs as she attempted to wrap them around his waist, but the force of her attack sent the two of them tumbling over the side of the dragon.

The breath rushed from Jade as the demon landed on top of her. Surprise flittered across his face a second before he trapped her shoulders against the ground. Her reaction was instantaneous. She latched onto his wrist and opened the gates of healing white light. The same instinct she had felt with Rell raced through her. She needed to heal. Their gazes locked while the chant commanded the power of healing into the demon.

Icarus convulsed with each tendril that burrowed into the blackness of his soul, but this time, the light moved much more slowly. The forest shifted to the glowing realm and once again all living things offered up their healing. A low keening turned into a growl.

At first, Jade thought the noise might be coming from her, but realized it was the demon. Icarus's eyes swirled from yellow to bright silver, the color similar to the white light emanating from her. His body shuddered. Again he growled, but this time the guttural sound formed into incomprehensible words. Jade's control over the healing light slipped.

The glittering world shifted back to the black tempest. Dense darkness pushed against her power, sending black threads into Jade's hands. Loneliness, sadness, and bottomless despair sucked at her light, extinguishing its pure essence. The creeping evil drank in her strength and goodness, leaving nothing but emptiness behind. Like drowning in hopelessness, she tried to claw her way to the surface, but only sank deeper.

All was lost.

Icarus catapulted backward, nearly yanking her arms from their sockets. Jade gasped, vaguely aware of the battle ensuing a few yards away. She had no strength to live, let alone stand and fight. Tears streamed down the sides of her face and glittering diamonds shifted back to black rain, sprinkling her face.

How evil must a creature be to survive in such a state of destitution?

She closed her eyes, not caring if she died. Death would be better than the endless misery she couldn't find the strength to fight.

Of their own accord, her eyes opened. *Traitorous willpower.* The last fringe of glowing embers framing the leaves above her winked out, losing their fight against the constant rain.

How long she lay there staring up at the night sky she didn't know, but slowly the silence drew her awareness. The fighting had stopped. Only the pounding rain against the leaves next to her head made any sound.

With more strength than she thought she possessed, Jade rolled over and pushed off the ground. Her gaze scanned the clearing. The dragon was gone. Several yards away lay a man.

"Luc?"

The dragon had clawed a large, shallow hole. Within the depression, he lay curled and unmoving. She crawled through the muddy furrows toward him. Streams of red ran from deep gouges in his back. She stopped, the understanding of what she saw slowly sinking in.

"Luc?"

She pushed the black despair away and scrambled the rest of the way to him. His clothes had been shredded. The leather vest he wore hung in pieces from his shoulders. Blood mixed with the puddle of rain he lay in.

Afraid to move him, she gently brushed long blonde strands of hair from his eyes. "Luc, can you hear me?"

His chest rose and fell in labored breathing.

She knelt and lowered her face to his, examining the gashes on his neck. His eyes opened and focused on her. "Thank the Sainted Ones."

"That—" His voice grated from his throat.

Jade leaned closer. "Don't try to talk."

"That was the…" He swallowed.

She lifted her hand to wipe the rain from his eyes. "Shhh, it's all right. I'm going to help you."

Determined to speak, he swallowed again. "That was the stupidest thing I've ever seen."

Jade's hand froze an inch above his forehead. "Excuse me?"

"You…attacking Icarus." Luc coughed. "Stupid."

She blinked several times, not sure if she'd just been insulted. From the irritated look on his face, she had.

Jade braced her arms on either side of Luc's body and hovered above him. "I saved your life, jackass."

"Saved me?" He wiped a trickle of blood from the corner of his mouth. "I had things well in hand."

"Really? Was that when you were thrashing about like a fish out of water or when Icarus was peeling your flesh like a ripe orange?"

He pushed to a sitting position, sending Jade scrambling backward in an effort not to touch him. She noticed how his eyes cut to the sky and back to her. Maybe he wasn't as confident as he pretended.

"Where is Icarus?" She scanned the sky. "What happened?"

"I pulled him off of you." Luc leveled a stare at her. "Whatever you did weakened him, but he was still strong enough to escape."

"I think I tried to heal him." The night's events began taking hold again and her head spun. "Almost like I didn't have a choice."

Luc rolled to his hands and knees but rose no further. His head hung as if he was mustering the strength to stand. He definitely wasn't all right.

"You need healing." She inched toward him. "Can you walk?"

"I'm fine."

"No, you're not." She knelt and wedged her shoulder into his armpit. "I'll help you into the chapel. We'll be safe there and I can heal you."

"You're too weak." He tried to push her away, but she wrapped an arm around his waist.

Anger drained from Jade. As much as it irritated her to admit it, he'd saved her life. What would have happened to her if Luc hadn't arrived? Would Rell have handed her over to Icarus? Another thought dawned on her. Had they known Luc would follow her? She pushed away the thoughts of betrayal and her conflicting fear that her sister might be dead.

It took what strength she had left to raise him to a standing position. Though he didn't complain, she could tell by the amount of blood covering him that his injuries were quite painful.

They slipped on the slick grass and stumbled the few yards onto holy ground. Luc motioned for her to stop. His chest heaved from the exertion. Grateful for the respite, she waited. After a minute, he nodded and they continued into the chapel.

The stone walls dampened the sound of the storm. Jade helped Luc lean against the wall while she bullied the old wooden door shut, dropping the bar to keep it in place. Blessed silence filled the holy chamber, casting a much-needed sense of peace.

She led him down the center of the church and onto the small rise below the round stained glass window. This had been her sanctuary, a place to hide away from the world of demons. The thought of sharing her private haven with anyone had always set ill with her, but as she helped Luc down to her makeshift pallet, the reality of having him here wasn't so bad.

He eased to his side and exhaled, the tension flowing from him. She shifted, not sure what to do to help him get more comfortable. Her hands suddenly felt awkward, so she settled them in her lap and waited, trusting he'd tell her what he needed.

A smile quirked at the corner of his mouth.

She raised her eyebrows in question. "What is so funny?"

"Not funny—ironic."

"Fine, what's so ironic?"

"You." He winced and adjusted his position. "First you try to kill me and then you try to save me."

Unable to sit still under his scrutiny, she fumbled with the tattered blanket, tucking it around his shoulder and making sure not to meet his eyes. "I must have had a lapse in judgment."

"Which time?"

She couldn't help but smile back. "Perhaps both times."

"Perhaps." His smile widened and his eyelids drifted shut. "Are you to heal me then?"

"I'll try." She reached to lay her trembling hands on his neck and arm. "But first I need to know." She swallowed the bile rising in her throat. "Did you kill my sister?"

CHAPTER TWELVE

He didn't want to open his eyes, but she'd just saved his life. He owed her an answer. When he did, everything he'd expected to see stared back at him; anger, control, and maybe even hope.

"No, I didn't kill her. She's a Bane and I'd need an immortal weapon to vanquish her."

Jade's shoulders sagged with relief. "I was afraid..." Her voice caught and she cleared her throat. "I mean, it looked so—" She glanced at him. "Final."

"Yes, it was quite a sight, wasn't it?" He took a deep breath and exhaled against the burning ache gripping his body. "I don't know where they go, but the demons always return—unfortunately."

Jade smirked. "So..." She picked at a patch of mud on her pants. "You're a dragon."

"It would appear so." Shooting pains raced across the gashes on his back. He did his best to ignore them, wanting to continue their conversation. It was the first time they'd spoken without hurling insults at each other. "I must admit, I did *not* plan on transforming, but when I saw Icarus and realized you were in danger..." He shrugged and grimaced. "I changed."

"I'm flattered."

"Don't be. It was completely involuntary. I couldn't control the shift, and once a dragon, I couldn't control my own limbs." He curled an arm under him and rested his head. "Quite embarrassing, really."

"I don't know." She scraped her fingernail back and forth over the dirt. "Your flames were impressive and you didn't burn down the forest this time."

"It's a start." He closed his eyes. Silence stretched between them. They seemed to be on good terms for the time being. The last thing he wanted was to push too far and alienate her again. He tabled his questions about Rell. "You were impressive yourself."

When Jade didn't reply he opened his eyes. She was staring at him, a look of pure desperation on her face.

"Jade?" He rose to a sitting position, ignoring the burn across his neck and back. "What is it?"

"It was horrible." Her voice quivered, tears pooling and enlarging her green eyes. "Icarus."

"What about him?"

"How can he live with all that hatred?" Her eyes rounded and she shook her head. "So much despair." A shiver rippled through her body. "His hopelessness was so dense and vast, I…I can't describe it."

"He's a Bane." Luc covered her hand with his. "Demons thrive on the misery of others."

He cursed himself the second the words were out, but he didn't try to cover his thoughtlessness. Perhaps it was better if Jade accepted that Esmeralda was gone and only a merciless demon remained.

"I know." She looked at him. "For some time I've realized that my hope of Rell retaining her humanity was in vain." Her hand clenched under his. "How could she not have told me about our mother? Especially after she'd first been turned."

"Fear of being alone." His head began to spin. He pulled his hand away and lowered himself to the ground, once again resting his head on his arm. "Nobody wants to be forgotten."

"She's my sister. I could never forget her—even now."

He gave her an understanding smile but had no words of comfort. As far as he was concerned, Esmeralda had died the night she'd been turned to a Bane. Perhaps it was cold-hearted, but what he'd witnessed tonight confirmed that Jade was no longer safe with her sister.

There was only one solution for putting Esmeralda to rest, but he doubted Jade would agree. Maybe in time he could convince her that freeing her sister's soul would be the only peace either one of them would find.

"Here." Jade placed her hands on his arm and shoulder. "Lay on your stomach so I can try to heal you."

His body rebelled with each movement he made. Every inch of his skin felt as if it had been pummeled with a club. He grimaced and eased to his stomach. "Are you sure you know what you're doing?"

"Absolutely not." Jade's warm hands settled onto his neck and back. "But since I'm all you've got, I guess you'll have to trust me."

"Your honesty isn't comforting me."

She gave an unladylike snort.

Heat spread across his neck and back. Though his body relaxed and his eyes closed, his awareness of Jade did not dim.

A new scent permeated the small alcove. He inhaled. Like the warm breeze after a summer storm, freshly picked grass and the crisp taste of a mountain stream all rolled into one smell. He turned his head and inhaled again. The sweet aroma was so distinctly Jade.

He opened his eyes and scanned the interior of the church. There were no furnishings or embellishments beyond the colored glass window. A stone balustrade partially encircled the rise where they rested. Several of the spindles had crumbled and lay in chalky piles below the rise. Dried leaves hugged the crevices where the floor met the wall. Though bare, the chapel harbored a sense of peace. He understood why Jade had chosen it as her sanctuary.

White light expanded from somewhere above him when she began to chant, illuminating the chapel. Sparks of blue flared and faded like tiny fireflies inside the spreading glow. Ropes of gold and green filtered through the colored glass window and cracks in the door to swirl around the walls of the chapel.

Snaps of pain pattered across the gashes on his back. The wounds tightened, pulling the skin between his shoulder blades. Whatever she was doing, it appeared to be working. Luc recognized the ancient words. They danced around him like a ribbon of whispers. Unable to resist, he once again closed his eyes and sank into the healing.

A sensation of floating surrounded him, tipping and turning him head over heels. He stilled the urge to open his eyes, but instead placed his trust in Jade's abilities.

Like hot soup on a frigid day, warmth spread from his chest outward in both directions, burning away every ache and cut on his body. His heart beat in unison with her healing words, creating a song of life inside his head.

Memories of the past flittered through his mind, bringing with them an intensity of emotions as if they were happening again. Some were good: him playing as a boy, being rocked on his mother's lap, his father smiling at him with a pride not yet tested. The chant dug deep, unearthing memories he'd buried and never wanted to revisit. His throat closed with emotion and he was helpless against the tears that pressed and slipped past his closed lids. All his transgressions laid open to him, raw.

In his mind, the healing light washed over the heavy visions like an ocean wave, dragging the tainted darkness from it with each pass. The tightness in his chest lessened. He saw the pain in his father's eyes as he rebelled and the two of them drifted farther apart. Surprisingly, it wasn't the pain of failure etched on his father's face, but of the loss of a son. The visions faded, taking the majority of the pain with them. A lightness lifted his heart. He blinked and opened his eyes to stare at the damp stone beneath him.

He turned his head and looked at Jade. Her body swayed with the rhythm of the chant, her eyes closed. Lit from the healing light, her face glowed, making her look like an ethereal being. She was beautiful—and strong.

Something beyond respect and obligation rose in him. The little girl he remembered as a child was barely familiar. In her place was a woman, somebody like him.

She opened her eyes and their gazes locked. Her words slowed, the song dying. The warmth in her hands faded and once again the chapel was dark. She didn't remove her hands, only continued to look at him.

Silence stretched between them, his body growing cool again. Finally he stirred, expecting pain but feeling none. She pulled her hands away and he sat up. Her eyes were wide with questioning.

"I think you did it." Luc pulled what was left of his leather vest and linen shirt over his head and turned his back toward her. "How does it look?"

"Flawless." Her fingers glided across his back where he'd been injured. "I can't believe it." With a gentle caress, she stroked the side of his neck. "It was as if my body knew what to do even when I didn't."

"It seems we both need to learn how to control our power so it doesn't control us."

"Very well said." She brushed her fingertips up his spine and across his right shoulder. Perhaps it was the way her fingers slowed or maybe it was her warm breath on his back, but the mood between them shifted, turning the examination from that of a healer to one of somebody more inquisitive. "You're so smooth."

The statement carried a hint of maidenly curiosity. The awareness her touch provoked surprised him. She ran both palms across his shoulder blades and down the sides of his body. He lowered his chin to his chest and closed his eyes.

It felt nice to be touched. Each stroke brushed him with compassion and caring. Not empty like the past decade of encounters with other women.

Until now, he hadn't realized how much of his life the death of Jade's family had stolen from him. He prayed there were some happy endings in sight. Jade would reunite with her mother and meet the family she never knew existed. She would be free of her burden of protecting and hiding Esmeralda. Still, there were clouds on the horizon. They would have to deal with Rell, and that would be a heartbreaking prospect for Jade to accept.

As her palms caressed his biceps, he covered one of her hands with his, stopping its progress. She didn't move or speak, only waited. Luc turned slightly and looked over his shoulder. Large green eyes met his gaze.

"Thank you for healing me."

She gave him a little smile but said nothing, as if she knew he wasn't finished speaking.

"You're not alone anymore." He tightened his grip on her hand. "Whatever happens in the future, I won't abandon or betray you again."

There were more things he wanted to say, but fear made him hold his tongue. He wasn't used to putting his emotions on the line, at least not true emotions. Silver words to women he'd never see again flowed easily from his lips because they meant nothing in the light of day.

What little he'd just given Jade was far less than she deserved. After a life of serving a demon, she'd earned a peaceful existence. Unfortunately, he doubted that would come any time soon.

For a few seconds, she focused on his hand covering hers. Then she spoke just two words. "Thank you."

They were enough to let him know he'd said what she needed to hear and to sever one of the many cords of guilt that had kept him bound to an empty existence. Tonight she'd healed him in more ways than she'd meant to.

Their eyes met and her smile grew. Perhaps tonight he'd mended something inside her as well.

CHAPTER THIRTEEN

Rell perched on the large, flat boulder, her arms wrapped tightly around her legs. She rocked, keeping her gaze focused on a tiny green leaf rolling back and forth between two intermittent jets of air. Such a bright green gem and so full of life—for the moment. Soon it would wither, as all things did in the Shadow World. She wondered how the leaf had gotten there. Emptiness filled her. Like other things in the demon realm, the leaf didn't belong here.

One ragged wing lay against her body while the other slowly reformed from the stub protruding from her back. She grimaced against the ache radiating through her. This was the first time she'd ever been exploded by a Bringer, or *fractured*, as the Bane called it. Hopefully, it would be the last time. The sensation of reforming again was unpleasant and she had no desire to experience it again.

The constant hiss of warm air through the vents and the occasional burp of bubbles in the pools filled the strained silence between her and Icarus. He paced at the edge of her periphery, but she didn't dare look at him. Their ambush had gone horribly awry and she was certain he blamed her for the failure.

He stopped near a vent and spread his wings. Unable to help herself, Rell cut a glance toward him. The torn membrane of his wings had mended and he now looked no worse for his fight with Luc. He hadn't spoken since they'd returned to the cavern, only paced as he healed. With a slow pivot, he faced her.

Rell ceased her rocking and shifted her eyes to stare at the floor near his feet. The last of her frayed nerves threatened to snap. She jumped when his deep voice echoed over the din of the vents.

"I think that went rather well."

Her eyes traveled up his body and settled on his face. He didn't appear angry.

Icarus cocked his head. "Don't you?"

"I—I'm not sure." The points of her talons dug into her skin. She concentrated on the pain and pushed her apprehension far enough down to where it wasn't apparent in her voice. "It seems neither of us got what we wanted."

"On the contrary." He folded his wings and clasped his hands behind his back. With smooth strides he glided toward her. "I got exactly what I wanted."

"But Luc got away."

"Because I let him." Icarus examined his talons, flicking bits of debris from them. "Now they will come to us."

Rell released her legs and let them slide forward to dangle over the rock's edge. "Come to us?"

"Your Bringer is young and impetuous. He doesn't possess the patience to outmaneuver me." The demon lowered his arms and looked at her. "What he wants most in the world is to be a hero and make things right." Icarus tilted his head toward her. "You are the force that will draw him to us."

"Me?" She leaned forward, resting her hands against the rock.

"He cares nothing for me."

"You're wrong. He does care about you, but…" He leaned a hip against the boulder, his body brushing her arm. "He cares about your sister more."

His words hit her like a punch in the stomach. She stared at her knees and tapped her heels against the stone in a steady rhythm. The movement was meant to keep her from reacting, an emotionless reflex that let the denial and angry truths tumble in her mind. She'd lost her sister tonight and her world seemed to be unraveling. There was nothing she could do about it.

"I still don't understand." She gestured to the surrounding cave. "Why he would come here?"

Icarus said nothing, but the answer was reflected in his eyes.

"He wants to kill me." There was no question in her statement. She knew the words were true the second they left her mouth. "They have an immortal weapon."

"Yes." Icarus's voice was soft but steady. "In his mind, the only way to give you and him any peace is to release your soul."

Rell stood and paced a short path to the closest wall. "And Jade?"

"She is the wild card. I'm unsure where her loyalties lie."

"My guess is with the Bringers." She stared at the glistening streams of water trickling down the wall, wondering how best to broach the subject they'd yet to discuss—the fact that she too was a Bringer. "Jade has been brought to power and…she knows I lied about our mother. Why would she remain loyal to me now?"

"Your sister is still mostly human and humans are weak. At the critical moment it is the rare few who can do what needs to be done. We must play to her sympathies."

Rell turned and wrapped her arms around her torso to ward

off the stark reality of what Icarus proposed. Things would never be the same between her and Jade, but to manipulate her so ruthlessly would certainly destroy any chance she might have of winning back her sister's trust.

The memory of Jade's touch gripped her. The white light had burned through her, clearing some of the black web that kept her trapped inside the demon body. It was as if the white cleansing had finally given her the ability to put words to the constant battle that raged inside her. Despite the moist heat from the burbling pools and vents, a shiver ran through Rell's body.

With measured steps, Icarus circled the largest pool and stopped before her. "You appear distraught."

She flinched, his words drawing her from her memories. How much could she ask him and how much would he confide to her? It wasn't as if they were friends, merely two demons with a common cause. The saying *No harm in asking* didn't hold true in this situation.

Rell lowered her arms and focused on the vapors dancing above the burbling pool in the center of the cave. "How do you manage the darkness?"

He pressed the smooth curve of his talon under her chin, making her look up at him. "I don't understand what you are asking."

She swallowed hard and ran her hand up her arm. With curled talons, she scraped downward against her skin. "At times I want to peel the very flesh from my body. It's as if I'm trapped inside a black web that I can't get free from."

Icarus released her. She resisted the urge to rub where his talon had pressed. Without answering her, he turned and walked to the edge of the pool. Silence stretched between them but she didn't move, didn't try to fill the void. He was the only one who could give her the answer she sought.

He knelt and dipped his hand into the water. The small splash seemed exceptionally loud. Green light from the pool shimmered against his black skin, creating a glow around his body. Though beautiful on the outside, there was no doubt that it would be a mistake to believe his beauty penetrated deeper than his skin.

He lifted his hand and let the water slide from his palm through his fingers. Droplets pattered across the surface. "It is different for every Bane." He continued the mesmerizing action. "I've known others like you."

Rell furrowed her brow. "Like me?"

"Others who found it difficult to embrace the…" His talons hovered inches above the pool. Fat drops collected at their tips, growing round until they could no longer cling to the points. With a quiver, the watery gems fell to once again meld with the pool.

After several seconds, he lifted his head and looked at her. "Darkness, as you called it."

"What happened to them?"

"Some eventually succumbed to the Bane way and embraced their life as a demon." He stroked the water again. "Others sought out the Bringers and their immortal weapons, believing it better to be free of their demon form than trapped within it."

He had left something unsaid. She encouraged him to continue. "And the others?"

Icarus stood. "Disappeared."

Rell shook her head. "What do you mean, disappeared?"

His shoulders lifted in a slight shrug. "Disappeared, vanished, never seen again."

"Where did they go?" She took a step toward him, pushing the sparks of possibility and hope away. "Did you find them?"

"No." He dragged out the word as if recognizing her too-anxious tone. "It's a mystery I've yet to solve."

"Do you think…" She swallowed and inched forward to stand across the pool from him. "They were Bringers?"

She held his golden gaze. Her desire for an answer far outweighed the intimidation his piercing stare caused. A jettison of air erupted from the nearest vent, causing Rell to flinch.

After several seconds, Icarus gave her a single nod.

Possibilities careened through her mind and the question tumbled from her. "Do you believe that's what made them different than the other Bane?"

He stood and wiped his hand across his torso. The water glistened on the cut planes of his abdomen. "You're very astute."

As he approached her, she commanded her body not to retreat. She wanted more answers and he seemed willing to oblige. How far could she push him? "Were you a Bringer once?"

His bark of laughter split the air. He stopped inches from her. "Me, a Bringer?"

"You're unlike the other Bane, even from your own father. Your mind is your own, not like the puppets that swarm around Vile. You think beyond your next meal or victim. You're intelligent and clever. And you're…"

She bit her lip, having already said too much. Icarus moved in, crowding her body and forcing her to look up and meet his gaze.

"I'm what?"

Rell swallowed hard, trying to moisten her suddenly dry mouth. Her words came out raspy. "Beautiful and warm."

The smooth black curve of his talon lightly grazed her cheek and circled under her chin to keep her head tilted and her eyes on him. "You think I'm beautiful?"

"Yes."

His expression and voice softened. "Never has anybody dared to say that to me before."

Though unsure, he didn't appear to be angry.

"They probably feared you'd rip their head off."

The corner of his top lip curved into a smile. "Perhaps I would have, depending on who had said it."

Awareness of his body made her want to lean into him. She raised her hands and placed them on the sculpted planes of his chest. "What about me? Will you rip my head off?"

He snaked an arm around her waist to pull her closer. His smile widened. "That would be a horrible waste."

As she stared into his eyes, the telltale yellow of the Banes faded to a pale gray, making him look almost human. Breath caught in her throat. "Then what will you do?"

With more emotion than the first time he'd kissed her, his lips captured hers. She opened to him, thirsting for somebody else's strength. So often she was alone, even when she had been with Jade. Her sister couldn't understand the darkness she battled every hour of her miserable demon life. Though he hadn't said as much, she knew Icarus understood. Maybe she was a first for him as well. The first demon not to cower. The first to recognize he was different. The first willing to give the same connection and warmth he surely must crave.

His lips were searching but not brutal. His embrace cradled but didn't crush. She slid her arms around his neck and stroked the long black hair that spilled down his back. The silky strands threaded through her fingers, begging her to gently caress his back as she stroked him. Muscles rippled under her touch, quivering with each pass of her hand.

After several minutes of glorious contact, he broke the kiss. The deep timbre of his voice reverberated against her chest.

"There are many things I'd like to do with you."

Rell noticed he'd thankfully said *with* and not *to*. A minor phrasing that could mean the difference between pleasure and pain. "But?"

He traced the curve of her face with the point of his talon. "But we must prepare." His gaze lingered on her, his expression almost wistful. "Your sister and the Bringer will be here soon."

Cold, hard reality sliced into their intimate moment. She let her hands glide down his body to hang loosely at her side, and stepped away. The line had been drawn. She and Jade stood on opposite sides. Would she lose her sister forever?

Icarus strode to the arched doorway and turned to look at her.

Rell drew back her shoulders and followed him. "Yes, we must prepare."

CHAPTER FOURTEEN

The carved oak door may as well have been a fortress. Jade stood beside Luc as still as stone, offering no objection or encouragement. This should be a happy reunion, but the uncertainty of Jacob's reaction kept Luc on edge. Would his father think he was purging himself of responsibility for the violence of that night so many years ago?

He took a deep breath and rapped on the door.

Though the wood was thick, his father's voice penetrated the barrier. "Enter."

"Stay here." Luc didn't look at Jade or wait for her agreement.

The sturdy hinges groaned. He didn't shut the door behind him, wanting her to hear their conversation and gauge the mood.

"Luc." Jacob stood. "What a pleasant surprise." He stepped around the desk and pulled his son into a one-armed hug. "To what do I owe the pleasure?"

For once, he seemed to be in his father's good graces. That position could change in an instant, depending on what debauchery Luc had gotten himself into.

"I needed to speak with you."

"Sounds serious." Jacob indicated that he should take a seat.

Luc remained standing. "It is, but happy as well—I hope."

His father returned to his chair and eased against the seatback, folding his hands over his still-flat stomach. "I'm intrigued."

A hundred times Luc had played this scene in his mind. Not only did he need to reveal that Jade still lived, but also that he was now at full power. His father had always been supportive of Rhys's efforts, but when faced with his own son being more powerful, would he continue to be steadfast? "There's somebody I want you to meet."

Jacob cocked a brow. "A woman?"

His voice sounded hopeful. He knew it was his father's greatest desire to have him wed and settled into domestic bliss.

"Yes." Luc didn't elaborate. When he introduced Jade, no explanation would be needed.

His father leaned to the side, looking around him. "Is she invisible?"

"Sometimes," Luc said cryptically. The fact that Jade had followed him for months without his knowledge still grated on him a bit. "But today she waits beyond the door."

"Don't be rude, boy. Show the poor girl in."

His heartbeat quickened, sending a fluttering feeling through his chest and stomach. So long had he hoped for a way to regain his father's good opinion. With everything he had learned over the past few days about Jade and Rell, the man who had orchestrated the card game, and the immortal daggers, surely the new information would help put their turbulent past behind them. It seemed fitting that their new beginning should start with Jade.

Large, green eyes greeted him when he stepped into the

shadowed hallway. She reminded him of a deer with her blazing stare, giving the impression she would bolt at any moment. He held out his hand, silently offering her his support. She took it.

Luc entered first, pulling her behind him. Jacob rocked forward in the chair, his eyes narrowing when she stepped around Luc.

They stopped a few feet in front of the desk. Out of protective instinct, Luc wrapped an arm around Jade's waist and was surprised when she covered his hand with hers and smiled up at him. A surge of pleasure spread through him. Besides Ravyn, he had never developed anything other than a sexual relationship with a woman. But he and Jade had history and a common cause. He respected her—and she was very beautiful.

He glanced away, overcome by the revelation that he cared for her more than he'd realized.

Before Luc could make an introduction, Jade spoke. "Hello, Lord Le Daun." She gave a quick curtsy. "It's been a long time."

Jacob's brow furrowed, as if trying to place the face.

"Father," Luc said. "You remember Jade Kendal, don't you?"

The older man slowly stood. His eyes bore into her as if trying to reconcile the impossible. "But…" He drifted around the desk, keeping a hand on the edge for support, his head shaking in denial. "But you're dead."

She took a step toward him, slipping out of Luc's hold. "Not dead, Lord Le Daun, just missing."

His gaze darted from her to Luc and back, seeking more of an explanation.

"It's as she says, father."

The confused expression melted and his eyes rounded, softening and growing moist. Jacob launched himself at Jade, scooping her up into a tight bear hug. Tears coated his voice. "I can scarce believe you're real."

Jade grunted and laughed, but made no attempt to dislodge herself from the man. A knot pushed against Luc's throat. It wasn't just his father who gained from the reunion. A bright smile, one he'd not seen since Jade was a child, spread across her face.

"I assure you I am real." She grunted again as Jacob hugged her tighter. "And unable to breathe."

"Oh, my girl…" Instead of releasing her, he set Jade on her feet and clutched her by the shoulders. "Seeing you again has made me the happiest man in the world." He lowered his hands and sobered a bit. "And what of your sister, Esmeralda?"

Jade's smile faltered.

"Why don't we sit, Father." Luc placed his hand on Jade's back and guided her to a chair. "I have more to tell you and a favor to ask."

They took their seats in front of the desk facing Jacob. He settled back in his chair. Lines creased his forehead, making it obvious he thought Esmeralda dead.

Unable to see his father's pain, Luc said, "Esmeralda is not dead."

Relief eased his pinched brow. "Thank the Sainted Ones."

"I doubt that would help," Luc said. He glanced at Jade and she gave him a reassuring nod. "Father, Esmeralda is a Demon Bane."

Jacob's mouth opened and closed several times before forming coherent words. "A Bane? But how?"

That one simple question encompassed a hundred other questions. How was she turned? Why wasn't Jade made a Bane? Where had she been all these years?

"My memories are vague from that night. I was only six, and had been asleep." Jade's gaze shifted to her fingers toying with the lace of her tunic. "Esmeralda shook me awake, ordering me to be silent." She swallowed hard. "I remember men shouting and the smell of smoke. We raced out the back of the house and hid in the woods for what seemed like forever. Esmeralda kept me clutched to her, blocking out as much noise as possible and not allowing me to lift my head from the thicket that concealed us. She didn't release me until the screams faded and the flames from our house burned to smoldering coals."

Jade looked at Jacob, but her eyes seemed distant. "She ordered me to stay hidden until she returned." Her eyes shifted to peer directly at Jacob. "That was the last time I saw Esmeralda as a human or my father alive."

"Did the Bane kill Bowen?" Jacob's voice cracked, betraying the emotion his expression did not reveal. "Were they waiting for you?"

Jade pressed her lips together and slowly shook her head. "I don't know. Neither does my sister. She said there was only one demon searching through the ashes, but when she turned and tried to run, he captured her. Esmeralda didn't cry out because she didn't want me to reveal myself by trying to help her."

Luc covered her hand with his. "She protected you."

She stared at their connected hands and then looked at him. "Yes, and after she was changed, she came back for me. I owe her so much for that."

"But what about Willa?" Jacob asked. "Where was she when all this was going on?"

"I've always believed that she was in the house—that she died fighting next to my father. That's what my sister led me to believe." She detached her fingers from Luc's and sat forward. "Obviously I was mistaken, since I recently found out she's alive and remarried—

but I plan on finding out exactly what happened when I see her."

Jacob's eyes rounded and he shook his head, as if trying to drink in everything Jade had just told him. "I'm almost afraid to ask how you two met after all these years."

Luc decided to take the lead with telling the rest of their story. He unfolded the tale, reliving Jade's attempt to kill him, his encounter with Rell, and Icarus's attack. Details of how Ravyn had brought him to full power were tempered, leaving out his night of drunken debauchery. Jacob said nothing, only listened as he always did before forming an opinion.

Finally, Luc sat silent, waiting for his father's reaction. Jacob exhaled and rubbed his hands over his face. His shoulders sagged from the weight of the information, laying his forearms limply on the thick brocade pads covering the carved wooden arms of the chair. Luc could see his father struggled to take in the tale.

"Your sister's fate is a tragedy indeed. One I wouldn't wish upon my worst enemy." Jacob sat forward and folded his hands on the top of the desk. "But your mother's arrival is a source for great joy." He looked at Luc. "And you."

The thick censure in his father's voice had Luc sitting straighter in his chair.

"A full Bringer." Jacob's face split into a wide grin. "I never thought it possible." A tremor shook his last words. "What Ravyn and Rhys have discovered will truly benefit the Bringers and hopefully even the odds of battle." The corners of his mouth relaxed a bit, pride filling his eyes. "You've made me very proud."

Words he'd so desperately wished to hear for so long filled Luc's ears, but they sounded hollow. He was not the man his father perceived him to be. Though it was a miracle that Jade was alive, he hadn't brought her back from the dead or even found her. It had all been a bizarre twist of fate. And Ravyn bringing him to full power was more embarrassing than brave. He had ranted and accused her of taking his free will, never once considering that he might be worthy of his fate. The reality of how his life had unfolded was a far cry from heroic.

"You give me too much credit, father. Jade found *me* and Ravyn discovered the secret to bringing us to full power. I had *no* choice in the matter."

His father nodded. "Perhaps not, but you haven't run from the challenge, but instead have embraced a new destiny. No man could do more." Jacob placed his palms on the desk and stood. "Now, what was this favor you wish to ask?"

Something shifted in Luc. His father's words, though simple and direct, spoke volumes about Jacob's patience and wisdom. He saw beyond past deeds and focused on the good. Luc checked himself. Had his father always been like this while he'd been too wrapped up in his own guilt to see that forgiveness had happened long ago?

He glanced at Jade. Her gaze held steady with reassurance, but her half smile silently teased that she understood his new revelation. Luc looked back at his father and cleared his throat.

"With Siban taking the ship to fetch Willa, we'll need new lodgings." He reclined against the back of the chair and crossed his legs, placing his ankle on top of his knee. "I was hoping we could stay here."

Jacob tilted his head, his lips turning down in a pout. "Luc, this is your home. You don't need permission to stay."

"I didn't want to assume."

"And I appreciate your consideration, but please know you and your friends are always welcome here." He looked around the cavernous library. "This house has been empty for far too long. It will be nice to fill it with old friends and family again."

"Thank you, Lord Le Daun." Jade stared at her hands folded in her lap. "I never thought I'd hear those words." She looked up. "I'd hoped, but never believed I'd once again have friends and family."

"It looks like it's a new start for many of us." Jacob glanced at Luc. "A truly joyful day indeed."

Luc clenched his jaw, trying to stem the wave of emotions coursing through him. The appropriate words escaped him. He stood and Jade followed him to her feet. "I'll go tell Rhys and Ravyn the happy news."

Jacob trailed them out. "How many will there be? I'll get cook on preparing a light evening meal."

Luc stopped, counting up the growing group in his head. "Eight, I believe. Ten once Willa and Siban return."

"Excellent." Jacob clapped and rubbed his hands together. "Finally, some excitement."

Jade shifted uncomfortably on the straight-backed settee. Luc and Jacob Le Daun's bodies crowded against her, their thighs taking up most of the space and pinning her knees together. She gazed longingly at Delphina's son, Hayden, playing on the thick wool carpet at her feet. *Lots of room down there.* Perhaps she could slide from between the two men without appearing rude.

"Thank you for opening your home to us, Jacob," Rhys said.

The older man smiled and waved a hand. "It's my pleasure. This house needs people." He laid his arm across the back of the settee, wedging Jade in tighter. "It's nice to hear the laughter of children in the halls again."

She glanced at Jacob and noticed how his eyes lingered on

Delphina. Could it be that the lord of Le Daun Manor was smitten with the woman? Delphina glanced up from the sleeping baby in her arms to Jacob and back at her child. The gaze had lasted a second longer than appropriate.

Jade repressed a smile. There was no doubt that the woman had blossomed since retiring from her less than savory profession. When they'd first met, Jade had thought the whore to be near forty. Now scrubbed up and no longer bearing the burdens of a harsh life, she looked no more than thirty.

In a sorry attempt to disguise a laugh, Luc coughed, the sound quickly transitioning to him clearing his throat. "I'm grateful as well, Father."

Behind her, Jacob gripped Luc by the shoulder. "I'm just pleased you had the foresight to ask, son." Jacob's voice softened. "Unfortunately, from what you've told me, I fear Le Daun Manor won't be enough."

"I'm afraid not," Luc agreed.

The mood grew heavy as everybody seemed to contemplate the future. Nobody commented, but Jade noticed the guarded glances cast toward the children. The clatter of wooden soldiers and Hayden's quiet commands filled the silence. After a moment, Delphina leaned forward in her chair.

"Serena?" The young girl glanced up from the table, where she sat sketching on a small sheet of parchment. "Would you please take Hayden and Jenna to your room and get them settled?"

The girl set aside her thin piece of chalk and stood without question. "Of course, Mama."

Delphina shifted the sleeping baby from the crook of her arm and handed her to the girl before standing. Soft grunts issued from the child, but she didn't wake up. Chubby, limp legs dangled over

Serena's skinny arms, and with the ease that came from hours of cradling a child, the older girl tucked her baby sister safely against her nearly flat chest.

Delphina brushed the hair from her eldest daughter's eyes and softly cupped Serena's head with both hands. She kissed the girl's forehead, lingering as if to drink in the moment. The girl didn't pull away, but instead leaned into her mother.

The exchange between the two caused a knot to form in Jade's throat. She swallowed and blinked several times, looking away in a feeble effort to give them privacy. On a small level she understood what it must be like to finally be able to send your children to bed, knowing they would be safe.

"Thank you, my sweet. I'll come check on you in a bit." She released her daughter and turned to the boy at her feet. "Take your toys and go with your sister."

Without argument, Hayden followed his mother's instructions. In one hand he clutched the wooden soldiers, and with the other, he twined his fingers with Serena's and let her lead him away. This family worked together, which was probably one of the reasons they had survived their harsh life.

Once gone, Delphina turned to the group and smiled. "Now," she said, settling back into the chair. "Why don't you tell me exactly what's going on?"

Jade raised her eyebrows and looked around. To her knowledge they hadn't revealed much to the woman. Of course she was smart enough to realize how very different things were among this group. For the love of the Sainted Ones, she had witnessed Luc's annihilation of two men and a forest. Though his fire could have been mistaken for simple earth magic, Delphina didn't seem the type to accept things at face value.

Jade ran her hands up and down her thighs, wondering who would explain. Certainly not her. She was the newest member of the group and least capable of putting into words what the Bringers were about.

"I suppose an explanation is in order," Ravyn said. She looked around. "After all, the only way to stand united is to understand who and what we're fighting for."

"I agree." Rhys leaned forward and rested his elbows on his knees. "Delphina, have you ever heard of the Bringers?"

Delphina's eyebrows shot up in surprise. She glanced around, taking each one of their measure. Warmth stole through Jade. It was odd to be assumed part of this amazing group. Something akin to pride made her meet Delphina's gaze.

"Yes," the woman finally said. "I've heard of the Bringers." She mirrored Rhys's bent posture. "And I've also heard of the Bane." Her gaze narrowed. "Are you telling me all of you are Bringers?"

"More or less," Jacob chimed in.

"What do you mean, 'More or less'? You either are or aren't, yes?"

"We are all Bringers," Ravyn said. "But some of us are not yet at full power." She pointed to Rhys. "Rhys and Luc are full-powered Shields."

Delphina gave a quick shake of her head, indicating she didn't recognize the term.

"We protect," Rhys said. "Our powers allow us to fight with fire and…" He glanced around the room. "Change into dragons." He pointed to Ravyn. "She is also a Shield, but changes to a phoenix."

Shock registered on Delphina's face, her mouth dropping open. A smile tugged at one corner of Jade's mouth, thinking that it probably took a lot to awe a woman like Delphina.

"But I have other powers as well," Ravyn continued. She held up her palms to show the sun tattoos. "I'm a Redeemer. As is Jade. Which means we can heal others." She pointed to the blue-black line on her chin. "But I'm also a Tell, which so far means I know when something is false or true. My Shield powers seem to be the strongest, then Redeemer, then Tell."

Delphina's gaze narrowed. "Are there others like you? Who have all three powers?"

"Not that we've discovered," Rhys said. "But we're looking and hoping."

"And the Bane?" Her question echoed the dread they all felt about their foe.

"Real," Jade said. This part of their situation she knew very well. "And deadly."

Luc gave her a sympathetic smile. Maybe he understood more about her turmoil than she had originally thought.

"Vile, the Demon King, has assassinated all the original Bringers as far as we can tell. Only Rhys and I survived," Ravyn said. She glanced at him. "As he is much older than I am, we believe there may still be full-powered Bringers among us."

Delphina cocked her head. "How much older?"

Uncomfortable shifting and evasive gazes rippled around the group.

Luc covered his mouth with a fist and coughed. "Three hundred years."

"I'm sorry." Delphina leveled her gaze on him. "Did you say three hundred years?"

"Is that what it sounded like?" he said innocently.

"Yes, I'm three hundred years older than everybody here, give or take a decade or two." Rhys settled against the back of his chair.

"My parents were some of the last to be killed by Vile, the last of the full-blooded Bringers—besides me. By the good graces of the Saints, I survived."

Ravyn placed her hand on his knee and rubbed. "And now we're building the Bringer army again, albeit slowly."

"How?" Delphina asked.

This was the very question Jade had wished to ask.

"We can't reveal that right now," Rhys said. "The Bane are too unpredictable and it's the only edge we have against them."

A twinge of disappointment poked at Jade. She understood why they didn't reveal the process to her. After all, she had lived with a demon and had tried to kill Luc. Still, the fact that she hadn't yet gained the level of trust she desired made her feel like a bit of an outsider.

"Understood." Delphina leaned back in the chair and stared at them as if resigning herself to the idea. "I knew there was something odd about this group. I just never imagined…" She took a deep breath and exhaled. "So what's the plan?"

"Correct me if I'm wrong, Rhys." Jacob stood and walked to the hearth. "But we need to turn our focus to Vile."

"You're not wrong, Jacob." Rhys shook his head. "But it won't be easy."

Jacob placed his hand on the mantel and stared into the flames. "Indeed. While the Bane grow stronger, the Bringers fight among themselves. We've lost our history, our weapons." He curled his fist and lightly thumped the wood. "And now our own people."

Jade eased to the left, taking the spot he'd vacated. No longer crammed against Luc, she was able to cross her legs at the ankle and relax.

"What do you mean, 'You've lost your people'?" Delphina

asked.

Jade refocused on the conversation. *Yes, what did he mean?* During the years of hunting Luc, she'd come across Jacob, but only from a distance. Always he seemed jovial and flamboyant. Tonight she was seeing a different side of him.

"There is a place a few miles from here called Illuma Grand. Have you heard of it?" Ravyn asked.

The woman contemplated her question. "The big estate, kind of secretive?"

"Yes, it's run by mixed-blooded Bringers. Those who have descended many generations from the original Bringers and have very little power."

Again, Delphina looked properly impressed.

"Some of the Bringers from Illuma Grand are missing," Rhys supplied. "We fear the Bane have taken them."

"What else could it be," Jacob growled. "They've no need to run away. Everything they could want is provided for them at Illuma Grand."

"Except freedom." Luc mumbled the statement loud enough for everyone in the room to hear.

Jacob turned and faced the group. "I will be the first to admit that Fromme Bagitta has made things difficult over the last few years, but not bad enough for these Bringers to disappear without a trace." He shook his head. "No, something far more sinister than Fromme's quest for power is behind this."

"Well, we can't sit idly by and wait for the Council to do something," Luc said.

Jade studied him from her periphery. Annoyance laced his words and the steady drumming of his fingers emphasized his opinion on the matter. "What *is* the Council?" she asked.

"The governing body at Illuma Grand," Jacob said.

"A bunch of bureaucratic ignoramuses," Luc added.

"Watch your tongue, boy. I'm a Council member." Jacob's stern tone held a hint of humor.

"Right." Luc smiled sheepishly. "Sorry, Father."

Heaviness pressed against Jade's chest. As their discussion progressed, the reality of her own situation with Rell became more oppressive. She uncrossed her legs and sat straight, as if good posture would push away the pain of her sister's lies.

This was not the time to lament her family situation. The one conclusion she'd come to since healing Luc was that she'd been given a gift. No matter what that meant for her and Rell's relationship, Jade knew she wouldn't be able to sleep at night if she didn't hold true to her destiny of being a Redeemer.

"You're right, Luc," Rhys said. "The Council is not the answer. They are unwilling to help. But neither Siban nor I have been able to discover anything about the Bringers' disappearances." He looked at Ravyn. "I think we need to go to Illuma Grand and see if we can find anything that might help us locate the Bringers."

"Search the entire compound?" Ravyn said.

Rhys nodded.

"But Siban has left to fetch Willa," Ravyn said. "Won't we need his Tell powers to help?"

A thrill raced through Jade at the mention of her mother's name.

Rhys twined his fingers with Ravyn's. "Not when we have you. I'd like you to explore the Council chamber. Look for secret doors, weapons, anything you wouldn't normally think out of place."

The color drained from her face. "You know what happened the last time I was in there."

"What happened?" Jade blurted out the question, wanting to fill in the empty spaces between the time she'd left Ravyn at the ship until a few days ago.

Luc snorted. "Ravyn erupted in flames and blew up Fromme Bagitta's atrocious portrait."

It was Jacob's turn to cover his laughter with a well-disguised cough.

"It wasn't my fault." Ravyn slumped back against her chair, reminding Jade of a pouting child. "There's something off about that room."

"That's why we need to search it." Rhys twisted to look at her. "Without Siban, you're the only one with Tell powers."

She glowered at him. "Take Luc."

"I'm not a Tell." Luc tapped his chin, indicating the blue-black tattoo that ran under Ravyn's lower lip. "Sorry."

The sound she made was a cross between a groan and a whine. "You have no idea how much that hurt and I've handled a lot of pain in my life. But that…" She waved her hand in the air but didn't finish her statement.

"At least your sister isn't a demon," Jade tossed at her. She cocked a brow at Ravyn, daring her to retaliate with a more grievous burden. "Well, it's true."

Ravyn grunted and crossed her arms over her chest. "You're a dirty fighter. Fine, I'll do it, but I won't like it." She pointed a finger at Jade. "And don't think you can keep tossing that card on the table every time."

Jade smiled, oddly comforted by their friendly banter.

"Your sister?" Delphina's question reverberated around the room. "A Demon Bane?"

After she and Luc had returned from their incident with Rell and Icarus, Jade had told the Bringer group everything about growing up inside the Shadow World. Until now, she'd forgotten that Delphina hadn't been included in the discussion.

Her smile tightened, uncomfortable with being the center of focus. "Uh, yes. It happened when I was six."

"Quite remarkable really," Jacob added. "Her sister raised and protected Jade from the other Bane."

Jade appreciated his attempt to lessen what must sound like a horrific childhood. Unfortunately, it was too much to hope that they would turn the conversation to a different topic.

Delphina's eyes gleamed with unasked questions. "Bless the Sainted Ones, I thought I'd lived a dangerous life."

She'd never considered her life that dangerous. Mostly it was lonely and burdened by her sister's demands, but not really dangerous. "I would choose living among the Bane over what you've survived." She held Delphina's gaze. "You are a far braver woman than I am."

"Having children will do strange things to a person. It makes us braver than we really are." She folded her hands in her lap. "It looks like you and I have something in common."

Jade's eyes widened in question. "And what would that be?"

"Only by the grace of the Sainted Ones are we both still alive."

"I think that goes for everybody in this room," Rhys said.

Jacob lifted his goblet of wine. "Hear, hear."

The sensation of somebody staring at her poked at Jade. She turned to look at Luc. His blue eyes searched her face, and though not completely sure, she thought he was silently asking if she was all right. She smiled to let him know she was fine, and then added a teasing quirk to her lip to lessen the serious mood between them. It was probably best to keep Luc Le Daun guessing about her state of mind. That way he'd never take her good nature for granted.

The deep gong of a tall, slender pendulum clock in the corner chimed. Ravyn yawned, which seemed like some secret signal for Rhys to stand.

"The hour grows late," he said, offering his hand to Ravyn. "We've much to do tomorrow and more plans to make."

Jade noticed the way his gaze caressed Ravyn and how she in turn blushed and took his hand. Some involuntary need made Jade glance at Luc. He took a drink of his wine, but didn't look at her. When she made a move to rise, his hand slid across the settee and lightly gripped her wrist. Did he not want her to leave? She relaxed against the back of the settee again and waited for his lead.

"Delphina, my dear," Jacob said. "May I escort you to your room?"

"I'd be honored, my lord." She stood and looped her arm with his. "Thank you all for your honesty. I will do whatever I can to help the Bringers."

"Very good, my dear." Jacob patted her hand. "Thought we might have frightened you off."

She gave a gruff laugh. "It takes a lot more than a few demons to scare me off."

Jacob's grin spread. "Touché." He guided Delphina toward the door. "Bank the fire, would you, Luc?"

"Yes, Father."

Rhys and Ravyn said their good nights and followed Jacob and Delphina out the door, leaving Jade and Luc alone.

Luc stood and walked to the fireplace. How did he tactfully bring up his plan to Jade? What he intended was careless, but he didn't see any other way around giving Jade the life she deserved. In an ironic twist, his plan would free both her and Esmeralda.

"I think your father carries a torch for Delphina," Jade said.

"Really?" He leaned an arm against the mantle and looked at her. "I hadn't noticed."

"Maybe you didn't want to notice." She gave him a sly smile. "She can't be much older than you."

"Trust me, I'd embrace any woman and call her 'Mother' if she drew my father's attention away from me."

"At least you have a father who cares."

Instead of replying, he squatted and gripped the metal poker. With the pointed tip, he prodded the embers and spread them across the floor of the hearth. Yes, at least he had a father, and she had a mother. If they didn't do something about Rell, Jade wouldn't live long enough to meet Willa.

After a minute he set the poker back in the rack, but remained crouched, staring into the fire. "When we were in the chapel you mentioned the despair you felt in Icarus. Do you remember?"

Her voice sounded tight and wary. "Yes."

"Did you feel the same when you touched Rell?"

He watched the tiny flames dance and disappear around the edges of the red-hot coals. Several seconds passed and she didn't reply. He glanced over his shoulder, but Jade wasn't looking at him. Instead, she stared into the fire, unblinking. Her arms were crossed in what looked like an effort to shield herself from the unpleasant memory.

Luc stood and faced her. "Jade?"

She glanced at him, as if pulled from a trance. "Yes."

Since she hadn't phrased her reply as a question, he assumed it to be her answer. "Can you describe it for me?"

"Like screaming, but nobody can hear you." She swallowed hard, her gaze traveling back to the fire. "Like walking on the edge of madness. Like knowing that your mind is slipping away and there's nothing you can do to stop it." Her eyes grew wide. "Like running from someone but you can't stand or see where you're going. Desperate, hopeless." Her voice trailed off. "Insane."

"I'm sorry." His voice cracked, but he didn't try to hide the emotion her description raised in him. Jade needed to know that even if he couldn't fully comprehend what she'd experienced, he did understand what it meant. More eloquent words escaped him. "I'm sorry."

"I believe you." She gave a tight smile and scooted to the edge of the settee as if to stand. "Now, before we start sharing our feelings too much, why don't you tell me why you kept me here."

He recognized sarcasm as her way to avoid unpleasant confrontation. Perhaps the direct approach was the best way to deal with Jade.

"You're losing her." He walked to the chair across from her. "After your encounter with Esmeralda and Icarus, surely you see that."

She braced her hands against the cushions and watched him settle into the chair. Her teeth worried her bottom lip and her right index finger scratched absently against the wood. It didn't appear she would come easily to the same conclusion he had.

"I understand how difficult this is for you, Jade." Luc leaned forward and lowered his voice, attempting to coax her with kindness. "She's your sister, the only family you've had for most of your life." He held her gaze. "But she's dangerous."

The tapping finger stilled. Jade's gaze narrowed. "She's a Bane.

She's always been dangerous."

He stood and slowly paced the length of the library. "Not like now. With Icarus in the picture, I'm afraid…"

"Afraid of what?"

It was a challenge. He heard it in her tone. But what was the dare? A challenge to express his emotions? A challenge to voice what Jade needed to hear? A challenge to betray her and Esmeralda again?

"Afraid that she's too far gone."

Jade eased from the settee, not breaking her gaze with his. "And if that's true? There's nothing to be done about it."

Another challenge. "We can do something to protect you."

Her head began to shake with slow denial. "What, stay on sanctified ground the rest of my life? No matter where I go, Rell will find me."

"You know that's not what I'm proposing."

"You're asking me…" She dragged her gaze away from him and turned to walk to the hearth. "To kill my own sister?"

His heart tightened against the anguish in her question. A solution she'd obviously contemplated but couldn't bring herself to entertain in its entirety. "Esmeralda is already dead."

Jade hugged herself again, her shoulders hunching against the truth of his statement.

"And now that she and Icarus have formed an alliance," he continued, "I fear for you more than ever." He joined her at the hearth, but she didn't look at him. "Until now it's been you and her, but no longer."

"But what if we're wrong?" Her eyes rounded, pleading with him to find another answer. "What if Esmeralda is locked inside, screaming to get out, but nobody can hear her?"

He stilled the urge to touch her. "I would love nothing more than to restore your sister to the girl I once knew. But that's not going to happen."

Jade's voice raised an octave. "It could."

"It can't." He picked at the wax of a candle sitting on the mantle. "And even if we could, we don't know how. Every day that she remains in Icarus's company, she becomes more Bane, more dangerous." He hesitated. "More hopeless."

His last words seemed to have the desired effect. Jade exhaled and trudged back to the settee. She sat and cradled her head in her hands. "I can't kill her."

Warmth from the fire radiated against his legs, penetrating some of the chill that had invaded his bones at the very thought of traveling into the Shadow World. "Not you, me."

He didn't expound on his plan, only waited, letting the full scope sink in, but what he truly wanted was her permission to do what needed to be done.

Jade lifted her head and stared at him. Everything from repulsion to calculation flitted across her face. "With an immortal weapon?"

He nodded and continued to wait for her to work out his suggestion.

"How?" she asked after a few minutes.

"I'll go to her—in the Shadow World."

Jade's eyebrows rose to her hairline. "You realize the Shadow World is full of demons and Icarus."

"Yes, but they won't expect me to infiltrate their realm. They feel safe there and will be more vulnerable."

"So you propose to sneak into the Shadow World, corner Rell, stab her with an immortal weapon to release her soul, and walk out unharmed?"

He shrugged. "It could work."

"Have you informed Rhys and Ravyn of your plan?"

"No." He scooped the wax shavings into his hand and tossed them on the dying embers. "I don't know if I will."

Jade crossed her arms and cocked her head. "Why?"

"Because…" Luc dusted his hands against his pants. "Somebody needs to lead the fight against the Bane, and—" He met her gaze. "Kill *me* if I'm turned Bane."

The breath rushed from Jade, her mouth falling open at the prospect. Her arms hung limply at her side, as if he'd drained all the fight from her with his last sentence. "You have truly gone around the bend if you think I'm going to give you my blessing to not only kill my sister, but to quite possibly be turned into a demon yourself."

"Hypocrite." Luc pointed at her and chose his words carefully. "You won't release your sister's soul even though the very idea of being a Bane is incomprehensible." He took a step toward her and she reared back against the settee as if he was going to slap her. "You've felt Rell's desolation, yet you won't let me free her from her physical prison." He continued to stalk toward her, his voice growing louder. "Surely you can see that there are worse things in life than death."

Jade stood, her words barely topping a whisper. "She's my sister."

"And a Bane." He backed her against the wall and held her in place by fixing a hand at each side of her head. "And under Icarus's influence. How long do you think it will take him to figure out that if he manipulates Rell enough, she will hand you over?"

Tears pooled in Jade's eyes. "She wouldn't do that to me."

"Maybe not before." His hands slid down the smooth wooden

wall and rested on her shoulders. "But you're at full power. Both Icarus and Vile need a converted Bringer. You've become a pawn and Icarus will stop at nothing to have you." Soft flesh gave way under his kneading fingers. "And now that you know your mother lives, the only way Rell can keep you is to turn you."

A tear slid down Jade's cheek and her conviction crumpled. She closed her eyes and leaned her head against the wall. "I know."

Unable to watch her pain, Luc gathered Jade to him. She went willingly and encircled his waist with her arms. He held her, silently showing her that he understood what it took for her to concede, and admitting to himself they were now connected by a quest neither wanted to undertake.

He rested his cheek against the top of her head. She was so small, tinier than Esmeralda had been. But whether from the years spent trying to survive or a life forged from distrust and suspicion, Jade possessed a strength Esmeralda had never had.

"When do we leave?" Jade asked.

"'We'?" He pulled away from her. "You're not coming."

"And how are you going to stop me?" There was a definite challenge in her stare. "I'll just follow you."

By the gods, the woman was maddening. He rubbed his finger across her cheek. "And what of your mother? Would you chance her having to relive your death?"

"We never enter into battles believing we'll die. But the cause is usually worth the risk." She swallowed hard but continued to stare at him, the conviction burning in her eyes. "It's far less cruel to take the choice out of my mother's hands than to one day force her to make the decision. Hate and anger are much easier to live with than guilt."

"You're a good daughter."

She gave him a weak smile.

"And a giant pain in my arse, you know that."

She lifted her chin a fraction of an inch and her eyes softened. She leaned into him again. "I know."

Even though subtle, it was an invitation. He lowered his mouth to hers and gently kissed her. His hold was loose, wanting her to know she could stop at any time. But she didn't stop. Instead she opened to him, rocking up on her toes and wrapping her arms around his neck.

She was soft and pliant, a side he had rarely seen of her, a side he doubted she allowed herself to show, a side he wanted more of.

Their lips lingered, drinking each other in slowly. Desire stole through him, presenting him with two questions. What did he want to do and what should he do? What he wanted was to drag her to his bed, but the timing wasn't right. Passion born out of desperation to feel alive wasn't what he wanted anymore, and she deserved to know she meant more to him than any other woman.

He pulled away and she didn't resist. Her eyes searched his face as if calculating his reaction. Danger and possible death was their future. To promise her something that might never come to fruition would be cruel.

He cupped her face with his hands. "You deserve so much better."

Like him, she seemed unable to fully express what she was feeling. She covered his hands with hers. "I don't want better."

"When this is over…"

She nodded. "Yes, when this is over."

He wanted to kiss her again, but knew he wouldn't stop if he did. "Come on." He took her hand. "Tomorrow is a big day."

Chapter Fifteen

A quiet rustle pulled Jade from her dream. She opened her eyes and stared at the dark beamed ceiling, trying to locate the intruder by sound. Another soft swish whispered to her from the foot of her bed. Her eyes darted along the wall but with the curtains drawn, the room was too dark to see clearly.

The pile of blankets covering her obscured everything from the mattress down. Somebody could be sneaking up from below her and she wouldn't be able to see. She inched to the left side of her bed. A quick glance over the edge revealed no intruder. She rolled a half turn and dropped to the floor. The cold stone absorbed most of her movement—but not all.

Measured footsteps clipped across the floor. From the sound of it, they had stopped approximately three feet beyond where she crouched. Before Jade could react, the drapes were flung back, blinding her with brilliant sunlight. She threw an arm across her eyes.

"Are you all right, miss?" a soft, feminine voice asked.

Jade blinked away the white dots dancing across her vision and lowered her arm. Any advantage she might have had against an attacker had been easily spoiled by the simple act of opening the curtains. She was losing her touch.

"Yes." She pushed up from the floor to stand and straightened her nightshirt. "I'm fine."

The young woman Jade recognized as one of the servants tipped her head to the side. "Did you fall out of bed, my lady?"

"No, I was just…" She struggled for an answer that didn't make her sound like an idiot. "Stretching." She raised her hands over her head. "I like to do that before I get dressed. It works out all the kinks."

The woman nodded as if contemplating the practice. "Well, when you're finished, Lady Ravyn would like you to join her and the men in the great hall."

"Very good." She lowered her arms.

"My name is Penny. I'll be your lady's maid while you're here." She bent and picked up a gown the color of newly sprouting leaves from the bed. "Would you like me to help you dress?"

Jade pointed at the gown. "That's not mine."

Penny smiled and ran her hand down the long skirt. "Lady Ravyn asked that you wear it today. Said it would be better received than what you usually wear." Her face tightened in a slight scowl. "Not sure what that means."

"She probably wants to make sure I don't wear my street clothes." It appeared they were leaving for Illuma Grand today and playing the role of a proper lady must be part of their plan. Jade feigned a smile of excitement and widened her eyes like she'd seen other women do when they saw something pretty. "Lady Ravyn needn't have worried. How could I resist a beautiful gown like this?"

The statement sounded overly dramatic, but Penny didn't seem to notice.

"Very good, my lady."

One comforting fact was that Ravyn would be dressed similarly. The last time Jade had worn a gown was before the Bane had taken Rell. It wasn't that she was against wearing such feminine garments—it was that she wasn't sure she knew how. Penny grabbed the hem of Jade's nightdress and hauled it over her head, tossing it on the bed.

Jade crossed her arms over her chest, partly due to the chilly morning air and partly out of modesty. It felt odd to have somebody dress her, but under Penny's polite directions and coaxing, she relaxed and gave over to the servant's expertise.

The first layer was a soft, lightweight chemise. Over that fell a floor-length apron that covered the near transparent shift, settling Jade's modesty to a comfortable level. Last was a heavier brocade coat two shades darker than the green of the apron. Large, velvet cuffs turned up at her wrists and two velvet loops hooked around metal toggles at her waist to allow the apron beneath to show through. The gown was more beautiful than anything Jade had ever worn.

Penny led her to a carved bench and pulled a wooden comb from her hip pocket. With short strokes, she tugged at the knots in Jade's hair, relentlessly working each snarl until the narrow teeth ran smoothly from crown to tip. After that, she deftly braided the mass in a flurry of hand motions.

Her quick actions reminded Jade of the shell man in the market. He displayed three cups, placing the small shell under one of them. With sleight of hand, he would rapidly switch the position of the cups, swirling them across the makeshift tabletop. Each time she had been certain she knew where the shell lay, but each time she was wrong. Though she'd never seen him cheat, nobody was that good and his hands were too swift to be sure.

When finished, Penny moved to stand in front of Jade and folded her hands. "All finished, my lady."

Jade stood and walked to the looking glass. The image before her was nearly unrecognizable. Gone were all traces of the street rat or sailor. In their place stood a woman, someone who was part of something bigger than a life spent scraping by.

Her words were simple, but certainly heartfelt. "Thank you, Penny."

"You're welcome, my lady." The servant curtsied and walked to the door. "I'll inform Lady Ravyn you'll be down shortly."

Jade turned toward the woman, but she was already gone. "Efficient."

Unable to resist, she examined herself in the mirror again. The green of the gown accentuated her eyes, giving them a vibrant glow. She tugged at the edges of the coat, but the material didn't give. She'd put on weight since joining the Bringers. Though only a pound or two, it did a lot to fill in the hollows below her cheeks. Or maybe that's what happened when you came to full power. Whatever the cause, she had to admit, she looked healthier and felt better than she could remember.

It took careful steps and planned movements to maneuver down the winding staircase. The layers of material wound around her legs and slid under her feet. She glanced around, and seeing the area empty, grabbed a handful of fabric and hoisted it above her ankles. With quick steps she descended the steps before anybody saw her less-than-ladylike behavior. At the bottom she dropped the material and smoothed the front of her gown.

Everyone was in attendance in the great room. Jacob reclined in an ornately carved chair at one end of the table and the rest of the members spilled along both sides in various degrees of repose.

She couldn't help notice how Luc sat straighter when she entered, his eyes following her progress across the room. All heads turned toward her, the conversation stopping.

"Good morning." She forced her gaze around the table, making sure not to linger on Luc. "Sorry if I kept you waiting." The men rose from their chairs. She stopped, confused by their action. "Damn, did I miss breakfast? Are we leaving already?"

Ravyn laughed. "No, you're right on time. The men are practicing their manners."

Jade scrunched up her face. "Well, stop. It makes me nervous."

"You'll have to get used to it," Jacob said. "Manners are of the utmost importance at Illuma Grand."

Luc stood and pulled out the chair next to him, indicating she should sit. She hesitated for a second and then accepted his offer. "Thank you."

His hair hung damp around his shoulders and the clean smell of rainwater and soap tickled her nose. Clad in a dark blue doublet and black pants, he looked like a proper lord of the manor.

A wave of surrealism washed over her. Not a week ago, she was sleeping in a deserted chapel and plotting his death. Now, not only were they living under the same roof, but the feelings she had for Luc were at complete odds with the past thirteen years of her life. It was almost too much to take in.

Last night she'd been accepting of his plan. It had made sense. No matter how difficult it would be, it was necessary and she had put down her foot, demanding to go with him. But in the light of day, the idea of releasing Rell seemed stark and ruthless. It was hard to know what was right and wrong, especially when he looked at her the way he was. The intensity of his stare muddled her reasoning.

She pasted on a tight smile and addressed the group. "Sleep well?"

"Not really." Luc's tone caressed her.

Neither had she. After he had left her at the door, it had taken an hour before she had felt ready to climb in bed and another hour after that before she had fallen asleep. Images of their kiss had left her fidgety and a little conflicted.

"I think most of us had a restless night," Jacob said.

Luc continued to appraise her like a tasty piece of mutton. She shifted uncomfortably, wishing he'd be a little more subtle about his interest in her. When he smiled at her, feelings she shouldn't be having stirred, giving her crazy ideas about a future too tenuous to contemplate. Guilt immediately extinguished any further forbidden thoughts.

Unable to stand it, she turned to glare at him and whispered, "Why are you staring at me?"

"You look beautiful." He'd spoken the words quietly, but not so much so that the others didn't hear.

"I agree." Ravyn leaned on her elbows and rested her chin on her fists. "The second I saw that gown, I knew it was perfect for you."

Finding it safer to ignore Luc, she turned her attention to Ravyn and ran her hand along the brocade sleeve. "I prefer pants, but if I must dress like a lady, this makes the effort worth it."

"I'm glad it pleases you. I think the Bringers at Illuma Grand will be more accepting of us if we cause less of a stir among the women."

Ravyn wore a similar ensemble in deep purple. Instead of wide cuffs, her sleeves were fitted and trimmed in short, black fur, which was echoed at her collar. She donned gowns and jewels as naturally as she sported leathers and daggers, seemingly comfortable in any situation.

Penny set a trencher of eggs and crisp bacon in front of Jade and then filled a goblet with weak wine. It seemed the woman was meant to serve her in every capacity.

"Thank you," Jade said, not sure she'd ever get used to having her needs anticipated.

Penny bobbed once and bustled out of the hall.

"So we leave for Illuma today?" Jade shoved a spoonful of eggs in her mouth. Bless the Sainted Ones, she was hungry. When had she eaten last?

"We hope to leave for Illuma within the hour." Rhys leaned forward and folded his hands in front of him. A single braid at his temple fell forward and brushed the table. "We've gotten word that the Order of the Saints will be leaving tomorrow. Paying respects to them seems like a plausible reason for our arrival."

Jade took a bite of bacon and slowly chewed, her attention wandering. Bless the Sainted Ones, Rhys was a beautiful specimen of a man. As he continued with his instruction about their travel plans, she scrutinized his high cheekbones, sculpted brows, and long silky strands of black hair that spilled around his shoulders. The unbidden question of what it must be like to have somebody look at her the way Rhys looked at Ravyn floated through her mind.

She picked up her goblet and drank. The tart bite of wine slid across her tongue. She continued her appraisal of him, enjoying the wine and image.

"Luc, Jacob, and I will divert Fromme's attention, while Ravyn and Jade search the Council chamber," Rhys said.

Jade set her goblet on the table and picked up the slice of bacon, taking another healthy bite.

"Fromme Bagita is always distrustful when I'm around, so we need to be about our business quickly," Rhys continued.

"Plus, any attempts I've made to find out more about the missing Bringers has been met with stony silence."

"But wouldn't they want to find their missing people?" Jade asked.

"You would think as much." Jacob drummed his fingers on the table. "Another red flag that all is not as it seems."

"If he doesn't already, Fromme will have his eyes and ears out once he hears we've arrived."

"How long will we be staying?" Luc asked.

"One, maybe two nights. The Order of the Saints superiors are slated to leave tomorrow. It makes sense that we would come to pay our respects, even if only out of curiosity. If we stay much longer, Fromme will become suspicious of our motives." He leaned back in his chair. "I'd like to keep him guessing as to our intentions."

"This will be an excellent chance for Luc to assert his authority as my son." Jacob tapped his finger against the base of his chalice. "It is assumed that he will eventually take over my position at Illuma, so there should be no questions about his intentions." He smiled at his son. "Be vague and noncommittal."

"That shouldn't be difficult," Luc said. "There is a festival planned for tonight in honor of the Orders' departure. I find tongues loosen when the wine begins to flow." He smiled at Jade and Ravyn. "And female wiles are the best weapon to pry forth guarded secrets."

Jade slapped a hand over her mouth, preventing the wine from spewing everywhere. She swallowed hard and beat on her chest with a fist, forcing the liquid to go down. A fit of coughing racked her body.

"Was it something I said?" Luc pounded her on the back, but

she waved him away.

Little by little she sucked in gulps of much-needed air. After a few deep breaths she said, "I am the least skilled person when it comes to flirtation."

Luc considered her for a few seconds. "That is true." He rubbed the back of his skull. "I know from experience."

She'd knocked him over the head with a shovel when the Bane sirens had attempted to lure all the sailors on Rhys's ship to their watery graves. "To be fair, I did save your life."

"Yes, remind me to thank you for that one day."

His words sent a prickle of uneasiness through her.

"Jade's right," Ravyn said. "Neither of us have much experience with the opposite sex. I don't think that plan will work."

"What about the women at Illuma Grand?" Jade asked.

"Well, I'll certainly do my part." Luc wiggled his eyebrows.

"I'm sure you will." She graced him with a look of utter disgust. "But that's not what I meant." She turned to Ravyn. "Didn't you say you caused a stir with your leathers?"

"Yes, the women were quite intrigued."

"As I see it, those women will probably seek you out. We strike up a conversation, get them trusting us and extract information from them."

"Sounds easy, but how do we do that?" Ravyn asked.

"I find the only thing most people love more than talking about themselves is having somebody listen to them talk about themselves. Trust me. It will take little effort to get those repressed women to spill their secrets." Jade popped the last bite of bacon in her mouth and sat back.

"Diabolical," Luc said.

She gave him an evil smile.

"And brilliant," he added.

A twinge of satisfaction passed over her. Some of the best plans were the simplest.

"The female mind." Jacob gave a heavy sigh and shook his head. "That is one opponent no man can conquer."

"So now that we have our immediate plans decided, I'd like to discuss the Bane." Luc looked at Jade. "Namely Esmeralda, Jade's sister."

Jacob steepled his fingers under his lower lip. "I know that look. You've got some plan in the works."

"I do, Father." He took a swig of wine and then shifted in his chair to lean forward, setting his goblet on the table. "Rhys had mentioned going into the Shadow World to engage Vile."

Jacob's gaze snapped to Rhys. "That's madness, man."

"We need to stop him before he opens the Abyss of Souls." Rhys's voice remained steady but the firm tone brooked no argument. "The best way to do that is to take him unaware."

"Before you attempt this, Luc and I would like the chance to go into the Shadow World." Jade took a deep breath, forcing the next words out. "To release my sister's soul with one of the daggers."

Jacob's mouth dropped open. "Have you all been struck stupid? To charge into the Shadow World is death—or worse. Then where would the Bringers be?"

"That is why I wish to go in first," Luc said.

Jade faced him. "*We* wish to go in."

"That is why I wish to go in first, and Jade has demanded to join me," Luc amended.

Rhys eyed him. "If we take Vile out first, the rest of the Bane will be easier to manage. You can have your chance then."

"And what if you can't vanquish him and don't return? What if you are turned like Esmeralda or he uses *you* to open the Abyss?" Luc tapped his index finger against the table. "The tides of war will shift in the Bane's favor. Who among the remaining Bringers will be strong enough to vanquish not only Vile, but Icarus, you, and Ravyn?"

Silence filled the room. Luc's words filled Jade with dread. Though she'd understood the risks for Rhys and Ravyn, she hadn't completely thought it through. For them to enter the Shadow World was unthinkable.

"Let us go." Her voice broke the tension. "And if we return, we will help you. I've lived in the Shadow World and know of a way in that will not alert Vile." She paused. "But first, we need to release Rell so that she does not become a tool for Icarus and possibly Vile."

Rhys glanced at Ravyn, lifting his brows. She stared at him for a long time, unblinking.

Finally, Ravyn turned toward Jade and Luc. "I don't like it. There's nothing telling me you will be successful."

"But there's nothing telling you we won't be, right?" Luc said.

"Usually I feel something, but with this there's only—" She hesitated. "I don't know how to explain it. As if destiny is holding its breath, waiting."

"Let's table the idea until after Illuma Grand." Rhys stood, indicating the discussion was over.

"Perhaps we'll uncover something at Illuma that will be of help." Jacob also rose. "Then we'll be able to reassess more effectively."

Luc's father looked like a man given a short stay of execution. It couldn't be easy to watch your son gallop into danger.

Luc said nothing more, but pulled out Jade's chair and offered her his hand. She took it and was surprised when his fingers threaded through hers and didn't let go. His eyes lingered on her face, holding her gaze for a second before looking away. From his expression, this debate was not over.

She gave his hand a gentle squeeze in a show of silent support. Whatever he decided to do, she would follow. Setting her sister's soul free was something they had to do before either of them could move on.

Chapter Sixteen

They were on the road within the hour. Not used to riding, let alone sitting sidesaddle, it took a good mile before Jade felt confident in her seat. She ignored the ache in her back caused by the horse's gait and concentrated on the beautiful day.

The crisp morning air bit at her nose and steam rolled from the horse's nostrils. Sunlight illuminated the leaves, rimming them in yellow light. Wood smoke from the chimneys of the cottages filled the air, bringing with it a sense of home. All harbingers of the impending winter.

Conversation was light and the road uncommonly busy. Shortly after noon, they turned off the main road and passed beneath the iron arch of Illuma Grand.

Posh carriages, single riders and throngs of walking people clogged the roadway.

"What is going on?" Luc said.

"Damn fool." Jacob pulled his horse to a stop. "Bagita has opened Illuma Grand to the masses."

"Aren't the Bringers to remain anonymous?" Ravyn asked.

"Yes." He lowered his voice so only their small group could hear. "The Council voted against this proposal at the last meeting, but it appears Fromme doesn't need Council permission any longer."

"He grows bold indeed," Rhys said. "But to what end? Is he vying for control of Illuma Grand?"

"I think it's bigger than that." Jacob glanced around them. "At first his actions were confined to the Council, then the Bringers who lived here." He shifted in his saddle and leaned in. "I've heard rumors that Fromme has formed an alliance with the Order of the Saints."

"Rumors?" Luc asked.

Jacob shrugged. "From a reliable source." He lifted his head in the direction of the crowds. "Now he throws open the gates as if Illuma Grand were his own home. I can only assume the rumors are true."

"It sounds like he's positioning himself politically," Luc said.

"But why?" Ravyn asked. "He's not part of the Order and the royal seat has been empty for…"

Jade watched the quiet exchange between Jacob and Ravyn, comprehension dawning. Unable to resist, she whispered, "Do you think he means to be king? To claim the throne?"

She stared at Luc's father until he slowly nodded his head. "Of course, he's going to reinstate the crown."

The caravan rolled forward a few feet and stopped again. Rhys sat straight in his saddle, his expression set hard. "The repercussions of his success would be disastrous."

Jade only knew Fromme Bagita by reputation, but what she had heard was disturbing. Overbearing, ruthless determination and an elitist, somebody she had no wish of running into. The crown had been decommissioned by the Order of the Saints more than a hundred years ago. Most believed the Order did it to solidify their control. What did they gain by putting a puppet on the throne again?

As if reading her mind, Luc said, "What kind of deal could he have possibly struck that would be beneficial to the Order?"

"Certainly one that does not serve the people," Jacob said.

A sneer pulled at Luc's top lip. "One that betrays the Bringers to the church."

Nobody spoke as their retinue crept forward, each lost in their thoughts. The responsibilities of being a Bringer weighed on Jade. She and Ravyn's search for information in the Council chamber and the looming expedition into the Shadow World made the current problem of Fromme Bagita seem less pressing.

She exhaled and tried to relax. The last time she'd been on the grounds of Illuma Grand, she had been seven. Never venturing onto the property, she'd played near the estate's boundaries, usually when she was hiding from Rell. Something about the place had called to her. Now she understood that even then she had been a Bringer and this was part of her heritage.

"No matter the strife within the Council," Ravyn said, "one can't argue that Illuma Grand is magnificent."

Jade nodded. Symmetrical trees lined the cobblestone roadway, spaced equal distance apart. Between their foliage she caught glimpses of carved statues in various poses. Flowers lined the walkways and marble columns towered over the heads of the approaching crowd. "It is truly beautiful."

A group of women stepped aside to let them pass. Most appeared to be near her age and all wore drab gray gowns. A redheaded woman glided behind the group, following them as they passed. Something about the woman struck a familiar cord with Jade. She struggled to place the woman, searching her memories.

A smile spread like thick molasses across the woman's mouth. She grabbed the arm of one of the women standing at the edge of the group and pulled her down the path, following them. When she moved level with Jade, the redhead stopped and held up her right hand, her palm facing away from Jade.

"Somebody you know?" Ravyn asked.

"I can't believe it." Jade stared at the familiar greeting and then returned the salute, smiling. "I played with her as a child." She lowered her hand and looked at Ravyn. "That girl was my only friend—Beatrice." She hadn't spoken the name in years. "She would sneak me food and we would play for hours at the edge of the grounds. Until I found the chapel in the woods, Illuma had seemed like the only place safe from the Bane."

As the line moved forward, she glanced over her shoulder. Beatrice and her friend had fallen behind, but still watched her.

"Perhaps you will have a chance to get reacquainted," Ravyn said.

"I'd like that."

The party stopped at the base of the wide marble steps. Stable hands waited to take their horses, each one dressed in gray tunics and britches.

Luc dismounted and moved around his horse to stand below her. He placed a hand on either side of her thigh. "May I help you down?"

Her first reaction was to say no and to attempt the dismount herself. But when she glanced around, she noticed that a large crowd had gathered. Several pointed at them or whispered behind their hands. The throbbing in her lower back spread up her spine when she twisted toward Luc. This confirmed it. She was not a horse person.

Misinterpreting her grimace, Luc smirked. "I promise I won't kiss you?"

"And why is that?" She gritted her teeth and leaned slightly forward. "Do you think your kisses frighten me?"

He grabbed her by the waist and with what seemed like no effort at all, eased her from the mount. Jade's body slid down his, gliding along hard muscle before alighting on the ground. Vibrations rippled through her legs, threatening to set her off balance. His hands lingered at her waist and his face hovered inches above hers. "I certainly hope not."

It was impossible to look away from his fiery stare. Blue eyes peered into hers, stirring all the emotions she tried desperately to keep harnessed. With a slow downward stroke along his biceps, she lowered her hands and stepped back.

Tremors rippled along her legs, setting her off balance. She stumbled, knocking into the horse, but Luc caught her. The animal shifted. Jade placed her hand on its haunch to not only steady the horse, but her nerves as well. Luc's hold loosened and he lowered his hands to his side.

"You do like to pox me, don't you?"

He gave her an innocent smile. "I have done nothing."

With all the calm she could muster, she straightened her aching spine, lifted her skirts and stepped around a pile of horse dung. She brushed past him, lowering her voice. "Perhaps that is your problem."

Not waiting to hear his response, she moved to stand next to Ravyn. She saw Ravyn look behind them and then back at Jade. She cleared her throat but said nothing. A thin smile played on her mouth and she looped her arm through Jade's in a show of amused support.

Jacob led the procession through manicured grounds and into the Grand Entrance. It was everything Jade had dreamed it to be. Polished stone walls soared to unimaginable heights. Archways branched off into what looked like endless lines and disappeared down murky corridors. Sunlight cast tall domes of light through each of the arched windows, creating brilliant white pools on the marble floors.

The upper class and merchants claimed most of the attention in the hall, while the common folk crowded against the walls, seemingly happy to just be near the promised pageantry.

Somewhere beyond her sight, a choir sang. The magical music lilted around them, blending with the ever-growing din. Twenty-foot-tall tapestries hung on the towering walls, each representing a different hunting scene. Jade examined the hangings. The works, though beautiful, could have been hanging in any castle in the kingdom and seemed inconsequential to the Bringers' history.

Her gaze tracked down the wall and stopped on an ornate tile set to the right of one of the hangings. She squinted and stepped toward it, trying to get a better look.

"What is it?" Ravyn said, moving up beside her.

"Do you see that tile?" She motioned with her head, not wanting to point in case somebody watched them. "The one beside the tapestry of the boar hunt?"

"Yes."

"I recognize that symbol from the book I sold to the curiosity shop."

Ravyn scrutinized the square. "I've seen that before too. On my tome from the abbey."

As Jade glanced around to make sure they weren't drawing attention to themselves, her eyes landed on the next tapestry. She flicked her head toward the hanging. "Look."

Another square with a different symbol peeked from behind the curtain. "It means something." Ravyn's eyebrows arched upward. "It can't be a coincidence."

"I agree." Jade dipped her head, indicating the hangings further down the wall. "Each tapestry has a symbol."

"What are you looking at?" Rhys wrapped his arm around Ravyn's waist.

She leaned into him. "Those tiles beside the tapestries."

Before he could answer, Luc and Jacob joined them.

"What are we looking at?" Luc asked.

Rhys pointed and Ravyn slapped his hand down. "Don't point."

"See the tiles beside the hangings?" Jade said.

The men examined the square, each nodding.

"Those are Bringer symbols." Rhys glanced at Jacob. "Have you ever noticed them before?"

"Walked by these old hangings a thousand times and never noticed those once," he said.

"Probably because we didn't know what they were until we had the books." Luc nodded. "I bet nobody else has noticed, either."

"Jacob." A male voice boomed behind them. They all turned in unison to face the man. "And Lord Blackwell."

The approaching man had to be Fromme Bagita. A sumptuous scarlet brocade and fur robe framed a wide chest laden with heavy gold chains and a large jewel-encrusted medallion.

"Fromme, just the man I wanted to see." Jacob clasped his hands behind his back in a show of displeasure. "As I recall, the Council voted down the proposal to open the doors of Illuma Grand. And yet when I arrived, the entire county was streaming through the gates."

"Jacob." The man's tone held no hint of an apology. "If you had remained at Illuma Grand, you would have known about the secondary assemblage I called."

"Why?"

Fromme looked perplexed. "Why what?"

"Why did you call a secondary assemblage? We voted and the answer was no."

"Yes, well, Lady Whitefeld hinted to me that she'd had a change of heart about her vote." He shrugged. "Poor dear, what did you expect me to do? It was her dying wish."

"Lady Whitefeld is dead?" Luc asked.

Even though Jade knew nothing about the workings within Illuma Grand, Fromme Bagita's story seemed laced with lies.

"Died in her sleep last week." He gave an exaggerated sigh. "She'll be sorely missed."

Probably so, but Jade imagined not by Lord Bagita. The hair on the back of her neck bristled. She didn't like this man. His arrogance and oily speech fueled her distrust.

"You'll be looking for a new Council member, then?" Luc asked.

"Yes, yes." Fromme's head bobbled up and down, his chins flattening against his chest with each nod. "There are several fabulous candidates. Any of which would make a fine member."

"Excellent." A brilliant smile spread across Luc's mouth. "Add me to the list."

Fromme's confident expression tightened. "Really, I hadn't pegged you as the political type."

Not missing a beat, Jacob chimed in. "Oh yes, he's been talking about it for years. Said it was time for him to take his rightful place among his peers."

Jacob slapped Luc on the back. Since she and Luc were planning a mission that could possibly end in their deaths, she presumed he was simply calling Fromme's bluff.

"And you, Lord Blackwell?" Bagita's eyes narrowed, the forced smile spreading no further than his mouth. "Do you plan on running as well?"

Jade glanced at Rhys. His expression was unreadable and his voice flat. "I don't play well with others."

"Luc will definitely have our support, but we have more important matters to deal with, Lord Bagita," Ravyn said. "Matters that take us outside Illuma Grand."

"Still on about the Bane, are you?" He shook his head. "Well, best of luck with that."

The man's haughtiness prodded Jade like an angry bee. "Ignoring the Bane won't make them go away."

For the first time Bagita turned his attention on her. "I know everybody else, but you I've not met before."

"Fromme," Jacob cut in. "This is Jade Kendal."

Large, bushy brows drew together and he pursed his plump lips. "Kendal? Why does that name sound familiar?"

A note of pride and a thread of menace laced Luc's answer. "She is Bowen Kendal's daughter."

Fromme's face went slack, his mouth opened and closed once. "But I thought his family was killed."

Jade held her arms out to the side. "Obviously not."

"Her mother lives as well," Luc added. "Incidentally, she's on her way to Faela as we speak."

"Alive, why that's imp…incredible." His face transformed into a mask of unconvincing excitement. "Is it possible that your father lived as well?"

There was nothing hopeful in his question. "Unfortunately, no," Jade said.

"And there was an older sister." He turned his gaze to Luc. "You were courting her, were you not?"

"Gone as well," Jade cut in, not liking the way the man took every opportunity to throw a verbal barb.

Luc glanced at her, giving her a wink. The simple action reinforced the fact that these were her friends and he'd do anything to protect them—especially from somebody like Lord Bagita.

"Jade?" a woman said behind her.

She turned to see her old friend, Beatrice, standing behind her. A tentative smile played on her mouth and her hands were clasped at her chest, as if she were afraid Jade wouldn't recognize her. Even though Beatrice had transformed from a tomboy into a beauty, her freckled nose and coppery locks gave her away. Her tan skin glowed with health and her huge brown eyes sparkled like a cup of weak tea.

"Beatrice." Jade smiled and opened her arms and hugged her. "I'm so happy to see you."

She hugged Jade back. "I wasn't sure it was you, but when you waved, I knew." She released her and slid a hand along Jade's braid. "Besides, who else has hair like this?"

"Beatrice." Fromme's voice broke into their reunion. "I'm glad you're here."

She let go of Jade's hair and folded her hands in front of her. "Yes, my lord."

"Fetch his lordships' and the ladies' refreshments. We'll be at the Superiors' table in the Great Hall. Deliver them there."

"Yes, my lord." Her gaze cut to Jade. "Perhaps we can catch up later."

"I'd like that very much."

With a quick curtsy to the group, she turned and wove her way through the crowd.

"Come." Fromme held his arm out, presumably in the direction of the hall. "There's someone I'd like to introduce you to."

Instead of waiting for their consent, he pivoted and bullied his way through the crowd. Luc moved up behind Jade and placed his hand on her waist. At first she thought he was being forward, but once amid the jostling mass, his hand steadied and guided her.

The air thickened, becoming warmer the deeper into the crush they progressed. The din of the crowd rumbled in her ears, making it impossible to hear anything distinctly. A thousand different odors clogged her nostrils, none of them good. She coughed and covered her nose with her sleeve. Too short to see over most of the heads, Jade gave up trying to get a glimpse of where they were going and let the flow take her.

After what seemed like an eternity, people's attire transformed from threadbare to sumptuous and the smell of unwashed bodies lessened. She lowered her arm and was struck with the savory tang of roasted meat. Two more arches passed overhead and with each one the crowd thinned.

They entered the Great Hall and Jade's breath caught in her throat. Her eyes followed the soaring dome-shaped ceiling upward to an expansive mural of the sky. Planets and celestial bodies she couldn't name stretched overhead, giving her the feeling of being outside. Never had she seen anything so spectacular.

Though hundreds of people milled about the hall, it was obvious that only the richest, highest ranking, and the most elite were allowed near the Superiors.

Lord Bagita led them through the center of the room to a

long table stretching across the length of the hall. Men and women cloaked in black robes hovered around the dozen or so people dressed in white. They approached a white-clad figure. From her size, Jade deduced it was probably a woman.

"Ascendant Meran?" Fromme stopped behind her.

The woman turned and Jade was immediately struck by the color of her pale blue eyes, which was all that could be seen beneath the white layers of the veil covering her face.

"Lord Bagita?" The woman's voice was soft and surprisingly low for her size.

"There are some people I'd like you to meet, Ascendant." He stepped to the side, giving Jade a clearer view of the woman. "You've met Jacob Le Daun, I believe."

Jacob tipped his head in greeting. "Lovely to see you again."

"You as well, Lord Le Daun." Her gaze traveled over the group and stopped on Luc. "And this must be your son. The resemblance is quite remarkable."

"Luc, my lady, and yes, he is all mine."

The veil over the Ascendant's mouth shifted and lines around her eyes crinkled into what Jade assumed was a smile. She looked no older than twenty, but Jade knew that most Ascendants were in their thirties or older. The Ascendant position within the Order of the Saints was given only to those Sisters who possessed the gift of prophecy. Jade had to wonder how powerful Ascendant Meran's gift was to have garnered such a high position at such a young age.

"One of our less frequent visitors," Fromme said, drawing the attention back to himself. "Rhys Blackwell, and his companion, Lady Ravyn Mayfield."

"I've heard a lot about you, Lord Blackwell." The Ascendant's words held a hint of amusement.

Rhys cleared his throat. "All good, I hope, my lady."

"But of course." Her pale blue gaze leveled on Ravyn. She took a step forward and reached for Ravyn's hand. Gasps and whispers rippled around the hall. "Lady Ravyn, I had hoped to meet you."

Jade watched the unprecedented exchange. It was death to touch an Ascendant. To have one initiate the contact had never been heard of, as far as she knew. Ravyn stiffened at first touch, obviously aware of the law and just as surprised. All traces of humor had vanished from Rhys's expression and now he wore his unreadable mask. Luc slid Jade a glance, silently warning her to be ready if somebody tried to enforce the law.

"There are so many questions I wish to ask you about your life in the abbey and how you came to be with this wonderful group."

"I would like that very much, Ascendant." Ravyn gave her a genuine smile and the tension within the group seemed to melt. "I'm at your call."

The Sister released her grip and slid her hands into the voluminous sleeves of her gown. "Would you and Lord Blackwell join me for a private dinner before the festivities begin?"

"But my lady, dinner is being served in the south dining room within the hour." Fromme held his hands out as if her plans were set in stone and gave her a pleading smile. "You are to be honored during the feast."

"You can honor me afterward, Fromme. I rarely get the opportunity for girl talk and I won't miss the chance." Her tone brooked no argument.

"Of course, Ascendant." He executed a half bow, which bordered on groveling.

"We would be honored," Ravyn said.

By the look on her friend's face, Jade knew that Ravyn enjoyed putting Lord Bagita in his place. She had shared with Jade on the ride to Illuma Grand that there was no love lost between her and Bagita ever since the Council had interrogated her. That had been the day she'd erupted in flames and she and Rhys had nearly ended their relationship. There were many bad memories, and most revolved around Fromme's condescension and unwillingness to believe in their cause—that the Bane were on the rise. Jade understood Ravyn's dislike.

"Excellent. Shall we say eight o'clock?" said the Ascendant.

"We will be there, my lady." Ravyn gave her a brilliant smile.

Somebody called the Ascendant's name and Jade could have sworn the woman gave a tiny eye roll.

"If you'll excuse me." She curtsied and pivoted to gracefully drift across the room in a cloud of white robes.

"I like her," Rhys said. "Not at all like the other Superiors I've met in the past."

Bagita harrumphed. "If you'll excuse me, I have other guests to attend to." With a flip of his robe, he spun and stormed out of the hall.

"Don't think that went quite as he had planned," Luc said.

"I'm not sure what he'd planned," Jacob agreed. "But if you can capture the Ascendant's ear, you may have yourself a powerful ally."

"I can't believe she touched you." Jade reached and covered Ravyn's hand, wondering if it now felt different. It didn't. She pulled back. "And you're still alive."

"My first impulse was to yank my hand away, but insulting an Ascendant would have been just as bad." Ravyn glanced around them and then leaned in. "That whole exchange was very odd, don't you think?"

"Odd," Jade agreed. "But maybe something is finally going in our favor."

"Perhaps we'll find answers during dinner." Jacob pointed to a table filled with food. "Until then, let's enjoy ourselves and socialize."

CHAPTER SEVENTEEN

"Jade?"

She turned to see Beatrice weighed down with a huge silver tray containing goblets of wine. "Bless the Sainted Ones, let me help you."

Jade picked up the two nearest goblets and handed them to Jacob and Rhys, continuing to pass them around until everybody had a drink. Beatrice set the tray on the Superior's table and rejoined the group.

"Sorry it took me so long." Red tinged her cheeks. "I waited until Lord Bagita was gone. Otherwise, he would have found another task for me and we'd never get the chance to chat."

"Smart girl," Jacob laughed. "Well, I will leave you to it. Lots of elbows to rub."

"I will find you later, Father," Luc said to his departing back. Jacob waved a hand in the air to signal he'd heard. "Rhys and I have a few things to take care of."

"Fine, go," Ravyn said. "I'm sure we can keep ourselves occupied without you."

Rhys leaned in and kissed her on the cheek. "Stay out of trouble."

Jade gave a snort, but quickly covered it when Ravyn pinned her with a stare.

Where the men were going or what they had planned, Jade didn't know, but most certainly it was to ferret out any information about the missing Bringers and Lord Bagita's pact with the Order of the Saints. Suddenly she was grateful for their simple task of exploring the Council chamber.

She turned. "Ravyn, this is my friend, Beatrice."

The two women exchanged greetings. It felt strange to make introductions in such a civilized manner. It was almost as if she were a real lady.

"It's so good to see you," Jade said. "How is your mother?"

Beatrice's smile slipped. "She died two years ago."

"Oh, no." Jade reached out and touched Beatrice's arm. She knew a lot about the loss of a parent, the void it had created inside her, and all the years wasted trying to fill it. "I'm so sorry."

"Thank you." Her friend gave a little shake of her head and sniffed. "I'm getting along. Everybody here has been very kind and supportive. I've built my own life now." She paused, her eyes quickly roaming the people standing near. "But there is something I'd like to speak to you about." Her gaze cut to Ravyn and settled back on Jade. "Both of you."

"Of course." Their childhood connection pushed Jade to answer without considering what Beatrice might want to talk to them about, already deciding that if it was within her power to help, she would. Though they hadn't seen each other for more than a decade, it seemed like only yesterday. "Is there some place private we can talk?"

Beatrice smirked. "Probably not, especially with the Order here, but perhaps I could give you a tour of some of the less crowded areas of Illuma Grand."

"That would be wonderful." Ravyn folded her hands in front of her and donned an innocent smile. "I've wanted to show Jade the amazing doors on the Council chamber."

"Right," Jade lied. "I hear they're amazing."

They both stared pointedly at Beatrice. The corner of her mouth quirked as if resisting the urge to smile. "Well then, follow me."

Beatrice worked her way through the crowd smiling and introducing them to various people whose names Jade was certain she'd never remember. One thing could be said for their hostess, she was a consummate actress. In a slightly louder than normal voice, Beatrice described the massive paintings depicting grand celebrations inside the Great Hall. She regaled them with forgettable details about the people for whom the statues were carved, all the while leading them toward the staircase that spiraled to the lower levels.

The crowd of people spilled down the first level of the steps and milled about on the landing. Disguise was one of Jade's fortes, but acting was not. She lifted her skirt to avoid tripping and tried to wrestle the yards of material under control without appearing clumsy. Seemingly one with *her* gown, Ravyn stopped to contemplate an alcove that was lit from above by a hole running two stories above.

"How does the light get this deep? Aren't we below ground?" Ravyn asked.

"Mirrors." Beatrice pointed up inside the tube above a small statue of a scholarly figure holding a book. "They are angled to reflect all the way down. There are several of these light tubes throughout Illuma."

"That's amazing," Jade said, truly impressed with the ingenuity.

Ravyn turned and flinched. Jade spun, expecting to see someone suspicious following them, but the area behind them was empty.

"Is everything all right?" Beatrice asked.

A shudder rippled through Ravyn. Jade gave her a questioning look.

"Sorry." Ravyn glanced around and lowered her voice. "Ghosts."

Beatrice's eyes rounded. "Ghosts?"

"Yes." Ravyn rubbed her arms as if to get warm. "You have quite a few of them here, and one in particular seems very interested in what we're doing."

Jade looked around but saw nothing. She didn't know which part of being a Bringer gave her friend the ability to see spirits, but she was glad she hadn't been *gifted with* that talent. "What does he want?"

"She," Ravyn said. "And I believe she wants us to go to the Council chamber." She stared into empty space for a second. "Yes, definitely the chamber."

They turned to Beatrice, who hadn't seemed to recover from the initial ghost announcement. She blinked a few times and nodded. "All right then."

She turned and continued down to the next level. The crowd began to thin and it was easier for Jade to catch snippets of conversation. Nothing seemed too nefarious, just complaints about who was receiving more attention, excitement over the festivities, and the impending dinner. By the third level only the occasional gray-clad Bringers were present, bustling in and out of a pair of solid wooden doors.

"That's the back entrance to the living quarters," Beatrice

said, indicating the slowly closing door. "We rarely use them unless there's a gathering. It's easier to avoid the crowds." She lowered her voice. "And avoid more chores after your shift is over."

Jade snorted and nodded in understanding.

They spiraled down the next flight of stairs, which was empty. Beatrice held her arm out, blocking their descent, and slowed her step. She crept to the bottom and peered around the corner, then motioned them forward.

"It looks empty." She descended the last step and stopped, turning to look at them. "I wanted to speak to you about the missing Bringers."

Jade tried to keep her face passive, but couldn't stop herself from glancing at Ravyn.

"You've heard about them?" Beatrice looked over her shoulder to make sure they were still alone. "Do you know anything about their disappearance?"

Unsure how much to say, Jade waited for Ravyn to take the lead.

"Only that they're missing," Ravyn said.

Beatrice's expression fell. "Nothing more?"

"No, I'm sorry."

"I was afraid of that."

"What's happened?" Jade said, sensing this was more than just curiosity on Beatrice's part.

"There's a man." A flush crept over her friend's cheeks. "He's missing."

"Your beau?" Ravyn asked.

Tears gathered, magnifying the woman's doe-like brown eyes. She nodded and swallowed hard, wringing her hands together. "Marcus Tobin." She sniffed. "I've asked around and all they tell me is that he's left Illuma."

An uneasy feeling slithered along Jade's spine. "And you don't believe them?"

"He wouldn't have left without saying something." A tear ran down her cheek and she brushed it away. "The night before he disappeared, he asked for my hand." She shook her head. "At the very least he would have left me a note. He wouldn't have just abandoned me."

Ravyn pulled Beatrice into a hug. "We'll do whatever we can to find him. I promise."

Jade rubbed her friend's shoulder. "We promise."

"Thank you." Beatrice stepped out of Ravyn's embrace and wiped her tears. "I know there's more going on than anybody is telling me."

Jade and Ravyn exchanged glances.

"We agree," Ravyn said.

Beatrice straightened. "You do?"

"That's why we need to search the Council chamber." Ravyn paused. "But it must be kept a secret. If somebody is trying to cover up the Bringers' abductions, it means there's a traitor among us."

"A traitor? I don't understand," Beatrice said.

"Neither do we." Jade took her friend's hands. "But I promise we'll do everything we can to find out."

Her conviction to go through with Luc's plan strengthened. People's lives were being affected by Bane, and whatever she could do to stop the growing threat, she would do—starting with her sister's deadly alliance with Icarus.

Ravyn cocked her head, peering at Jade with clear pale blue eyes that seemed to see into her soul. Too late Jade realized her mistake. Though Ravyn may not have been able to read her exact thoughts, it was obvious from her friend's expression that she had gleaned enough understanding about Jade's intentions.

"We'll talk later," she said and moved past Jade.

Jade propped her hands on her hips and exhaled, cursing her wayward thoughts. Hopefully she hadn't botched Luc's plan. She turned and followed the two women.

The clip of their boot heels echoed around the cavernous area. The air carried a nip, the few lit braziers doing very little to add heat or light. Black soot climbed the polished walls behind the sconces and the acrid tang of tallow and pitch hung heavily on the bottom level. The outer chamber was devoid of the grandeur that had been displayed on the levels above. Only deep alcoves with carved benches adorned the walls.

Shivers ran along Jade's arms. There was something off about this place, as if it watched them and knew the reason they were there.

Beatrice held up her hand and tiptoed forward. From where Jade stood, the Council chamber appeared empty. Awareness ruffled against her and she suddenly had a sense of being drawn forward. She grabbed Ravyn's arm to steady herself, stifling the urge to drop all her defenses and plunge into the room.

Ravyn looked at her. "You feel it too?"

She nodded. "What is it?"

"The presence I told you about." Ravyn slid a glance toward Beatrice. "When I burst into flames."

"I'll go in first," Beatrice said.

Jade tensed when she entered the chamber, expecting some reaction, but there was no hesitation in her friend's step. Jade leaned toward Ravyn. "She seems unaffected."

"Interesting." Ravyn moved forward. "Guard your mind."

Guard her mind? The urge to giggle bubbled up inside Jade. She snickered, but quickly tried to suppress the impulse.

Ravyn looked over her shoulder and scowled. "Guard your mind. Trust me, bursting into flames is not pleasant."

That thought instantly sobered Jade, pushing any urge to laugh to a tolerable level. She inhaled and closed her eyes, visualizing a solid wall around her mind and body. The strength of the presence lessened. She opened her eyes and nodded. "That's better."

"Psst." Beatrice waved them forward. "It's clear."

Wasting no time, they walked toward the chamber. Large doors stood open. Jade's step slowed and stopped, her eyes rounding. Carved in the bottom panels of the doors was a forest surrounding an arched doorway, its doors flung wide. Above it spiraled a phoenix and a dragon. She looked at Ravyn, her mouth hanging open.

"What do you think?" Ravyn caressed the phoenix. "Coincidental, or a direct link to the full-powered Bringers?"

Jade touched the dragon. "This cannot be coincidental."

"No." Ravyn ran her hand across the door and smiled. "I don't think so either."

Dry heat fluttered against Jade's skin when she stepped into the Council chamber. Energy swirled around her, raising the hair on her arms. She stopped and looked at Ravyn, who was staring at her as if to gauge her reaction. Jade nodded.

"If you can feel it, I suggest you don't step into the center of the circle."

The shape had been laid out in an intricate arrangement of tiles. In the center was a smaller sphere and above the circles soared four stone arches. The hair on Jade's legs prickled and a buzzing sensation ran through the bottoms of her feet and up her body. She shimmied her shoulders and rotated her head from side to side, trying to fend off the subtle attack from the presence in the room.

"This ghost is very persistent." Ravyn skirted the circle for several yards and stopped. Her hands stroked the polished stones as if searching for something. Though Jade couldn't hear her, she could see Ravyn's lips moving, obviously chatting with the spirit. After a second she continued around the room, staying close to the wall and away from the tiled circle.

Jade examined the room. Nine portraits hung above corresponding chairs. Fromme Bagita's painting was quite a bit larger than the other Council members' portraits and held the center position. Jade grimaced at his pretentious pose. "I thought Fromme's painting had been destroyed."

"I'd heard rumors," Beatrice's gaze slid to Ravyn, but spoke to Jade. "Are you like her?"

Jade smirked. "No, there is nobody like Ravyn."

They moved in a counterclockwise direction to Ravyn, but Jade wasn't sure what she was supposed to be looking for. She ran her hands along the stones, but felt nothing odd.

"That's too bad." Beatrice said from behind her. "We could use all the help we can get."

"'We'?" Jade asked.

"Those who think my uncle is becoming dangerous."

Jade stopped at the Council table and turned toward her friend. "Uncle?"

"Fromme Bagita."

"I remember you talking about him when we were girls." Her brow furrowed. "But I never realized he was your uncle."

"He is my father's brother, but there is no love lost between us."

Ravyn approached from the opposite direction. "But you're family."

"Fromme never approved of my mother." She shrugged. "Or of me."

"I'm sorry," Jade said. "I didn't know."

"Because it never mattered." She looked at her uncle's portrait. "Until now, I think."

"What do you mean?" Ravyn stopped beside Jade.

"My uncle has always been very concerned about appearances and power. That's the reason he never approved of my mother. She was from the wrong family." She turned and leaned against the table. "That's the reason for all the pomp since the Order has been here."

Ravyn crossed her arms over her chest. "Do you know why the Order was invited to Illuma Grand?"

Though Ravyn's face held nothing more than mild interest, Jade knew that her abduction by the hand of one of the Order still weighed on her. Perhaps she and Luc weren't the only ones with a personal agenda.

"None of us know why my uncle would host the Order. It's never been explained and from what I understand, many of the Council opposed it."

"We've heard that as well," Ravyn said.

"I have a theory." Beatrice frowned. "It may be nothing."

"You probably have better insight than anybody else," Jade said.

"I agree." Ravyn's stare turned intense. "The things you hear may have different meaning for you than somebody who doesn't know Fromme Bagita as well."

Beatrice glanced toward the door and lowered her voice even more. Jade and Ravyn leaned in. "I have another uncle who is a superior in The Order of the Saints."

"Is he here?" Jade whispered.

"No." Her scowl deepened. "That's what struck me as odd. It's possible he was too busy, but Uncle Feildon rarely passes up the chance to compete for attention with Fromme."

"What are your thoughts?" Ravyn said.

A whiff of compulsion brushed past Jade. She slid a glance toward Ravyn, who ignored her.

"Quite a while ago, I was clearing the noon meal from my uncle's desk. There was a parchment lying partially open and I saw Feildon's signature." A blush crept up her neck. "I opened it, curious to see what news my uncle had sent, but all the message said was *Support guaranteed.*"

"Any idea what it means?" Jade couldn't help but feel the message had a direct correlation with Jacob's theory about restoring the crown.

"None, but I don't trust either of them."

Voices wafted in from the outer foyer. Beatrice gasped and jumped to her feet.

"Don't worry, I'll see who it is." Without a second thought, Jade jogged across the room, passing directly through the tiled circle.

Sparks snapped against her skin. She stumbled and slowed, biting back a loud curse. With each step she took closer to the sphere in the center, the more intense the flash of pain grew. She wasn't sure, but she thought she heard Ravyn speaking to her.

The edge of the circle seemed to yawn backward, growing away from her. Her foot brushed the edge of the black sphere, sending a bolt of what felt like lightning through her body. The sharp edge of her teeth bit into her tongue with each convulsion that rocked her. She couldn't move.

Arms grabbed her from behind and hauled her out of the circle. The pain faded and a loud hum in her ears continued to buzz like a hive of angry bees. Thankfully, Beatrice still held Jade upright, otherwise she'd be face down on the floor. Bone-deep tremors traveled through her body, lessening by degrees with each pass. She looked at her friends moving, but nothing made sense.

Ravyn moved up beside her and placed her hands on Jade's arms and sent healing heat into her. The buzzing cleared and a modicum of strength returned to her legs, though her fingers continued to tingle.

"What the shaggin' saints was that?" Jade said.

Ravyn lowered her hands. "I warned you not to step in the center."

Beatrice released Jade and stepped away, her eyes as round as liats. "There was lightning."

Jade took a deep breath and released it. "Was there?"

She opened her mouth to say more, but a male voice cut her off.

"Lady Ravyn. What a surprise."

Jade schooled her features and concentrated on turning without falling.

"Sir Gregory." Ravyn's smile didn't quite reach her eyes. "I didn't expect to see you here."

"Likewise," he said.

"I was giving them a tour of Illuma Grand," Beatrice said. "Explaining some of its history."

"Wonderful." His eyes remained on Ravyn. "I hope it's been informative."

"Very," Ravyn said with a genuine smile.

Jade scrutinized the man's handsome face and turned to scan the portraits. His likeness claimed the last position on the right. Besides the painting, he was completely unfamiliar to Jade and she was certain she wouldn't have forgotten him. His close-cut goatee highlighted sculpted cheekbones, and thick black lashes framed eyes the color of nickel. His hair was so black it seemed to absorb the light from the flickering braziers. He emanated power and danger, a combination she'd always prided herself on staying away from—until recently.

"You have changed much since we last met." His eyes glided along the tattoo on Ravyn's chin, and then turned to look at Jade. "And you are?"

Unsure whether she should answer, she glanced at Ravyn, who gave her a single nod. "Jade Kendal."

"A beautiful name." He reached for her hand and lifted it to his lips.

The kiss he placed was chaste and she thought nothing of it until he flipped over her hand to reveal her palm. Ravyn gasped and Jade snatched her hand away but it was too late. He'd seen the sun tattoo.

A knowing smile tugged at the corner of his mouth and suddenly Jade wanted to be anywhere but with Sir Gregory. Beatrice eyed them both, a slightly confused expression playing across her face.

"I believe your uncle is looking for you, Beatrice." He gave her a sympathetic smile. "Something about serving at the head table tonight."

"Damn." She slapped her hand over her mouth. "Beg your pardon, Lord James."

He gave her a truly dazzling smile. "Quite all right."

The dichotomy of this man was not lost on Jade. His presence gave her a sense of warning, but he seemed genuinely amused by Beatrice's lack of etiquette. Another strike against him. She never trusted people she couldn't read.

"Jade…" Beatrice placed a hand on her upper arm. "Will I see you before you go?"

"I don't know, but if we don't get another chance to catch up, I'll come back when..." She paused. "Things are less hectic."

"I'll hold you to it." She gave Jade a hug and then bustled out of the chamber and up the stairs.

Gregory turned his attention back to Ravyn. "Are you staying at Illuma Grand again, my lady?"

"No." Ravyn hesitated. "Lord Le Daun has been kind enough to put us up while Lord Blackwell's ship is being repaired."

"A lovely estate." He gifted them with another brilliant smile. "I should visit sometime—soon."

"I'm sure Jacob would like that very much."

His left eyebrow lifted ever so slightly, his smile settling into an amused grin.

Ravyn gave him a single, slow nod. "As would we, of course."

"But of course, my lady."

She looked at Jade. "We'll, we really should be getting back."

He stepped aside to let them pass. "Yes, I heard you're to have dinner with Ascendant Meran."

Ravyn took a step but stopped. "You heard that already?"

"It's quite unprecedented, Lady Ravyn." His gaze was steady. "But I'm sure you know that, having grown up in an abbey."

His statements seemed clear and unmasked with innuendo, but Jade couldn't shake the impression that Sir Gregory's words were not so simple.

"Yes, I do know that." Ravyn said nothing more about the dinner. "It was a pleasure to see you, Sir Gregory."

"As it was to be seen, Lady Ravyn." He didn't move, obviously expecting them to take the lead. "Lady Jade."

She gave him a tight smile and tipped her head in reply. Resisting the urge to glance back at him, she followed Ravyn out of the room. Neither spoke until they reached the next level, but made sure to keep their voices low.

"He's a member of the Council," Ravyn said. "And was with the woman I was telling you about—the one who looked like me."

"Well, one thing is certain. Sir Gregory knows exactly what these tattoos mean." Jade held up her palms. "Somehow he knew they were there."

"I think you're right."

A group of richly dressed men glided down the stairwell, speaking loudly and gesturing with their hands.

She and Ravyn moved to the side of the stairs and waited for the men to pass. Several appreciative looks drifted over her, but she ignored them. Too many ideas were churning through her head. Though they'd discovered nothing of significance inside the chamber, hopefully Beatrice's thoughts would give them a new direction to follow in finding the missing Bringers.

"Let's find the men." Ravyn gathered her skirts. "We've got a lot to tell them."

Jade glanced down the stairwell to see Sir Gregory staring up at her. The man was a mystery, one she had no desire to try and figure out.

Yanking up the yards of fabric, she jogged up the steps after Ravyn.

CHAPTER EIGHTEEN

A hand slipped over Jade's mouth. Her eyes popped open, but darkness blanketed the room. All she could make out was the large outline of a man. With her legs trapped under the blankets and the stranger, she fisted her hand and punched in the general direction of the attacker's neck.

Her hand hit solid muscle and rebounded. Curses followed the loud grunt and the stranger fell sideways to lie on the bed.

He gasped a few times, and then said, "Why do you keep doing that?"

"Luc?" Jade pushed the covers off and crawled to her hands and knees, feeling her way toward him. "Why can't you just gently shake me awake instead of hovering over me like a nefarious attacker?"

"I was trying to be quiet. I didn't want you to scream."

"And you thought covering my mouth would achieve that?"

"Obviously I didn't think this through." She could see the dim movements of Luc rubbing his neck.

"Obviously. Why are you here?" She sat back on her heels. "Couldn't this have waited until morning? I didn't get to sleep until late and am tired."

"No." He rolled to a sitting position. "We need to leave before the others rise."

"Leave for where?"

His voice dropped to a whisper. "The Shadow World."

Cold reality washed over her. "Now? What about Rhys and Ravyn? Are they coming?"

"No." He slid to the edge of the bed. "It's better if we depart now before they wake up."

"But—"

"Listen Jade, Rhys and Ravyn mean well, but if we wait to—" He paused. "Deal with Rell, we might lose the opportunity. I know Rhys. He'll plan things out to the last detail in order to protect us."

Jade wrapped her arms around her knees. "That's not such a bad thing."

"No, but in doing so we'll lose the element of surprise." He released a long sigh. "I owe Rhys everything, but I need to do this. Esmeralda deserves peace."

She didn't speak, contemplating his words, understanding everything he said and a lot of what he hadn't. Esmeralda deserved peace, but so did they. The thought of Luc going into the Shadow World alone made her heart race and cold dread pump through her veins. "All right. Let's do this."

He was silent for a second and when he spoke, his words rasped with emotion. "All right." The bed dipped beneath him as he pushed up to stand. "After the Order leaves, the roads will be clogged with travelers. Hopefully it will slow Rhys down if he decides to follow."

"But I only have gowns." She scooted to the side of the bed. "I'll be killed trying to maneuver through the caverns. I can barely walk down the hallway without tripping."

"I've thought of that." Three footsteps sounded before a small pack hit Jade in the chest, dropping into her lap. "Here."

"Ouch." She groped for the bag, recognizing it as hers by the frayed leather strap. He must have gone into her room at the manor to get it. Had he pawed through her meager belongings, touched her private items? The idea thrilled and irritated her. She bit back a retort, thankful for the change of clothes, but if they lived through this, she'd have a few things to say about privacy. "Can we at least light a candle? That's not going to wake anybody."

"Fine." Footsteps shuffled across the stones and were punctuated by several loud thunks and even more muffled curses. "Damn."

Since he couldn't see her in the dark, Jade smiled. Any injury he received served him right. The stupid man had scared the daylights out of her when he woke her up. Even though her survival skills seemed to have slowed since leaving the streets, Jade doubted she'd ever be rid of the instinct to react before thinking.

More thumps and profanity issued from his direction. The sound of a metal poker being dragged across the stone pinged near the hearth, followed by the swish of Luc stirring the nearly dead coals in the fireplace. The sound of blowing preceded the small flicker of light. His silhouette glowed briefly when the coals flared.

She smiled and crawled to the end of the bed. Despite his grumbles, he'd done as she asked. The hollow thump of a log hitting the dying ashes sounded to the right of her.

She waited for the logs to catch fire, blinking into the darkness. Her thoughts turned to Rell. Rationally, Jade knew it would be better to get their dealings with Rell over with. Her sister would no longer live in darkness and Icarus would have no chance to use her. Still, she couldn't help but wonder if her mother would forgive her. That was, however, if Jade made it out of the Shadow World alive and not as a demon. Her doubts intensified. Maybe it was better this way. No tears. No regrets. No connection before she faced death.

The fire crackled to life with enough light to allow her to see.

Luc stood. "I brought you clothes."

She glanced at the forgotten pack and reached for it. Inside was a complete set of leggings, tunic, an undershirt, and boots. The feel of them calmed her. They were familiar and in them she knew who she was.

"Rhys is planning on returning to the manor tomorrow. We've gathered what information we could, which turned out to be nothing." Luc walked to the bed and sat. "We should be able to gain a few hours of riding time by leaving tonight. Otherwise, we'll be backtracking."

It was sound reasoning. "But…I can't help but worry about the group. Won't they worry when they realize we're missing?"

The orange glow from the fire framed the tight line of his mouth. "Probably, but they know of our plan." He paused. "And they know me."

She nodded. "But, wouldn't it be better to explain our intentions and ask them not to follow?"

"No." He stood and gave her a pointed stare in the dim light. "They would follow us. Rhys and Ravyn are leading a new generation of Bringers and this war needs them. I won't endanger my friends." He stopped at the end of the bed, towering over her. "And if I thought for one second you would stay put, I'd leave you behind. But I promised I would never betray you again and that means not lying about my intentions." Orange light danced in the reflection of his black pupils, intensifying his next words. "I'm still going to the Shadow World. Stay here, I beg you. I dare you."

She bristled at his words. They were equal parts bitter and

sweet. Did he care about her more than he let on or did he believe her incapable of committing to the task? With or without her, he would try to kill Rell. In the end, going with him and sending her sister through the Veil was the right thing to do.

"Sorry, but I'm coming." She gathered the clothes. "Wait in the hall while I get dressed."

His gaze caressed her, his expression changing as if he'd just noticed she wore nothing but a thin shift. "It's better if I wait in here while you change. There are people sleeping in the halls. I'm sure to be noticed lurking by the door."

"I'm not changing with you gawking at me." She clutched the tunic to her chest in sudden modesty.

Luc walked to the hearth and peered into the fire. "I won't look. Now hurry."

She didn't move for a few seconds, wondering if he could be trusted not to peek. Would that be so bad? A hot flush crept over her body and she chided herself for the rogue thought.

He harrumphed. "Are you getting dressed?"

"Yes." She scrambled from the bed and crept to where the light from the fire didn't reach. "Don't turn around."

He gave an impatient sigh. "Hurry."

Cold air nipped at her skin and numbed her toes. She bounced from foot to foot, keeping an eye on Luc while trying to maneuver into her clothes. A pair of woolen stockings lay folded between the shirt and leggings. Jade gave a sigh of relief. Wet, cold feet could be the death of a person. These would keep her feet warm under the worst conditions.

She jammed her foot into one of the legs of the pants, hopped twice while she yanked, and then donned the other side. After tying them at the waist, she gathered the shift around her hips and sat at the edge of the bed to pull on the stockings. They hit her at the knee and instantly warmed her feet. Next came her boots. Within a minute, she was dressed from the waist down.

She stood and yanked the thin nightdress over her head. Shivers raced up her spine when the cold air brushed her naked torso. Not wanting to leave the shift behind, she folded it and walked to the pack at the end of the bed. Luc turned, his eyes staring at her half-dressed state.

"Luc!" She hugged the inadequate square of material to her chest. "You promised."

"I heard your boots and thought you were…" His mouth sagged open and he stared at her, making no pretense to turn around.

She gritted her teeth and glared.

The way his eyes lingered much longer than necessary transformed her irritation into response. He took a step toward her but stopped. Awareness sizzled between them. Her forbidden attraction to him expanded, spreading a flush across her chest and up her neck like warmed honey. Her cheeks heated and she swallowed hard. The fact that she was a woman and he was a man hung between them.

The words grated from her throat, sounding far too breathless. "Turn around—please."

With one last appraisal, he pivoted to the fire and braced his hands on the mantel.

Had he been as affected as she had been?

Mentally shaking herself, she grabbed the pack and pulled it to the head of the bed. With another glance at Luc to make sure he still faced away from her, she shoved the shift into the bag and snatched the undershirt off the bed. The extra-large garment slipped easily over her head, giving her a false sense of protection. After adding her leather tunic, she was fully dressed. "I'm ready."

A lock of hair fell forward, brushing just below Luc's chin when he glanced over his shoulder.

Jade cocked her head and squinted. "You cut your hair."

He turned, self-consciously ran a hand through his now short, blonde mane. "Yes, long hair has proven to be a liability. I figured shorter would be better."

There had been many times when she'd yanked his braid— usually when she was ass-end-up over his shoulder. The new cut made him look less feminine, more formidable. "I like it."

She couldn't be sure, but she thought a smile briefly touched his lips.

"Your approval means everything," he said in a dry tone.

"Fine." She tipped her chin up. "I hate it."

He turned and sauntered away from her. "Too late. You can't take it back."

Her gaze bore into his back and she willed herself to have powers of fire. If she could just blast him a little bit, maybe to just set his leather vest on fire, he wouldn't be so arrogant. It didn't happen, and for her hesitancy she received another disgruntled look.

"I need to leave Ravyn a note. I can't stand the thought of her worrying." She held up her hand to cut off the objection forming on his lips. "I will only tell her not to worry."

His lips pressed together in a tight line but he didn't argue with her. She hurried to the desk and scribbled out a note before he could change his mind. Waving the paper in the air to dry the ink, she contemplated where to leave it. When she didn't show up for breakfast, or at the latest, noon repast, Ravyn would check her room.

Jade pulled the shift back out of the bag and laid it on the bed. After a couple more waves, she folded the note and slipped it between the folds of the garment. As an afterthought, she spread the gown out on the bed. Ravyn might miss the small nightdress, but the gown was a clear indication that something was amiss.

"There." She picked up the pack and walked to Luc. "I feel better."

He shook his head and then gave her arm a light punch. "You're a good friend."

Unsure if he was being glib or genuine, she chucked him back. "You too."

He didn't reply, simply pressed a finger to his lips and opened the door. The hinges gave a tiny squeak of protest. He poked his head into the corridor, his hand groping behind him until he found her wrist. Warm fingers wrapped around her and pulled her out of the room. Though she was quite capable of exiting her chamber by herself, she let him lead her but extricated herself once in the passage. His touch had a tendency to unsettle her and make her do stupid things. This was no time to be distracted.

People sprawled along the hallways. Some were wrapped in cloaks. Some cradled children to them. All were of the lower classes. Illuma Grand was big but not big enough to accommodate everybody. She had to wonder where the merchants and noblemen slept.

Jade skirted a man who lay toward the center of the passage. This life she understood. The only bed she'd known for years was a cold, hard stone in the Shadow World. The soft ticks she slept on now were some of the things she liked best about her new life among the Bringers. A twinge of shame nudged her. Though her room was not grand, she could have shared it with a mother and her children. The thought hadn't even occurred to her. How easy it was to succumb to a life of entitlement.

If she got out of this mission alive, she would do more to help those less fortunate. Her stride slowed. She could actually do that now, help people. No more plotting. No more scrounging just to survive. No more hate and darkness.

Luc stopped, waiting for her to catch up. "Are you all right?"

She nodded. "I'm fine."

He eyed her as if to make sure she wasn't having second thoughts. She shooed him forward and whether he believed her to be committed or not, he continued on.

Outside, tents had been erected along their path. Some were lavish, some the most basic shelter. Nobody stirred and for the first time she wondered what time it was. There was no hint of sunrise in the sky. She didn't ask because the only thing that mattered was that they were able to leave unseen.

Another question arose. She jogged a few steps to catch up to Luc. "How are we getting to the…" She glanced around. "Where we're going?"

He smiled down at her, turned the corner of a building and stopped. A moan escaped her when she saw a young Bringer holding the reins of two saddled horses. Luc stared at her, almost daring her not to go.

"You won't get rid of me that easily," she said between clenched teeth.

He gave a quiet snort of laughter and continued into the stable yard.

Jade silently groaned. The thought of getting back on her mare made her backside hurt. From the ache that still ran down her legs, she was almost certain she sported several bruises in that tender area.

Luc took the reins and in exchange placed a small bag in the man's hand, the clink of coins revealing its contents. "Thank you, Thomas."

"Always a pleasure, my lord." With a quick nod, the young Bringer pocketed the payment and walked back into the stable.

She watched until he disappeared inside. "Aren't you afraid he'll alert somebody?"

"About what?" He handed her a set of reins. "That we've left? They'll know that much by breakfast."

"Right." She supposed he was right. The man couldn't reveal what he didn't know, and if Luc hadn't shared details, then what would it matter if he told or not?

She gripped the leather straps and eyed her horse. From their trip to Illuma Grand, she knew the animal to be gentle and easy to guide. It didn't make the prospect of traveling by horseback any better. She tied her bag to the back of the saddle and moved to the side. With one fluid motion, Luc mounted. Much less gracefully, Jade hoisted herself up and swung her leg over to settle slightly off balance. She held onto the pommel with a white-knuckled grip and righted herself, glancing at Luc to see if he was watching. He was.

"Ready?" he asked, his brows rising in question.

"Of course." She bobbed up and down a few times, trying to find the most comfortable position. "Lead on."

From the look on his face he didn't believe her, but after an assessing second, he signaled the horse forward and her mare automatically fell in behind. If left to her own navigation, she would have been lost within the first mile. Perhaps it was the darkness or how much the trail had changed over the years, but the forest no longer resembled the same place where she used to play. Time had a way of altering all things.

They rode in silence and the slow rock of the saddle lulled her into a doze, only to be jerked awake when she started to slip from the horse. With a frantic grab, she gripped the pommel of the saddle and righted herself, glancing up to check if Luc had seen her. He still sat straight, his head occasionally rotating from side to side and above, searching for danger. The sky slowly lightened from black to pinkish gray, signaling a new day.

Her stomach growled. "I'm hungry. Did you pack food by any chance?"

Luc reared back on the reins to stop his horse and opened the bag tied to his saddle. Much to her pleasure, he produced a bright red apple and tossed it to her. "Your wish is my command."

She fumbled for the fruit, nearly dropping it, but managed to keep hold. Though his offering might have been meager, she was grateful for it. There had been times when she'd eaten a lot less. "Thank you."

"You're welcome." He dug an apple out for himself and bit into it, holding it between his teeth while he retied the bag. Juice dribbled out of the corner of his mouth.

Jade licked her lower lip and watched the thin line of liquid slither down his chin. She was neither able to look away nor stop the desire spreading through her chest.

Luc bit down, wiped the juice with the sleeve of his tunic and signaled the horse forward, blissfully unaware of the effect he had just caused. She jammed the apple in her mouth and chomped down, taking off a sizable hunk and almost choking herself. Juice sprayed and trickled down her chin in a far less seductive way than Luc's had. She wiped her arm along her mouth and urged her horse into motion.

They didn't stop again until after noon and then only briefly to eat and relieve themselves. Jade's backside throbbed and she stifled her irritation that Luc seemed unaffected by the ride. Though she refused to complain, the thought of sitting down was too much to bear, so she opted to eat standing up. While Luc stepped away to attend to his private business, she leaned against a large oak and attempted to heal herself. A small buzz hummed in her head and for an instant the world shimmered and brightened, but just as quickly faded. Even though the display had been unimpressive, her radiating pain did seem to lessen somewhat, but it still took all her willpower to get back on the horse.

A twisted tree that reminded her of a dancer came into view. Its large leaves draped around the lower branches like a skirt of green. She smiled, now knowing their location. This was the familiar trail she had used in and out of the Shadow World. They were close, maybe two hours from the entrance. She goaded her horse with her heels to come level with Luc.

"We should be there in another few hours."

"I'd rather go in tomorrow when we're both rested. Do you know of a good spot to camp?"

She knew the perfect spot next to the hot spring. "About an hour and a half farther on foot, there's a pool fed by an underground spring that's cool enough to swim in. I've never run into the Bane there."

"Perfect." They entered a small clearing. "You should lead."

She moved ahead. "We'll need to leave the path up ahead. I've done my best to conceal the trail."

"That's wise, both for your safety and others who might wander near the opening."

A gnawing bite hit so suddenly Jade nearly fell from her horse. She gasped and clutched her arm. Luc sprang from his mount and grabbed her around the waist, hauling her to the ground.

"Get into the trees." He gathered the reins and led the horses to cover.

The animals shied away, their nostrils flaring. He looped the straps loosely around a sapling. The burning sensation expanded across her shoulders and down to her fingertips. She leaned against the tree, flexing her hands.

"They must be close." She scanned the woods but saw nothing.

"It's getting worse." He gritted his teeth and reached in his boot, pulling out the immortal dagger. "Wait here."

She opened her mouth to protest but he was gone. "Idiot," she mumbled.

He crept forward, staying to the shadows one tree back from the clearing. Jade crouched, her fingers digging into the soft bark. This very position reminded her of when Rell would hunt her. Leaves rustled overhead. Her gaze snapped to the canopy, searching within the branches for a lurking demon. Was it Rell?

Luc circled the clearing, raking the trees for the faintest hint of the Bane. He'd learned his lesson from his run-in with Rell and Icarus. They could be anywhere.

A loud thrashing of underbrush broke the silence. Luc ducked behind a tree and looked over at Jade. He held up his hand, signaling her to stay put. She nodded, for once complying without argument. Several scenarios ran through his mind. What if the noisemakers were humans and the demon lay in wait? He would have to save the unsuspecting humans and destroy the Bane. These were his duties now, protect people and rid the world of Bane.

Laughter broke through the trees and the Demon Bane

emerged. Their huge forms hunched forward, their arms nearly dragging the ground. Bulbous heads sat on top of shoulders twice as wide as his. Right away he noticed that neither creature had wings. He sent up a prayer of thanks. At least this fight would stay on the ground. Though he knew these to be simple-minded minions, they were some of the largest demons he'd ever seen and they were headed directly toward Jade.

Luc crept forward until he stood behind a tree to their right. He glanced at Jade. She stared at him, her eyes wide. Obviously sensing his plan, she shook her head, trying to stop him. He ignored her and stepped clear of the tree.

The two demons stopped and stared, seemingly confused by his appearance.

"Afternoon, gentlemen." Luc leaned a shoulder against the tree, making sure to keep his right arm behind him, hiding the dagger. "I seem to be lost."

Though he wasn't that adept at battling as a dragon, once he transformed, the sight of the creature should be enough to send these two Bane running.

Black lips stretched in a fanged smile across the largest demon's mouth. "Too right you are."

"Looks like we got ourselves dinner," said the smaller Bane.

The two demons laughed.

Luc smiled, chuckling along with them. "So you plan on killing me?"

"Killin' ya and eatin' ya," the smaller demon said.

"We'll be killin', roastin', and eatin' ya," the other added.

Luc shrugged. "Once I'm dead it doesn't matter what you do to me. I won't be able to feel it."

The demons glanced at each other as if mentally conferring.

The smaller said, "Then first we'll capture ya, torture ya, and then we'll roast you alive."

"Yeah," the larger one chimed in. "And then we'll kill ya."

"Frightening." Luc gave an exaggerated shudder and edged away from the tree, moving in the opposite direction from where Jade hid. An odor that smelled like a mixture of sulfur and rotting meat wafted off the creatures. "And you two look just the type to do it."

The creatures beamed at his praise, straightening their hunched forms as much as possible.

"Done it lots of times before." The small demon circled as he talked, following Luc's course. "Even ate a Bringer once."

"A Bringer?" Small sticks snapped under Luc's feet as he continued to inch away. He shook his head and furrowed his brow. "I find that hard to believe."

"It's true," the smaller demon continued. "I hit him over the head with a rock. Dropped him just like—" He tried to snap his crooked fingers, but the misshapen phalanges wouldn't connect. "That."

"How do you know he was a Bringer and not just a man?"

The demons glanced at each other, again as if mentally discussing their answer. Perhaps it took two of their brains to form a complete thought. Finally, the big one said, "Tasted different."

"Yeah, like chicken," the little one added. "Humans taste like mutton. Bringers taste like chicken. He was definitely a Bringer."

"Hmm, I never knew that," Luc said. "I've learned something new today."

"All this talk makes me hungry." The larger demon took a step toward him. "Time to eat."

The Bane's foul breath wafted toward him. Luc coughed,

crouching, ready for the attack. The large demon lumbered toward him and swiped with a hugging motion. The movements were slow and capture easily avoided. Luc dove to the side and rolled to his feet a few yards to the right of him.

The smaller demon charged, moving much quicker than his companion. The sharp points of his talons raked across Luc's tunic, shredding the material but not touching his skin.

The larger demon spun to face the direction where Jade hid and lifted his nose to the air. Large nostrils flexed, sniffing. Luc spewed a war cry, drawing the creature's attention away from Jade. With a demon on each side, the only direction he could move was toward Jade or backward.

Fire rippled down his arms and burned along his fingers. He gripped the dagger, trying to stem the flow. Burning the demons would be a temporary fix. What he wanted was to release their souls. From what Ravyn had told him, all he had to do was stab them with the blade. Easy.

They rushed him. He dove forward into the clearing, landing hard but managing to gain his feet and spin. The larger demon barreled toward him, arms spread wide like a giant bear. Luc faked a move to the left and the demon followed. Before the creature had a chance to right himself, Luc snapped back and thrust the blade up and into the monster's heart.

The demon froze, his watery yellow eyes round, his black lips going slack with surprise. Luc yanked the dagger free and jumped backward to crouch for another attack. The creature's knees buckled and he dropped to the ground.

The smaller demon skidded to a stop, his eyes darting from Luc to his kneeling companion. "What did you do to my brother?"

Luc straightened and produced the knife, holding it up for the

Bane to see. "Set him free."

The big demon's body folded, crumpling in the grass. His brother stumbled forward and dropped to the ground. He scooped up the bigger demon and cradled his brother to him.

"It's so beautiful, Colin." The bigger demon's gaze stared at the empty space above him. He swallowed hard and struggled to speak, his hand clutching at his heart. "So light. No dark."

"You gotta stay with me, Seth." The smaller creature gave him a hard shake. "You can't leave me alone."

Seth's reptilian gaze slid to his brother's face. "Coooome."

White vapor slithered from the wound in his chest and slid around his black talons and swirled around Colin's arms, enveloping the demons' torsos. His eyes grew wide, a small shriek escaping him. He released his dying brother and scrambled away from the sparkling wisps, swiping at the fog. A draft of air captured the white mist, spiraling it upward until it disappeared from sight.

A heavy breath rushed from the large demon, the final exhale rattling his body. Yellow eyes clouded and turned white. The gray, leathery skin paled and began to peel like bits of old paint.

A warm wind blew across the clearing. The demon's body softened and turned to ash, flaking away with the circling breeze. Colin cried out and grabbed at the blowing bits, but the ash turned to powder and when he opened his hands they were empty.

He looked up, his expression so stricken it made Luc's throat tighten. "What will I do now?"

"He wanted you to follow." Luc took a step and the demon recoiled. "No more darkness, only light and freedom." The need to console Colin overwhelmed him. This was not like anything he'd ever experienced or anything he'd expected. The dagger made everything different. "Instead of death, I can give you life."

The demon struggled to his feet, locking eyes with Luc. His lips curled in a snarl. Harsh, as if he struggled against some inner foe, the words fought to get free. "Do it—quickly."

Without hesitation, Luc stepped forward and thrust, but before the dagger could pierce the thick hide, the creature caught his hand. Pressure like a vice crushed Luc's wrist and as he stared into Colin's eyes, he saw the change. Muddy brown swirled to the color of cognac and began to fade. His chance was nearly gone.

Calling the fire, Luc felt the heat build in his hand. The creature's neck was too thick to wrap his hand around, so he clamped down on the muscular shoulder. Heat radiated from his palm, searing the demon's flesh.

The Bane reared back, roaring in pain. Luc thrust the dagger into the demon's heart. Instantly, the fire cooled and the massive body slackened, dropping to the ground. Luc pulled the dagger free and crouched next to Colin.

A look of peace settled on the demon's face, his mouth stretching into a smile of pure wonder. "So beautiful." His gaze shifted to Luc. "Thank you."

Luc covered the taloned hand pressed against Colin's chest. This was not a happy moment, but one of necessity. The lives of two brothers had been forever changed by the Bane. A senseless and cruel fate. One he had put right to the best of his ability. "Go in peace."

Like his brother Seth, Colin's vaporous essence seeped from his body, passing through the Veil and the monstrous form disintegrated into ash.

The snap of twigs cracked behind him signaling Jade's approach. He squared his shoulders before facing her.

She crept forward to where the demons had fallen and knelt.

"Look at this."

Tiny white flowers spread in a perfect circle, marking the spot. He stroked the petals, which opened to him, responding to his touch.

"They're together and happy." Jade placed her hand on his thigh. "I truly believe that."

He nodded. The experience had awakened the Shield inside. To give all converted humans the same peace was a quest worthy of his life.

"Come, let's find the camp site before it gets dark." He took her hand and stood, pushing away the question of whether he would be able to give Esmeralda the same peace he'd given the brothers when the time came. "I could use a nice soak."

Chapter Nineteen

The horse slowed, and Jade groaned. Dull pain radiated up her calves and thighs. Her shoulders ached from the constant tension of holding the reins and pommel all day. Without looking, she suspected that the top layer of her skin had been rubbed raw on the inside of her legs. Whoever invented riding horses was a fool.

She sat atop the horse and stared at the ground. The prospect of reaching solid earth without falling from the saddle seemed like an impossible feat. Luc slid from his horse with the expertise of an experienced rider. She silently cursed him. When they'd agreed to undertake this mission, she hadn't imagined that her equine experience would be her downfall.

Luc turned and propped his hands on his hips. "Are you getting down?"

"Yes." Her head seemed to be the only body part willing to work. "Yes, I am."

When she didn't move, he crossed his arms over his chest and cocked his head to the side, narrowing his gaze. "Well?"

Maybe if she could slide from the saddle, she'd be able to make it to the ground and he'd be no wiser to the fact that she was so inexperienced. She tilted to the left, squeezing the pommel in a white-knuckled grip while trying to bring her left leg high enough to lift over the horse's back. One minute she was balanced, naïvely believing she could perform the maneuver, and the next she was face down on the hard earth.

"Jade!"

Blades of grass tickled the inside of her nose and prickled against her throbbing cheek. The weight of her body trapped her arms beneath her, but she didn't have the strength to push herself up. Luc's hands wrapped around her upper arms and hauled her to her feet. Every muscle in Jade's body protested against the movement, causing a throaty growl to erupt from her.

"Are you all right?"

Her knees buckled, but he held her up until she found her legs. "Yes, just a little stiff from riding."

He released her and stepped away, watching her as if she could topple over any minute. She rubbed her cheek and turned toward her horse, praying he said nothing more about her ungraceful dismount.

It took all her effort to lift her arms and untie her bedroll from the saddle. Even her fingers hurt. When the bundle dropped to the ground, she groaned and stepped back. Luc still stared at her. There was no possible way her aching legs would support her if she crouched to pick up the blanket. Perhaps she could just bend at the waist a fraction.

Spasms rippled across her lower back in protest. An involuntary gasp escaped her and she straightened. Her gaze snapped to Luc. From the expression on his face, she hadn't fooled him for a second.

Her shoulders relaxed. "Fine, maybe I'm not all right."

He smiled and picked up her bedroll. "A bit sore?"

"Not a bit." She scowled. "A lot."

"I know just the thing." He wrapped his arm around her waist and led her to a large, flat rock.

"Please don't make me sit again." The idea of putting any more pressure on her rear end made her want to cry.

"I've got something better." He tossed her bedroll on top of the rock and turned to face her. "Take off your clothes."

Jade blinked back her surprise. "Excuse me?"

He pointed to the hot pool. "You'll probably heal naturally by morning, but the water will soothe your muscles and relax you."

"I'm not taking off my clothes." Heat crept up her cheeks. "Especially in front of you."

"Don't be ridiculous." He bent and grabbed one of her legs, lifting it off the ground. "We're about to enter the Shadow World and face the Bane. We need to be at our best. Now is not the time for modesty."

Jade grappled for something to hold on to. With nothing but Luc within range, she grabbed his waist. He yanked, tugging her boot off. Before she could protest, he removed her other boot. Now barefoot, he targeted the ties of her pants.

"Stop that." She slapped at his hands. "I can undress myself."

He raised his hands and stepped back. "Right, sorry."

They stared at each other for several long seconds. Propriety warred with common sense. To enter the Shadow World injured in any way would be foolish, yet being naked around Luc Le Daun seemed equally imprudent.

"Turn around." She held her arm out in front of her and circled her finger. "And don't peek."

A coy smile spread across his face but he pivoted and walked toward the pool. Jade's mouth dropped open when he tossed his vest to the side and pulled his shirt over his head. All that smooth skin she remembered from her healing in the chapel rippled with his movements. He stopped at the edge of the water. Jade couldn't tear her eyes away, and when he slid his pants over his hips, her stare grew wide and her mouth dry.

She should have looked away, squeezed her eyes shut, done something other than watch his hands glide over his muscular rear end and down his thighs. Sweet mother of the Forgotten Gods, the man had a body made for sin.

She turned away and stared at a nearby bush, but the image of his naked body lingered like an unwanted guest. If her powers had consisted of fire vision, the shrubbery would have erupted in flames.

The sound of slapping water let her know he had entered the pool. Not sure how she could ignore his advice to soak, Jade tugged her tunic over her head. She'd lost track of the number of times she'd bathed in this exact pool. His reasoning to heal was sound. It was her own tangled web of emotions that had her questioning not only his, but her motivations as well.

She removed her pants with as little movement as possible, but decided to leave the thin linen shirt on. Since there had been no reason to hide her identity, she hadn't bound her breasts. Once wet, the shirt would be worthless in hiding her body. For now, the garment would be good enough to get her into the pool with her modesty intact.

It was a man's shirt, something she had stolen from a laundry basket more than a year ago. Though she was grateful for its long hem that brushed her mid-thigh, the wide neck hung off her left shoulder and nearly exposed her breast. She turned toward the pool.

"Are you done yet?" Luc stood facing away from her, the water lapping just below the dip above the curve of his cheeks.

She swallowed and brushed a hand across her forehead. "Nearly."

With no other reason to stall, she walked to the edge of the pool. He slowly turned and faced her. Bless the Sainted Ones, but the glimmering blue algae clung to him like a second skin, outlining his thighs. She cleared her throat and shifted her gaze to his face.

"I used to bathe here when I was a child," she said, trying to make conversation. "Since it's on the other side of the mountain from the main entrance of the Shadow World, it was fairly safe."

"That's good to know." Luc sank into the water. "Hopefully we won't be disturbed."

She watched the blue algae glisten and swirl around him.

"Coming in?" He pushed off the bottom and glided toward her. "I promise you'll feel better."

"Yes, just give me a chance to ease into it."

"I find…" A few feet separated them. "The best way…" With little movement, he effortlessly cut through the water. Jade's eyes raked his body. "To get in…" He stopped at the edge and peered up at her. "Is to jump."

A warning flashed through her mind a second before his hand snaked out of the water and latched onto her foot. She shrieked, but her cry barely escaped her lungs before she found herself hauled off the bank and tossed into the water.

Bubbles erupted around her and her muffled scream was cut off when she instinctively inhaled. Her feet found the bottom and she pushed, launching out of the water in a cacophony of sputters and coughs. Her hands tangled in her thick mass of dripping hair when she attempted to push the strands from her face.

She continued to cough and Luc gave her a few hard pats on

the back.

"Swallow some water?"

She shoved his hand away, coughed again, and spit out the remainder of the swallowed water, not caring how unladylike the action was. Her nostrils burned from the sulphury liquid she had snorted. She rubbed her knuckles against her eyes to clear her vision and glared at Luc.

"Thanks to you, jackass."

He gave her a smile that was pure rogue. "You're welcome."

She scowled. "I wasn't thanking you."

His eyes blazed a trail down her throat and stopped at her breasts. His voice took on a seductive tone. "You're welcome anyway."

Her nipples tightened under his gaze. His expression darkened at her reaction to him. This time her propriety warred with curiosity. She liked the way his eyes revealed what he was thinking and the curious stirring he caused inside her. Besides Rell, he'd been in her life longer than anybody. But the situation between them had changed—no longer enemies, but allies.

A twinge of guilt poked at her. They were on a mission, in essence, to kill her sister, and here she was lusting for the one man she'd been trained to hate.

Exhaustion swamped her. She was tired of maneuvering through the menagerie of emotions that came with having Rell for a sister. For once she wanted to experience something wonderful with no thought to consequence or guilt.

Her expression must have cued Luc to her thoughts. "Turn around."

Without argument she did as he said. Luc moved up behind her and wrapped an arm around her just below her breasts, lifting her. Every inch of her body pressed against his, leaving no doubt about his desire. She closed her eyes and leaned her head against his shoulder, drinking in the feel of being taken care of.

He carried her to the edge of the pool and released his hold, but didn't stop touching her. His hands slid down her arms, giving her goose bumps even though she was feeling anything but chilled. His fingers twined with hers, closing into fists. He slowly extended her arms, his chest pressing against her shoulders, and placed her hands against the rocky ledge. More shivers rippled down her neck from his warm breath brushing against her ear.

His voice was pitched low. "Hold on."

Other than her fingers digging into the rocky edge, she didn't move. She let him take the lead, deciding for once to not overthink things but instead trust him.

His erection and hips pressed against her backside, but she didn't pull away. She focused on his fingers, which had begun a soft rotating motion on her shoulders, working out the stiffness and knots.

Jade melted under his touch. A delicate mewl she would have thought impossible for her to make eased from her lips. From the way Luc's body responded, she knew he liked her reaction.

His massage moved along the tops of her arms and returned from underneath, paying special attention to her wrists, elbows, and upper arms. He spread his hands against her ribs. His fingers brushed the sides of her breasts while his thumbs dug into the muscles around her shoulder blades.

Saints help her, but she wanted him to touch her, wanted his fingers to stray a little closer to her breasts, to stroke her. She hung her head and gazed along her body. His sculpted hips protruded beyond hers and the tips of his fingers hovered enticingly close to where she desired them to be. But he didn't take advantage of her vulnerability, even though she believed he felt it. Instead he continued his trek downward, keeping to his promise to help heal her.

His arm slid around her hips to hold her in place. With the heel of his hand, he pressed against her lower back, massaging the aching muscles with skill. She moaned and all the lustful thoughts melted from her mind. The abused area slowly relaxed, releasing the tension and letting her back elongate. She sagged in ecstasy, her face lowering to inches above the water. Never had anybody taken the time to heal her before.

Luc tightened his grip. "You like?"

She groaned again in answer and then gasped when he knelt in the water and began to massage her thighs. The urge to pull away nearly overwhelmed her when his fingers drew dangerously close to her private area. So far he'd done nothing to warrant her panic. That would have been her usual response. Escape before things went too far. That was the old Jade. Like she'd thought a hundred times since the night she'd tried to kill Luc, things were different now.

She gave herself completely over to him, and as she knew he would, he proved to be a man of honor. His hands worked their way down her thighs to her tender calves. When he was finished, he stood and helped her straighten. She slowly turned, keeping her eyes leveled on his chest.

"Thank you. That was amazing."

"Do you feel better?"

She glanced at him. Did she feel better? "I think you've banished *nearly* every ache in my body."

He smirked, as if he caught her innuendo, but he didn't act on it. Instead, he raised his hands over his head and fell back in the water.

Jade caught a brief glimpse of his erection before his lower body submerged. Respect for him grew. It must have taken a lot for Luc Le Daun, womanizer, to not act on his obvious urges.

Jade ducked into the water, hiding her body. Flaunting her near nakedness just seemed cruel. They floated in the pool for several minutes, unspeaking. The chirping of the night crickets infused the quiet with a peaceful cadence. Both she and Luc seemed unwilling to spoil the calm moment.

Neither of them knew what tomorrow held. They could be killed, turned, or accomplish what they had set out to do. Exhaustion stole her ability to be firm.

After several more minutes of blissful silence, Luc stood. "We should get some sleep. We have a big day tomorrow."

She released a heavy sigh and straightened, crossing her hands over her chest, and walked to the ledge. A tingle from the water's rejuvenating effects, or maybe it was the close proximity to a naked Luc, skittered across her skin. He grasped her waist and lifted her to sit on the edge of the pool. Their eyes met, her hands lingering on his shoulders. So badly she wanted to kiss him, but to allow herself that one indulgence would ratchet the stakes of their success.

She already cared too much and she knew his intimate caress would push her past the point of rational thought. If something happened to him in the Shadow World, she would forsake their plan to save him. No, she needed to keep what little distance was still left between them.

She lowered her hands. "Thank you."

As if reading her signal, he stepped away, respecting her wishes. Even though every inch of his lower body had spent the last ten minutes bumped up against her, she kept her eyes averted. He'd had the sense and strength of will to rein in his desires, and she feared that the least provocation from her would initiate more intimate moments she didn't think she'd be able to resist.

They both dressed and worked in silence, unsaddling the horses and setting up camp. When they'd eaten and cleaned up, Jade hunkered under her bedroll with her head resting against the root of a tree. Luc took first watch, but sat close. Things between them had changed tonight. They'd crossed into unknown territory. Because of Rell, Jade couldn't be happy about the feelings Luc stirred inside her. Despite Rell, she couldn't regret them either.

CHAPTER TWENTY

Morning mist blanketed the ground below the rise on which Luc stood. Pebbles crunched under his feet, the sound echoing against the small opening carved into the side of the mountain. The entrance sat fifteen feet above the ground and a thick covering of vines hid it from view. Unless a person knew where to look, they'd never know the door was there.

He pulled back the plants and eyed the opening. It was questionable whether he'd fit through the narrow passage. That was an obstacle Jade hadn't considered. Her hand slapped the small ledge and she pulled herself the rest of the way onto the outcropping. Too engrossed in examining the entrance, Luc made no effort to help and she refused to ask. Though still a little sore from riding yesterday, she was able to scale the face of the mountain with ease. Pride had made it difficult enough for her to let him lead the way into the Shadow World. After all, this was her domain, but he had insisted.

Rocks skittered along the ledge and skipped into the dark hole. They both froze, waiting to see if the Bane lurked beyond sight, waiting for their prey. No sound or movement issued from the blackness. Luc let out a slow breath and looked at her. She smiled up at him with an apologetic grimace. To be stopped before they ever got started was the last thing they needed.

Jade hauled herself the rest of the way onto the rock shelf and dusted off the knees of her britches. She straightened. "It's smaller than I remember."

"Or I'm bigger."

She nodded. "That's probably it. You are rather…massive."

He smirked and her stomach did a little flip. Even with his hair short, he was strikingly handsome—maybe more so.

"Ready?"

The mood grew serious and she took a deep breath. "As ready as I'll ever be."

He nodded. There were no words to comfort her in this deed they had to perform. The doorway's span was only a few feet. Luc turned sideways and inched in. Once Jade entered the corridor, darkness surrounded them, her body blocking out the light. Stifling humidity invaded the small opening. Sweat beaded on her forehead, but there was little room to lift her hand and wipe it away. A solid black wall separated them and she felt, more than heard or saw, Luc in front of her. Not only his size, but his presence filled the space. Even though she'd been raised in the Shadow World, this was the first time she'd ever felt a sense of security upon entering the demon realm.

The passage curved and a pinprick of light glowed at the end. Luc eased toward it, his body outlined faintly by the distant light. She took extra care not to kick rocks and possibly alert any waiting demons. Rell could be there. After all, this was her home—her world. The prospect of releasing her soul in a place that had in essence been her prison seemed wrong. But believing Rell would agree to come with them so they could perform the deed among loved ones was an even more foolish idea.

To her surprise, Luc's fingers brushed her hand. He latched on and squeezed. Despite her bravado, the anxiety of facing her sister tested her resolve. She intertwined her fingers with his and returned a reassuring squeeze.

They stopped just inside the shadowed doorway. The cavernous room yawned before them, empty. Moist heat coated her skin, making the clothes she wore cling.

Shadows cast along one side of his face when he looked at her. "Empty."

His whisper filled the passage, too loud for the stealth they were attempting. With no reason to wait, they stepped into the cavern. The soft hiss from vents in the floor and the slow bubble of some of the pools created enough noise to hide somebody's approach through the passage.

Jade entered behind him and stopped. He looked at her, as if gauging her reaction, probably wondering if being back in the Shadow World would be enough to make her abandon their mission. It wouldn't. She surveyed the chamber, but saw nothing out of the ordinary. She loosened her fingers and pulled away. Luc didn't resist. From here on out they needed to be ready for an attack.

He moved around a burbling pool. "I wonder where she is."

His statement echoed Jade's thoughts. Traveling deeper into the Shadow World was not what they had hoped for. Still, if Rell wasn't here, they couldn't afford to wait very long.

"You're getting careless." The demon's voice drifted down to them.

They both spun and scanned the soaring ceiling. Perched on a high outcropping twenty feet above sat Rell. In her current pose, she reminded Jade of a distorted stone statue carved for the cathedrals of The Order of the Saints. The creatures were meant to keep evil out. Large wings opened and Rell launched herself from the ledge.

Tattered membrane flapped as she spiraled to the ground. Jade moved to stand in front of Luc, her right hand ready to retract the dagger from her boot when needed, her body tensed for attack. She watched her sister's descent with the intensity of a shepherd dog watching its flock.

Luc stood a mere pace behind her, waiting. No matter what the cost, they would accomplish this disagreeable mission together.

Rell folded her wings and dropped the last few feet to the ground with a heavy thud. Holes speckled the membrane of her wings and Jade noticed that she favored her left side when she straightened. Guilt tempted Jade to relax her stance and give her sister solace, but she pushed her emotions down, burying them under duty.

"Come to free my poor tortured soul?"

Rell's statement threw Jade off guard. An inkling of dread ran up her spine. Had she known all the time they would come? Had they walked into a trap? She opened her senses and searched for other demons, but inside the Shadow World their presence was too great to recognize one demon from a horde.

When Jade didn't reply, Rell sneered and turned away to limp toward a large flat rock, as if their presence was of no concern. "As I suspected."

Luc remained at Jade's back, letting her take the lead. The gesture left her grateful and horrified. She knew he thought it best to get this over with, but as hard as she tried, she couldn't separate all her feelings. There was so much she wanted to say. Things she needed to understand about why Rell had not told her about their mother. Things she wanted her sister to know. Would it matter? She doubted Rell would listen or try to comprehend them.

"I love you." Jade's soft profession fell flat.

"Ah, yes, love." Rell circled behind the rock and stopped, propping her hands against the top. "That would be the reason you're here? Because you love me so much?"

Jade's throat worked up and down, trying to swallow past the growing lump. Luc stepped up behind her and placed a hand on her back. Together, they presented a united front, but would it be enough?

"I felt the darkness, Rell." She hugged herself, the memory sending a chill deep into her heart. "Nobody should be forced to live with such desolation."

"Did you come to this conclusion on your own, or was it — " She flicked her horns toward Luc. "His idea?"

"No." She wouldn't let him take the blame for their situation any longer. His irresponsibility might have had a hand in the events that had happened thirteen years ago, but he was not at fault for the horrible things that had followed. Somebody had plotted against her father, and the entire family had paid. "I wanted this." She moved toward the demon. "Ever since that night at the chapel, I realized our life has been a lie."

Rell's lower lip turned down in an exaggerated pout. "Finally realize I was a Demon Bane?"

"No." Jade shook her head. "That I could accept. What I can't accept is that you've lied to me about our mother."

Understanding of why her sister had kept that secret flittered just out of Jade's reach. She tried to put herself in Rell's place, but she couldn't fully grasp a rational excuse. And that one concept is what drove her to complete this mission. There was no rational excuse, no answer that would ever satisfy her.

The arrogant look on Esmeralda's face slipped. "Was your life so awful?"

"I know you did the best you could." Jade paused. "But it wasn't a good life—not what I could have had with our mother."

Rell sneered. "She left us. Why did she not try to find us?"

"Why would she when she thought we were dead?" She pointed at Rell. "Why didn't you tell me she was alive instead of hiding me away in this cavern?"

"Look at me." Her sister held her arms out to her sides. "Do you really think she would have accepted this for a daughter?"

"You never gave her a chance."

"It doesn't matter now. What's done is done."

Jade reached into her boot and removed the dagger. "And what has to be done must be done."

"Will you be the one to send my soul through the Veil, sister?" The demon hopped on top of the boulder. "To hold me as I turn to ash?"

Luc didn't move, his hesitation like silent words of encouragement. Would she be able to release her sister and lose her forever? "Yes."

With that one word, Luc edged to the right to block Rell's path so she couldn't escape through the door and flee deeper into the Shadow World. Jade tensed, her every instinct screaming to strike. But before she could lunge, Rell leapt off the boulder, clearing Jade's head by three feet. Surprised by the lightning-fast movement, she and Luc spun to follow the demon's movements.

Rell landed behind them on the other side of a pool, but remained crouched. Unwittingly, she'd pinned herself in between the water and the sheer rock wall. There was no escape besides flying.

Jade glanced at Luc. "This is going to be a lot more difficult than we'd planned."

"I never thought it was going to be easy." He looked back at the demon. "But I know you can do it."

His unsolicited praise gave her courage the boost it needed. She turned back to Rell. Living with her for more than thirteen years gave Jade insight into her sister's actions.

They circled the pool, each moving in a different direction. When they were within a few yards, Rell leapt away from them and landed on the large flat rock closer to the entrance of the cavern. Jade ground her teeth. Her sister was playing with them. This was like chasing a mouse around a circular room. Just when you thought you had it cornered, the rodent slipped through your hands.

Sharp talons scraped along the stone as Rell settled, glowering down at them. "Two against one, that doesn't seem very fair." She smiled. "For you."

Obviously tired of being played with, Luc sprinted toward her and dove. Like a jettison of steam, she shot into the air, but she hadn't anticipated Luc's determination. Using the rock as leverage, he leapt onto the boulder and pushed off, the leap taking him high enough to reach the demon's ankle. His arms wrapped around her legs and knocked her off balance. The two plummeted to the ground and smacked into the earth with a heavy thud.

Jade raced toward them as Luc released his hold and jumped on top of Rell. He rolled her face down on the ground and using his knee, pressed her into the floor. Jade skidded to a stop, unsure what to do or how she could help.

Luc straddled the demon and bent over her to keep her wings crushed against her back and her shoulders restrained. With his

other arm, he wrapped it around Rell's tiny waist and hoisted her
off the ground. Once upright, he compressed both her arms against
her side in a snakelike hold. Despite her petite size, her wings were
taller than Luc and her feet swung free, slicing at his pants with her
talons.

"Stab her!" On an inward swing of her legs, he tried to pin her
clawing feet between his knees, but Rell was too fast.

Her screech reverberated off the walls. "Let me go!"

This was the moment. Rell was helpless. Jade could release her
soul and they could go home. Tremors shook Jade's hand when she
lifted the dagger and drew it back.

"Please Jade, don't do this." Rell's eyes widened and for the
first time ever that Jade could remember, large tears pooled in her
sister's eyes. "I don't want to die."

A whimper escaped Jade. "You're already dead."

At those words, Rell's pleading yellow eyes narrowed. She
dipped her chin forward and flung her head back, smashing the
back of her skull into Luc's face. Blood spouted from his nose and
streamed over his mouth and chin, but he didn't let her go.

"Do it!" He spit a mouthful of blood on the ground. "I can't
hold her much longer."

Jade stepped forward, determined to send her sister's soul
through the Veil. Rell's eyes grew round again and tears spilled
down her cheeks. She ceased her struggle and closed her eyes. "I
forgive you."

Before Jade took her first step forward, she knew she wouldn't
be able to stab Rell. Her voice cracked. "I can't do it."

"You must." Luc pushed the demon forward, moving her sister
within range. "Now, Jade. Be strong."

"I can't, Luc." She shook her head. "I thought I could, but I can't."

"Jade." Her name sounded like an accusation. "I can't hold her *and* release her soul. You must do this."

Reason and foolish loyalty fought for dominance. Love for her sister won control of Jade's heart and she opened her mouth to refuse Luc's command when she noticed her sister's expression. Rell's lips quirked at the edges and one brow lifted ever so slightly in a triumphant arch. A performance, that's all these newly displayed emotions were. Anger rushed through her.

"You're not capable of forgiveness or remorse." Jade lifted the dagger overhead. "And I won't let you dwell in darkness."

The smile spread across Rell's lips. Jade lunged, but before she could drive the dagger into her sister's heart, Jade was yanked off her feet and lifted in the air. The dagger flew from her hand and hit the wall, clattering to the floor. A scream ripped from her throat, her fear of heights being smothered by the stark terror of the demon that held her.

Icarus's thick black arm snaked around her neck, pulling her against his body. Muscles rippled against her back with each stroke of his wings. Unlike when Rell hunted her, Icarus's movements were calculating and smooth. He settled on a ledge that was only big enough for one large-winged demon—and nobody else. Her legs dangled twenty feet above the ground, swinging madly in an effort to find a foothold.

Icarus's voice reverberated against her back. "Let the demon go."

Luc stared at them, unmoving. The arm tightened around Jade's neck, cutting off air and making her gasp. Needle points of his talons settled against her heart and pressed through the rough fabric of her tunic to pierce her skin. She cried out.

"Let Rell go or I will drop her."

Luc's gaze darted to the dagger and back.

"Please, Luc," Rell pleaded. "He'll kill her."

"As if you care," he said, jerking her to the left as he inched toward the knife.

"I do." Rell hung limply in Luc's arms. "Of that one thing you should have no doubt."

"You have a strange way of showing it." He maneuvered them closer to the knife.

"One more step, Bringer, and I drop her."

Icarus's hold loosened and Jade slipped. She clawed at his arm, this time trying to hang on instead of getting free. "*Luc!*" Her intention had been to tell him to let Rell go, but what came out was completely different. "Release her soul. Don't worry about me."

"She's very sweet, isn't she?" Icarus called to Luc. The talons dug deeper. Warm blood flowed down her torso and pain seared across her chest. The pressure increased, making it difficult to breathe and impossible to speak. "Perhaps I should drink her soul."

His words registered a second before what felt like an icy blade sliced through her body. Her head lolled forward, her chin resting against her chest. White threads that looked like smoke spiraled from her body and around Icarus's finger. Heaviness weighed her eyelids and it became a struggle to keep them open.

"Icarus, no!" Rell's shrill cry pierced Jade's slide into unconsciousness. "You promised you wouldn't hurt her!"

"Only if the Bringer cooperated." He nuzzled her neck. "She smells so sweet, almost too good to resist."

The reality of what was happening penetrated the haze building in Jade's head. Darkness pressed around her, sucking her into the endless black void. Luc shoved Rell away from him. She stumbled forward, landing on her hands and knees, and scrambled for the knife. Her black talons curled around the hilt and she lifted it, holding it over her head like a prize.

"I have it, Icarus, and we have him." When he didn't respond, she walked toward him. "Let her go. I have kept my side of our bargain."

He pulled his talons free from Jade's chest and the white tendrils slithered back into her body. The pain dulled and awareness returned just as Icarus stepped off the ledge.

She tried to scream but the noise lodged in her throat. His huge, black wings flared, catching the air current to slowly lower them to the ground.

If it hadn't been for the bulky forearm still crushing her neck, she would have vomited.

"Release her." The promised retribution in Luc's voice was unmistakable.

Rell walked to a rock and lifted a thick chain and pair of manacles. "Put your hands behind your back."

"No." Jade's plea rasped from her throat and Icarus's grip tightened. "Please."

"It was either Jade or you." Rell snapped the bands around Luc's wrists. "You see, I really do care about my sister."

"Your friend's fate is sealed," Icarus whispered in Jade's ear. "But your fate is still undecided."

"Let me go." With great effort she dragged in the air. If she could get to Rhys and Ravyn, there might be a chance to save Luc. "I will serve you."

The deep timbre of Icarus's laugh rumbled against her back. "Liar. No, I will keep you in reserve." He inhaled again, rubbing his cheek against her neck. "In case my attempts to open the Abyss of

Souls fail. Full-powered Bringers are difficult to come by, but now I've got two." He paused. "Lucky me."

All the fight went out of Jade. The demon's arm loosened from around her neck and lowered, brushing across her breasts and down her arm. Determination pulsed through her veins. She would not let the Bane have *two* people she loved.

Talons circled her arm, dragging it behind her. Rough metal clamped around one of her wrists and cut into her skin. She gave no resistance, but her eyes remained locked with Luc's, telling him this battle was not over. He dipped his chin in the slightest show of solidarity. They were in this together—to the end.

Rell knelt and shackled both of Luc's ankles and then nudged him forward. Chains scraped against the stone floor with each shuffling step he took, reminding Jade of the slave market of Faela. Like the poor souls who were sold or traded for a few coins, her life and Luc's had just become as expendable.

She caught Rell's stare and held it, silently telling her sister that the game wasn't over. A sliver of satisfaction coursed through her when Rell broke eye contact first, unable to hold Jade's gaze.

"Follow them." Icarus shoved Jade forward. "We have something special in store for you."

She looked over her shoulder and gave him a humorless smile. "I can hardly wait."

CHAPTER TWENTY-ONE

The icy stone slab of the table pressed against Luc's back, his body quivering uncontrollably from the cold and pain. Metal cuffs burned at his wrists and ankles and a leather strap bit into his chest, making it impossible to fight during his torture. Blood coated his body and pooled beneath him, coagulating into thick puddles. Blue light flickered from the braziers but provided no warmth to the cavern. This was a place of death, a place where one went to lose his soul, a chamber for the damned.

Knives, hooked blades, and axes lined a narrow table against the wall, unused. No need for weapons when Icarus's talons were more than efficient at ripping.

"How were you brought to full power?" The demon stood over him and ran a talon down the center of his chest, piercing the skin and laying open the flesh. A thick line of blood spilled over his ribs. "I really must know."

Stinging pain fanned across Luc's chest. He pressed his lips together, refusing to answer the same question that had been asked a dozen times before. He inhaled, trying to focus his healing along each cut the demon had made. Concentrating was becoming difficult. Weakness crept through his body, his will power chipping away with each slice the demon delivered, and the wounds weren't healing fast enough.

How long had he been on the table? Hours? Days? He'd drifted in and out of consciousness, praying that he wouldn't beg or reveal the secrets Icarus so badly desired.

"Rell, please!" Jade's voice broke through the haze that clouded his waking moments. "How can you do this?"

He wanted to tell her everything would be all right and not to be afraid, but she would know he was lying.

"Tell us how you were converted." Rell's voice sounded almost pleading. "And all this will end."

"I've told you a hundred times, I don't know. I'd been shot with an arrow. When I woke up, I had my full powers."

Luc opened his mouth to tell her not to speak, but Icarus's talons clamped over his heart, penetrating his skin. He gasped and tried to pull free of the hooks pinning him, but the strap and cuffs immobilized almost all his movement. Blood gurgled in Luc's throat.

Icarus's eyes narrowed, his nostrils flaring. The sensation of a cord being pulled ran from Luc's feet, up his legs and out of his chest. The air in his lungs turned to ice. He coughed against the tightening in his throat. From the five points where the black talons dug into Luc's chest slithered white vaporous threats. They curled along Icarus's fingers and wrapped around his hand, as if drawing Luc into a dense, black hole. Confusion filled him, his sense of self melding with the endless void of agony and desolation.

Icarus leaned over him, his face only inches away. "Tell me how you were converted and you can keep your soul."

Luc lingered at the edge of oblivion. If he tumbled, he would be lost forever. He rallied what little strength he had left and spit, coating the demon in blood and saliva. "Fuck you."

Icarus barely flinched, slowly straightening.

"So brave and loyal." He sneered. "How loyal will you be when I devour your soul and turn you into my puppet?" He pushed the tips deeper into Luc's skin. "How brave will you be when I make you kill your friends?"

For the first time, Luc cried out, the pain slicing into his chest all the way to his backbone.

"He doesn't know!" Jade rattled her chains. "We're not lying. He doesn't know."

"He knows." Icarus's wings snapped open. "And you are both fools to think I won't do everything to get that information."

"You're wrong." Tears clogged Jade's voice. "That's why we decided to come and not tell the others. If something happened to us…if we were captured, we wouldn't be able to tell you anything. It's only our lives we lose."

Darkness crawled around the edges of Luc's vision. Jade's words drifted across him, their meaning only partially making sense. The pressure and agony suddenly disappeared from his chest, tendrils of heat raced back into his body. He coughed again, bringing up blood. He turned his head and spat.

Time had no meaning. An hour or an eternity, there was no distinction and no escape from the pain. Prayers for death played through Luc's mind, but he knew they would go unanswered. Icarus would not give up his prize to something as mundane as death.

More pressure eased from his chest when the strap was released and he found himself lifted off the slab. This would have been his one chance to fight, but his limbs would not obey. Even his head refused to rise and he struggled to keep his eyes open. Images of

Jade stretched to the end of her chain on all fours flashed in and out of his vision.

Icarus released him, letting his body drop face down on the ground. The breath rushed out of him and pain ricocheted through his body, but nothing like he'd already endured. A firm kick rolled him to his back and he was dragged upward by one arm. His body slammed against the icy rock wall and his wrists yanked outward to be clamped to shackles in the wall. Ankle cuffs snapped around his leg, once again restraining him in a nearly immobile state.

Rell hovered behind Icarus, her arms wrapped tightly around herself. "What are you doing?"

"He grows too weak." He peered at Luc, assessing him like a flank of venison. "I will not have him die before I'm finished."

"But what of the other demons?" Rell's voice dropped to a whisper. "Sha-hera? Vile?"

"These chambers have not been used in years. Nobody will find them." Icarus crouched. "So scream all you want, Bringer. There's no one to hear." A sneer pulled at his upper lip. "Rest up. We're not finished yet."

Blood seeped into the corner of Luc's right eye, but he held the demon's gaze. "Looking forward to it."

Several seconds passed, neither willing to show weakness. The demon's sneer spread to a smile. "As do I, Bringer. And when you have shared all your secrets, I will use your power to open the Abyss of Souls." He leaned in. "And destroy everybody you love—starting with your woman."

Icarus stood and stalked toward the door. It took everything he had to stay conscious, but Luc forced his head up to watch the demon disappear from the chamber. When Icarus was gone, he let his head sag forward and gave over to blessed unconsciousness.

Jade strained against her bonds. The chain around her wrist only extended far enough for her to reach Luc and only if she angled her body. She stretched and pushed back his hair with her free hand. Rocks dug into her knees and the palm she braced on the ground, but she ignored the discomfort and focused on Luc.

Blood trickled from a cut at his hairline. That should have stopped from his natural healing process. The fact that it hadn't revealed just how weak he was. Desperation pushed the healing chant from her and she mouthed the words so Rell wouldn't hear. Immediately, the bleeding ceased.

A shiver shook her body. The cold this deep in the Shadow World was like none she had ever felt. It sliced to the bone, making her entire body ache. Her fingers were numb and sore, her lips cracked. She needed water. Hunger pangs had died away long ago and now the very thought of food made her want to vomit.

She sat back on her heels. He was unconscious again and his breathing weak. She needed to heal him as much as possible before Icarus returned. The demons' presence had been constant since they'd been captured. Neither had left the cavern, instead waiting for Luc to regain consciousness when he passed out from the pain. She hadn't had the chance to heal a single scratch until now, and she refused to let Rell know what she was doing. The demons desperately wanted information and had watched Luc and her for anything that would hint at their powers or how they'd come into them. After all they'd done to Luc, she'd be damned if she'd give her sister even the tiniest clue. What she needed to do was to get rid of Rell.

The demon perched on a low ledge about a foot off the ground.

She watched Jade, her yellow eyes intense and anxious.

Jade shook her head. "How could you do this? How could you betray me like this?"

"I am not the one who came with the intent of killing her sibling." Rell sneered. "I am not the betrayer."

Jade gave a harsh laugh. "You were waiting for us. You knew we were coming."

"Icarus knew." She jumped from the ledge and took a step toward Jade. "I did not believe him." She paused. "I did not want to believe him."

"I do this out of love, Esmeralda." Jade wrapped her arms around her chest and rubbed her upper arm, trying to bring some warmth back in her body. "What is your excuse, since you are clearly incapable of love?"

"Yet I am the one who has cared and provided for you nearly all your life."

"Lied to me, don't you mean? Or have you forgotten that our mother still lives?" Jade pushed against the wall and crawled to her feet. "All this time we could have been together, but you chose to lie."

"Together?" Rell's face twisted with scorn. "You mean you and our mother together, while I was left here."

"If you loved me you wouldn't have subjected me to a life in the Shadow World."

"And if you loved me, you would understand how much I didn't want to be alone." She walked to the door and stopped. "It's too late now. We've both done things that can't be undone."

With that she walked from the chamber. Jade finally realized that was why Rell had done what she had. Her sister's words hurt, but right now the most important thing was to heal Luc.

She knelt again and examined his wounds. There were so many. Tears burned behind her eyes. She swallowed back the helplessness threatening to overtake her and placed her hand over the slashes on his thighs. Dark stains spread across the fabric, the dried blood making the edges of the ripped material stiff. He didn't stir, even when she applied pressure.

Again she let the healing words wash through her, but the expected wave of healing she'd experienced in the chapel didn't come. She squeezed her eyes tighter and whispered the chant. Heat slithered down her arms like cold molasses, thick and sluggish. She opened her eyes, continuing to speak. Luc didn't respond.

The cavern glowed with a dull yellow light, nothing like the brilliant gold ribbons that had danced around them in the chapel. There seemed to be no life to pull energy from down here. A thin strip of white light spiraled from the dark corner. Jade concentrated, calling it forth. Whatever hid in the shadows was giving freely and she would gladly accept the gift.

The warmth spread to her fingertips and connected with Luc's body. He convulsed but didn't wake. She focused her healing but each push of power took so much effort her energy drained before she could close all the wounds.

She slid to the floor and twisted so she was able to rest her head in Luc's lap. Exhaustion weighed her eyelids and she drifted into a restless sleep. Occasionally, she would awaken to close a seeping wound or aid an already mending cut as best she could. Each attempt took so much out of her, she would drift back to sleep until rousing again to repeat the process.

Their time was running out. It wasn't just Icarus and Rell they needed to worry about. If any other demon found them chained, they would be helpless. From the way Icarus had explored the cavern and examined each of the weapons along the wall, Jade got the impression that this lair was not his. And if it wasn't Icarus's, then it had to be Vile's or Sha-hera's.

They were still alive because Icarus needed them. He had mentioned using Luc's powers to open the Abyss of Souls. Is that why Vile had tried to capture Ravyn? Were father and son in a race for power and the full Bringers the key to their success? If that was the case, not just the Bringers but the entire world was tottering on the brink of dark destruction.

Luc had been strong enough to withstand the torture, but that too would not last much longer. She needed to figure out a way to escape. That…and a very big miracle.

CHAPTER TWENTY-TWO

Cold seeped through the leather seat of Luc's pants and into his bones. Stiffness had seized his body while he slept and now each movement sent a radiating ache across his hips. His eyelids slid open, the dark, silent cavern greeting him. Lethargy made it difficult to remain awake and he had to fight to keep his eyes open. The wounds Icarus had inflicted continued to drain him of energy, keeping him weak.

He attempted to wiggle his toes but nothing happened. Next, he concentrated on circling his ankle. Numbness seemed to have paralyzed his limbs. How long he had been unconscious, he didn't know and it really didn't matter. In his condition he wouldn't be going anywhere.

With great effort, he managed to lift his leg a few inches off the ground and flexed his foot. The shackle around his ankle rotated slightly, biting into his skin. Fat chain links stretched and gave a low clank. The rattle of metal seemed overly loud in the silent chamber. Hopefully the noise hadn't alerted Icarus or Rell that he was conscious.

Luc looked at his lap. Jade lay with an arm draped over his thighs and her head cradled against his groin. At any other time, this would have been a pleasant surprise, but their situation was dire and their chance of escape seemed beyond bleak.

The shackle binding her right wrist was stretched tight and her body bent at an awkward angle to allow her to reach him. He didn't know when she'd moved, but suspected it was after the demons had left them. At some point he had passed out from the pain and though he currently felt far from good, he didn't feel as bad as he should. Jade must have tried to heal him in his unconscious state.

He swallowed the emotion that rose inside him. He wondered if she had been scared. Without too much thought he knew that if in the same situation he would have been frantic to heal her.

Deep, steady breaths told him that she slept heavily. Shadows cast across her face, making the hollows of her cheeks and the dark smudges under her eyes seem more pronounced. His chest tightened at the thought of Jade exhausting herself while trying to heal him.

He raised his hand to brush a tangled lock from her face, but the chain didn't extend enough to reach her. He flinched when the metal recoiled and the sharp edge of the band cut into his wrist.

Jade stirred and opened her eyes. She blinked several times and then stared straight ahead. He lowered his arm and watched the unguarded expressions play across her face. It was disorienting to wake up in a cold, dark place. Then again, she'd grown up in the Shadow World, so maybe it was a scene she was used to.

With a little huff, she pushed off the floor. The chain around her right wrist tightened and pulled in the opposite direction. She groaned and settled back onto his lap. *That* sentiment he did understand.

"Morning."

She craned her neck and looked up at him. "You're awake."

"Unfortunately." He shifted his back against the stone wall. "I'm beginning to think my unconsciousness was bliss."

"Sweet Sainted Mother." Her voice pierced the quiet. She flexed her hand and moaned. "My fingers feel like they're on fire."

Luc glanced at the entrance and listened. No crunching footsteps reverberated down the corridor. He tried to bend his knee to give Jade a push upright, but a sharp pain shot along the back of his leg. His body seized and his head thumped against the wall. It took all his willpower to not cry out. He stared at the ceiling and released a long slow breath, concentrating on exhaling the searing fire.

"Luc?" Jade scooted toward the wall where she was chained and sat upright. "Are you all right?"

He grunted more than spoke the words. "I will be in a minute."

Desperation laced her question. "What can I do?"

He shook his head and continued to stare at the ceiling, trying to wrestle the pain back into submission.

A shadow on the far side of the ceiling caught his attention. He watched the dark stain move along the edge of the wall and disappear. His eyes narrowed, trying to bring the area into view. Another shadow appeared, skittering along the ceiling to the other side of the chamber. A glint reflected off the black circle but disappeared.

"Do you see that?" He lowered his chin but kept his eyes trained on the corner, his pain finally abating to a tolerable level.

Jade looked in the direction he was staring and scanned the area. He watched her gaze skate across the ceiling and stop. She had the natural skills of a warrior, with patience to seek out her quarry before asking questions. He looked back at the shadow.

"I see it," she said.

A second shape slithered along the top of the entrance from the outer corridor and moved across the chamber. Then like the other, it suddenly vanished.

"What is that?" Jade whispered.

"I was going to ask you the same thing."

She squinted. "Imps, maybe."

"Are they magical?" He rested his head against the wall, making it easier to peer at the farthest corner. "Do they have the ability to appear and vanish?"

Jade shook her head. "I don't think so. I only saw two or three when I was growing up. They're like giant bats with big, black eyes."

That would explain the glint that caught the light of the blue flame. "I've never heard of them."

"From what Rell told me, they usually stay close to Vile, but she might have been wrong."

"Watch." He flicked his head at one of the shadows inching its way toward the far side of the chamber.

The shape hovered near another dark spot, and then scooted around it to the very edge of the wall and disappeared.

Jade's mouth opened in surprise. She looked at him. "Where did it go?"

"If they're not magic, then I think there must be a doorway." He paused. "Maybe a way out."

Her mouth rounded and she glanced back in the direction the imp had disappeared. She raised her right hand and swept the chain out of the way, climbing to all fours. "Maybe I can get a better look."

She crept forward. The clink of metal hitting the stone wall tinged. Jade stopped and spread her hands on the ground, systematically searching the area in front of her. Her chain pulled tight but she gave a whispered whoop of triumph, obviously finding what she had been looking for. Bracing her hand against the wall, she stood. Dark shapes darted away from her and disappeared.

"What is it?" Luc squinted, trying to see what she held in her hand.

"My lock pin, and maybe the answer to our problems. I thought I'd lost it." She braced her hand against the wall and stood. "I think you're right." She looked over her shoulder. "There's definitely a passage, or at the very least, an alcove." She turned and shuffled toward him. "If we can get these chains off, maybe we can hide."

He loved her optimism, but the possibility of breaking the chains was nil, especially in his weakened state. "A good plan, but how?"

She held up the straight piece of metal. "With this, but first I want to try and heal you again. Then we'll concentrate on escaping."

Luc didn't have the strength to ask questions. She knelt as close as she could and laid her hand on his knee. Without explanation, she closed her eyes and began to chant. Warmth flooded his leg and moved through his body.

Jade's whispered words cloaked him in a dull white light. The protector in him wanted to stop her. From the dimness of her healing, he could tell she was exhausted, but the determined set of her jaw let him know that arguing would be pointless.

He closed his eyes and rested his head against the wall, opening himself up to the healing and trying to aid her. He'd been too weak after Icarus's brutal treatment, but perhaps now he had regained enough strength to be of some help.

Like a gentle wave, Jade's light ebbed and flowed, gradually burning its way through his body. Luc concentrated on her words, committing the chant to memory. The mantra took form in his mind, transforming into a living entity.

He began to speak. Without force, the healing light sparked inside his chest and spread up his neck. Cool tingles, like the bite of the yucamint plant, snapped along his jaw and across his tongue. Through slitted lids, he watched his whispered words flow from his lips and turn to vapor.

A thin mist formed around him and Jade, thickening with each line he spoke. Jade's golden light brightened and connected with his faint blue glow. The intensity of the link would have buckled his knees if he'd been standing. His back arched away from the wall, his breath lodging in his throat. Thick mist spewed from him as the healing chant took control.

Golden light poured from Jade's hands, illuminating the chamber and casting a yellow glow onto the figures hovering on the ceiling. Large, black eyes stared at them through the ever-solidifying mist.

Feeling returned to his feet and the ache at his shoulders and wrists dissipated with each word Jade spoke. Energy filled him and clarity returned to his mind. The need to exhale pushed against his chest. He raised his head and blew, releasing the last of the icy breath in his lungs and filled the chamber with fog.

The warmth inside him faded, but he could still feel Jade's hand pressed against his leg. Mist swirled around them, obscuring his vision. What had happened?

"Jade?" His words sounded muffled. "Are you all right?"

"Yes." She paused, her breathing labored. "How did you do that?"

He shook his head even though he knew she couldn't see him. "It just...happened."

A gentle push against his leg told him she was sitting up. "This would have come in handy before."

Luc could think of a lot of times the ability to cause mist would have come in handy. Fleeing an angry husband, fleeing an angry tavern owner, fleeing the magistrate's men when he had been a boy poaching deer. Perhaps it was better that he hadn't had this ability before now.

"I wonder what other useful talents I have that I'm not utilizing."

Jade's chains rattled and then her hand pressed against his calf. "Can you bring your ankle closer to me?"

He shifted to lean against his left hip and bent his right knee, drawing his leg as close to her as the chain would allow. Her fingers slid down his calf to settle near the shackle around his ankle.

"What are you doing?"

"Putting my years on the street to good use." Her fingers fumbled along the edges of the metal. "If this lock hasn't been infused with magic, I might be able to pick it."

His eyebrows raised in surprise. "You're a woman of many talents."

She gave a little snort. "You have no idea."

He could just imagine. Perhaps when he was better he'd test her skill. As it were, he had neither the energy nor the stamina for witty banter. He let the onslaught of inappropriate remarks remain unspoken. Now was not the time.

"Damn." Her curse hissed through the mist.

"What's wrong?"

"I need both hands."

The links of her chain clanked and she scooted away from him. Several minutes passed, which were punctuated with a plethora of colorful expressions, until the sound of iron hitting the ground echoed through the chamber. Luc leaned forward, hoping she'd just accomplished the impossible. Suddenly she was before him, a wide smile spreading across her face. She held up her arm and shook it.

"I never doubted you," he whispered.

She scowled at the lie and moved down his leg to the shackle. After a few silent minutes, the band opened and dropped to the ground. With single-minded determination, Jade crawled to his right hand and freed his wrist. He pressed his back against the wall, surprised when she threw her right leg over him to straddle his lap. The intensity on her face made him want to kiss her. She was so stubborn even iron shackles couldn't best her when she put her mind to it.

In an effort to get a better angle, Jade leaned into him, pressing her chest to his and rolling her hips forward. Surely he would burn in the Abyss for the thoughts racing through his mind. All blood and reasonable thought raced to his groin. His penis stiffened. He pressed his knees together and leaned slightly forward, trying to reposition her.

"Uh, Jade."

She shoved against him. "Shhttt."

Her command cut him off. He closed his eyes and relaxed against the wall. *His father, cats giving birth, mistakenly walking in on his old nanny bathing herself.* He tried to visualize anything unpleasant and shivered at the image of his nursemaid.

The last shackle fell away and Jade grinned down at him. He returned a strained smile and shifted again. Apparently, she was oblivious to the havoc she was causing him. After a few seconds, she climbed off and stood.

It took a minute for Luc to regain his composure, but the urgency of their situation extinguished all evidence of his condition. He rubbed his wrists while flexing his leg, eventually rolling to his hands and knees. Dizziness threw him off balance and he caught himself against the wall. Jade crouched and shored him up with her shoulder. He silently cursed his weakness. She'd already done so much and was in no state to carry the burden of their escape.

"I'm fine." He stood and leaned against the wall, removing his weight from her. "Give me a minute."

She blocked his path, her body tense, as if she was ready to catch him if he fell. Pride surged through him. He'd be damned if he would be the cause of them getting recaptured. He straightened away from the wall. The dizziness had abated and much of the pain had been extinguished by Jade's healing.

He grabbed her hand and took a step toward the passage doorway. Though not completely sure of the way out, he was confident between the two of them they could find the path back to the hot pool caverns and out of this nightmare.

The sharp edge of the table materialized out of the mist. He gripped the edge and followed it around until he stood where Icarus had stood while torturing him.

"What are you doing?" Jade tugged on his hand. "We need to leave."

Pulsing energy thumped against him. Maybe it was part of being a Shield, but it was as if the weapons called to him. "Patience."

He could almost hear her grinding her teeth in frustration, but this was too important to leave. Cold metal grazed his fingertips and he smiled. He dropped Jade's hand, searching for the handle of the weapon. Smooth wood caressed his palm and he clutched at it, lifting what he could now see was an axe.

Wings of a dragon cradled the blade against the black, polished handle. Two deadly hooks that resembled the spikes on a dragon's back curved from the opposite side. The blade arched like a talon and ended in a point. Every aspect of the weapon was created for killing. Low vibrations hummed through his hand, causing the beast inside him to stir, returning the weapon's greeting. As he suspected. Another immortal weapon.

He shoved the handle into the waist of his pants, making sure to hook the point on the outside of the material, and continued to search the table. Again his hand brushed cold metal, his fingers coasting along the filigree hilt of his dagger. He snatched it up and shoved it in his boot, then froze.

The sound of footsteps crunched from somewhere beyond the room. With only one way out, whoever approached blocked their escape. He turned and moved along the wall, dragging Jade behind him. She didn't resist. Never had he been so grateful for her survival instincts—or her silence.

Perhaps they should have stayed and fought, but with neither of them being at peak strength and not knowing how many demons drew near, they were better off waiting for their chance to escape. Too many unknowns put a warrior at a distinct disadvantage.

His hand fumbled over the rough, icy stone, searching for what he hoped would be another passage or at the very least, a hiding place. As the footsteps drew closer, the beat of his heart quickened. The wall seemed to go on forever. He pushed forward as quietly as he could, trying not to alert the forthcoming demon of their existence.

One minute his hand pressed against solid rock and the next he was falling sideways into a passage. Relief washed through him. In order to slide into the narrow entrance, Luc had to turn sideways. Jade gripped his hand, stumbling over his heels behind him. Once inside, their vision cleared. The mist hung over the opening like a blanket, but it didn't penetrate the passage. Luc followed the curve of the wall until he was certain they couldn't be seen by anybody in the chamber.

He stopped and signaled for Jade to do the same. It was difficult to hear what was happening beyond the passage. The thick walls of their hiding place muffled much of the sound and light.

They waited, neither moving nor saying a word. The sound of their chains being picked up and most probably examined jangled. Jade looked at him, her eyes wide. The clatter of the shackles being dropped and a stifled curse was followed by the stomp of angry footsteps, which exited the chamber and faded down the corridor.

Luc looked at Jade and pressed a finger to his lips. He didn't completely trust that the demon was gone. She nodded but released a breath, her shoulders relaxing slightly. He made a motion for her to follow him. Now that their escape had been discovered, their original exit was not an option.

He ventured deeper into the passage. The air grew even colder. Jade rubbed her arms and shivered, letting him know the drop in temperature wasn't his imagination. The passage widened and a dull blue light glowed up ahead. It appeared that the conduit made a sharp right.

Luc stopped at the bend and pressed his back against the wall. The telltale bite of the Banes' presence didn't increase, but it was difficult to differentiate one demon from two or three. Zero was the only acceptable number of demons he wished to encounter.

There was no guarantee the path beyond the turn was an exit and from the feel of the air, they were probably traveling deeper into the Shadow World instead of out. He didn't voice his concerns to Jade, but she was smart and more than likely had already formed her own opinion.

Luc poked his head around the corner, quickly surveyed what

lay beyond, and ducked back in. He glanced at Jade and held up his hand for her to wait where she was.

She silently mouthed, "What is it?"

He shrugged and pointed to his eyes, and then toward the passage. She nodded in understanding. He was struck with the realization of how well they worked together, always on the same page with their approach to situations—despite their bantering.

With tiny steps, Luc crept along the wall and peered around the corner again. The chamber appeared empty. From where he stood there were no other passages or doorways. A waft of cold air, like stepping out into a winter day, hit him. He held up his hand, trying to feel where the breeze came from. Perhaps it was a way out. There was no discernible direction and no obvious vent.

Blue light glowed in measured patches along the rocky walls of the chamber. Though the ceiling was low, the room stretched for what looked like more than a hundred feet before fading into darkness. Only the areas of blue light, which shrank to small pinpricks of light in the distance, lit the chamber.

Luc scanned the low ceiling, searching for imps, but the room seemed devoid of all life. The rock walls glistened with a thin layer of ice and a fine white powder that looked like frost dusted the stone floor. Not looking, he reached behind him, searching for Jade's hand. She clutched at him and laced her fingers with his. The eerie glow against the wall sent chills along Luc's spine. Foreboding filled him. It wasn't so much about the danger they were in, but the wrongness of this place.

A cloud of mist blew from between his lips and thinned. They stepped into the chamber, drawing near the first glowing patch. Jade's other hand slid over the top of the one she already clutched. He glanced at her and gave a little squeeze of reassurance. At first

Luc thought it was a window, but as they drew closer he could see that the area was not glass, but a thick layer of ice. Blue light emanated from within.

The beast inside him suddenly roared to life, sending fire down his arms and into his hands. Jade gasped and jerked her hands away. Taken completely off guard, Luc stopped and fought to control the dragon.

He clenched his fists, inhaled deeply, and commanded the beast to settle. Now was not the time to transform. Control slipped back to him, but the animal didn't blindly obey. It was more of a case of acquiescing to Luc's request, but the beast paced, ready to defend. Where had it been when he was being tortured by Icarus? Once he felt he had regained the majority of control, he turned to Jade and nodded. "I'm all right."

She inhaled and returned his nod. "What is this place?"

Their words sounded dense and flat, as if the walls absorbed all sound. Another blast of cold air ruffled his hair and sent shivers skittering down his spine.

"I don't know, but it triggered my dragon, so it can't possibly be good." He turned back to the blue light. "Ice." He touched it. The clear sheet burned his fingers and his own fire flared again. He snatched his hand back, examining the white blisters rising on his fingertips. "Don't touch it."

Jade grabbed his hand, whispered a few words, and blew on his fingers. Instantly, the pain was gone, but the white patches remained.

He smiled. "You're very handy to have around."

She shrugged. "Told you I had many talents."

"Indeed."

He lowered his hand and surveyed the ice. It looked like a window, tall and oval shaped. He stepped in front to peer straight in.

"Holy Sainted Mother."

"What is it?" Jade wedged her body in front of his and gasped. "Oh my gods."

There before them, frozen in ice, was a man. His eyes were closed and his hands folded over his chest, as if presented for burial. From the color and style of his dress, he was most definitely one of the missing Bringers from Illuma Grand. Luc stepped around Jade, trying to get a better view. "I know him."

"Who is he?" Jade stood on her tiptoes and pushed against his side.

He gave way. "Marcus Tobin, Lady Tobin's grandson."

Jade gasped. "And Beatrice's fiancé."

He scowled and turned toward the corridor of blue lights. Nausea rolled through him. Like wading through mud, he struggled to the next window of ice, knowing what he would see, but still praying the oval would be empty.

A young woman with long red hair stood in the same position. Again, her clothing indicated she was also from Illuma Grand. "I think the mystery of what happened to the Bringers has been solved."

Jade stopped beside him but said nothing as she stared at the young woman who was probably no older than she was. Her gaze searched the length of the room, the reality of what each window held taking hold of her. She turned and walked to the opposite wall. "Another one." She moved to the next window, leaving small boot prints in the frost. "And another."

Her steps quickened and she began to jog from one icy window to the next, saying nothing, only stopping long enough to peer in and then move on. Luc followed. Some of the Bringers he recognized. Most he didn't.

"Luc!"

He spun and ran toward her. She was pressed as close to the window as she could get without touching it. Her hands hovered in front, shaking. He slid to a stop and stared, the blood draining from his face.

Jade looked at him. "Is it?"

"No." He said the word, but for a fraction of a second, he wasn't sure he was correct. The woman encased in ice looked so much like Ravyn it took his breath away. "No, it's not her."

"Are you certain?"

"Positive." He understood Jade's confusion. The resemblance was striking. He inhaled and blew warm air on the ice, then quickly rubbed with his sleeve. Ice crystals floated from the surface, giving them a clearer view. "She's older. See the streak of gray at her temples."

"She looks so much like Ravyn. Who do you think she is?"

"If I didn't know any better, I'd think it was her mother." He shook his head. "But she's dead."

"What if she isn't? What if…" Jade pivoted and ran to the next window, zigzagging her way down the line.

Luc took another look at the woman, committing her face to memory, and followed Jade. Before he could reach her, she slid to a stop and cried out, her knees buckling beneath her. He raced to where she knelt and froze.

A woman he thought long dead stood in peaceful repose, as fresh as the last time he'd seen her. "Esmeralda."

"Get her out." Jade's voice cracked, cutting through his shock. She stood, the look on her face so full of rage she looked unbalanced. "Get her out!"

She slammed her fist against the ice. The sizzle of burning skin hissed but she didn't seem to notice the pain. Luc grabbed her arm before she could touch the window again and pulled her away.

"We've got to get her out." She barreled forward, intent on attacking the ice again. Luc wrapped his arm around her waist and lifted her off the ground. She kicked and fought to get free. "Let me go."

"Not until you calm down." She clawed at his arm, but he held fast. "Jade, you're not going to get her out by beating on the ice and injuring yourself." He gave her a hard shake. "Do you hear me?"

Rational thinking seemed to slowly return and she ceased her struggle. "Yes."

He set her on her feet and released her, turning his attention back to the woman in ice. If Esmeralda was here, who was the demon who had raised Jade? It didn't make sense. Each secret they uncovered seemed to only end in more mysteries.

"What are we going to do?"

She sounded so heartsick, the last thing he wanted to do was let her down, but how could he get Esmeralda out of the ice *and* get them to safety?

"Step back."

Jade did as he asked. "What are you going to do?"

"I'm not sure yet. Maybe nothing."

He pulled out the axe from his waistband and clutched the handle with a double-fisted grip. This weapon was immortal. Maybe it did more than just send the Bane to the Abyss.

Luc drew the axe back and brought it down in an overhead arc. The blade struck the ice and bounced off. He stepped close, but the strike didn't appear to have any effect or even leave a mark. He tried it again, battering the surface with four hacking blows. Nothing.

"Damn."

Jade watched him, her fingers pressed to her lips as if praying for success. His determination grew and suddenly giving her what she wanted so desperately was the most important thing in the world to him. The dragon stirred inside, giving him what he hoped was the answer for getting Esmeralda free. He leaned the axe against the wall and refocused on the ice, tapping into the beast.

The animal pushed for dominance, wanting complete freedom to transform and conquer. He pushed back but allowed the beast to stretch. Luc sent a mental request to the dragon for help, asking for guidance in the quest. The beast calmed and answered with fire.

Unlike the uncontrollable blasts that had ignited the forest the night Jade had been shot, this fire was intentional. Like an extension of his arms, the flames, the dragon and Luc became one.

Energy raced down his arms. He opened his hands and spread his fingers, wearing the white-hot heat like a pair of gloves. With a tentative touch, he brushed his palm across the surface of the ice. A rivulet of water ran down the front of the window and the hiss of steam spiraled up from his hand. He raised his other hand and swiped in the opposite direction, again melting the ice.

"It's working." Jade took a step back as his movement became bigger.

The process was slow and he wasn't sure what he would do when he got close to Esmeralda's body. He worked in silence, always aware of Jade hovering a few feet away. To her credit, she never once offered advice or suggestions. This was his gift, part of being a Shield.

When only inches separated him from Esmeralda, he once again asked the dragon for guidance. The intense heat faded to merely hot. Awareness of the beast lingered at the back of Luc's mind, as did its awareness of him. Working together, guiding the heat, they were able to accomplish a miracle.

Luc glided his hand along Esmeralda's leg. A loud crack popped behind her body and her limbs crumpled, sending her toppling out of the ice. Jade leapt forward and Luc managed to catch most of Esmeralda over his shoulder. He eased backward, inching his way out of the window. Jade guided him and then lifted much of her sister's dead weight so he could get his footing.

Together they gently laid her on the ground. Her skin was cold and white, her lips blue. With tentative hands, Jade brushed back the chocolate brown locks from her sister's face. She seemed unsure what to do or how to help Esmeralda.

Luc laid his head on her chest. Damp cloth pressed against the side of his face. He lifted his head, tore at the laces on the front of her gown and repositioned his ear.

"What…" Jade clutched her sister's hand to her breast. "Are you doing?"

He held up a hand for silence and closed his eyes, listening—hoping. Then he heard it, the faintest beat. Not fully trusting his hearing, he pressed two fingers against her neck, then her wrist, each pulse point telling him the same thing. He sat up. "She's alive."

Tears brimmed in Jade's eyes, spilling over and streaming down her cheeks. "Are you certain?"

He took her hand and laid it against the side of Esmeralda's neck. "Feel that?"

She shook her head, her words rasping from her throat. "I don't feel anything."

"Close your eyes." He covered her hand with his and pushed her index and middle finger deep into her sister's neck. "Wait."

It took several seconds, but Jade's eyes popped open. "I felt it." She sat a few seconds longer, the smile spreading across her face.

"It's a miracle she's alive."

She twisted and threw her arms around Luc. He caught her up, pulling her tightly against him. A miracle? He wasn't sure. The fact that there was a demon walking around with Esmeralda's soul wasn't happy news.

He didn't voice his thoughts when he released Jade. She was brave and had been incredibly resourceful on this mission, but he suspected seeing her sister's body had pushed her past the point of reason.

He stuck the axe handle in the waist of his pants at his back and tugged the strings of Esmeralda's bodice together. Their situation had just gotten a lot more difficult. In addition to his already weakened state, escape had already been questionable. Now he had a body to carry. He scooped up Esmeralda's limp form and stood. "We need to get out of here—now."

"I'll check if there's another way out." Jade jogged to the end of the room, disappearing into the darkness.

He waited, shifting under Esmeralda's weight. The seconds ticked by and still she didn't return. As he crouched to lay the limp form on the ground, Jade reappeared.

She slowly walked back, surveying the walls. "It dead ends."

"Then we leave the way we came." He readjusted the body and looked around. "It doesn't feel right leaving them here."

"I know." Jade rubbed her arms vigorously. "But there's only two of us and a whole army of Bane."

"Another time?"

She smiled. "You can count on it."

They moved back into the corridor and crept along the wall. The air grew warmer but nowhere near warm. Luc turned sideways and repositioned Esmeralda's body in order to fit through the narrow passage. They halted at the entrance and listened. All seemed quiet. Jade tiptoed forward to peek into the chamber.

Luc looked up. Three feet above him, a lumpy black shape clung to the ceiling. Dark eyes as round as quarried onyx stones stared back at him. The creature didn't move or send up an alarm, but the way it looked at him, unblinking, gave him an uneasy feeling. As though there was more to the imps than just resembling huge bats.

Jade eased back to where he waited and mouthed, "Empty."

He nodded, hefted Esmeralda's body, and tilted his chin toward the door, giving Jade the signal to lead. They inched forward into the chamber. The fog had completely disappeared and the path to the doorway was clear and thankfully empty. They skirted the chains and were almost to the door when a figure stepped out and blocked their way.

"Leaving so soon?"

CHAPTER TWENTY-THREE

A wicked smile quirked at the corners of Sha-hera's mouth, showing off her pointed white fangs. She cocked her head. "What do you have there?"

Jade positioned herself in front of Luc and tensed, ready for an attack. Nothing was going to stop her from getting Esmeralda's body out of the Shadow World. "Step aside, Sha-hera."

"I don't think so." She gave Jade a disgruntled look. "At least not until you answer my questions."

The demon glided toward them. Both Jade and Luc retreated several paces. There was no other escape but through the door Sha-hera blocked.

The demon bent and snagged the chain that had shackled Luc's ankle, holding it up. "I assume these were for you." Her yellow gaze rested on Luc and then slid to Jade. "And this…" She kicked the band that had imprisoned Jade. "Was for you?"

Neither answered her question. Jade kept her body between Luc and the demon, ready to fight if the bitch so much as twitched a wing.

"Since we are such good friends, Jade..." She drew out the name and paced back to the door. With a dramatic pivot, Sha-hera faced them and flared her wings, completely blocking their only escape route. "I will make you a deal."

The demon couldn't be trusted in the simplest of matters, but they had no other choice.

"What kind of deal?" Jade asked.

Sha-hera crossed her arms over her ample chest. "You answer my questions and I will let you go."

Jade smiled sweetly. "As simple as that? You'll just let us pass?"

The demon held up her hand. "I swear it."

"A Bane promise holds little weight," Luc said.

Sha-hera lowered her hand and shrugged. "True, but really, what other choice do you have?"

"Why?"

"You have information I need and I'm willing to compromise. But decide quickly. I'm not very patient."

It would be a waste of time to press the demon into the promise of keeping her word. She either would or wouldn't and they would have to deal with the consequences. Jade glanced at Luc. He nodded.

She faced Sha-hera. "Ask your questions."

"Good." The demon straightened. "Somebody held you prisoner, yes?"

"Yes." Jade said.

Sha-hera's eyes narrowed. "Who?"

Loyalty warred inside her. If there was a chance to escape and get Esmeralda's body to a safe place, then she would do anything. But what if the demon Rell really did embody her sister's soul and the limp form in Luc's arms was a trick or an illusion? Jade swallowed her doubts and made her decision. "Icarus."

A finely sculpted brow arched, the singsong note in the demon's voice telling Jade she knew Icarus was not the only abductor. "And?"

"And Rell."

"So the two of them are working together." She glared at Jade. "Why?"

Too late Jade remembered the tattoos on her hands. She pressed her palms against her thighs and slid them around her back. The demon watched her movements, understanding slowly dawning on her face.

Sha-hera lunged forward and grabbed Jade's arms, yanking her hands up to look at them. "How did you get these?"

Jade circled her arms, twisting to pull free. "That I will not tell you."

"It matters not." Sha-hera's smile turned to a sneer. "I know how it was done, but I venture that Icarus does not, correct?"

Neither Jade nor Luc answered her.

"No, that is why he tortured you—to get information." Her smile was one of genuine delight. "One last question." She turned and glided away from them. "Did Icarus mention the Abyss of Souls?"

Jade gritted her teeth, sure her answer would give Sha-hera a distinct advantage. The situation between Rell and Icarus was pulling Rell deeper into the struggle. With the discovery of Esmeralda's body, Jade knew that putting her sister in danger was the last thing she wanted.

She looked the demon squarely in the eye and lied. "No, he didn't. What is the significance of the Abyss?"

Sha-hera waved a finger back and forth. "No, no, I am the only one who gets to ask questions."

"At least tell me why Esmeralda's body was frozen in ice."

Sha-hera stepped to the side, giving them a clear path to the door. "You will have to be satisfied with an unhindered escape." She tipped her small blue horns toward the limp form in Luc's arms. "And your useless prize."

No matter what the demon inferred, Jade would not believe her sister was dead. She couldn't give up that hope. Not yet. "Then we are free to leave?"

Sha-hera held her arm out to her side, indicating the doorway.

"Just like that?" Jade said. Nothing was ever this easy with a Bane.

"I said I would keep my word." She lowered her arm. "Go."

"And you will not follow us?" There was a trick within the demon's actions, but Jade couldn't put her finger on it.

"I will not follow and Vile has forbidden all demons but me to enter these caverns, so there will be no Bane to pursue you."

"What about Icarus?" Luc asked.

A malevolent smile crept across Sha-hera's mouth. "Yes, he's been a very bad demon. Won't Vile be angry with him when he finds out that not only did Icarus violate his private realm, but also let you two escape?"

Jade's stance relaxed a fraction. "Ah, I understand now. We escape, you tell Vile, he becomes angry with Icarus and you are once again in the king's good graces."

"Not as dumb as I thought." Sha-hera leaned a shoulder against the wall. "But you'd better go before Icarus returns." The demon's gaze turned hard. "Or I run out of patience and claim you as my own prize and present you to Vile."

"Why not do that anyway," Luc asked. "Would you not still gain his favor?"

Jade turned and glared at him, but he ignored her.

"I thought about it," Sha-hera said. "But this plan gains the same favor and thwarts Icarus." She moved to block the doorway. "I assume you can find your way out?"

Slowly she pivoted. "And I'll be sure to let your sister know you found her body."

The demon's light footfalls echoed in the passage before fading.

"Let's go." Jade jogged to the entrance. The passage was indeed clear.

Luc joined her at the opening, shifted Esmeralda's body to lie over his shoulder and exited first. She followed him down the corridor. As the distance between them and Sha-hera widened, hope that they might actually escape grew.

Their course turned upward. The heat and the tang of sulfur hung in the air. They rounded a corner and Jade recognized the jutting stone at the top of the passage. It had been her boundary as a child, the marker at which she was not allowed to venture beyond.

She pointed. "We're almost there." As they approached the opening to the cavern, she grabbed Luc's arm. "I'll enter first. Wait until I signal you." She squeezed past him. "If Rell is in there, I don't want her to see her body—not yet, anyway."

"Be careful." He walked so close the toes of his boots kept kicking her heel. "Check the ledges and the ceiling."

"I will."

"And make sure she's not bathing in one of the pools." He kicked her again. "Some of the bigger boulders could hide her."

Jade gritted her teeth and stopped. Luc barreled into her, sending her stumbling into the wall. She spun and glared at him. "I know what I'm doing." He opened his mouth to argue, but she cut him off. "Shhhtt!"

Not waiting for his unwanted response or look of disapproval, she spun, took a deep breath, and crept to the entrance of the cavern. Her heart fluttered like moths beating against the glass of a lantern, erratic and out of rhythm. A veil of wet heat lay like a blanket in front of the door. She glided slowly forward, leading with her shoulder, and stepped inside. Her eyes darted around the roof of the cavern. No dark shapes huddled in the shadows and no grating nips flared on her body. There was no indication that Rell was in the chamber.

The slow burble of bubbles in the greenish-blue pools continued to roil and the vents hissed. This cavern would forever remain unchanged, no matter if its occupants lived or died—left and returned—were happy or battled great darkness. Until some cataclysmic event transformed the face of Inness, her childhood home would stay hidden from most of the world, unaffected by time.

The large, flat rock she used to sleep on stood like a silent reminder of her past. Jade squared her shoulders. Perhaps this would be the last time she would ever set foot in this place. She smiled at the thought.

Jade motioned Luc forward. He turned sideways and ducked to enter the chamber. Not wasting any time, they skirted a ring of boulders and traversed the thin bridge of rock between two pools. The narrow crevice lay directly in front of them. Luc stopped and lowered Esmeralda's body to cradle her.

"I don't think I can carry her and fit through the passage. Once we make the turn, the opening narrows."

Jade glanced down the dark passage and then walked to where he stood. She hoisted one of Esmeralda's limp arms around her neck and settled her sister's dead weight solidly on top of her shoulders. "Maybe if we balance her between us, we'll be able to slide through."

Luc gave a quick nod and draped Esmeralda's other arm around his neck so she hung between them. "It's worth a try."

They sidled into the passage. At first their movements were awkward and Jade found herself repeatedly slamming into her sister like an expanding and contracting accordion. But as the light dimmed and they were forced to use their other senses, a rhythm emerged.

Sweat dripped down Jade's temples and into her eyes. She blinked away the irritating moisture and tilted her head to wipe the side of her face on the sleeve of her sister's gown. Their labored breathing bounced around them and was occasionally punctuated by a grunt when one of them hit a protruding rock. Jade blew a lock of hair out of her eyes, swearing Esmeralda was getting heavier with each shuffle they took.

The path turned and the opening narrowed even further. Their pace slowed considerably. Though now in complete darkness, she could hear the rasp of Luc's leather as he maneuvered through the constricted opening. A hint of fresh air brushed her face and she inhaled, turning her head to capture every wisp.

The linen shirt she wore under her tunic stuck to her like a thin layer of wet paint on a canvas. Again a puff of cool air circled around her heated cheeks. "I think we're getting close."

"Let's hope so. I don't remember the passage being this long." Luc said.

"That's because we weren't hefting another person."

Luc grunted but didn't reply further. They shuffled around the last corner and were enveloped in cool air. Sighs of relief escaped them. Jade stopped and leaned against the cold rock wall. Luc did the same without complaint.

An oval of gray light marked the end of the tunnel. How long

had they been held captive? Tears threatened to well and her nose
tingled at the sight of freedom no more than a few yards ahead. She
swallowed hard, frantically blinking back her swelling emotions.
The word rasped from her throat. "Light."

He seemed to understand the importance of that single word.
"A miracle."

Even though she couldn't make out his face, she looked at him.
"Are we like Siban now? Survivors of the Shadow World? Forever
scarred by the Banes' torture?"

"No." Luc was quiet for a few seconds. "What we've been
through is nothing compared to the cruelty that Siban suffered, but
I do understand him better, his watchful suspicion and need for
solitude at times."

"And respect him more."

"Yes." Silence stretched between them until Luc said, "Let's go
home."

The warmth of happiness spread through her. "Yes, let's go
home."

At the end of the passage, Luc repositioned Esmeralda's body.
"I think I can carry her from here. Check for Bane. I don't feel any,
but it's difficult to tell so close to the Shadow World."

Jade released her sister and exited the opening, blinking against
the sunlight. The day looked barely changed from the time they'd
entered the Shadow World. Again she wondered how long they'd
been held captive.

She scanned the woods and sky. All seemed quiet and nothing
appeared out of place. She motioned him forward.

"Climb to the next ledge and I'll lower her. If you can balance
her until I climb down to you, then we can work our way to the
ground."

"All right." The dead weight would be difficult to wrestle and Jade prayed she wouldn't tumble over the edge, but she couldn't think of a better plan. Whatever she could do to get them safely back to the manor, she would.

Healing Luc had drained more energy than she cared to admit, but she didn't regret doing it. Hollow dips and dark smudges under his eyes told her he still wasn't well. There would have been little hope of escape if she had left him in his weakened condition. At least now they had a chance and the odds were looking better with each obstacle they conquered.

Poor Esmeralda. The descent was none too smooth and their handling of her even less gentle. If by some chance they were able to revive her, she would bear the aches of scrapes and bruises. Finally, Jade's feet touched solid ground. Their descent, no matter how uncoordinated, was a success for the simple fact that neither of them had fallen to their deaths.

Luc scooped up Esmeralda and carried her into the trees, indicating Jade should follow with a roll of his head. The long furrows caused by scraping against jagged rocks burned across her torso. She pressed her hand to her side and limped behind him.

She wanted to moan—wanted to cry like a little girl. It was still a mile to the horses and their gear if the horses hadn't wandered off. Then there was the act of riding the blasted animals.

With great strength of will she repressed the urge to whine. They'd just escaped a fate worse than death in the Shadow World. The rest of this trip would be easy in comparison and the last thing Luc needed was to hear her complaints. She might sleep for a week, but until her head hit the pillow, she would not grumble.

Luc laid Esmeralda on the ground. "I have a plan."

"What is it?"

She liked plans.

He rolled the shoulder that had been supporting Esmeralda. "You're not going to like it."

It was difficult to keep the half smile from slipping, but she managed it. "Try me."

"I don't think I have the strength to carry your sister the entire distance, especially if the horses are gone." His words echoed her very concerns. "We need help."

She nodded her head. "Fine. Do you want to go or should I?"

"Neither."

Her spine stiffened, her chin lifting in a huff. "You don't mean to leave Esmeralda behind, do you?"

She'd just gotten her back. Even if she had to drag her sister's limp body all the way back to the manor, she wouldn't leave Esmeralda.

"No." Luc held up a hand before she could continue her tirade. "So calm down."

"What, then?" She didn't trust him. His voice sounded suspicious.

"We fly."

The words circled around her and she mentally swatted them away. Her response was simple and brooked no argument. "No."

"Jade, be reasonable. If I transform I can carry you and your sister."

"No." She hugged herself, only flinching slightly at the spark of pain that raced across her abdomen. "No." She took a step back, trying to put distance between them. "No."

He followed, pacing her step for step. "I need you to put aside your fear and think."

Think? Be reasonable? He wanted her to climb onto the back

of a dragon and fly—high—where people didn't belong. Bile rose in her throat. She waved him off, her head shaking frantically of its own accord. She turned and began quickly walking away. To where she didn't know, but she had to get as far as she could from the possibility of flying. "I'll go get the horses and be right back."

Footsteps thundered behind her. She began to run but Luc was faster and lifted her off the ground before she'd picked up speed. Kicking and her attempts to bite him didn't seem to dampen his determination. He tossed her over his shoulder and stomped back to where Esmeralda lay. With very little consideration, he tossed her on the ground and stepped on her chest. The more she fought, the more weight he applied.

Her unladylike name calling wheezed from her throat and her feeble slaps were useless against him. He had size and patience on his side. After exhausting herself with very little effect, Jade lay spread-eagle on the ground, panting.

He stared down at her. "Days of being tortured in the Shadow World, starved, cold, thinking death was near, and you remained calm. I ask you to fly and you completely lose your mind."

It was impossible to keep the quiver from her voice. "I'm afraid of heights."

His eyes narrowed and then widened. For a second he looked as if he would say something, but then his gaze narrowed again. He pursed his lips and stared down at her, his foot still resting on her chest. Finally, he stepped back and offered her his hand. Unsure what the truce meant, but having no fight left in her, she accepted it. He pulled her to a stand.

"You must trust me."

"I want to, Luc." Her throat tightened. "But I can't do it."

"Close your eyes."

"That won't help." Heat spread in a small patch on her neck. She stared at Luc, willing him to change his mind. Tiny bumps rippled under her fingertips when she rubbed her neck. Hives, a most unpleasant result of her nerves. "I can't do it."

He clutched her shoulders, his icy blue stare commanding her to act. "I have faith in you."

Damn him. She pressed the heels of her hands to her eyes, taking a deep breath. Could she do it—for him? Her head began to shake, her words coming out in a desperate plea. "I can't."

"Jade, I don't know how much time we have." He lowered his hands. "Despite what she said, Sha-hera will most definitely be after us. As will Icarus, Rell, and probably the entire succubus army."

His words broke through her panic. He was right. There was no guarantee she would die while flying, but if they didn't return to the manor and warn the others, she could die right here.

She nodded. "I know." Though the intensity of her fear didn't lessen, the importance of them getting home quickly increased enough for her to think rationally.

"We are still in a lot of danger."

She nodded her understanding of the situation, the motion all she could manage.

"I promise if you do this, I will never make you fly again."

Her mind screamed no but her mouth said, "All right."

The look on his face was one of pride and appreciation. He drew her to him, wrapping her in his strong, reassuring arms. She returned the embrace, closing her eyes to drink in his strength. She was going to need as much as she could get for what she was about to do.

He released her and stepped away. "Let's hope this works."

She crouched next to her sister and watched him walk deeper

into the trees. The forest wasn't as thick here, and once in dragon form he should be able to move without much problem. This would be the first time she'd ever seen him transform. He stood in the middle of a small clearing with his eyes closed. His lips moved with silent words. Like her, he seemed to be learning about his powers through trial and error—unfortunately.

His change was truly magnificent to behold. It happened much quicker than she'd anticipated. Though she hadn't given it much thought, she assumed he'd lie on the ground and undergo some painful stretching of bones and muscle. Graceful, that was the first word that came to mind. Golden light flared and engulfed his body. She shielded her eyes from the brightness, but the light quickly dimmed to a million glittering sparkles.

In the middle stood Luc. Another form swirled around him in a whirl of glistening streaks. With each pass his body transformed, lengthening.

Luc faded and in his place stood the golden dragon she remembered from the night at the chapel. Scales the size of serving platters swept along his haunches in waves of white light. As the animal's neck extended, ridges rose along its spine. Oval nostrils flared and flattened against a wide snout and two thin horns spiraled upward from the low, sloping head. A spiked tail flowed away from the creature's back like a deadly train and wings sprouted from its sides, unfolding like a butterfly breaking free of its cocoon.

Lights faded and Luc was gone. The dragon exhaled, expelling a thick cloud of mist much like the fog that filled the chamber where they'd been chained.

"Dragon's breath," she whispered. It was a story her father used to tell about the dragons of old and how their breath could befuddle their attackers. "Not a fairytale, it would seem."

The dragon turned its head and held her stare. Its eyes were the color of pale blue river ice. An ancient awareness radiated from the beast. Luc might be part of this magnificent creature, but he was not its whole. This was an entity like she had never known, powerful and raw. It was clear now that her father's stories had been so much more than just fantasy for a little girl. This creature could conceal the world with its breath or destroy it with its fire. It offered tolerance but not kindness and without the Bringer bond, its need for dominance would enslave any whose will was weaker.

The dragon twisted its body within the tight confines of the trees and lumbered toward her. Instinct had her cowering next to Esmeralda, even though logically she knew the animal wouldn't hurt her. Warnings from her father's tales rang through her mind. How predictable could a dragon be, even if Luc lurked inside?

The animal stopped a few yards away from where she crouched. Curled talons pawed at the ground. It lowered its head and gave a look that questioned her resolve to go through with their plan. She licked her lips and eased to a stand, holding the white-blue gaze. Her feet felt as if they were made of iron and her body rebelled against cooperation.

Another jet of steam erupted from its nostrils. The corner of the creature's upper lip curled upward. Was the dragon growling at her? She took a step back and it advanced until reaching Esmeralda. With movements more gentle than Jade thought possible, the dragon lifted the limp body and cradled her next to its chest. Sitting slightly back on his hind legs, it unfolded its wings, extending one of them to where Jade stood with her back pressed against a tree.

Curse the Sainted Ones, but she didn't think she could do this. The tip of the wing tapped her ankle, coaxing her to climb on. She shook her head and the dragon growled again. Unlike Luc, who tried to reason with her, the dragon seemed less patient and not nearly as inclined to concede to her fears.

That thought was nearly as frightening as the idea of flight. If she didn't climb onto the dragon's back, it could grip her by the mouth and carry her, or worse, take hold of her ankle and fly the entire distance with her dangling head down over the rushing ground.

Her breath stuttered in her chest. No, better to be a willing prisoner and keep a small amount of control. She pushed away from the tree and forced one foot in front of the other until she reached the dragon's haunch.

The creature craned its long neck to watch her. Encouragement and something akin to pride flickered in the dragon's otherwise stern expression. It was the first hint of Luc she'd seen since his transformation. Knowing he was aware and supportive gave her the boost of courage she needed.

With one hand, she grabbed the thick cartilage that framed the wing and with the other hand braced her palm against the bent leg. She jumped and propelled herself onto the haunch. After getting her balance, she eased to a stand. Even ten feet off the ground, her heartbeat quickened. The scales provided good traction. Unlike what she originally thought, they weren't smooth. Long ridges arced from one side to the other and held her feet in place as she made her way along the spiny back.

A cleared spot lay at the base of the dragon's skull. She crouched, holding onto a thick spike behind her, and let her legs slide over the sides of the thick neck. And she thought riding a horse had been uncomfortable. She searched for something to hold onto, knowing she'd fall off if left to balance herself. As if sensing her dilemma, the dragon tilted its head back, placing two feet of horn within her reach. She hesitated. The creature grunted and shook its head. Its message was clear.

She took hold of each horn and slid forward. Wedged between the head and slope of the neck, the position gave her stability. The horns were a solid brace and if she gripped with her thighs, which she would probably do out of sheer terror, she should be able to stay on.

She swallowed hard and let out a heavy and somewhat desperate breath. "I'm ready."

The words had barely left her mouth when the dragon reared on its back legs and launched them all into the sky. The first leap took them just above tree level, which allowed the large wings to give a deep stroke downward. Her knees dug into the dragon's neck in an effort to remain seated in their nearly vertical position. The scream lodged in her throat and the effort to not pass out became a struggle.

After what seemed like an hour of pulse-pounding ascent, they leveled off and Jade was able to regain a secure seating. The ground below them rushed by and she chose not to look down but instead focus on the horizon. A band of orange spread across the sky. Sunset was approaching. She inhaled and sent up a prayer of thanks for their freedom, even if it meant riding this damned dragon.

Her panic and fear eased the longer they flew. If she didn't think about how high they were, she was able to view things from a point of appreciation. The world was a different place from above. Roads turned at different angles from what she'd always believed and the river wasn't nearly as wide. She wondered how many people would see a dragon in the sky tonight.

They swooped low over their campsite at the hot pools, but there was no sign of the horses. That revelation gave her decision to fly a little more credence. Hopefully the horses had wandered back to the manor and maybe even alerted the others to their plight.

Brisk air and mind-numbing fear of falling off kept Jade alert. After a while, she started anticipating their movements, riding the downward stroke of the dragon's wings and sensing which direction to lean in order to stay seated. Flying wasn't as bad as she'd expected—but that didn't mean she wanted to do it again. She was certain that constantly squeezing her legs would leave her every bit as sore as riding the horses had. Her hands ached from the chilled wind rushing over them and her inability to relax her grip.

The sky darkened, the orange band spreading to a bluish pink. After what seemed like hours, they crested the rise and the manor spread out before them. Joy pounded through her veins. She gave a whoop and the dragon released a roar and a jettison of mist in reply.

They landed hard in the front garden, its back legs taking all the force. Jade slid sideways, but caught herself, preventing a fall. The animal settled Esmeralda on the ground and lowered its body to a crouched position. Unsure if it was going to move again, Jade sat for a second. The thick sides heaved in and out. She could feel the fast pace of its heart thumping against her calf and suddenly she felt bad. All this time she'd only been thinking about her own welfare. Never once had she considered how difficult it would be to carry two people to safety.

She released the horns and leaned over the top of the wide head. "Well done, dragon." She gave a tentative pat on its protruding brow ridge. "Well done."

A grunt that sounded more like Luc than the dragon rumbled from its throat.

With more grace than she'd managed when dismounting her horse, Jade stood and wove her way around the spines running along the back. Her legs trembled from exertion but she remained upright.

She'd just stepped onto the dragon's bent thigh when loud voices erupted from the house. The creature's head swung in the same direction. Another low grumble reverberated from deep inside the animal.

Taking its warning, she jumped down. Her legs buckled and she went to her knees. There she stayed, watching her friends sprint toward her across the open ground. Heat bristled along her skin and a flash of white light flared. In a blink of an eye Luc was lying prone beside her. He turned his head in the direction of the advancing horde, gave a half smile, and passed out.

Praise the Sainted Ones, it was good to be home.

CHAPTER TWENTY-FOUR

Icarus's shoulders nearly spanned the width of the narrow corridor. He walked with purpose, never hesitating in his goal. Rell followed, but the closer they drew to the chamber where Jade and Luc were chained, the slower her steps became. The need to reap her revenge on Luc had driven her for so many years, but seeing him tortured, and Jade's pleading for it to stop, had tempered her anger.

Despite the doubts that plagued her, there was no turning back. She'd severed the remaining cords from her past with Icarus's plan and killed whatever loyalty Jade had for her. The Shadow World and the darkness would be her only companions for eternity.

Icarus turned into the chamber and stopped. Tension rippled along his muscles, his spine straight and stiff. She instantly sensed the change in his mood and halted in the doorway, bracing one hand at the edge for support. What would she see?

"They're gone." His words drifted to her and he slowly turned. His eyes narrowed to stab her with accusations.

"I didn't release them." Relief assaulted her and she struggled to keep her confused expression in place. She moved beside him to see the chains for herself. They lay in a pile, empty. "I swear, Icarus."

"Did you have a change of heart?" He coiled his fingers around her neck. "Decide to save your lover?"

She clawed at his hand as the pressure increased. A single word strangled from her throat. "Please."

Deep laughter echoed from the shadows at the far side of the room. Icarus's hold loosened and released her, spinning to face the intruder. Rell coughed, sucking in deep breaths of air, and stumbled backward to crouch near the wall. A whimper rose in her throat but she pushed it down. This was the end.

Vile and Sha-hera glided from the darkness and stopped a few yards from Icarus. The king's face was uncharacteristically expressionless, only his penetrating gaze revealed his anger, while Sha-hera's triumphant malice glittered in her eyes, undisguised.

"Lose something?" Vile glided along the opposite side of the stone slab table. "Or should I say—someone?"

Rell couldn't see Icarus's face from where she cowered, but his spine stiffened, his wings slowly unfolding.

His father stopped at the center of the table. "When I heard my own son had captured—" He held up two fingers. "Not one, but two full-powered Bringers and didn't tell me—" He lowered his hand and leaned his arms against the slab. "Well, I didn't want to believe it."

Sha-hera shifted to lean a shapely hip against the table, but Icarus made no other movement. Rell struggled to remain motionless, not wanting to draw the king's attention.

"Now why wouldn't my son, my second in command—" In a grand display he held his arms out to his sides. "The captain of my entire demon army, not tell me about the Bringers?" He lowered his arms. "He knew I needed them to open the Abyss of Souls, so the only thing I can assume…" Vile's expression turned dark, all pretense of ignorance gone. "Is that he's trying to usurp my throne."

The ignorant smirk melted from Sha-hera's face, but still Icarus did not speak. The king's fist slammed down on the thick stone slab, splitting the table in two and causing Rell to fall backward. She scrambled to the corner like a crab. The heavy chunks fell inward and crashed to the floor to lay broken at Vile's feet. Sha-hera inched away from the king, but Icarus did not flinch.

The two powerful demons stared at each other. Silence stretched tight through the room. Rell closed her eyes and sent up prayers to the Sainted Ones, chiding herself for her foolish decision to follow Icarus. She opened her eyes.

"Your attempt would have impressed me if it hadn't been so inept," Vile said. "Where are they?" Again he held his arms out to his sides. "Gone."

For the first time Icarus moved, slowly pivoting toward Sha-hera. "Where are they?"

The she-demon's expression softened to one of convincing innocence. "Why would I know where your Bringers are? I was doing a security check and found this room in disarray. Do not blame me for your incompetence."

A chill of apprehension ran across Rell's shoulders. By asking Sha-hera the question, he'd admitted his guilt. She braced for the king's reaction, but the violence never came. Icarus faced Vile.

"So what happens now, Father? Will you consign me to be tortured or perhaps vanquish me to the Abyss? Or maybe both?"

Greed burned in Sha-hera's gaze. It was obvious the demon would love nothing more than to watch Icarus suffer.

"No, Icarus." Vile's words were laced with victory. "I have something more fitting planned." His gaze cut to Rell. "You and your whore are banished from the Shadow World."

Sha-hera stepped forward, her eyes wide. "But my king, that is no punishment. He thirsts for your throne. Banishing him will not stop him."

Vile's gaze never left Icarus. "He would not be the king I've groomed him to be if he tucked tail and ran so easily."

"King? You've groomed me to be nothing but a dog under your heel." Icarus's wings flared. "Rest assured, I will not sleep until I see your reign destroyed."

Sha-hera's wings flared and her body tensed. "You will have no army to command and no sanctuary where you can hide from the Bringers. The mighty Icarus will be brought down and crushed into ash beneath the hooves of their horses, and all memory of the once-mighty demon will fade." She took another step forward. "I will see to it."

Rell's gaze cast over the three demons. Rage radiated off Icarus and Sha-hera, but the king's demeanor was far less antagonistic. As the two demons squared off, a smile tugged at Vile's lips and she could not shake the feeling that there was much more to his punishment than she could decipher.

On the surface, banishment for a demon like Icarus was no punishment at all. He could easily convert an army. His skill in battle was legendary and he was clever. All things Vile already knew.

Rell's gaze cut to Sha-hera. She was Vile's lap dog, always sniffing to get into the king's good graces. Though cunning, she was also reactionary when it came to Icarus. The action before her crystallized. Vile was playing Sha-hera, setting a scene and allowing her to respond as she naturally would. She probably didn't even realize that she was his puppet.

Icarus spun and stalked to the entry, but stopped to glare at his father. "This is not over."

"I certainly hope not," Vile said.

Icarus turned and stomped out the doorway. His footsteps reverberated down the corridor and faded. Rell didn't move, unsure if she should follow him. Where would she go now? Banished and having turned Jade against her left her outlook bleak. Never had she felt this alone. The darkness inside surged forward as if sensing her acceptance was imminent.

"I think that went very well," Vile said. Without looking at either Rell or Sha-hera, he quit the chamber.

The succubus watched him leave, her gaze confused. Rell didn't move, hoping Sha-hera had forgotten about her. No such luck.

"You align yourself with deadly allies," Sha-hera said. The demon turned her yellow gaze on Rell. "You're naïve to think Icarus will triumph over Vile."

"I only wanted my sister back." If the demon thought she was naïve, then Rell would play the part. She wrapped her arms around her torso and hugged herself. "I didn't think he'd hurt her."

Sha-hera snorted and shook her head. "Like I said, naïve."

Rell crept forward with slow, cautious steps. "What should I do?"

The succubus was silent for a few seconds, as if calculating how to best benefit from the new developments. "I think we can help each other."

Rell crawled a few more inches and slowly stood. At this point she had nothing to lose. "How?"

"Follow me." A smile that reminded her of the cat that had caught the canary pulled at Sha-hera's full mouth. The succubus walked to the shadowed corner on the far side of the chamber and stopped to glance back at Rell. "I'm about to show you something that will change your world."

Rell's common sense raged against following. The demon could not be trusted. She forced her expression to remain passive and her steps moving forward. Would this be the day she died at the blade of an immortal weapon? Was Sha-hera going to be the one to send her to the Abyss? As she closed the distance between them, she couldn't help but marvel at the irony of fighting so hard against Jade's attempts and walking freely into Sha-hera's clutches.

The demon moved forward and disappeared. Rell stopped, holding out her hand to find the wall. Rough rocks scraped her palms and then were gone. A doorway. She had not noticed it before. She followed, feeling her way along the dark passage. The air grew cold, much colder than even the lower level. She shivered, partly from the icy temperature but also from the unknown.

Blue light from somewhere beyond the next turn lit the end of the passage. Sha-hera stopped and looked back at her. Even though every nerve in her body demanded she turn and run, Rell continued forward. The succubus disappeared around the corner and like a fool, she followed.

A blast of chilled air hit her when she stepped into the chamber. The blue light emanated from oval windows that lined both sides of the room. "What is this place?"

"This room…" Sha-hera spread her arms wide. "Holds the secrets of the Bane."

Unsure what to do or say, Rell walked toward the first sphere of light. She glanced at Sha-hera, but the demon hadn't moved. Her eyes remained fixed, as if waiting for her reaction.

Ice created a type of window. Rell stopped, her mouth opening and her eyes grew round at the sight of the man frozen in perpetual perfection. She managed to form a question and sound somewhat in control. "Who is he?"

"A Bringer." Sha-hera moved to stand beside her. "Captured by Vile."

A feeling of unease slid through her. She walked to the next window, knowing she would find a similar scene. This woman had thick copper-red hair, her skin as smooth and white as a porcelain doll owned by the children of the most elite. On she moved. An older man probably in his fifties. Another woman who bore a striking resemblance to the Bringer woman, Ravyn. Her pace quickened as she continued down the line. Another woman—two more men—and then... The ice was gone, the window empty, and she knew this was what Sha-hera wanted her to see.

"Who?" Had it been her father or somebody she knew? She turned and met Sha-hera's eyes. "Who was here?"

The demon stopped inches away and cocked her head. "You."

"Me?" She said the word but it had no meaning. *Her?* She shook her head. "I don't understand."

"When you became this..." She indicated Rell's demon form. "Your human body was preserved here." She turned and crossed to the opposite wall. "All Bringers are brought here unless they're killed in battle."

The purpose of such a thing was unfathomable. "Why was I brought here?"

"Vile loves his trophies." Sha-hera gazed lovingly into the ice window containing a man. "And you never know when they may come in handy."

"I don't understand. Where is my body? Why do you keep these?" She pointed to the frozen Bringers, trying to make sense of it all. "Is my human body dead?"

"To be honest, I don't know." Sha-hera crossed to where she

stood and ran her hand along the edge of Rell's wing. "Vile has yet to share the secret of his frozen trophies with me, but everything the king does is for a reason." She lowered her hand. "Your sister took your body."

Words failed Rell. Where had Jade taken her body? How had they found it in the first place? Had it all been a ploy to retrieve her human form? Did Icarus know of this place?

She tabled all but one of her questions. "Why do you show me this?"

"As I said, I think we can help each other." She sauntered toward Rell. "I help you and in turn, you help me." Sha-hera stopped and cocked her head. "Without the protection of the Shadow World, you're going to need all the allies you can get."

This peek into the secrets of the king was no gift, but neither did Rell have any other alternative than to play along with the demon. "What do you want?"

"Nothing really. Just keep me informed of Icarus's whereabouts and activities." She snagged a lock of Rell's hair and ran it between her fingers. "Maybe in time, if you've been helpful, Vile will bring you back into the fold."

The urge to yank her hair from the black talons and run pushed at her, but Rell stayed the urge. Bring her back into the fold? The very idea drained the last bit of energy from her. Exhaustion weighed her limbs down and a heavy presence pushed on her chest. She would rather be sent across the Veil than live an eternity in Vile's good graces, doing his bidding.

Sha-hera lowered her hand, her expression menacing. "There's a battle coming, Rell, and you'd be wise to align yourself with the demon who can do the most for you—which would be me."

"What about Icarus?"

"Icarus." Sha-hera spit on the ground. "He plays at war but knows nothing of what is truly happening."

A perception of knowing pushed against Rell. She could almost feel the truth in Sha-hera's words. It was a sensation she didn't like. Playing two sides against each other was a dangerous game. "And what is actually happening?"

Sha-hera gave her a placating smile, but her eyes narrowed. "You're different, Rell. I need more Bane like you in my army."

Everything she'd tried to avoid for the past thirteen years was for naught. Once Sha-hera set her sights on a demon, they were loath to break free of her hold. "The king has banished me."

"You are resourceful and smart, if a bit misguided." Her gaze caressed Rell's body, like one would appraise a horse before purchase. "I'm sure you can come up with a way to get back into Vile's good graces, and your loyalty to me would be greatly rewarded."

"And if I decide to go with Icarus?"

The demon's gaze was steady. "That would be most unwise."

Death infused the air and the walls of the chamber began to narrow. The past week's events were taking its toll on Rell. One thought continued to shove against her—the need to see her body. She schooled her voice. "I understand."

"I hope you do." The demon walked to the empty window. "So sad that they stole your body." She ran her hand around the edge of the opening. "You were one of my favorites, you know."

It took every ounce of Rell's control not to launch herself at Sha-hera. Like a menagerie to be ogled, these Bringers were forever preserved for the benefit of the king, and she had been one of them.

When she didn't reply, Sha-hera turned and scowled. "Doesn't my praise please you?"

"Very much." She forced a smile.

The demon seemed to relax. "As it should."

Rell shivered and rubbed her arms. "I'm getting cold."

"Ah yes." Sha-hera nodded. "Your kind do."

"My kind?"

The demon pivoted and headed toward the passage without answering her question. "Remember what I said, Rell. Know where the true power lies and align yourself."

Sha-hera turned the corner and disappeared.

"You can bet on it, Bane." Rell glanced around, making sure nobody heard her. The frozen Bringers were her only audience.

She shivered again. If Luc and Jade thought they were done with her, they were sadly mistaken.

CHAPTER TWENTY-FIVE

Somebody grabbed Jade and pushed her hair away from her face. A thousand frantic questions bombarded her. The person seemed familiar, the blond hair and green eyes that peered into hers. Hands gently cupped her face. "Jade?"

"Mama?" The fact that she was staring at a face she had thought long buried refused to be understood. She covered the woman's hands. "Mama?"

Warm arms enveloped her, the scent of lavender dredging up her childhood memories. She clung to Willa, pressing her face into her neck and crying. Years of believing her mother to be dead bubbled to the surface. A lonely childhood spent in the caverns of the Shadow World. Her sister, caught between life and death. Like a torrent, all of it poured forth.

Loving words of comfort whispered from Willa, her arms gently rocking Jade as if she were a little girl again.

How long they stood there, she didn't know, but finally the tears slowed. She stepped away from her mother in the twilight and looked at her.

The years had done little to diminish her beauty. Faint lines played at the corners of her eyes, but her skin was as smooth and flawless as Jade remembered. As a child her mother had always reminded her of a fairy. Now she was Jade's angel.

"I can't believe you're alive." Willa pushed a spray of tangled hair out of Jade's eyes. "Saints forgive me, but I thought Siban was lying when he arrived and told me you lived."

Jade smiled. "I can imagine."

Her mother's gaze roamed her face and she cupped Jade's chin in her hands. "You are all grown up." Sadness pinched her features and her voice cracked. "I missed it all."

She covered her mother's hands with hers. "Rell took care of me."

"Rell?" Her features hardened slightly. "You mean Esmeralda?"

Jade nodded. "Did they tell you about her?"

"That she's a Demon Bane? Yes." She lowered her arms and took Jade's hands in hers. "And that she knew I was not dead."

"I was angry at first too, but we can't blame her." Jade gave her hands a squeeze. "She battles unimaginable darkness." She took a deep breath. "I went to release her soul—to send her through the Veil." She shook her head. "But I couldn't do it. Does that make me a bad sister?"

"No." They turned and slowly walked toward the manor. "Both actions make you the best kind of sister."

"I feel like I failed her."

"You brought back her body." Willa looped her arm through Jade's. "We'll figure out what to do next together."

It was the first time the burden of Rell was lifted from Jade's shoulders. Her friends were wonderful, always willing to accept her and help, but her mother was the only one who felt the same pain and betrayal as she did. "Perhaps, after I rest. Terror and torture takes a lot out of a girl."

Willa cursed under her breath and wrapped her arm around Jade's shoulder. "You are a lot like your father and I can see you will put me in an early grave."

Luc's low voice reached her through her riot of emotions, calming her. He was all right, too. Though he'd briefly passed out when they landed, he seemed to be awake and functioning.

Jade pulled back and smiled at her mother. "We'll talk later."

Willa nodded.

Without warning, Rhys lifted Jade into his arms and strode across the grounds toward the house. Willa raced beside them, giving Rhys directions, chattering that everything was going to be fine now that they were together.

Jade leaned against him, resting her chin on his shoulder and glanced back. Delphina and Jacob were helping Luc to his feet, and Siban and Ravyn crouched beside Esmeralda's body. The breath caught in Jade's throat. Would they be able to save her sister?

"Rhys." Her heartbeat quickened. "Rhys, please stop."

He halted and turned to watch Ravyn and Siban. Willa's hand gently caressed Jade's arms as they watched Siban lift and cradle Esmeralda to him, his cheek resting lightly against her forehead. He looked up, their eyes meeting. Without breaking eye contact, he strode past them and into the house.

Rhys told her and Luc that they had been missing for more than a week. The time had seemed much longer when they were being held captive, but now safe within the manor, the experience faded to surreal memories that she wasn't yet ready to examine. Even with Ravyn's healing, exhaustion quickly claimed Jade and once her head hit the pillow, she slept hard. No dreams, no nightmares, just body-healing oblivion.

When she finally awoke, long shadows stretched across the floor of her chamber and the muted light of the afternoon sun filled her room.

"Thought you were going to sleep the whole day away."

She turned her head. Luc lounged beside her bed, looking decidedly better than the last time she'd seen him. Fresh from a bath, damp tendrils of hair hung around his face. His feet were propped up on the mattress and crossed at the ankle in a relaxed pose.

She wondered how long he had been sitting there. "Have you been watching me sleep?"

He held up his index finger and thumb. "Only for a while."

A dimple dotted his cheek and she was instantly struck with the desire to kiss it. "I hope I didn't snore or drool."

He held up his fingers again. "Just a little."

She gave a little grunt, hoping he was teasing her. She burrowed deeper in the blankets in an attempt to hide the tinge of heat creeping across her cheeks. "Where is everybody?"

"Gathered in the great room. Dinner is in an hour if you're hungry."

She sighed and rolled to her side, propping her head on her hand. "What did you tell them?"

"Everything." He leaned forward and tilted his head as if trying to gauge her well-being, as if more than a little concerned about her. "Well, everything I could remember."

She held his gaze, the mood between them shifting. That was probably inevitable considering what they have been through. There was something intensely personal about facing death with someone. The deep connection that had formed erased everything she thought she knew about him. In its place now sat the man before her, someone who had risked his life to do the right thing.

He gave a strained smile. "Why are you looking at me like that?"

"It's strange, isn't it?" She picked at a thread on the duvet.

"What?"

"How things have worked out. A few weeks ago I tried to kill you. Now I…" She let the statement hang.

He cocked a brow. "Don't hate me?"

That far understated what she felt for him. But how would he react if she told him that somewhere between the night at the chapel and now, she'd fallen in love with him? If he didn't feel the same way, it wouldn't be fair to burden him with yet another Kendal woman's affection and the guilt of not returning it this time.

She attempted a nonchalant smile. "More than don't hate you."

He slid a little farther forward in the chair. "Would you go as far as saying you like me?"

The way he was looking at her made her mouth go dry. She rolled to her back, but continued to gaze at him. Her words came out more serious than she'd intended. "Very much."

Her heart raced when he knelt beside the bed, coming eye to eye with her, and laid his arms on the mattress. He inched his hand toward her until his fingers touched her arm. With the lightest touch he caressed her wrist with a delicate swirling motion. "I'm glad to know you don't hate me." His finger trailed a path along her arm, over her bare shoulder and up her neck, laying a thin line of heat along its course. The blue of his iris darkened and his thumb strummed her cheek. "Very glad."

This felt right, him touching her, looking at her with desire, not malice, and her wanting more. She turned her face and kissed his fingers. His eyes watched her every move. In a daring move she nipped at their tips, making sure to add the gentle brush of her tongue. The words she longed to say still wouldn't come, but she needed him to know she was open to them as a couple. "Me as well."

Her heart fluttered when he leaned in and lowered his mouth to hers. Their lips touched and her breath caught, her eyes closing against the onslaught of desire that washed over her. Only faintly did she register the bed bowing beneath her until Luc's body blanketed hers. His weight was the most glorious thing she'd ever felt. Heavy, pressing, hot.

On instinct she opened her mouth. Luc's tongue slowly swept along her lower lip, his teeth gently tugging before covering her mouth fully. He deepened the kiss, swirling his tongue against hers. Sandalwood and mint teased her nose and the faint hint of wine tingled along her tongue.

Her arms wound around his neck, pulling him closer. There were too many blankets. She needed to be closer. His hand followed the contours of her body and cupped her breast through the thin shift, drawing his thumb across her nipple. She gasped against his mouth and arched into his hand. Nothing had ever felt so amazing, so sinful, so right. The rigid line of his erection pressed between her legs and she struggled to open for him, needing to feel his skin against hers.

A knock at the door jolted her from her building desire. With a frantic shove, she pushed against his chest, using her legs for leverage. Still caught up in the passion, Luc rolled off her and tumbled over the side of the bed. A loud grunt erupted from the floor.

"Sorry," she whispered.

The knock came again. He sat up with a scowl and climbed back into the chair. Trying to hide his erection, he folded his hands in his lap. She grabbed a square decorative pillow and tossed it to him, and then turned toward the door. "Come in."

Willa opened the door a crack and peeked in. The sight of her mother's smiling face filled Jade with happiness. So much had happened, some of the memories blurry. It soothed her to know that her mother had not been a hallucination her exhausted mind had played on her.

Seeing Luc, Willa opened the door wider and came in. "I just wanted to check on you."

Jade stretched, putting on a convincing show of having just awakened. "I'm feeling much better." She patted her stomach. "And hungry."

"Good." Her mother clapped her hands. "Let's get you dressed. Dinner is almost ready."

Luc stood and tossed the pillow on the bed, all traces of his previous affliction gone. "I will meet you ladies downstairs." He walked to the door. "We have a lot to talk about."

The door clicked shut and Jade looked at her mother. Before her courage left her she asked the question that had been burning inside her. "Where were you the night of the attack?" She swallowed the resentment that surfaced with surprising speed. "Why weren't you at the house to help us?"

Willa sat on the edge of the bed but made no attempt to touch Jade. She took a deep breath. "That night, after you'd been put to bed, Timothy McCarty showed up at our house in a frightful panic. His wife was in labor and he'd left her to come fetch me." She toyed with the hemmed edge of her tunic. "There was no reason for me not to go since your father was home. It was a difficult birth and Sarah McCarty didn't deliver until late the next afternoon, but by that time…" Her voice fell to a whisper. "I searched frantically for you, but I know now your sister had already taken you away."

Jade nodded, not mentioning the fact that Esmeralda had known all the time that Willa was alive. She reached out and covered her mother's hand. "It's all right. You couldn't have known."

"I think I went mad for a while." She peered at Jade in a way that felt like sharing a secret. Perhaps her mother had never admitted this to even herself. "I clawed through the ashes until my hands blistered, and when I didn't find you near the house I began searching farther away." She shook her head. "I didn't eat. Didn't sleep. I didn't know how close to the edge of insanity I'd come until Orvis found me."

"Orvis?"

Her mother's face transformed, softening with the glow of love. "Orvis Giles, my savior. I stumbled upon his inn, asking about you and your sister." She smiled and squeezed Jade's hand. "He's a kind man, Jade. I'll always love your father but Orvis breathed life back into me."

The words hurt. It was difficult to understand how anybody could replace her father. He had been bigger than life. "And your children?"

"And the children." She gave Jade's hand a little shake. "Your brothers and sisters. Ten of them."

Jade blinked several times. "All yours?"

"All mine now. Orvis was a widower and five oldest were from that marriage. The five youngest are your half brothers and sisters." She paused. "How do you feel about that?"

Several seconds passed as Jade dissected her feelings. How did she feel about having an entirely new family to get to know? "I'm happy you had somebody to help you and I'm happy to finally have a family, even if it's not with Father."

Willa's smile turned sad. "I know it's a lot to take in, Jade, and I'd never force you to accept Orvis and the children, but I'm so happy you're willing to try." She took a deep breath. "Now the only unfinished business I need to deal with is your sister."

Dread wound its way back into Jade's good mood. Neither Icarus nor Rell would leave things as they were and if Sha-hera had meddled, as Jade was sure she had, they could expect Rell at any time, and more than likely with the Bane following close behind

"It will all work out." Jade hugged her mother. "But now we need to prepare."

CHAPTER TWENTY-SIX

Luc watched Jade pace in front of the hearth, wanting to tell her to sit down. The plan had been for everybody to act normally, go about their business as if they weren't expecting a Bane attack, but that idea had quickly gone by the wayside. The tension seemed to be taking its toll on Jade.

She stopped and scrubbed at her arms. "She's out there. I can feel her."

"Are you certain it's not another demon?" Ravyn asked, slipping a bolt into her crossbow.

"Yes, I've been with Rell long enough to know her irritating bite." She walked to the window and peered out. "What is she doing out there?"

"Waiting," Luc said.

She paced back to where he stood. "For what?"

"Until she's ready to confront you." He stood and took her shoulders in his hands. "Are you ready?"

Jade held his gaze for several seconds. "I have to be."

They'd spent the day preparing the manor for the impending

attack. Jacob had insisted that Delphina move the children to the inner chamber, where there were no windows. Using the instructions Ravyn had deciphered from the tomes, she'd warded the door. After that, she and Jade had cycled through the manor, weaving protection at any opening big enough to allow in the Bane.

Willa called forth her earth magic and cast protective spells around the grounds. Unfortunately, the manor spread for hundreds of acres. Even the gardens surrounding the manor were too big to fully ward. Many spots would not keep out the Bane.

Luc and his father had scoured the outbuildings, scavenging items they would need to construct an effective prison for Rell. After hours of discussing the connection between Esmeralda's lifeless body and her demon form, Ravyn had convinced them that with the help of other Redeemers, there was a possibility they could transfer Esmeralda's soul back into her Bringer body. Both Jade and Willa had only needed to hear this idea once before joining in on the preparations.

To construct a prison strong enough to hold a Bane was a daunting task. Though Luc could estimate Rell's strength, having fought her, he didn't know the full spectrum of her powers. In the end, they rigged an old bird cage–style brig, salvaged from one of Jacob's ships, to hang from the ceiling in the middle of the drying house. Jade and Ravyn had left the cage unwarded. Once inside, the only way for Rell to get free would be for somebody to carry her out. In that same vein, the only way to get her into the cage was for somebody to carry her in. Luc doubted one of them could do the job on his own.

"It will work," he said, holding Jade's gaze. It didn't matter if he believed that or not. She was ready to jump out of her skin at the slightest noise. "Trust us."

"It has to work." The last word rasped out.

He wanted to take her into his arms, but with everybody around, he didn't know how she would react. He opened his mouth, but a shout from the front of the manor cut him off.

"Give me back my body."

Everyone jumped to their feet. Delphina ushered the children into the room and shut the door. With no magical powers to draw on, they would be the most vulnerable. Willa would be next, but hopefully being Rell's mother would stay the demon's hand against her.

"I know you have it!" Anger laced Rell's words. "Sha-hera told me."

"Of course she did." Luc strode toward the front door and flung it open.

Rell waited on the stretch of grass beyond the cobblestone drive, her wings flared. A faint path had been worn on the lawn where she had prowled back and forth. She stopped and glared at him. When Rhys, Ravyn, and Jade joined him, her bravado faltered, but it was Willa who stopped the demon in her tracks.

They needed to draw Rell closer, lure her within the range of their trap. If she sensed it was a trick, they would lose the element of surprise. Now everything was up to Jade and Willa.

Willa stepped toward the demon. "Hello, Esmeralda."

"Mother?" Rell took a step forward, but stopped. "Why are you here?"

"For us." Jade moved to stand beside Willa. "So we can be a family again."

Rell shook her head. "Not us, you and her."

"No, Esmeralda." Willa kept her voice even, using Rell's name to draw her in. "I love you both."

The demon sneered. "You love this?" Rell held her arms out to display her demon form. "Everything Father used to fight against?"

"It's not your fault," Jade said. "We can help you."

For the first time since Rell had barreled into his life, Luc saw real yearning to be accepted. "How—by freeing my soul?"

"Yes, but not by sending you through the Veil." Jade and Willa took another step toward her. "Your body lives."

Willa opened her arms. "Let us heal you and make you a Bringer again."

Rell drifted forward. Only four more feet and she would be where they needed her to be.

"That's not possible." Three more feet. "And I will never be the daughter you lost."

"I don't need you to be the daughter I lost. I need you to be the woman you can be—without the darkness."

Two feet. Luc glanced into the tree, where Siban waited, ready. He'd volunteered to take first shift after dinner and Luc had worried about how he would react when he saw a Bane. Not a few short months ago, Siban had refused to leave Alba Haven. Now here he was confronting the very creatures who had held him captive for nearly two years. Luc could not possibly comprehend the intractability it took for Siban not to slide into insanity, but he did grasp the strength the man possessed.

The Tell stared at the demon, unmoving, as if ready to pounce. Luc glanced away, not wanting to draw attention to the tree and praying that Siban stuck to the plan.

One foot. Rell stopped.

"And if this does not work?" the demon asked.

Neither Jade nor Willa were ready for that question. Their second of hesitation was all Rell needed to know that one way or another, she *would* be rid of her demon form. She crouched, preparing to launch. In a blur of movement, Siban tossed the net over Rell.

The Bane's screeches pierced the night. Luc and Rhys leapt from the steps and tackled her as she thrashed about under the thick tangled webbing. Her clawing talons gouged at the men's arms, but they managed to roll the net more tightly around her and finally pin her arms under the mass of rope.

With Rhys at her feet and Luc at the head, they hefted the net like a game bag and carried Rell toward the outbuilding. Her body convulsed and thrashed like a large fish out of water. The net slipped from Luc's hands, his fingers clutching painfully at the net before Rell hit the ground, her curses spitting at them like venom from a sand cobra. He repositioned her body and secured a more firm finger hold before continuing toward the outbuilding.

Jacob ran ahead and opened the door. "You'll need to get her out of the net first."

"Easier said than done," Rhys grunted when Rell gave a particularly firm kick.

"Watch out for her horns," Luc said over Rell's screams. "Father, we need manacles."

Jacob ducked into the outbuilding while he and Rhys lowered her squirming body to the ground.

"Roll her over so she's face down." Luc straddled her and turned to Jade. "I need you to cut the rope just enough for me to get the shackles around her wrists."

Jacob returned, dragging two thick sets of chains and manacles. Ravyn moved to stand on the other side of Luc and reached for the bonds. Working as a team, Jade cut a small hole in the layers of net near Rell's hands while Luc immobilized her arms. Once finished,

Ravyn took Jade's place and snapped the restraints around the demon's wrists.

"Now her feet." He motioned with his head toward Rhys. "Do the same thing."

Within minutes, Rell had been efficiently restrained and the net removed. To be on the safe side, Luc wrapped several lengths of rope around her chest to prevent her wings from opening. She now sat on the ground, silent and glaring.

Luc crouched in front of her, careful to not get within striking distance. She was still dangerous even though she was bound. "I am going to pick you up and carry you into this building. Inside is a cage where you will be housed until we can attempt to heal your human form."

"And what makes you think your prison will hold me?" Rell hissed.

"Understand this." His gaze held hers. "Once inside, you will not be able to touch anything but the cage that holds you."

Fear flickered in her eyes but disbelief quickly replaced it. "You lie."

"The entire building is sanctified." He didn't bother telling her the details of how it had been done. She didn't need to know the nuances they'd discovered about warding. "If you place one talon on the ground, wall, door, or roof, your body will be incinerated." He flicked an imaginary speck of dust from his sleeve. "I can't say where you would end up, but I guarantee it won't be pleasant."

If she was not already the color, Luc would have sworn her complexion flushed to pale green. "So you wish to torture me now? For payback?"

"You will learn, Esmeralda, that some things you are forced to do are for your own good." He risked her compliance and brushed a lock of hair over her shoulder. "Sometimes they are tough lessons, but ones that change your life."

She made no reply and didn't fight him when Jacob and Rhys helped Luc hoist her over his shoulder. He waited for her sharp fangs to sink into his back, but she did nothing, no attempt to get free, not a single complaint, not even a snide remark.

Jade and Ravyn held the cage steady while he lowered her inside. There was enough room for her and her wings, but no room to expand them. Rhys and Jacob reached through the bars and hauled her backward by the arms, allowing Luc to lock the door. Next Jade removed the rope from around Rell's chest. Never once did the demon utter a word. Her gaze remained focused forward. She refused to look any of them in the face.

Luc released the manacles at her ankles while Rhys unlocked the bands at her wrists. Still she didn't protest, merely rubbed her wrists and leaned against the bars.

Jade approached the cage. "You'll thank us when this is over."

The yellow reptilian gaze slowly moved to Jade, holding for a few seconds, and then refocused on the distant corner. Willa approached, but from the sizable distance she kept, Luc knew she was struggling with coming to terms with her Bane daughter.

"I do love you, Esmeralda." Willa sniffed. "I don't know what I'll do if I lose you again."

Rell swallowed, clenching and unclenching her jaw. She may have been using silence as her defense, but Luc thought perhaps her mother's words were having an effect.

"Rhys!"

Siban's shout cut through the tense moment. Fire flared along Luc's arms and instantly the Bringers broke into action.

Luc barreled out the door, shouting over his shoulder to

whomever remained. "Lock her in."

Screeches pierced the darkening sky. Luc skidded to a stop, the sight of swarming demons nearly paralyzing him. Jacob grabbed his arm and pulled him along behind him. "We need to move."

A demon swooped, narrowly missing Jade. In one smooth action, Luc pulled the axe free from his waistband and threw it. With a heavy thud, the blade buried deep in the demon's back, knocking it out of the sky. The creature hit the ground hard and exploded. A million sparks gathered and swirled, the first signs of a fiery vortex.

The smell of sulfur burned Luc's nose, the heat from the flaring cloud searing his eyes. He grabbed Jade's arm and scooped up the axe, dragging her away from the increasing pull of the spiraling band of fire. "Run!"

Everybody raced toward the manor, where Siban stood ready. Jacob and Siban would be at a disadvantage not having been brought to full power, but each could still be effective in the fight. The plan was that Jacob, Willa, and Delphina would defend the manor and give any aid they could, while Jade and Siban fought from within the warded areas.

"So this was Sha-hera's plan," Luc said. "To follow Rell and trap us all in one place."

"We knew something was coming," Jade picked up a crossbow and a quiver of arrows. "I just didn't expect this many Bane."

"It looks like her entire army," Ravyn said.

Rhys scanned the sky. "At least now we have an idea of how big her forces are."

The beast inside Luc roared with frustration at being kept contained. He shook his arms. "My dragon is being quite insistent."

"I know what you mean." Rhys turned to Siban and Jade. "Stay within the protected areas and send as many Bane as possible back to the Shadow World. Hopefully the warded weapons will have some effect on the demons."

Siban turned and sprinted toward one of the hidden caches, but Jade hesitated, her eyes fixed on Luc. "Don't be a hero."

He pulled her to him and kissed her. Desperation and fear poured from her. She snagged her fingers in his tunic, clinging to him, and returned the kiss. But the moment was short lived. A demon dove and Ravyn spun, blasting the creature out of the sky.

Luc released Jade. "Don't you be a hero either."

She nodded, stepping away from him. Her stare drank him in for another second before she spun and dashed for the front of the manor.

Terror at the thought of losing her ripped through him. He *would* be back for her.

Luc tore his gaze from her departing back and turned. Rhys and Ravyn were already changing. The claws of Rhys's black dragon pawed the ground, shredding the grass beneath them. Gigantic wings snapped outward and stretched, ready for flight. It swung its head to watch Ravyn, who was racing across the yard.

Luc had never seen her change and the sight was more glorious than he could have imagined. Ribbons of fire trailed from behind her, spreading orange light that crackled and popped along the ground. Demons swooped but banked away from her as if they had been burned. Fire sizzled along her body with a million glowing sparks. The flames flared and enveloped her like the closing petals of a flower. An instant later a phoenix burst forth and took to the sky.

Rhys pushed off the ground, lifting his immense body with deceptive ease. Luc's own dragon cried out again for release. He gave over, letting the creature take control. White heat coursed through his veins, bringing with it the transition. Power filled every inch of his body and any fear he'd been harboring slipped away.

His vision shifted and the Bane transformed from winged creatures to colors and shadows. Some possessed small white orbs that pulsed at the center of their chests, while others harbored a more muted glow, but devoid of the white light. Either way, the demons were easy to track.

He launched himself into the sky, nearly colliding with a diving Bane. Without thought, he spewed a stream of fire at the demon, the action thundering through his head. The monster banked to the left, narrowly missing being incinerated. Screams and intermittent flashes of fire filled the sky. Where he and Rhys directed their attacks through jettison blasts, Ravyn rose high in the air and spiraled downward, laying a trail of fire across the sky. Demons propelling too quickly dove into her line of fire and exploded into a million sparks. The embers swirled, collecting into a spinning vortex and smashing into the ground to burrow and disappear. The acrid smell of singed flesh and sulfur mingled with the scent of charred wood and earth.

So focused on the demon circling to outmaneuver him, Luc didn't see the attack until it was too late. Claws tore across the thick hide of his dragon. Stinging gashes burned along his flank. Red rage filled him, blotting out all human control. The dragon whipped his tail around and slammed the demon with its jagged spikes. The talons dragged across his back, shredding the flesh as they lost their hold. A solid blast of fire dispatched the Bane, sending it back to the Shadow World.

Pain ripped through Luc and the dragon roared. He struggled to maintain control of his creature. The beast balked, wanting nothing more than to destroy everything in the sky. This was the delicate balance. The power of the dragon melded with the compassion and reasoning of the man.

Stinging heat radiated across the animal's back with each twisting move it made. Luc focused his awareness on the injury and sent his healing consciousness to the wound. Flesh mended and the thick hide knitted, delivering immediate relief.

The dragon spiraled toward the ground, the wind deafening in his ears. He swerved to avoid a fiery funnel cloud. Flames licked along his underbelly but could not penetrate the dense scales.

Luc's attention snapped to Jade. She raced across the front lawn. A demon trailed her, skimming no more than three feet off the ground in pursuit. She dove and rolled, releasing a bolt from the crossbow. The arrow whistled through the air and lodged in the demon's shoulder, the force nearly jerking its body to a complete stop in midair. Its talons bit into the earth and the creature toppled, rolling toward Jade.

The Bane growled, struggling to gain a kneeling position, and yanked the arrow out of its shoulder. Jade scrambled backward, her panicked breathing registering with Luc's heightened hearing. The demon rose to its feet and advanced on her. The warded weapons weren't working as expected.

Luc's dragon body twisted and dove, extending its hind legs. Jade's gaze cut upward and her eyes widened. Before the demon could turn and avoid the attack, the dragon speared the Bane from behind with razor sharp talons. A tortured cry ripped from the demon. The dragon flipped the creature forward, tossing it into the sky. Not giving the Bane a chance to spread its wings and right its tumbling course, the dragon spewed, engulfing the creature in flames. With a brilliant burst, the demon exploded.

Luc sent an order to the dragon to return to Jade, who had

repositioned herself on the top step at the front of the manor. A line of crossbow bolts lay in a line beside her. White light glowed from her hands and her mouth moved rapidly. The ancient healing words she uttered caressed his ears.

Two demons dove toward her, obviously thinking she was an easy target. Again the dragon twisted, bashing its tail into the closest Bane. The hard spikes sunk into the much softer flesh, causing the demon to stick. With a quick spin, the dragon catapulted into the sky.

Undaunted, the second demon continued its attack on Jade. Panic raced through Luc and the dragon roared when it was unable to turn fast enough to stop the diving creature. Jade leveled the crossbow, but didn't shoot. Luc's mind screamed for her to release the bolt. Just as the dragon was about to fold its wings and dive, the demon smashed into what looked like a net of fire.

Its body writhed and flames lapped along its body, bubbling the mottled green flesh. Jade loosed the arrow, delivering the blow directly into the creature's heart. Instead of immediately exploding, threads of brilliant white light tore through its body. With the dragon's vision, Luc could see the dark shadows surrounding the white orb burn away. When the stream of light connected with the pulsing circle, the demon shattered into a million white sparkles. Unlike the times they blasted the Bane with fire, this demon didn't spiral into a vortex. As each spark blinked out of existence, the almost inaudible tinkle of a bell chimed.

Without hesitation, she notched another bolt, ready for the next attack. The dragon veered and shot upward. If she didn't move beyond the ward, Jade would be safe. More Bane had arrived. The sky swelled with demons. As much as he didn't want to admit it, the three of them were outnumbered.

Five Bane raced after Ravyn. Even by banking quickly in a tight circle, she couldn't incinerate all of the demons. Rhys battled three on his own, defending with his tail, talons, and fire. Though maintaining the advantage, if the attacks increased, he would be overtaken.

Out of the dark, Sha-hera and two of her succubi dove at him. He laid a trail of fire, but they darted around it to continue their assault. The two demons flanked Sha-hera and then broke off in an effort to cut him off. They were faster and more skilled than most, probably Sha-hera's seconds in command.

The demons dove, crisscrossing paths and sinking their talons into whatever part of the dragon's flesh they could. Their high-pitched screeches pierced his head, setting him off balance. Though the dragon landed a few solid hits with his tail, it could never deliver a direct hit of flames. Their cackles echoed around him with each missed attack he attempted.

Luc turned control over to the beast. This was what his Shield powers were meant for and why the dragon existed. Its calculations for attack flickered along Luc's awareness, too fast to comprehend all the details, delivering just enough to let him know what the dragon intended.

It folded its golden wings against its sides and dove. Two of the demons followed him, but Sha-hera held back, her skills as a warrior obviously sensing the trap. He flared his wings twenty feet off the ground and swooped toward Jade. Unsure how high the ward extended, he skirted as low as he could, aiming for the front of the manor.

Never slowing in their pursuit, the demons spiraled and dove to keep up. To the dragon Jade shined like a brilliant white light, but within Luc's consciousness, he saw her human features. She looked up from where she knelt, her eyes widening, and then understanding dawned. She snatched an arrow from the ground, shoving it in the pocket of her tunic, and leveled the crossbow in his direction.

The ground four feet beneath him raced past and the distance between him and Jade quickly narrowed. Still she remained motionless and ready. Ten feet from where she stood, the dragon extended its legs and pushed off the earth, at the same time thrusting its wings downward. Their tips dug into the soft ground, providing the needed push to quickly rise. The creature soared over the top of the manor, its talons raking the timber shakes of the roof. The demons followed directly in its path, but where the dragon was free to pass through the ward, the Bane slammed into it like a brick wall. The fiery net extended beyond them and Jade dispatched each demon with a direct shot to the heart.

Twice more they were able to run the same plan, but it didn't take long for the Bane to catch on. As if tired of all the cat and mouse antics, the Bane converged on Rhys, Ravyn, and Luc, swarming them like angry bees. They weighed down his dragon's wings, forcing him toward the ground. Jettisons of fire lit the sky and the thunderous roar of two full dragons reverberated through the night. No matter how the dragon thrashed, it could not get free of the teeming demons. Movement became impossible and all hope of escape seemed lost when the sky erupted in a blaze.

Fireballs pelted the demons holding Luc and instantly they exploded. Screeches filled the night, the Bane releasing him to escape the onslaught. Luc crashed to the ground, his gigantic body tumbling tail over head, gouging a deep furrow as he slid. Unhurt, he climbed to his feet and searched the sky. Dragons battled the Bane; not just Rhys, but Shields he'd never seen before. There must have been fifteen, but the exact number was hard to gauge.

A black dragon circled down to land heavily at the corner of the grounds. Another red Shield alighted to the left of him at the corner and a large blue dragon settled at another corner, creating a lopsided triangle. The compulsion to join them pushed into Luc's mind. Unsure what to do, he once again gave full control to the dragon.

By taking its place at the final corner, the position of the four dragons created a square that encompassed the manor. The black dragon lifted his snout toward the sky and blew. The red and blue dragons did the same, shooting a stream of fire into the air. More compulsion to comply rippled through Luc and the dragon. As he blew, streams of flames branched out and converged, creating a dome of fire over the manor.

Several Bane attempted to crash through the protection, only to be incinerated in the fiery web. Those demons caught inside were easily dispatched by the remaining Shields. Shrieks from the demons echoed across the open expanse of the grounds. Ash and sparks filled the sky. Though a few lingered, most of the creatures shot into the night with what looked like no intention of returning. The four dragons ceased the fire and the remaining Bringers pursued the last of the Bane, sending them back to the Shadow World either by fire or fear.

Luc struggled for dominance, demanding that the dragon relinquish control. Praise of the creature's keen fighting skills did much to soothe its pride and garner its cooperation. His body shifted in one smooth move, transitioning dragon back into man. The lightness of his limbs was somewhat disconcerting at first, but after a minute he felt like himself again.

Rhys landed and shifted, followed by Ravyn. One by one the unfamiliar dragons landed, morphing back into men. Some he recognized. Some were unfamiliar to him. Siban and Jade raced toward them to join the crowd. Jade skidded to a stop next to Luc and he wrapped his arm around her waist, pulling her to him. Without pause, she wound her arms around him and stared into his face.

"Are you all right?" Her eyes were wide with worry.

"Fine. And you?"

"Fine." She gave him a squeeze. "Now."

He smiled, their connection filling and finally setting the last missing stone of his life in place. This is where he was supposed to be—with Jade, as a Bringer, fighting the Bane. Though the series of events had started over a decade ago, tonight his journey had coalesced and created a future.

The last dragon landed and transformed.

"Sir Gregory," Ravyn said. "What a pleasant surprise."

A wry smile pulled at his lips. "I did say I was going to visit the manor soon, Lady Ravyn."

"You picked a most fortunate time," Rhys said, grasping the man's forearm. "Though I now have many questions I hope you will answer for us."

The front door of the manor slammed open and Jacob, Willa, and Delphina raced across the lawn to join the group, while the children hovered in the entry.

"Sir Gregory," Jacob panted. "If I hadn't seen it with my own eyes, I never would have believed it."

"Perhaps it would be best if we went inside," Gregory said. "There is much to discuss." His gaze tracked around the group. "And someone who wishes to join our cause waits inside."

CHAPTER TWENTY-SEVEN

"I'd like to check on Rell first." Jade twined her fingers with Luc's, hoping he'd offer to come without her asking. "Make sure she's all right."

"Rell?" Sir Gregory asked.

Jacob slapped him on the back. "We've got more to discuss than you think."

"I'll go with her and we'll meet you inside," Luc said.

"May I join you?"

The group pivoted to face the feminine voice. Shock rippled through Jade as the white veiled figure approached. She glanced at Luc. His brow was furrowed, obviously as surprised as she was by the appearance of the Order's Superior.

"Ascendant Meran?" Ravyn's gaze darted to Gregory and back.

"You were supposed to wait inside," he said.

The Ascendant glided past him to stand next to Jade. "I'm needed here."

Jade shifted to the left, to make room for her. Luc laid his hand on her hip and tugged her toward him. The firm foundation of his body pressed against her back, grounding Jade with the reality that he would not leave her.

Sir Gregory glared at the Ascendant but finally conceded to her wishes.

"We will meet you inside after we check on Jade's sister."

With confused glances but no argument, the rest of the group made its way to the manor. The Ascendant faced her and Luc, holding her arm out in the direction of the outbuilding.

"Shall we?"

A dozen questions flittered though Jade's mind. Why was a Superior of the Order at the manor and how did she know about Rell? She bit her tongue, hoping they would get the answers after they rejoined the group.

About fifteen yards from the outbuilding, the grating irritation of the Banes' presence bit. Jade slowed. The Ascendant stopped, giving her arms a shake.

"Something is off," Luc said.

"There's another Bane here." The woman scrubbed her arms and looked at Jade. "That's not just your sister's presence I feel, correct?"

Jade shook her head. "No, there's definitely another demon." They crept forward until the building came into view. Perhaps a demon had been injured in battle and hadn't been able to escape. Or perhaps Sha-hera had returned to claim Rell. A movement caught Jade's attention and she pointed. "There."

The demon paced in front of the outbuilding door, searching the front. Jade's blood ran cold.

"Icarus." She made no attempt to whisper the word.

He pivoted and glared at them. "Where is she?"

Luc stepped forward. "Some place where you can't reach her."

Again Icarus turned and held his arms out, running them back and forth in front of the door. His fingers hovered at the plank that barred the door, as if sensing his inability to touch it. Jade tensed. If the ward didn't hold, he would free Rell and she would be lost to them.

The demon inhaled and laid his fingers against the metal handle. His body jolted and he yanked back his hand, stumbling away from the door.

"You can't have her." Jade moved to stand beside Luc. "We know about the bodies and we're going to heal her." Her voice held more conviction than she actually felt about what they were going to attempt.

Icarus slowly pivoted. No longer an unreadable mask, his expression radiated confusion and desperation. He massaged his left hand with his right. "What bodies?"

"The ones we found in the Shadow World. The Bringers," Luc said.

The demon cocked his head and Jade could tell he didn't know what they were talking about. "Where in the Shadow World did you find these bodies?"

Jade glanced at Luc. If the demon didn't know, she certainly wasn't going to tell him. The firm set of Luc's jaw told her he thought the same thing.

He looked back at Icarus. "Ask Sha-hera."

The demon's eyes flared at the mention of the succubus. "She knows of these bodies?"

Jade nodded.

"And," he said, inhaling as if reining in his rage, "she freed you?"

"No," Luc said. "But she did allow us to escape."

Jade couldn't repress the snort of laughter. After everything that had happened, she'd grown numb to danger, and facing down Icarus on warded ground seemed like the safest thing she'd done in weeks. The urge to poke the sleeping lion was irresistible. "She seems to have it out for you. Said the king would be interested in knowing you'd held us prisoner."

She thought that tidbit of information would infuriate him, but instead, Icarus ignored her jab. "This body you found." He paused. "It is Rell's human form?"

His question was asked with such open vulnerability that Jade was loath to refuse him an answer. "Yes."

Ascendant Meran stepped forward. She looked tiny compared to Icarus's massive frame, but the look on his face told Jade that he feared her more than she feared the demon.

She stopped several yards from him. "What do you seek?" She pointed toward the building. "Not Rell." She inched forward and he retreated a step, his reptilian eyes rounding. "But you want something."

"Ascendant Meran." Luc took a tentative step. "It's not safe."

She ignored him and continued to close the distance between her and Icarus. Mere feet separated them. Jade's fingers itched to be holding her bow and arrows. To finally put down the demon.

Meran halted within reach of Icarus. His eyes bore into her. Tension rippled through Luc's body and he shifted as if preparing to attack. Icarus paid no attention to Jade or Luc but kept his gaze riveted on the woman.

"You carry a great burden," her voice whispered. "Not right. Not as it should be."

The Ascendant reached for Icarus and ran her hand along his arm much as one would do to calm a spooked horse. Like a stone statue, he let her hand caress him.

"So dark." She stepped closer and gripped his bicep. "So alone."

Luc took another step forward, his action drawing Icarus's stare. Yellow eyes swirled to silver. Jade squinted, certain they glowed, but just as quickly the silver faded back to gold.

The demon pulled his arm from her grip and crept backward. "I will be watching you."

His gaze slid to the Ascendant and for a second he looked like he would say something more. Instead, he spread his wings and launched into the sky.

The fiery burn faded, leaving only the familiar rub of Rell's presence.

Jade walked to where Meran stood, unmoving. "Ascendant, are you all right?"

For a few seconds she didn't respond, but finally she turned. "Yes. I'm fine."

Jade stared at her for a few seconds, knowing what she was feeling, understanding how imperative it was to rationalize the debilitating desolation. "It doesn't go away."

Pale blue eyes peered at her. "What doesn't?"

"The darkness. You will never forget it. There is nothing that can wash it away and forever you will know that this is what the demons...what my sister—what Icarus—lives with...always." Jade gave a heavy sigh. "It is a fate worse than death."

Meran rubbed her arms and swallowed hard. "I never knew."

That was all that needed to be said—the only thing that really *could* be said after one had touched the dense hopelessness. Jade said nothing more, but walked to the door and lifted the brace.

Rell was there. Her back faced them and she made no move to turn around.

"Are you all right?" Jade asked.

Silence.

"Sha-hera attacked with her army." Jade glanced at Luc.

Still no reply.

One of Rell's legs dangled over the edge of the cage, swinging back and forth with tiny kicks. The impulse to go to her pushed against Jade. Her sister seemed so forsaken, as if she had nothing left to hope for. There were no words that could console her. Until they healed or released her, she would more than likely remain angry and despondent.

Jade sighed and turned away. "Let's go."

The Ascendant wrapped an arm around Jade's shoulder. "All will be well."

No longer surprised by the other woman's actions, she nodded. "Thank you."

Luc relocked the building, and the three of them moved wordlessly toward the manor. The night seemed oddly quiet in comparison to the battle that had raged less than an hour before. Cool air brushed Jade's face and the intermittent glow of lightning bugs dotted the darkness as they did every night, oblivious to the monumental events of the evening.

"Sir Gregory, now there's a surprise," Luc said, disrupting the companionable silence.

Both Jade and the Ascendant smiled at his attempt at casual conversation.

Jade shook her head. "I did not see that coming."

"Oh yes," Meran said. "He's full of surprises."

All eyes turned toward them when they entered the great hall.

"Sir Gregory was just telling us the most remarkable thing," Ravyn said.

Jade noted that her friend didn't sound all that pleased.

"Really?"

"Yes," Ravyn continued. Her back was stiff and her hands lay folded in her lap. "It seems Sir Gregory and all his men are Bringers." She tapped her index fingers together in rapid succession. "Not just mixed-bloods or Bringers who have been brought to full power, but real, live, from-the-other-side-of-the-Mystic-Arch Bringers."

Jade's mouth fell open, her mind trying to wrap itself around the ramifications.

Luc voiced exactly what Jade was thinking. "Where the bloody Saints have you been while we've been out battling the Bane?"

Gregory cocked a brow at Luc and his men shifted uncomfortably, their eyes darting to each other.

Rhys coughed and sniffed, obviously covering a laugh. "In the interest of preventing you from sticking your foot any further in your mouth, I should tell you that Sir Gregory has informed us he is the rightful heir to the Bringer throne."

Luc's gaze darted around the group. "Him? King?"

"Rightful heir," Gregory corrected.

"But I thought Ravyn's father was king?" Luc asked.

"A lie told by Vile to disarm Ravyn. Lord Mayfield was my most trusted advisor. Many times he acted in my stead." His voice softened. "He was the father I never had."

Jade glanced at Ravyn, wondering what her friend was thinking. She knew a bit about the jealousy of finding out that other children had received her parents' love and attention. Ravyn's posture relaxed and she smiled at Sir Gregory. The kindness that radiated from her expression made Jade feel guilty for the twinge of envy she'd felt after hearing Willa had another family. She looked at her mother, who was staring at her. An expression of understanding played at Willa's mouth. None of that mattered now. She returned the smile.

"Your mother," Gregory continued, "was my strongest Oracle."

"Oracle?" Rhys asked. "I'm not familiar with this term."

"An Oracle possesses all the powers of the Bringers—Shield, Redeemer, and Tell. They also see beyond this dimension."

"Spirits," Ravyn added.

Sir Gregory smiled. "Among other things, but yes. Oracles are rare." He leaned forward and rested his elbows on his knees. "You are an Oracle, Ravyn."

Luc moved to an empty chair and sat, pulling Jade down on his lap. "Well, that explains a lot."

Rhys nodded. "Yes, it does. This is why Vile wants her so badly."

"Absolutely. An Oracle is the only person who can open the Abyss of Souls."

Jacob bristled. "Then we must protect her at all costs."

"Yes," Gregory said. "It would be the end of the Bringers if Vile controlled the Abyss." His gaze slid to Rhys. "You may already be aware that Oracles are difficult to…manage."

Quiet laughter rippled around the group.

"Excuse me," Ravyn said. "I am not difficult."

"You are," Luc said.

She glared at him.

"I mean no disrespect, Lady Ravyn." Gregory ran his fingers through his black chin-length hair and glanced at the Ascendant. "You come by it honestly."

The Superior propped her hands on her hips and glared at him. Though all that could be seen were her eyes, it was quite enough to get her displeasure across. The attention of the group turned toward the Ascendant. After a few seconds, she raised her hand and unhooked the veil that covered her face, letting it fall.

A collective gasp filled the room. Under her lip ran a blue-black tattoo exactly like Ravyn's. Something else registered with Jade. Though the woman's complexion was lighter and her brows more brown than black, she looked remarkably like Ravyn.

"You're her sister." The words popped from Jade's mouth. Ravyn's gaze snapped to her. Jade pointed at the unveiled woman. "She's your sister."

All eyes turned back to the Ascendant. Ravyn looked at Meran and rose. "Is it true?" Ravyn asked.

The Ascendant nodded. "Yes."

As if she was afraid she'd break the delicate thread of destiny that had just given her a living, breathing family, Ravyn moved forward and wrapped her arms around her sister. Meran returned the hug with surprising gusto.

"Why reveal this now?" Rhys said.

The women separated but remained holding hands. He stood and ushered them to his seat. They crowded together next to Willa.

"It's a long story, so let me first give you a bit of history," said Sir Gregory. "The battle for the Bringer throne has been ongoing for over a thousand years. After my father died, my half-brother disappeared, which meant I became next in line for the throne, but I was too young to rule." He leaned back in his chair, resting his hands in his lap. "I won't bore you with the saga of regaining the throne, but after I came of age, I decided to reopen the Arch and bring home our people. What we found was that the Bane had returned and our people were dead or missing."

"Why not gather an army and put down the Bane once and for all?" Luc asked.

"That had been our plan, but unfortunately we were unable to return through the Mystic Arch."

"Why?" Jade asked, getting caught up in his story.

"Only the rightful heir can open the portal," Gregory said.

Luc's gaze narrowed. "But aren't you the rightful heir?"

"I was." Gregory hesitated. "On the other side of the portal."

"But how can that be?" Rhys asked.

"There's only one answer. My half-brother is still alive and somewhere on Inness." He gave a heavy sigh. "I've been trying to find him, but have had no luck."

"All right, back to my original question," Luc cut in. "Where have you been while we've been battling the Bane?" The corner of Luc's lip curled up. "Besides holding court at Illuma Grand."

"Luc." Jacob's voice was full of warning.

Jade slid her hand into his, giving him silent support.

"It's all right, Jacob. It's a valid question." Gregory sat forward in his chair. "We've been waging a quiet war, positioning the Bringers we know we can trust, and sniffing out others. We've infiltrated many areas—Illuma Grand, the Order, and key cities across the land." He waved toward Jade and Luc. "That's how we knew about your escape from the Shadow World."

Rhys stood and paced in the space behind the chairs. "How many Bringers total are with you?"

Sir Gregory's stare was unwavering. "One hundred."

"One hundred!" Luc leaned forward, nearly pushing Jade from his lap.

"If Vile knows I am here, he will move against us and our efforts will have been for naught. Until we were ready to strike, I had to stay low."

"What about tonight?" Siban asked. "Why show yourself now?"

Jade turned to face him. She hadn't noticed the Tell when they'd entered the hall. Even though he leaned against the corner wall, his stance still emanated barely-maintained control. His eyes held hers for several seconds before cutting back to Gregory. She returned her attention to the conversation.

Sir Gregory flicked his head toward Ravyn. "She alerted me first."

"What did I do?" she asked.

Gregory ran his index finger from his lower lip to his chin, indicating her tattoo. "I wager you bear all three marks of the Bringers, correct?"

Her mouth dropped open but she snapped it shut. "Yes. How did you know?"

His eyes drifted to settle on Meran. "She bears the three marks as well."

Ravyn looked at her sister.

"We are what is called The Trilation." Meran's thumb rubbed small circles on Ravyn's palm. "Three to battle the darkness."

"Three?" Ravyn glanced to Sir Gregory and back to Meran. "There's another?"

"Yes." Meran smiled. "Three sisters. I am the youngest, you are the middle child, and Juna is the eldest."

"Juna," Ravyn said the name slowly and looked at Gregory. "She was at Illuma Grand. I saw her."

He nodded. "You and she favor your mother."

"Practically look like twins," Meran added. "Though I think she's more stubborn."

Rhys snorted. "That's hard to believe."

Ravyn glared at him. "I'm not that bad."

"Yes you are," Luc added unhelpfully.

Questions bubbled inside of Jade. The revelations of the evening were too vast to understand completely. "And there's another," Jade blurted. The entire group turned to look at her. "In the Shadow World."

"She's right," Luc added, all traces of humor gone. "There is a woman—in the ice. She looks just like Ravyn, only older."

"I assure you it's not Juna," Sir Gregory said. "And there are only three sisters."

"You say the woman is older?" Ravyn asked.

"Yes." Jade brushed her fingers against her temple. "Her hair was touched with gray."

Ravyn turned to Gregory. "Could this woman be our mother?"

Instantly, Rhys was behind her, placing his hands on her shoulders in a show of support. Though it was vital they have the information, Jade almost regretted giving her friend what might be false hope.

"I don't see how," Gregory said. "Surely I would have known if she was still alive."

"Not necessarily." Jade's words came out cold, their meaning clear. "I've learned the Bane are capable of many deceptions." Ravyn appeared calm and accepting of what she was being told. Maybe it was her Tell powers that allowed her to understand the situation, but Jade had no such gifts. "Perhaps it's best to assume the worst when it comes to the demons."

"But if she is our mother, and she was a powerful Oracle, why didn't the Demon King use her to open the Abyss?" Meran said.

Gregory smirked. "First, because your mother would have found some way to foil his plan, of this I have no doubt. But another reason is that for all his knowledge of the Bringers, Vile doesn't know everything. It takes three Oracles to open the Abyss, the Trilation. It is a secret the royal family shares with only their most trusted." He looked around the room. "I feel confident after everything that's happened, my decision to share this information is sound."

Ravyn met his gaze. "Then my sisters and I can command the army of souls?"

"Perhaps, or you may never be faced with that decision," Gregory said.

"Let's pray not." Meran gave a tiny shiver and rubbed her arms. "The very thought gives me nightmares."

"We need not deal with this now." Rhys massaged Ravyn's shoulders and she placed her hands over his. "But I think it's obvious what our next step should be."

Jacob provided the answer. "The Shadow World."

Rhys nodded. "We must know what we're facing."

"Yes." Luc's hand rested firmly against Jade's hip, his fingers curling into her flesh. "It's time we take this war to the demons."

Silence stretched through the room. Jade's stomach roiled at the thought of reentering the Shadow World, of battling the Bane and perhaps dying. The weight of their future pressed too heavily around her. Not wanting to think about what would be needed of her, she struggled to lighten the oppressive mood.

"Have you always known about Ravyn?" She asked the question of Meran, but it was Gregory who answered.

"I have, but Ravyn and Meran were unaware of their connection or each other's existence. For their own safety, we separated the girls when they were very young. Both were sent to the Order to serve because on warded ground they would be unreachable by the Bane." He gave an apologetic smile. "Or so we thought. Brother Powell was a miscalculation."

"Luckily, Rhys was there to save me." Ravyn glanced up, her expression filled with love.

"Yes," Meran said. "We are so thankful for you, Rhys."

He shifted in his chair. "I still didn't prevent her from being kidnapped."

"Nor did we," Gregory said. "Actually, it was Ravyn seeing Juna that gave Powell the opportunity to abduct her. I did not pick up on his presence and that is something I will never forgive myself for."

"It wouldn't have mattered." Ravyn looked at Gregory and then Rhys. "If not then, he would have found another time to take me. He was driven."

"What about Juna?" Jade asked, wanting them to get back on the subject.

Gregory sighed, as if mustering great patience. "Even as a child Juna had a mind of her own. She was four when your parents were killed and she refused to be cloistered within an abbey."

Meran smirked. "I've been told she climbed a tree and tied herself to the highest branch, refusing to come down until Gregory agreed to keep her."

He nodded. "Like I said—stubborn."

"Where is Juna now?" Willa asked.

"She had some business to finish up." Meran's gaze landed on Jade. "But she'll be arriving tomorrow."

The woman's look made Jade uneasy and her question came out more suspiciously than she'd intended. "Why?"

"Jade," Willa said. "Don't be rude."

She opened her mouth to defend herself but her mother's expression brooked no argument. She harrumphed and leaned back against Luc, crossing her arms. "I was just asking," she mumbled.

"She's right to inquire." The Ascendant stood and moved to stand beside Siban. She turned and faced the group. "We would like your permission to try and heal Esmeralda." Though she looked at Willa, the question seemed to be asked of everybody. "There are other Redeemers besides Ravyn, Juna, and me. Jade, we would like you to help."

Luc's hand ran up her back and caressed her shoulders. She slowly turned her head and peered at him. He neither encouraged nor offered her advice. This was a decision she had to make. Would she be able to control her powers? And even if she could, what would she do if the healing didn't work? In the Shadow World she'd been unable to free her sister's soul. Would she fail her again?

Hope radiated from Willa, making Jade's decision for her. "Yes, I will help."

Siban shifted away from the corner and stepped forward. "You said there are other Redeemers?"

Meran faced him. She didn't speak at first. Instead, she looked at him as if she were puzzling something out. "There are other Redeemers among those Bringers who followed Gregory through the Arch. All are powerful and I think we have a very good chance of healing her."

Siban gave a single nod, then turned and left.

A tiny kernel of hope sparked inside Jade. Tonight, when the demons had swarmed across the sky, their situation had seemed grim. Now there were a hundred full-blooded Bringers ready to fight and help heal her sister. A thought occurred to her. She turned to Gregory. "You know everything. The language, the history, what we've done right and what we've done wrong. You can teach us what we need to know."

A murmur of approval traveled around the room.

Sir Gregory nodded. "Yes, we can benefit from each other's knowledge. You and Luc can share what you learned from your time inside the Shadow World. Unfortunately, until we find my brother, we are stranded without further aid."

"Then we make every move count," Luc said.

"But not tonight," Jacob said. "There will be enough time for that tomorrow." He stood. "We've had quite a night and I for one am starving. Might I suggest dinner?" He gave Gregory his signature charismatic smile. "Your Highness."

Gregory cocked a brow. "That's a good idea, Jacob. I think a little wine is in order if you've a bottle or two to spare."

"There's always wine to spare."

The group stood and began filing out of the room. Jade rose, her mind trying to wrap around all she'd learned.

Willa approached. "How is Esmeralda?"

Jade bit her bottom lip, searching for the right words. Should she try to soothe her mother by sugar coating her sister's state? Emotional weariness pressed around her. "Despondent. Alone. Feeling betrayed."

Willa wrapped her in a gentle hug. "She could have asked for no better sister than you."

Jade pulled back. "Me? I've done nothing to help her."

Her mother gave her a look of patience. "You have done everything for her. Perhaps after tomorrow you will have even given Esmeralda her life back. You stood by her even though she is a Bane. You loved her even when it was the most difficult."

Jade shifted from foot to foot, uncomfortable with Willa's praise. If she had done any of those things it had been with a lot of grumbling and lamenting her life. "You would have done the same."

"But she didn't allow me to." She gripped Jade's upper arms. "No matter what happens, please believe that you have done everything you could for your sister."

Even though Jade doubted she would never feel that way, she nodded.

Her mother's intense expression relaxed. "Good, now go get cleaned up before dinner."

"All right." ·

She walked toward the stairs. Thoughts swirled through her mind. What would happen from here on out? Across the room Luc talked to Rhys. Her heart skipped a beat. Tonight he had protected her and as she thought back over the last several weeks it became clear that he did care for her. His relationship with Esmeralda had happened a lifetime ago. Since then, their worlds had been tipped upside down and she and Luc had been drawn together.

He turned and followed her ascent, his stare unwavering, just as his presence in her life had been since the day she had stabbed him. She smiled ever so slightly and his expression turned dark. Her breath caught in her throat at his purely male look of desire. She let her hand trail along the railing of the stairs, her fingers lightly grazing the wood. From his determined look, she most certainly would not be sleeping alone tonight.

CHAPTER TWENTY-EIGHT

Though Jade sat quietly with her hands folded in her lap and her legs crossed at the ankle, inside she paced like a caged tiger. Too much had happened tonight to take it all in. She needed to expend the pent up energy swirling through her. Going outside wouldn't be wise, not so soon after the battle. Who knew if the Bane still lurked at the edges of the estate?

There was always visiting Esmeralda, but that wouldn't do any good. Her sister seemed set against any solution that might actually solve their problems. Her weariness of always being at odds with Rell squashed the notion of seeing her tonight. There had been too much fighting. But she couldn't just sit here and do nothing.

Jade uncrossed her legs and stood. At the very least she could pace in her room while she wrestled with the magnitude of how her life had changed. "I think I'll retire."

Luc bolted to a stand. The chair scooted backward, sending the legs scraping along the floor. Everybody turned to look at him. "I'll walk you to your room."

Rhys cleared his throat, but thankfully didn't follow up with a comment.

A warm blush crept up Jade's neck. She avoided the gaze of everybody in the room and focused on Luc. A thrill raced through her. His stare was intense, demanding no argument. Since the battle, he had barely left her side. At first it had been somewhat irritating. Even using the privy was no longer a private affair. Though he didn't accompany her outright, when she exited she found him lurking at the end of the corridor. His hovering prickled her independence, but the fact that he cared tempered her ire.

Not willing to make a scene, she gave a slight nod. Before leaving, she walked to her mother to kiss her good night. She wasn't sure she'd ever get used to that.

Willa stood and opened her arms. Jade stepped into the embrace, her eyes automatically closing in the wake of emotions that washed through her. So many things in her life were perfect now. It almost made the bad situations bearable.

"Would you like me to tuck you in?" Willa asked.

The question brought a smile to Jade's face. No matter how old she got, she'd never tire of hearing those loving words from her mother. She returned the hug and released her. "I'm a little too old for you to keep putting me to bed, don't you think?"

"I've missed a lot of years." Willa's hand slowly rubbed Jade's shoulder, giving her the unspoken comfort and reassurance that she would always remain a part of her life. "And you'll never be too old to tuck in."

"It appears we've been given a second chance to make up for those lost years." For an instant she was a little girl again. Her childhood memory of her mother's loving smile merged with the older, but still beautiful version of her face. Jade hugged Willa again. "All of us."

She loosened her hold and stepped back. Their eyes met and Jade knew her reference to Rell was not lost on her mother. Heartache shadowed Willa's expression, but she gave a strained smile and nodded. Both Rell and her mother bore a lifetime of guilt and anger, but Jade was certain all would be well in the end.

The room had fallen silent. She turned to see all eyes watching their exchange. Her heart swelled at the sight of their compassionate gazes. No matter the outcome with her sister, she knew she'd make it through with their support.

"Good night, everyone." Jade wove her way around the chairs. "Sweet dreams."

A chorus of *sleep tights* and *pleasant dreams* followed her out the door—as did Luc. They walked in silence, but his presence was anything but calm. Awareness of him pushed against her like a blowing cape in the summer breeze. She didn't look at him or attempt to fill the quiet.

At this moment, he was where she needed him to be, alive and attending. They stopped at her door. Jade turned, keeping her eyes on his chest. She opened her mouth to say good night, but Luc reached around her and turned the door handle.

His body crowded hers and she took a step backward, but collided with the door. The smell of soap and wine wrapped around her and she couldn't help but look into his eyes. Passion, protectiveness, hope burned in their depths and she knew she would not deny him access.

Their gazes remained locked as he pushed open the door and backed her into the room. His hand snaked out and grabbed her arm, gently pulling her toward him. He kicked the door shut, pivoting to press her against the solid wood.

Her heart thundered in her chest and her mouth went dry. Luc gripped her wrists and trapped them against the door on either side of her head. There was no resistance in her. Good intentions had finally lost the fight to selfish desires. Whatever came from their encounter, she would accept it. If it was only one night he wanted, then she would give it to him and carry the sweet memory with her always.

He bent slightly, coming level with her face. "Tonight, I nearly lost you."

Jade swallowed, but the action was useless since there was no saliva in her mouth. "I survived."

He nestled his face against her neck and sniffed. "I thought I'd go mad when I saw the demon chasing you."

"I was—" Her voice cracked. "Fine."

"Barely." Luc pulled back to look at her. "Know this, I—" He captured her lips in a brutal kiss. His teeth nipped her upper lip as he pulled away. "Will never—"

He attacked her mouth again, stealing Jade's breath and all her willpower. She fought against his hold, needing to touch him, but he didn't release her. After a torturously wonderful minute he pulled away. Both gasped from the power of the kiss.

"Lose you," he panted.

She stilled her attempts to get free and stared at him, almost too afraid to believe he wanted to be with her. "What are you saying?"

His grip loosened around her wrists and he pulled her to him. Without thought, she wound her arms around his neck, never losing eye contact.

"I don't care if it's proper or not. You're mine." He kissed her again, as if afraid she would argue. With no ability to speak, Jade poured all she would have said into their kiss. He broke their connection to rest his forehead against hers. His voice came out in a rough whisper. "You're mine."

A smile tugged at the corners of her mouth. "Are you sure you know what you're getting yourself into?"

Her comment broke the tension he'd been holding within him. "Well aware." He pulled back and cocked a brow. "So you'll consider staying with me?"

Her face grew serious. He'd chanced so much by telling her he wouldn't let her go, and in her mind there was no question of his sincerity. This wasn't a one-night tryst. His words had been clear. This was for as long as she would have him.

She cupped his face in her hands and shook her head. "I want nothing more than to be with you—forever."

He stared at her and for a second she thought she might have said the wrong thing. Then he moved, swooping her into his arms and crushing the breath from her body. Laughter erupted from Jade as he whooped and spun her around.

"Luc, I'm going to throw up."

He slowed his twirl and lowered her feet to the ground. The room continued to spin but there was no chance that she would fall, locked tightly in his embrace. The joyous mood shifted, as did the look in Luc's eyes. His passionate gaze nearly sizzled her. Her mouth went dry again and she licked her lips. Luc's eyes followed the course of her tongue.

The intensity of his stare and the palpable heat radiating off him sent thrills of anticipation through Jade. She took a step backward. Luc followed. She stepped again, as did he.

"I've waited a long time to touch you," he said.

The bedpost stopped her retreat. She clutched the pole, steadying herself against the onslaught of arousal. Her words came in short gasps. "I seem to recall you touching me quite often.

When you saved me from Icarus. When you carried me through the woods." She lifted her brows. "In the hot pool."

"The hot pools." He growled more than spoke the sentence. Inches separated them. He reached and rubbed his thumb across her nipple. "I've been dreaming of these lovelies since that night."

Her breath hitched and her nipples hardened under his touch. She pressed into his hands. A tight tingle sparked from both breasts, joining below her rib cage to spear its way to her core. He tugged on the tie at the neck of her gown, opening it wide and pushing it over her shoulder to pool on the floor. A thin shift was the only covering between her naked body and his voracious touch. Her eyes closed and she let her head fall back to rest against the post.

His warm palm slid across her back and the other hand covered her breast. Moist heat replaced his fingers. Jade's lids popped open to see Luc's mouth pressed against the thin material, drawing her in. Her pebbled tip ached with each tug.

"Luc." She combed her fingers through his hair, not sure what she wanted to say. "Yes."

He burned a trail of kisses up her neck as he grabbed her shift and lifted the fabric. Without hesitation, Jade raised her arms and let Luc divest her of the barrier. Then it was his turn.

Feeling far bolder than she ever had, she unlaced one side of his jerkin and then the other, spreading the material to pull it over his head. Each clasp unhooked and each lace untied, slowly stripped Luc of his clothes and bared the sculpted muscle to Jade's touch.

She glided her hands across the smooth expanse of his skin. A small patch of golden hair grew in the dip between his chest muscles, descending in a tempting path that disappeared into the waistband of his pants. Her fingers itched to follow that trail.

Twice in her life she'd been with a man—well, boys really.

Neither had had any more experience than she. The encounters were awkward and, in the end, hadn't filled the empty void in her life. She'd stopped looking to men for comfort, seeing what happened to women who continued on that path.

Now she knew why those encounters had fallen flat. Love. Everything was different now. She wanted to give Luc everything. No more hiding. No more doubts. No more denial. With him a lifetime of happiness was hers for the taking.

Jade stepped away to stare at him. Chiseled planes and carved muscle flexed with his every movement. There was no doubt about his arousal. His erection pushed against the front of his pants. She wanted to see him—all of him. Girlish modesty had no place tonight. She wanted to touch him. Know the scent and taste of his skin. Feel his weight as he covered her, driving into her, filling her.

Jade knelt. She gingerly pinched one of the laces holding his pants closed, and pulled. His fingers threaded through her hair, brushing it away from her face. She glanced up. His stare burned and the heaviness of each breath he took sent a rush of power through her. He wanted this. During her years living among men, she'd often seen women use their mouths to bring men pleasure. Until now she'd never understood why they did it when the act wasn't done for money. Heat pooled between her legs at the thought of giving Luc pleasure. Hopefully, this was something no other woman but her would ever give him again.

She pushed his britches down, freeing his erection. Like the rest of his body, it was perfection. The smooth, glistening head beckoned to her. She exhaled, bringing her lips as close to his cock as she could without actually touching him. His penis flinched and his hands tightened in her hair.

"Jade." Luc said her name like a plea.

She melted at the sound, her body needing to please him and her mouth needing to taste him. The very thought of Luc above her sent snaps of heat racing along her skin. She shifted, moving against the desire building between her legs. Her lips parted and without urging, he arched into her.

Moist heat surrounded his cock. Luc watched Jade's mouth slowly take him in and then pull away. The rhythmic movements of her head made him harden even more. Sweet Sainted Ones, but the girl had a mouth made for love. The impulse to thrust nearly overwhelmed him, but he restrained himself. She may not be ignorant in the ways of a man and woman, but she was still rather innocent, of that he was certain. Becoming too demanding might scare her. Besides, they had all night and he had every intention of keeping her awake until the wee hours of the morning.

With one hand she held him in place, working the length of his shaft with her tongue. The other hand circled around his leg and scraped upward, lightly dragging her nails along the backs of his thighs. A shiver spiked up his spine and he gripped her head, giving a subtle push into her mouth.

A low moan of pleasure escaped Jade. She released his shaft and reached around his body to knead his cheeks. The pace of her mouth quickened, her hands controlling his movements as she pushed and pulled him in and out of her mouth. Sparks tickled the base of his cock and spiraled up his shaft.

Too soon.

With gentle pressure, Luc eased his hips back, detaching Jade's mouth. She looked up at him. He could see by her expression that she thought she'd done something wrong. A wicked smile crept across his lips.

"You're too good." He helped her to stand and drew her to him. His erection pressed against her stomach. "And I'm about to shame myself by finishing too early."

She slid her arms around his neck, her breasts flattening against his chest. "And that's bad?"

"Ask me that…" He brushed the white, blond swath of hair from her neck and bent to place a kiss below her ear. "After I'm finished pleasuring you."

Her body quivered under his touch. "Finally, a reasonable plan."

Luc scooped Jade up and laid her on the bed. Smooth, tan skin glistened in the pale golden candlelight. She arched toward him, sliding her hands over her head to stretch like a cat. She was desirable without trying, even when she had been dressed like a boy.

He reached for the foot she glided along her leg and crawled onto the bed. She watched him draw her foot to his lips. A coy smile played at the corners of her mouth and she gasped when he first kissed, and then licked her big toe. She yanked, but he didn't release her.

He traced the tip of his finger up the center of her foot. "Ticklish?"

She squealed and nearly levitated off the bed. "Please, stop." She sat up and tugged against his hold. His finger hovered above her foot again. "Please, Luc."

"I like the way you say my name." The way she pleaded stirred his desire. He bent and pressed a kiss on the inside of her foot and then rested her ankle on his shoulder. "I think I'd like to see you beg for more."

His hand slid up the inside of her thigh, his body following. Jade fell back against the bed as Luc soldiered forward, his finger inching dangerously close to the blond curls between her thighs. Her green eyes widened and her mouth opened as if anticipating what he might do next.

He lowered himself, planting moist kisses along her inner thigh. When he reached her sex he stopped. Stiff limbs quivered under the brush of his warm breath. Unsure whether she would rebound from the bed or coo with pleasure, he lowered his mouth to her wet lips.

A sigh filled with feminine delight drifted from Jade. Luc slid his tongue along her tight slit, which garnered another sigh and an easing of muscles. Her knees fell open, allowing him full access. He flicked the stiff nub that hardened under his ministrations. Jade's hips lifted toward his exploring mouth, asking for more.

He wound his arms around her thighs and pulled her slick lips to him, holding her in place. With a slow thrust, he dipped his tongue inside her and slowly withdrew, licking and spreading her lips. Before returning for another pass, he lingered at her clit, gently skimming and sucking.

She was sweet and untainted. Pure like a honeysuckle wine. Blush pink nipples teased him, bouncing as she rocked against his mouth. He released one leg and glided his hand up her stomach to cup her breast. Jade gasped when he rolled the stiff peak between his finger and thumb, plucking it with the same rhythm he licked and suckled her. She writhed against him, twining a finger in his hair and pulling his mouth more firmly against her.

The action nearly made him lose control. His cock tightened painfully. He released her breast and reached to stroke himself, cupping his balls and massaging. Sweet mother, he needed to be inside her, but not until she climaxed.

He released his cock and focused his attention on the small section around her clit. He slid a finger into her tight sheath, continuing to stroke her with his tongue. Her hips arched and bucked.

"Yes." Small pants replaced actual words. "A—ga—in."

He dipped a second finger inside her and licked. In and out. With each thrust Jade replied in kind, riding his hand and mouth, guiding him with a firm grip in his hair. Her sheath tightened around his fingers and her body arched. A muffled scream ripped from her throat, but she grabbed a pillow and hugged it to her face.

She was so beautiful. The way her body glistened with a fine sheen and ripples of pleasure danced across her skin. Her firm hold turned into a steady push against his forehead. He held onto her thighs, but Jade threw the pillow aside and pushed up on one elbow. With surprising strength, she propped one foot against his shoulder and pushed.

He let her go but gave her a devilish grin. "Sensitive?"

She fell into the pile of pillows at the top of the bed where she lay trying to catch her breath. "Yes, and you continue to torture me."

"Torture?" He crawled to her across the bed. "I've never heard bringing a woman to climax referred to as torture before."

"You're rather ruthless." She drew her knees together. "And unforgiving."

He crept up her body, hovering above her. In an attempt to get away, she pressed further into the mound of pillows, but he had no intention of ending this glorious torment. "Should I tickle you some more?"

Jade tightened into a ball, her eyes rounding with comical fear. "No!"

Trapped beneath him, she was at his mercy. He lightly circled her nipple with his fingertip. "Perhaps I should kiss you again."

Her shoulders relaxed and her back arched toward his tracing finger. He strummed this thumb across her nipple. She bit her lower lip and inhaled sharply. With swooping circles, he spiraled his finger down her stomach. He noticed the way her muscles tensed. Instead of prying her legs apart, which he'd never had to do with another woman and he'd be damned if he'd start now, he glided his hand along the top of her thigh and up his cock.

She watched his movements, her tongue absently sliding along her lower lip. He held the head of his penis and stroked himself.

"Or perhaps I should give you more pleasure." His gaze captured hers. "With this."

With a slow inhale, her chest rose. She dipped her chin, glancing at his cock and back to his face. She shifted, her legs relaxing to lengthen along the outside of his calves. "Perhaps you should."

The intensity of her stare reassured him that she knew what she wanted. For a split second he wondered who was playing the seducer and who was being seduced. With a few simple words, she had him rock hard with need.

"Not like this." He ran his hands up her hips and rolled her over. With a gentle tug he lifted her to her hands and knees. As he draped his body over her back, his erection pressed against her behind. "Like this."

She didn't deny him, though he could tell she was unsure what to do from her rigid posture. In an effort to relax her, Luc straightened and ran his hands along her back. She was so beautiful, creamy perfection. He worshiped her body with his eyes and hands, caressing her outer thighs, along her ribs and up over her shoulders.

He positioned himself so his cock rubbed against her sensitive flesh. Gently, he guided her legs wider, opening her to him. Jade looked over her shoulder, her gaze curious and heated. He brushed the head of his penis against her opening. She pushed back. Placing one hand against her lower back, he slid inch by glorious inch inside her.

His jaw clenched as he fought to control the tight ecstasy that closed around him. She pushed against him and wiggled. Sweet Sainted Mother, if she continued like that he'd never last.

Pride poked at him. He wouldn't let his lust end their encounter early. Again he stroked her, this time separating her lips. With his other hand, he cupped her breast and rolled her nipple between his fingers. She moaned, bending at the elbows to lower down to rest on her forearms and her legs slid further apart.

He pushed into her, working his length in until his hips met her cheeks. He closed his eyes, letting his head loll to the side while he enjoyed the erotic feel of him deep inside her. Unlike the other times he'd been with women, making love to Jade healed him. The touch of her skin, the quirk of her smile filled the part of him that had died so many years ago.

With inhuman patience, he pulled back to the head, holding for a second to enjoy the way her hot velvet fisted around him and massaged the sensitive spot at the tip of his cock. More quickly than he'd intended, he drove into her.

Jade straightened her arms and arched her back. She ground against him, gyrating her hips. Sparks of pleasure raced up his shaft at the sight of her uninhibited display. He pulled out and thrust again.

"Do you like that?"

She turned her head and gazed at him from over her shoulder. Her eyes burned bright with unshielded desire and a touch of mischievousness. "I'm undecided."

Vixen.

He gripped her hips and drove deep, pulling out and thrusting back in before she had a chance to recover. He reached around her and rubbed her clit. The nub hardened, begging to be stroked. Slick moisture coated his finger as he worked her.

Tingles turned to waves, his climax building too fast for him to control. Jade's voice rasped through the euphoric haze rolling around him.

"Luc, I can't—I'm going to—" Her words cut off.

Her hands balled the duvet and she rammed against him, matching him thrust for thrust. His body shook with the effort to control his own orgasm. He wanted them to come together. That revelation suddenly seemed more important than anything else in his life.

He bent over her, bracing one hand on the bed at her hip and slid his finger to where he entered her. Added pressure and swirling his finger back up to circle her clit had Jade moaning and bucking.

"I think you like it." He caressed, swirled, and flicked again, trying to keep the orgasm that raged for release at bay a few seconds longer. She was so close. "Let it go, Jade. Take your pleasure."

She panted, rocking and grinding against him. Luc pulled out and drove back into her with rapid-fire movements. At last her body seized and shuddered. A hoarse cry erupted into the duvet as Jade pressed her face to the bed and rode her wave of delight.

The sight of her writhing body sent Luc over the edge. He surged one last time, dropping his control and letting the desire take him. His climax rolled through him like a sand storm rushing across the Alba Plains, blanketing him with wave after wave of heated pleasure.

Shudders racked his body and his legs became weak, unable to support him. He fell across Jade's back and together they slid to the bed, him still inside her. Neither spoke, their heavy breathing the only words possible and needed.

How long they lay there he didn't know. Afraid his weight might be crushing her, he rolled to the side, slipping out of her to lie on his back. Dark wooden beams stretched across the ceiling. He watched tiny flickers of golden candlelight dance along the rafters. He blinked to bring the world back into focus.

Jade lay quietly, her head facing away from him. He propped up on one elbow and reached to brush her hair away from her face. Her eyes were open, their green intensity staring at the far wall. Luc scooted closer.

"Jade?" Cold dread rippled along his skin. Had he hurt her? "Are you all right?"

She said nothing for several seconds, amplifying his anxiety. In a low, flat voice she finally said, "I can't feel my legs—or my arms—" She turned her head to look at him. "I've never, ever, ever experienced anything like that."

Relief washed through him. She rolled to her back, but her arms still lay limply at her side. Luc scooted across the few inches separating them and threw his leg over her.

"That's what happens when you do it right." He bent to place a kiss on her rosy nipple. "You're welcome."

"And you're arrogant." She pushed his leg off of her and slowly sat up. "I've had better."

"Liar." He draped his arm around her waist and tugged her to him, placing a kiss at the crook of her elbow. "Maybe we should have another go if it wasn't that good."

He pushed her back onto the bed and climbed on top of her. Jade squealed and tried to wiggle out from under him.

"Are you trying to kill me?" She placed her palms against his chest, but the effort was ineffective.

"What a way to die." He nuzzled her ear and cupped her breast. The tip hardened under his touch. "Your body tells me you want more."

She gave an unladylike snort, but wound her arms around his neck. "They do the same thing when it's cold."

"So you're telling me you're cold?"

She scowled at him. "Freezing."

He knew she was lying, but her stubborn streak would never allow her to surrender so easily. Luc rolled off her, grabbed the edge of the duvet and dragged it over them. "Better?"

She snuggled against him. "Much."

The minutes ticked silently by. Her eyes were closed and her chest fell with an even cadence, making him think she had fallen asleep.

"Do you know what would make this perfect?" She opened her eyes and looked at him.

There wasn't one thing he could think of that would make this moment better. He furrowed his brow.

"Convincing Rell to be healed." She turned and mimicked his earlier action, draping her leg over his. "Will you come with me?"

"Now?" The last thing he wanted was to leave the warm bed and Jade's naked body.

"I won't be able to sleep unless I try one last time."

He gave her a languid kiss and pulled back to look at her, grinning wickedly. "Like I said, I have the perfect cure for sleeplessness."

"I will love you forever if you grant me this one favor," she said in a singsong voice.

His smile faltered. "You love me?"

The mood in the room turned serious. She curled an arm under her head and trailed a finger through the patch of blond hair on his chest, keeping her eyes trained just below his chin. The seconds ticked by as he waited for her answer. He had bared his soul but had not expected to hear the same from her. After all, she'd hated him for so many years, but he was determined to win her forgiveness, even if it took a lifetime.

Her eyes turned upward to his face. With an absent movement, her tongue darted out to moisten her lips. "I think I've loved you for quite a while, but wouldn't admit it to myself."

The words he wanted to say seemed to lodge in his throat.

She shifted against him, scooting higher to look directly at him. "Say something."

He gave a slight nod and swooped down, rolling Jade to her back and pinning her to the bed. His lips captured her mouth in a searing kiss. Now everything was perfect.

CHAPTER TWENTY-NINE

Rell's arms dangled through the bars of the cage. Each movement she made caused her metal prison to swing like a slow pendulum. She glared at Jade, her lip curling in a sneer. "You smell like sex—and Le Daun."

The euphoric haze that had lingered after her and Luc's lovemaking dissipated. Jade tilted her chin and straightened her spine, but didn't reply to Rell's accusation. Her sister no longer had control over her. She'd make her own decisions and her own mistakes.

"It's like that now, is it?" The demon leaned forward. "What do you want, then?"

The lump in Jade's throat swelled, making it difficult to speak. "Let us try and heal you."

A smirk tugged at the corner of her sister's mouth. Yellow eyes peered at Jade with a mixture of amusement and desolation. The creaking and grating of iron against iron was Rell's only reply.

"Why won't you let me help you?" Jade's voice cracked, her heart aching from the memory of what Rell lived with every day.

"Why won't you let *us* help you?"

The demon lifted her head and smiled more sweetly than Jade could remember. Despite the wings and horns, the expression made Rell look entirely human again. "My little sister, always ready to champion a lost cause."

"You are not lost." Jade took a step forward. "Please let me help you."

"Don't you understand?" She leaned her head against the bars again. "There is nothing left for me in this life. I've been banished from the Shadow World and the only way to get back in Vile's good graces is to betray you." She looked away. "Allow me to pass through the Veil."

"You have me and our mother." Jade swiped at the escaped tear. "We've only just found her again. And there are healers who can save you. Please Rell, live for us."

The door to the barn opened and Luc stepped inside. He paused, his gaze darting between her and Rell and then settling back on Jade. "Are you all right?"

Unable to speak, she shook her head. From the time she and Luc had concocted their plan to enter the Shadow World, never had the possibility of Rell giving up on life been one of Jade's imagined outcomes.

Her sister waved a hand toward Jade. "She cannot accept that I no longer wish to live."

"Nor can I." He moved to stand beside Jade and slid an arm around her shoulder. "We have a chance to save you, Esmeralda."

"Not save me, merely assuage your guilt." She straightened away from the bars and pointed a black talon at him. "You have each other now. Let's put the past behind us and not play games. Our mother will never forgive me for lying to you and I no longer have a place in this world." She leaned her forehead against the bars. "Sister, let me go."

"Mother loves you and you kept me alive." The fight returned to Jade. "For that she will always be grateful."

"Grateful?" Rell gave a humorless laugh. "To build a relationship on gratitude is like building a house on shifting sand. With every swell and dip the foundation erodes and the house crumbles. Soon all traces of what was built are swept away by the waves."

"You prefer death over the chance to be healed?" Jade glided forward. "You would put your family through more pain when there's a chance at happiness?" She grabbed the bars and shook the cage, her voice growing louder. "You will sentence me to a life of wondering what if?" She leaned toward the bars and glared at Rell. "When did you become such a coward?"

Yes, trust had been betrayed, sister pitted against sister, lies uncovered, but they were family and those bonds were strong enough to bring them through any storm. Why couldn't her sister see this? It took every ounce of Jade's self-control not to shake Rell until she agreed to be healed. After all they'd been through, why would she give up so easily?

"I grow weary of fighting the darkness." Rell lifted her hand and caressed Jade's cheek. "It creeps around me, stealing my reason and compassion. I'm not afraid to die but I am afraid to live like this."

"But we can heal you."

"You have faith where I have none. If you release me, I *will* betray you."

Tears continued to flow down Jade's cheeks, burning an icy trail in the morning chill. She covered Rell's hand, holding it in place, drinking in its rough feel. This was the hand that had protected and provided for her. The hand that had brushed her fevered brow when she was ill. The hand that had soothed her when nightmares had stolen into her dreams. To accept her sister's choice and give her the freedom of death would be the ultimate act of love. She peered into the yellow eyes, wishing things could be so very different.

"Most of all, I will miss you." Rell brushed a strand of hair from Jade's face. "Please, free me."

An anguished whimper escaped Jade. She swallowed, blinking back the tears that blurred her vision. She gathered her strength and did the hardest thing she would ever have to do—she nodded.

A deep voice spoke from the open door. "Giving up so easily?"

Jade spun to see Siban standing in the doorway. His eyes were fixed on Rell and her human body lay cradled in his arms. Jade's impulse was to step into his path to protect her sister, but the look on his face kept her rooted in place. Determination? Anger? Passion? Never had she seen the man so animated.

The iron cage creaked as Rell inched herself upward into a crouched position, her gaze fierce, and leveled on Siban.

Luc stepped aside, giving the Tell room to enter. Tension crackled between the demon and the Tell, making the hair on Jade's arms stand on end. This was the first time Rell had seen her body and Jade chided herself for not thinking of the ploy before now. She watched her sister, realizing that it wasn't her old body Rell stared at, but Siban.

Luc bent to whisper in her ear. "Do they know each other?"

She wiped her tears away with the palm of her hand, sniffed and shook her head. "I have no idea."

Rell pressed her body against the bars, as if to get closer. "Si?"

"I guess that answers my question," Luc said.

So much emotion filled Rell's one word that new hope spread through Jade. She watched, unable to tear her gaze from the two.

Siban slowly approached, stopping inches from the cage. He held Esmeralda like a baby and angled the body for Rell to see. The demon's gaze drifted from his face to the limp form. Her hand reached through the bars and caressed the arm that had once belonged to her.

Tears spilled down Jade's cheeks, her breath catching in her throat. It was almost too much to hope that Siban could change her sister's mind. Family ties, loyalty, gratitude, duty—none of those could spur Rell to choose a chance at life, but this was something Jade had never considered. Rell was in love. The very thought almost made her laugh. She pressed her folded hands to her mouth and leaned into Luc. He pulled her against him.

Pieces of the mystery surrounding Siban tumbled into place. Years before, Rell had cryptically spoken of a man but refused to explain who he was when Jade had questioned her. Siban had been held prisoner in the Shadow World—that must be their connection. The night on the ship when he'd almost captured Jade, he'd called out to Rell because he had recognized her, not as a ploy to lure them back. He'd practically jumped at the chance to bring Willa to Faela and Jade would bet her life that it was in hopes of finding Rell. It all made sense and from the way he stared at Rell now, he obviously loved her too.

Rell's caress drifted upward and she cupped Siban's face with both hands. She tilted her head and pressed against the bars. Siban leaned forward, meeting her halfway. Ever so gently their lips touched, lingering as if drinking in the feel of each other.

Siban pulled back and looked at Rell. "Please don't leave me again."

Rell's yellow eyes swirled to green. "Never."

Jade looked at Luc. A half smile played at the corners of his mouth, his head shaking ever so slightly in disbelief. He looked at her and flicked a glance toward the door. She nodded. Tonight she would sleep well, wrapped in the arms of the man she loved and knowing that for these few short hours all was right in her world.

ACKNOWLEDGMENTS

First and foremost, I'd like to thank my fabulous editors, Kerry Vail and Erin Molta. You guys complete me. Thanks to CJ Ellisson, who tirelessly gives her support in every aspect of my life. Friends like you are hard to find. And to Heather Howland, you have my undying gratitude for the fantastic covers you continue to gift me with. You are a visionary.